Also by Rosalyn McMillan

Blue Collar Blues
Knowing
One Better
Flip Side of Sin

ROSALYN McMillan

A novel

This Side of Eternity

POCKET BOOKS

New York London Toronto Sydney Singapore

This book is a work of fiction. Names, characters, places and incidents are products of the author's imagination or are used fictitiously. Any resemblance to actual events or locales or persons, living or dead, is entirely coincidental.

POCKET BOOKS, a division of Simon & Schuster, Inc.
1230 Avenue of the Americas, New York, NY 10020

Copyright © 2002 by Bold Brass and Class, Inc.

Originally published in hardcover in 2001 by The Free Press

ISBN: 0-671-03436-7

First Pocket Books printing April 2002

10 9 8 7 6 5 4 3 2 1

POCKET and colophon are registered trademarks of Simon & Schuster, Inc.

For information regarding special discounts for bulk purchases, please contact Simon & Schuster Special Sales at 1-800-456-6798 or business@simonandschuster.com

Front cover illustration by Jody Hewgill

Printed in the U.S.A.

*This book is dedicated
to the city of Memphis, Tennessee,
and the two deceased sanitation workers,
Echol Cole and Robert Walker.*

Acknowledgments

Dr. Dorothy Jeffries was of great assistance in helping me to understand individuals who suffer from mental illness. I appreciate her wisdom and patience.

My sister-in-law, Beatrice Smith, was especially helpful when she shared a story with me about her friend who suffered from spousal abuse. Also, my sister-in-law, Pastor Allene Jackson, was always available any time or day to offer her limitless knowledge about the Bible.

I'd like to thank the librarians who work in The Memphis Room at the main branch of the Memphis Public Library. Their tireless support was essential in researching the city during the tragic years of the civil rights movement.

I acknowledge and honor my creative writing teacher, Mrs. Sandra Sutherland, for her insistence that I learn and understand poetry.

SRVS, the Shelby Residential and Vocational Services, is a nonprofit local agency that aids developmentally disabled people. Mrs. Tabitha Mathews, the head of admissions and discharge coordinator, took the time to share with me her knowledge about the SRVS program and gave me a tour of the wonderful facility. Thank you so much.

My daughter, Jasmine, who has a very creative mind, was always there to help me with my metaphors. Thanks sweetheart.

I was fortunate to have the support of my friends, Margaret Hall, Pamela Williams-Guinn, Veronica Busby, Simone Cooper, Chenise Lytrelle-Williams, and my very special cousin, Sonja William-Jones.

My cousin, Wanda Walton (the bombshell), kept me laughing when we reminisced and reflected about the music, fashions, and mindset of people during the sixties and seventies era. On a more serious note, Wanda has worked as a social worker in the mental health field for nearly twenty years. Her knowledge about individuals having seizures and coping with their handicaps was key in the writing of this novel.

And finally, as always, I'd like to thank my husband, J. D. Smith. Know that I am yours this side of eternity. And let me dream that love goes with us to the shore unknown.

Contents

Metropolis of the American Nile   7

1980
Racial Politics at the Crossroads   109

1991
We Are Coming   193

2000
At the River I Stand   313

This Side of Eternity

THE MISSISSIPPI RIVER, a Nile to the North American continent, was the "Great Inland Sea" of U.S. economy in the nineteenth century. It incorporated the waters of the great Missouri and Ohio River systems before it reached the rich alluvial flood plains of its delta.

At the apex of that triangular deposit, safely above the flood stage, and prior to its 1819 founding, a great city would rise.

The city of Memphis.

Named for the capital of ancient Egypt, the city outstripped its river rivals and emerged as the premier port of the mid-Mississippi.

Roads, stage lines, and railroads enhanced the city's commercial importance. In the 1850s Memphis grew faster than any other major American city and was a contender for the eastern terminus of the transcontinental railroad.

Although federal occupation early in the Civil War spared Memphis the devastation inflicted on other southern cities, war was only a prelude to plague.

Memphis was savaged in the 1870s by three major yellow fever epidemics. A decade later, the city had lost most of its population, its prosperity, and its good name.

By 1892, like the phoenix of old, Memphis was reborn on the site of devastation: the Great Bridge across the Mississippi. The city diversified economically, becoming the world's hardware lumber center as well as its greatest inland cotton market.

By the turn of the century, and with a population of more than 100,000, like most large cities, urban problems set in.

Saloon interest dominated the city. Crime rates soared, and Memphis won the dubious title of Murder Town, U.S.A. In that same vein, W. C. Handy captured the essence of this freewheeling era of blues music for which the city and Beale Street became famous.

Under reform mayor E. H. Crump's leadership over a forty-year reign, he reduced the city's crime rate and instituted a positive image that would last for decades. Memphis became known as the nation's cleanest and quietest city—it developed educational and cultural institutions of which all residents were proud.

By then, in the 1950s, the population had grown to nearly 400,000 people.

Racial strife, explosive crime rates, center-city decay, and suburban flight have all characterized the half century since World War II.

Yet by the beginning of 1968 Dr. Martin Luther King's civil rights movement forced more changes in the status of black Americans than any actions since the Emancipation Proclamation freed the slaves.

The potent gospel that he preached and the endless verses of "We Shall Overcome" did little to dispel the onset of racism that was about to be set in motion in the city of Memphis.

On January 30, 1968, Walter Russell and his co-worker, Matthew O'Conner, both under the age of forty, were accidentally killed.

Walter Russell, a deacon at Baptist Memorial Temple and director of the local chapter of the American Federation of State, County and Municipal Employees, AFSCME, was well respected in the Memphis community.

Matthew O'Conner, a soft-spoken young man who'd just recently been hired, had joked to his co-workers who were bitching and complaining about the working conditions, "This is a step up for me. Last year I was walking behind two mules. This year I'm riding on the back of a truck. Who knows—next year I might be driving!" His sense of humor would be sorely missed.

On that horrific morning, a woman who was looking out of her kitchen window saw the incident happen:

"He was just standing there on the end of the truck, and suddenly it looked like the big thing [the compressor unit] had just swallowed him. He was standing on the side and the machine was moving. His body went in first and his legs were hanging out."

"The motor started racing and the driver stopped and ran around and mashed that button to stop that thing," said one of the crew that was riding in the cab of the truck. "I didn't know what was happening. It looked to me like one of them almost got out, but he got caught and just fell back in there."

"I didn't know at the time someone else had already been crushed in the thing," the woman told the Memphis Press-Scimitar. "It was horrible."

No one said whether it was Walter Russell or Matthew O'Conner who almost made it out before the edge of his raincoat got snagged in the grinder when the electrical apparatus on the compressor shorted out. The truck, a barrel-type unit called the wiener barrel by the men, had come to use ten years before and was being phased out, but six were still in use.

The sanitation workers had complained about the faulty equipment, but it fell on deaf ears.

There was no workman's compensation. Neither man had life insurance. The city paid the families back pay, an additional month's salary, and $500 toward burial expenses.

The men in the Department of Sanitation didn't talk about it much, but the tragedy tugged at the periphery of their thoughts like a nightmare on the edge of waking. They had seen the deadly hydraulic ram in action.

Several days after the two men were killed, the rumors of a strike in Sanitation began.

In the aftermath of death, the workers began a seemingly hopeless struggle against the city of Memphis, Tennessee, demanding dignity, respect, and a subsistence wage.

Since 1964, their charter Local 1733 was not recognized by the city and had little power.

Safety issues and lack of pay because of the rain were factors that had also caused a wildcat strike by the public works employees seeking recognition of their union.

Some folks in Memphis saw it as a prototype fusion of organized labor and minority groups for economic independence.

At the age of thirteen, Walter Russell's baby daughter, Anne, vowed to be an integral part of the civil rights movement.

None of the gory details that perpetuated the Memphis Press-Scimitar or the Hamilton Appeal mattered to the southern belle, or to the other members of the Russell family, who had to prepare, once again, for a funeral.

Walter Russell's body was so badly disfigured that they had to have a closed-casket funeral.

Yesterday, tomorrow, and unrequited todays and tonights rained on Anne's psyche.

It was a combination of everything that had happened over the past few weeks when Anne went to sleep, free-floating fitfully on a turbulent river of dreams.

Metropolis of the
American Nile

One

"WHERE'S MY DADDY?" Anne screamed. "What have they done with him? I want to see him! Why can't I see him! No! No! Please. Not like that!"

Clutching the edge of the brown wool blanket against her heart, her body shivered more from emotion than from the cold February night.

As she struggled to shun the horrible images of death, she felt a stiff hand roughly shaking her. The stale odor of hot cigarette breath against her face made her wince, as someone repeated her name over and over again.

Still half asleep, she made an effort to open her eyes.

"Annie Mae, will you please shut up!" her sister Vanilla Mae demanded. "You're going to wake up those damn brats."

The six surviving Russells lived in a modest low-income wood-frame house. It was all that their father had been able to afford.

Since the death of their older brother and his wife last summer, their two nieces and nephew slept in their younger brother's old bedroom, next to them. The walls were so old and dilapidated they could hear the bedsprings creak when any of the children made the slightest movement.

Anne believed that she heard a slight tremor just now. It sounded like someone was clapping his or her hands together.

"I'm sorry, Mae." Her throat was hoarse and scratchy.

"See," Mae said, after they heard a much more distinct sound in the next room, "she's up." They both knew who it was.

By then Anne's eyes had adjusted to the darkness. She looked across the room to the clock-radio on the dresser. It was nearly three in the morning. "I'll check on her," she said, exiting the bed they shared.

Turning on the hall light, she opened the children's bedroom door. First she spotted Wesley snoring softly in the bed near the closet—a drooping sage green army blanket, used as a room divider, was nailed to the ceiling. To her left, the two girls, Bentley Camille and Nikkie Anne, slept in a twin bed barely three feet away.

As she moved closer, she noticed that six-year-old Nikkie was sitting up, looking dead in Anne's face.

"Why you always making that noise?" Nikkie asked with eyes as innocent as flower petals.

"Shhh," Anne cautioned. "Aunt Anne has bad dreams sometimes."

"I never *dreams*. How come? How come I don't get to *dreams*?"

Nikkie was a special child. Taking care of her had been a huge challenge, especially for Mae, who quit school the year before to become her surrogate mother.

Sitting on the bed beside her, Anne said, "I don't know, baby. Some people never *dreams.*"

But Anne's dreams were not always bad ones. Sometimes she dreamed beautiful dreams about her mother. Anne would tell all of her secrets to the woman she felt was her best friend. She would have liked to share these special moments with Nikkie, but she wouldn't understand.

Even in the semidarkness, she could see Nikki's strong features. Like Anne, she had the wide-set Russell eyes and milk chocolate coloring. In her large, shadowed brown eyes lingered more pain and sufferings than a child her age should know.

"Are you sad your daddy died?"

"Yeah . . ." Anne reached out and rebraided one of her three thick pigtails that had come loose. "And I'm sad about your daddy and mommy, too."

"Uh-huh. Me too. Heaven must be getting pretty crowded up there."

Anne smiled, "I was thinking the same thing, Nikkie. And you know something? A famous poet named Cummings said it better than I ever could. He said that life wasn't a paragraph, and death, he thought, is no parenthesis."

"I don't know what that means."

Sometimes Anne forgot about Nikkie's handicap. She had a bad habit of talking to herself, as though Nikkie were her personal sounding board.

"I'm sorry, baby. I'm merely trying to say that life goes on, even in death. And one day you and I will get to see our loved ones. And then—well then, neither one of us will ever have to worry about dreams anymore."

"Hmm," Nikkie said, as if she were trying to grasp what Anne had said.

"Now hush. It's time for you to get back to sleep. You've awakened Aunt Mae. And we both know that isn't a good thing."

Nikkie shuddered.

Anne motioned for her to lie back down.

After Nikkie had turned on her side, she pulled the quilt up over her and Bentley's shoulders and blew Nikkie a kiss good night.

While tiptoeing down the hall to use the bathroom, she could smell the smoke from Mae's Camel cigarette on her way back up.

Though they'd kept it a secret from their father, and brother Kirk, Mae had been a chain-smoker since the age of thirteen. Worse than that addiction was her ever-increasing messiness. Ashes and dirty clothes were the dominant decor in their tiny bedroom.

"Haachew!" she sneezed as she entered their room.

"This nightmare shit has got to stop." Mae flicked the ashes off the sheer sleeve of her blue baby doll gown and glared at Anne. "I haven't had a good night's sleep since . . ."

"Daddy died," Anne said quietly. She stared at Mae's haggard face. A year ago she was pretty. Four years her senior, Mae and Anne both had thick manes of hair, Anne's dark brown, while Mae's was a shocking reddish brown. Mae's face was a perfect oval; Anne's was heart-shaped. Mae's dark brown eyes were a bit too close to her nose, while Anne's were bright and wide-set like their brother Kirk's. Anne's full lips softened her exotic features, but Mae's tight narrow lips that rarely smiled made her look ten years older.

Maybe that's why she doesn't look pretty anymore.

But giving credit where credit was due, Mae had been a godsend to the Russell family. Kirk, as well as their father, often complimented Miss Mae, as they oftentimes called her, about her unfailing maturity.

At age six, Mae cooked, cleaned, and baby-sat as well as a grown woman did. It was a duty that their father had reluctantly bequeathed on her three years after his wife, her mother, had died during childbirth with Anne.

And today, shouldering all of that responsibility had taken its toll. Mae smoked two packs a day, and had been sexually active since age twelve.

"Do you see Daddy crunched up in that machine?" she said in a high shrill voice as if she'd shared the same dream. "Is that why you're screaming?"

Anne nodded, her face lit by the glow of Mae's cigarette. "Uh-huh. And I see Stuart and Danielle's faces pressed against Daddy's chest with blood all over them. All of them are screaming for help."

STUART, ANNE'S BROTHER, and his wife, Danielle, were killed in a car accident eight months earlier.

Anne wondered how one family could endure so much tragedy.

Where was the God their father had always prayed to? The God that her father had said almost made their mother a saint.

And what exactly did a saint mean? Was it the same as a nun—a homely-looking woman in black clothing who didn't believe in sex?

Since their father's death, the church they belonged to had taken up a love offering so often it was becoming embarrassing to attend service. Mae said the family was cursed, but, in the three years since she first voiced that thought, she would never tell Anne her reasons why she felt that way.

"It's in the cards, child," she would always say. "Every one of us is going to suffer a horrible death. Just like daddy, Danielle, and Stuart did. You mark my words."

*If you believe that stupid bullshit, then why are you
inhaling cancer sticks as fast as you can light one?*

Nothing made sense. Her mother and father were
gone. Her brother and sister-in-law, whom she'd come
to love as a real big sister, erased. Still, something was
off. There were too many pieces missing in their tiny
puzzle of life.

"God don't like ugly," Anne said, breaking the thick
silence. She went to the dresser and fondled the Austrian
crystal beads that belonged to her mother. She wore
them to church every Sunday. "I remember the pastor
telling us that. You should stop trying to scare me, Mae.
Just because I'm younger than you don't make me a fool.
And just because I'm a sexually free young woman,
don't misinterpret that either."

"Stop it, Anne." She ground out her cigarette in the
ashtray and got back in bed, "you're getting on my
nerves. I don't want to have to put you on my *shit list.*"

Anne slid into bed and turned on her side. She was
tired of hearing about Mae's *shit list.* Nikkie seemed to
always be on it and occasionally Bentley. But as of last
year, when the list started, Anne hadn't managed to get
on it.

The long silence, as Anne listened to their exagger-
ated breathing, made her reflect and shiver. Both
Anne and especially Vanilla Mae hated their names.
Everyone called her sister Mae for as long as Anne
could remember. Mae was named after their mother's
sister, Vanilla Mae Jemison. Accordingly, Anne was
named after her father's sister, Annie Mae. No . . .
Annie Mae didn't quite brown her bread, for Anne.
She and Mae both felt that their names sounded like
servants' names, not like today's women who could
quote the latest fashion trends and knew the instant

that the per-pound prices rose or fell on pork futures.

As she closed her eyes and feigned sleep, she remembered her father's last words, while being interviewed by Channel 3 News.

"It was a combination of things that have been going on for years, such as low pay and discrimination," Russell said. "But discrimination was the thing that initiated and precipitated the strike."

Her father was almost correct, Anne thought. But she knew, like most others who read the *Hamilton Appeal* and the Memphis *Press-Scimitar* on a daily basis, that the problems really began the year before.

In 1967 three prominent blacks had won district seats on the city council, but when the mayoral elections were held, the city's racial polarization had been reinforced and intensified after Henry Loeb, the landslide mayor of Memphis in 1959, came out of retirement to defeat incumbent mayor Ingram.

During his single term in office, Ingram was popular among blacks. But in Ingram's bid for reelection, Henry Loeb captured 90 percent of the white vote, beating Ingram, who had nearly unanimous support of the city's blacks.

By the time the election was over, Memphis had become a racial powder keg. The summer of 1967 had seen sporadic incidents of race-related violence and destruction. White Memphians had made unprecedented purchases of firearms and ammunition in anticipation of possible race warfare in the streets. All that was lacking was a major incident to ignite the fuse; then all hell would break loose.

It wasn't until now, Anne reflected, that that fuse was once again lit—only this time by the sanitation strike.

Regardless, the *Hamilton Appeal*, as well as the Memphis *Press-Scimitar*, reported the news about the unprecedented purchases of arms and ammunition in the Memphis area.

God Almighty! was reverberated throughout the city.

Off balance. Off kilter. Off track. The headlines in the *Hamilton Appeal* told it all.

The city of Memphis was just *off*.

Whites and blacks were on edge in the city. Especially Anne's brother Kirk, who'd let slide in a weak moment that he felt that his father's death was no accident. He and Mae continuously exchanged guilty glances. Anne was kept out of the conversation, no matter how many times she questioned them.

Kirk, also a sanitation worker, had quit school in his senior year to help his father out financially. It was also during the time that their father was so distraught when his eldest son, Stuart, along with his wife, Danielle, were killed in an automobile accident, that he had to take a month's leave of absence at work. It cost the Russells three hundred needed dollars. Three small children were left parentless. Only the eldest, Wesley, twelve, understood the gravity of what had happened. Nikkie, five, and Bentley, four, were too young to understand.

In the meantime, Walter Russell's modest two-story wood-frame home was cramped to the studs to make room for his needy grandchildren. Meals were cut down to snack size.

Anne didn't care. She loved her nieces and nephew from years before, when she first volunteered to baby-sit them. Anne wasn't sure how her sister felt about them, although, when the first Social Security check came in, Vanilla Mae quit school and fired the fifty-year-old baby-sitter, who couldn't seem to deal with Nikkie's special situation. On weekdays, a special-education bus would pick Nikkie up in front of the house, but because of her having so many seizures, she missed a lot of school.

Anne remembered trying to talk Mae out of her decision. After all, their father only had a ninth-grade education and he desperately wanted all of his children to get their diplomas, and possibly attend college.

To Anne's dismay, Mae's mind was set on the sinful pitfalls in life, money and fornication—not her edification. Now, with Mae quitting school, and Kirk quitting a few months later, Anne was the only Russell left to keep their father's dream alive.

The following morning was Saturday. Usually Wesley was the first one awake. Around eight o'clock, he would help his sisters brush their teeth and fix their cereal while they watched their favorite Rocky and Bullwinkle cartoons. Anne would scurry downstairs about thirty minutes later.

Bentley and Nikkie had finished their breakfast and were already busy coloring at the kitchen table, with paper, crayons, and pencils spread out before them.

At five years old, Bentley showed the signs of becoming a talented artist. Her baby-soft skin was as rich and supple as that of a dusky deer. She wore her ten-inch-thick locks in a single Afro puff on the top of her head. It gave her elongated oval face a look of regality. Her Tootsie Roll brown eyes were alert and serious, but especially while she drew.

Anne asked Bentley if she could draw a teenager reading while preschoolers sat and listened. Her attentive niece winked a yes.

Thirty minutes later, Anne heard quick steps coming down the stairs.

"Anne," Wesley chimed in, pulling on a slicker, "I've got to make a run downtown to see if Max wants me to work today." He looked out of the front window at the rain that was still pouring down, figuring, as Anne did, that business would be slow today. "Can you keep an eye on the girls?"

Anne nodded yes and glanced back at Nikkie, who was scribbling angry black marks on her half-colored picture. After Wesley left, Anne changed the television station to the *Mr. Rogers' Neighborhood* early-morning show. In no time, Nikkie was smiling at his soft-spoken words and captivating humor.

While they worked, both Bentley and Anne took turns watching Nikkie, who was now asleep in front of the television. She'd had a seizure yesterday that lasted nearly eight minutes. If her seizures lasted more than ten minutes, which happened on rare occasions, they had to take Nikkie to the hospital.

Mae sauntered downstairs around eleven, gulped down her daily fix of Pepsi while she lit a fresh cigarette. Without caring who was watching what, she turned the channel on the set.

Forty-five minutes later, Wesley returned unhappily and handed Anne a used copy of the Memphis *Press-Scimitar*. He told her that there wasn't any work today and rushed upstairs to change out of his wet clothes.

"Stop. You stop," Nikkie screamed.

With a cigarette propped in the corner of her mouth, Mae proceeded to whip Nikkie with a switch. "You stupid little thang. I told you not to piss on that floor again. Didn't I?"

Just thirteen years old, and nearly as tall as Mae, Anne dropped the paper, and rushed to Nikkie's aid. Anne stepped in between her niece and Mae and yanked the switch from her right hand.

Mae's face was cold but her eyes were as hot as pepper, as Anne grabbed her arm and held it tight.

Wesley was down the steps in seconds. He stepped up until he was looking into Mae's face and said, "If you ever hit my sister again, I'll beat your brains out! You hear me?"

"Nikkie," Bentley yelled. "Help her, somebody!" Just then Nikkie's eyes began to roll back in her head. Her short legs jerked out straight, snapped back, and buckled beneath her like she had the rickets. Anne could feel the floor beneath her feet shake as she hurried to Nikkie, who was turning back and forth on her side. Drool ran from her mouth and fell on the front of her shirt as the spasms continued to engulf her body.

Anne checked the clock in the kitchen.

Just over a minute lapsed and Nikkie was still on the floor, shaking and thrashing her arms and legs. Chairs were shoved out of the way and the table pushed further back toward the corner.

Two minutes. Three. Five. Six, and Bentley began to cry. Anne held her in her arms. "Shhh. She'll be okay in a few minutes, honey."

"No thanks to her," Wesley mumbled beneath his breath.

This wasn't the first time that Mae had beaten Nikkie. They all knew that Nikkie needed medical attention, not a beating. She had at least two seizures a week. But without extra money, they couldn't afford to get the help she needed. The doctor that Social Security insurance paid for wasn't concerned in the least bit about his young patient.

In eight minutes it was over. Wesley helped his sister up from the floor and wiped her foaming mouth with a cloth. Reaching into the cabinet, he gave Nikkie a dose of her medicine, followed by a glass of water.

"You okay, now?" he asked her tenderly. Nikkie nodded and hugged him around the waist.

"Wesley . . ." Anne began.

Without uttering a word, he took the girls by the hand and led them into the living room. As hurriedly as he could, he began putting on Bentley's and Nikkie's coat and hat. Removing an umbrella from the closet, he spoke to Anne. "I'm taking them to the store and then to the park. We'll be back later."

"Hey, boy, bring me a Pepsi back," Mae demanded. She removed a single dollar bill from beneath the sofa seat, balled it up, and tossed it at his back.

Wesley wheeled back around, fists balled at the end of his short alligator arms. Nikkie picked up the money and innocently handed it to her brother. "You know, at first I started to say, 'Hell no.' " Opening the door, he helped the girls open the tattered umbrella. The girls stood on the steps, cuddling in the slowing rain. "I'll get it, though. 'Cause I was raised to have some respect for folks." He slammed the door behind him.

While Anne and Mae argued about the kids and Wesley's smart mouth, Anne pointed out that Mae wouldn't be able to afford her habit if it weren't for their monthly Social Security checks.

Less than five minutes later, Kirk came home, cussing up a storm. "Damn it. Just damn this shit!" he said, removing his hat. "We're all going to starve. If this strike goes on any longer, we won't be able to pay the mortgage or keep up the utilities."

Kirk was nearly as tall as the doorway. His keen brown eyes were wide-spaced like the pictures Anne remembered seeing of their mother. A wild and wiry mustache completely covered his top lip. His strong nose and angular jawline made him look older than his seventeen and a half years. His jet, naturally wavy, half-inch hair stopped a neat three inches above his crisp shirt collar. Some people said he resembled Jackie Robinson. Anne thought he was just sublimely handsome.

"Look," Anne said, running to the kitchen table and showing him the fliers, "I'm going to start a baby-sitting business."

"Hrrmph," Kirk snorted, and began taking off his coat.

Mae sat on the end of the couch with a smirk on her face, puffing on a Camel and sipping on her last Pepsi.

Taking a quick glimpse out the window, Anne noticed that the blue mists of morning made shadows on the tree trunks, leaving the tops free.

Anne worried that even though the rain had let up some, the temperature outside was still chilly. She hoped that Wesley's temper would soon cool so that they all would come back home.

Kirk handed Anne his coat, which she shook outside the door, then hung in the closet. The expression on his face was as cold as a Chicago winter, and nearly as long.

"The kids have got to go. They're way too expensive. And when I get back to work, there are things that *I* need."

"Not a bad idea," Mae added, tapping her foot on the wooden floor.

Kirk snatched a chair back from the table and took a seat. "I'm not giving up—"

"How could you say such a thing," Anne said sharply. "Daddy wouldn't rest in peace if he knew you two were thinking such selfish thoughts."

Mae cut in. "I agree. Those kids are more of a burden than they're worth." She cut her eyes at Anne. "Especially that pissy retard."

Kirk tapped his fingertips together. "You ain't said nothing but a word, girl. Like I said, they'd be better off in foster care. Monday morning, I'm going to make that call." He got up, went down the hall to his bedroom, and slammed the door.

Mae turned her attention back to the television with a half-smile on her face. Instantly, tears welled, then slowly slid down Anne's face. What could she do or say to change their minds?

She ran upstairs into her meager bedroom and, removing her father's picture from the dresser, fell on her knees. Kissing her father's celluloid face, she formed her hands in a steeple and closed her eyes.

Afterward, she remembered the words from one of her father's sermons:

> If God has taught us all truth in teaching us to love, then he has given us an interpretation of our whole duty to our households—We are not born as the partridge in the wood, or the ostrich in the desert, to be scattered everywhere; but we are to be grouped together, and brooded by love, and reared day by day in that first of churches, the family.

Anne cried bitter tears. What had happened in a week's time for their family to turn from love to hatred?

Two

"SIT STILL, NIKKIE," Bentley scolded. Habitually, she tucked in her bottom lip with her top teeth and began to suck the soft surface.

Nikkie mumbled something under her breath that Bentley couldn't understand. Releasing her lip, she asked, "What'd you say, baby girl?"

"I wanna go home."

"We'll be okay, sister. You need to mind Aunt Mae better. And stop entertaining her—"

Nikkie began to cry.

"What's wrong with you?" She stopped combing her hair.

"I'm wet."

"See what I mean." Bentley tried to sound mad. But how could she be upset at her beautiful sister? Nikkie didn't understand what she was doing. And probably, she assumed, couldn't help herself. If she didn't feel bad about wetting in her pants, then why did she cry?

"I won't do it no more. I promise."

"C'mon," Bentley said, helping her up from the floor. Bentley thought back on the time when she first learned of Nikkie's mental and physical difficulties; she'd just had a terrible seizure. Bentley had secretly cursed God for giving her a sister with so many problems. And it wasn't a year later when she heard herself praying, "Lord, why would you give me a sister so incredibly amazing? Why would you bless Wesley and me with a sibling with so much character and love? Because Nikkie is all about love. She *loves* to love us."

"I don't like it here. I want my momma and daddy."

"Me, too."

"When they coming back to get us, Bentley? We need to go back to our own house now."

Bentley's eyes misted as she searched through the drawers for a clean pair of Nikkie's underwear and pants. When she returned, she said as tenderly as she could, "Our parents are gone to heaven. They went to heaven to build us a new house. We'll see them someday. Meanwhile, we're going to have to learn how to make ourselves invisible. You know, like Casper the Friendly Ghost."

"I like Casper!"

"Everybody loves Casper. Even Aunt Mae."

"So if I act like Casper, Aunt Mae might like me better?"

"Um-hm."

"For how long? I don't want to act like Casper too long. I'm scareded I might go away forever . . ." She turned to Bentley, looking confused.

"I know what you mean. But it's just for a little while. In a few short years Wesley is going to get a real job and get us out of here. If that don't work out, Aunt Anne will help us. I know she will."

"Why's Aunt Anne gone all the time? She ain't never home. Don't she like us no more?"

"She *loves* us. Right now she's baby-sitting for the Moores across the street."

They tiptoed downstairs and, noticing that Aunt Mae was asleep in the couch, headed for the bathroom. After closing the door softly behind them, Bentley told her sister, "Now hand me those wet clothes, then clean yourself up at the sink. Afterwards you can put on these new clothes that Aunt Anne bought you." Bentley showed Nikkie a pair of pink nylon underwear and pink-and-white-striped pedal pushers.

Bentley bent over the tin tub and turned on the hot water full blast, then threw in the bar of soap. After reclaiming her lip with her top teeth, she accepted Nikkie's two articles and began to swish them around in the soapy water.

One of these days, she thought, I'm going to be rich and famous. Rich enough to get my sister out of this ugly house and get her a good doctor. She'll be just like me then. I know she will.

Three

KIRK TURNED EIGHTEEN on February eleventh. There was a small celebration. Still on strike and with very little money, they managed to find only one candle to put on the cake.

To Anne's relief, Kirk was only bluffing about sending the kids to foster care, and the subject hadn't come up again. Temporarily replacing his anger was the fact that he might be drafted into the army. Mae had told Anne, because Kirk was the head of the household, he would get a deferral, and not have to go to war like so many of their neighbors' sons had.

But worrying about the war wasn't the Russells' only dilemma. The strike situation had by now escalated out of proportion and had become a symbol of the city's two races deadlocked in a test of will. T. O. Jones's efforts thus far to organize a union had been largely unsuccessful. The working conditions and near minimum wages were far from optimum.

Militant as well as conservative ministers were not above hinting at violence as a solution to the stalemate. It was no surprise to anyone when the remaining sanitation workers walked out on February 12, 1968.

On February 15, the city began trying to hire replacements for the 700 striking Sanitation Department workers, who had let more than 10,000 tons of garbage pile up in the city. Memphis had transformed from being one of the nation's cleanest cities into one of its filthiest.

Kirk's pessimistic attitude was getting worse as the strike continued on and on. He walked the picket line and came home angry and more exhausted than he did when he worked a full eight-hour day. Mae always had his dinner ready and made sure that the kids were upstairs and out of his way.

By February 28, it had rained nonstop for three days. Sewer and drain workers had their workday canceled because of it. On that misty day, the black workers were paid two hours, while their white contemporaries were paid for the whole day.

When word got out about the pay disparity, all hell broke loose. An emergency union meeting was held.

After the second union meeting, more than 1,100 members of the sanitation workforce engaged in a wildcat strike, shocking the national union leadership as much as it did city officials. The strike would probably have ended quickly if the local NAACP and black ministers had not thrown their support and resources behind the strikers.

When the city began replacement hiring and tried to maintain minimum levels of garbage collection, militant blacks harassed and attacked garbage trucks in some black neighborhoods. Collections in those areas ceased. Open garbage piled up and became breeding places for rats and other vermin.

The work stoppage had now escalated out of proportion. The union paid them about $26.00 a week strike pay, and they would pay the workers' house notes.

AFSCME, the American Federation of State, County and Municipal Employees, then organizing Sanitation Department workers, issued demands for policies that many governmental workers considered basic: recognition of the union as the workers' bargaining agent, deduction of union dues from paychecks, a grievance procedure.

Deducting the union dues from a worker's paycheck would not only imply de facto recognition of the union, it would also give the union leverage for building its membership.

Other grievances included a fair promotion policy, adequate hospital and life insurance, sick leave and vacations, two weeks paid after one year of service—after ten years, three weeks, and after the fifteenth year of employment, four weeks paid vacation.

Mayor Henry Loeb called the strike illegal. There was no state law against public employee strikes, so Loeb relied on a 1957 Tennessee Supreme Court decision. It was a decade before the city council would pass an ordinance prohibiting strikes by its employees.

But now, with most of the white council members siding with Loeb, the members still worried that prohibiting municipal unions was as important as the risk of permanently impairing chances for racial harmony if the situation blew up.

Joining with the three black councilmen, the council attempted to override Mayor Loeb's refusal to concede the dues grievance. They failed.

On March 22, twelve inches of snow handicapped the city. It was the most snow in its history. A scheduled protest march with Dr. King was canceled.

During the weeks that the black sanitation workers had been on strike, whites were hired to collect garbage, most in white areas. To show their resentment toward those they felt were the main perpetrators, blacks had boycotted white-owned stores.

Anne was dismayed by the fact that as each day of the strike wore on, there was very little mentioned about her father's and his co-worker's deaths. Oblivious to the pain of their families and friends, the strike dragged on.

In spite of everything, the spring flowers and accompanying adornments were making their debut. Early yellow lilies in the Russells' front and side yard bloomed as vibrantly as ever. A lone bouquet of white zinnias from her father's funeral was planted in the center of the flowerbed. In the narrow backyard, the thick vines on the blackberry bushes were beginning to bud. Already Anne was imagining canning and selling jars of blackberry preserves for the fall holidays.

Presently, her brother and his co-workers were asking for a raise from $2.10 to $2.35 an hour as top pay for laborers and from $2.10 to $3.00 for crew chiefs.

After the strike began, but before the march was called, T. L. Dickerson Jr.—a member of the city council—thought a solution was at hand.

Council members had just met at the home of Councilman Milton Davies to try to come up with a settlement. It was before the state's open meetings law was passed, so only council members were present.

All but one council member agreed that the union be recognized as a bargaining agent, that a form of dues checkoff be permitted, and that the $1.80-an-hour wage be increased a modest amount.

The council members left the meeting feeling great.

Still, Loeb refused to concede the dues checkoff. In short, the council failed. The seven-member majority, like most white Memphians, wanted the strike broken and the union discredited more than ever now. The two halves of the city were on a collision course.

Both newspapers printed front-page stories about the strike on a daily basis. Citizens who weren't affiliated with the strike were beginning to feel the pressure of racial strife. They were bombarded by it morning, noon, and night.

Negotiations were at a standstill. Mayor Loeb would not begin new talks with the union until the 1,300 workers went back to work.

Still willing to negotiate, the sanitation workers sought a 15-cents-an-hour increase, while Mayor Loeb offered 8 cents.

At eight a.m. on March 28, an estimated 20,000 supporters of the sanitation strike rallied at Clayborn Temple near Hernando and Pontotoc. Once a glamorous street, the area was now dirty and tawdry. It had always been garish, but now the street was bombarded with illegal pawnshops, cut-rate liquor stores, and discount clothing stores. Around the temple was an area of rapid deterioration, decrepit houses with broken gutters and dirt yards and a few wilting trees.

Of the people who marched, many carried signs reading, I Am a Man.

William Lucy coined the I Am a Man slogan, which came to symbolize the strike. Lucy felt that the words had captured everything that they wanted to say from childhood up but had not been able to express.

Most people didn't understand that the reason the strikers held the signs that proclaimed I Am a Man was because of the fact that most of the laborers were black, poor, undereducated, and had to work under subhuman conditions. All of the supervisors were white—some of them were abusive. A number of these supervisors oftentimes used favoritism and intimidation. The black workers felt that the city didn't recognize them as humans. The signs represented a new sense of pride and dignity.

One had to read *The Defender* to find out what the black community was thinking. Few citizens read two papers and consequently the gap between the races grew wider.

A worker with fifteen years' seniority being interviewed by *The Defender* said: "We were working more than eight hours and not being paid overtime. We had been told that if you did not finish your route, you don't need to work the next day, because you were firing yourself. So we had to remain until we would complete our route, our assignment."

Another said: "I would get home to take a bath. . . .

One time there were two maggots right around my navel. I took a bath and they stretched out and fell off in the tub. And my wife said, 'Lord have mercy, honey, wait a minute and let me run that water out.'

"She ran it out and she came in and washed my head and everything, and (she) was pulling them out of my head. You see, that was in the summertime. I said, 'Well, I can't help it. . . . We got to try and make it.' "

Earlier that morning, at Hamilton High School, students reportedly threw rocks and bottles. There were also reports that a Memphis black power group of teenagers, calling themselves the Invaders, called Dr. King "Uncle Tom," mocked his nonviolent ways, and were giving instructions to the students on how to make a bottle-and-gasoline bomb called a Molotov cocktail.

When police moved in on students at the school, one female student was injured. Later, as the march began, rumors circulated that the girl had died.

That same day, Dr. King had flown in town along with numerous local labor and religious figures. Because his plane was behind schedule, Dr. King was thirty minutes late for a press conference.

At the press conference King said that he did not realize when he came to Memphis that there were those in the Negro community who "were talking about violence."

The march was supposed to be peaceful. The first of a printed list of instructions handed out to the marchers was: "The only force we use is 'soul-force,' which is peaceful, loving, yet militant."

Later that afternoon, as the marchers moved about six blocks and were on Beale Street approaching Main, only a few windows had been broken. As the marchers turned on Main Street, according to parade marshals, about fifty teenagers—some believed to be members of the Invaders—started running.

The march turned into a riot, and therefore, the city had good reason to fear more civil disorder if another mass march was held. The city justified going into federal courts on the ground of diversity of citizenship—in other words the named defendants were not residents of Tennessee—and by raising certain federal questions spelled out in various civil rights acts. The city said that it was also seeking the injunction as a means to protect Dr. King.

On that same afternoon, the Reverend Dr. Martin Luther King Jr. said that President Johnson or the congressional leadership might persuade him to call off his controversial Poor Peoples Campaign in Washington starting in April if he were given a positive commitment that they would do something this summer to aid the nation's slums.

When Anne returned home that night, Kirk was still up watching the eleven o'clock news. Outside, the sound of fire trucks threatened to keep the kids up again. As many as fifty to seventy-five fire calls a night weren't unusual. People were burning their trash. Most had no choice.

"What about Memphis?" Kirk yelled at the man speaking on the television screen. He turned to Anne. "Where'd your damn sister gone to? The kitchen looks like a hog pen."

Probably in the back of some man's car.

"I'll take care of it in a minute. Just be quiet," Anne said, "I want to hear this."

Kirk ignored her and took his anger out on Bentley.

He yelled at her to come downstairs and clean up the kitchen.

This time Anne didn't defy him. The smell of cheap whiskey on his breath was stronger than usual. She gave the sleepy-eyed Bentley a quick smile, trying to tell her with imploring eyes that this wasn't her idea. Dr. King's commanding voice brought her attention back to the set.

At yet another press conference, Dr. King said that he probably wouldn't be able to fly to Africa the week of April 14 on a peace mission to try to end the civil war in Nigeria. He said that he might send his friend and associate, the Reverend Ralph Abernathy, instead.

Dr. King and other leaders of his group conceded that the unexpected violence in Memphis was a costly mistake. But he vowed to return to Memphis to lead a nonviolent protest.

On Friday, the following morning of the abortive march, Dr. King was set to meet with the members of the *Invaders*. Charles Cabbage, Calvin Taylor, and Lorenzo Childress knocked on the door of his room at the Rivermont Motel. All three young men were angry that their group was being publicly blamed "for an already tense situation that just happened and exploded."

Dr. King was taking a shower. Taylor said: "When he came into the room it seemed like all of a sudden there was a real rush of wind and everything just went out and peace and calm settled over everything. . . . You could feel peace around the man. It was one of the few times in my life when I wasn't actually fighting something. Although we were sitting there talking about the previous day and its events, it was like it never happened. Somebody just woke up and we were talking about it like a psychotherapy session . . ."

When the meeting was over, the feeling was great. Later at a press conference Dr. King expressed his confidence in the young militants. They had agreed that the *Invaders* would help plan the strategy for the next march, and that the SCLC, Southern Christian Leadership Conference, would give "financial administrative assistance to help the *Invaders* in their program, because they were working with the poor people." Memphis would also provide some people for the Poor Peoples Campaign.

Dr. King left for Atlanta, arriving about suppertime Friday night. His wife described him as "sorrowful and disturbed," and not having had much sleep. Dr. King was wrestling not with the specific Memphis problem, but with what he now saw as a massive threat against his entire concept of nonviolence.

Stories circulated that Dr. King disappeared on Saturday—that he sought his own Gethsemane (in the New Testament, a garden of Eden near the foot of Mount Olive. It was the scene of Jesus's agony and betrayal). Because if nonviolence failed now, did that mean it had never been the right way and his life was an ultimate farce? And what about the people he had led? Did he lead them now into escalating violence that he detested, that was none of his making?

FOUR DAYS LATER, none of the previous strategies had mattered.

"Sister, Sister," Bentley yelled, coming up the stairs. "Something bad happened."

Nikkie was on her heels, smiling, and sucking on a piece of peppermint candy.

Anne stopped dead in her tracks when she heard the

statement from the television set: "Nobel Peace Prize winner Dr. Martin Luther King is dead. He was shot down at the Lorraine Motel . . ."

The news reverberated through the black community as shockingly as the assassin's bullet that killed him. Telephones were ringing off the hook. People were running out in the streets screaming and crying.

Anne felt even more disturbed than when her father died. Even then she still had hope. Now all hopes of prosperity and dignity for her family died with Dr. King.

Would they ever be able to rise above the poverty level and live like the rich people in Germantown? Was it wrong for her to wish that the Russells could be successful too?

When Kirk came home that night, he avoided her gaze. But when he took a seat on the sofa, Anne could tell by his red-stained eyes that he'd been crying. He said to Anne in a voice more humble than she ever remembered, "To me, it wasn't worth him dying. Dr. King gave more than the entire Sanitation Department because he lost his life for our well-being."

"Dr. King had to die to bring Memphis to the sense of its duty," Anne spat out in anguish, then rushed upstairs crying.

Shock waves of anger, grief, remorse, and guilt smote the nation. Riots broke out in 172 American cities, resulting in 43 deaths, 3,500 injuries, and 27,000 arrests. Memphis was in the forefront of the rioting, and a curfew had to be imposed to curb the lawlessness that King's murder unleashed.

A white man who had lived in Texas before moving to Memphis said, "The King assassination had more impact on Memphis than the Kennedy assassination did on Dallas, and would for years to come."

Yet King's martyrdom did aid the civil rights cause. Television networks flooded the nations with days of sympathetic coverage of King's life and the whole civil rights movement.

White Memphians, who had previously despised King in their ignorance and referred to him in negative terms, acquired a new understanding of him. They reexamined views they had held for decades, and most wanted to do something to improve race relations.

Dr. King's widow, Coretta Scott King, said that she would "see that Dr. King's spirit never dies."

On April 8, twenty thousand seats in the E. L. Crump Stadium were filled with a crowd that appeared to be roughly 60 percent white and 40 percent black.

Twelve days after King's murder, the sanitation workers reached a compromise settlement. The workers received a 10-cents-per-hour raise and a provision for collecting union dues through the employees' credit union. Union recognition and dues payroll deductions were later regularized. At a cost, victory went to the blacks. Later, however, many blacks were outraged when the increased cost of sanitation service was charged to individual users on their utility bills, rather than being passed to the more affluent in the form of higher property taxes.

Even through all the turmoil, and almost immediately after Dr. King's funeral, Anne noticed that there was a sea of change in the attitudes of both blacks and whites toward race relations.

It was seen in both big and little things, from settling the garbage strike to more frequent newspaper stories about black weddings and parties to mayoral appointments to the elimination of the venerable *Hambone* cartoon from all three newspapers.

These thoughts were on Anne's mind when she desired to be an advocate of the people by working on the newspaper staff as a representative of fresh views from a teen's perspective.

Her interviewer, Mrs. Dash, loved the angle. Within a week, she had locked up an interview for Anne with Eli Spreewell, the manager of the black paper, *The Defender.*

Mr. Spreewell agreed to give her a thirty-day trial period.

In a week, her column received hundreds of letters. Ninety-five percent of them were positive. At the eager age of thirteen and a half, Anne quit her baby-sitting job and experienced the joy of her first official paycheck.

Marvin Gaye's "I Heard It Through the Grapevine" was playing on nearly every radio in the city. In the midst of such tragedy the soulful lyrics were enjoyed by most everyone—especially the blacks. If there was anything that her people enjoyed, and could make them forget about their problems, it was music—good gospel music—jazz, blues, but especially soul music.

Climbing the charts and competing with Marvin's hit was "Sitting on the Dock of the Bay," by Otis Redding. The tragedy, Anne felt, was that blacks lost not only Dr. King; they lost Otis in a plane accident right before his number-one hit was released.

Because Dr. King was assassinated in Memphis, business owners were worried about businesses moving out of Memphis and about the backlash Memphis would receive from the rest of the country. They felt that the city would be held responsible for Mar-

tin Luther King's death—where a legend was crucified.

Only days after his death, a mass memorial march for
Dr. King was being organized. Men, women, and children participating in the processional were expected to
number between 5,000 and 20,000. These marchers
would take part in the two-and-a-half-mile procession
from the Clayborn Temple to City Hall and back to the
temple.

Among those who notified the organizers that they
planned to take part in the march were Dr. King's
widow; Dr. Ralph Abernathy, Dr. King's successor as
head of the Southern Christian Leadership Conference;
Walter Reuther, president of the United Auto Workers
Union; Percy Sutton, borough president of Manhattan;
Albert Shanker, president of the United Federation of
Teachers; Frederick O'Neill, president of Actors Eq-
uity; Harry Belafonte, the singer; Bill Cosby, the come-
dian; Sidney Poitier and Ossie Davis, actors; as well as
directors, bishops, city councilmen, and many other
high-ranking officials.

Even days after the strike had ended, ministers were
charging police brutality.

Council members said, "The ministers say that they
want more black policeman. While Mr. Holliman is
trying to recruit them, they tell young blacks, 'Don't
you dare join the police force. You'll be an Uncle
Tom.' "

Anne was horrified by their comments. Her brother
was finally back to work, and though things weren't
exactly back to normal at their home, she was optimistic.

When she accompanied the children to church on
Sundays she hoped and prayed that the Lord would lift

the world's heart higher and that the racism would end in her great city.

She remembered her history teacher preaching that courage consists not in blindly overlooking danger, but in seeing and conquering it.

Her nightmares were becoming less frequent now, but even during her waking hours, she could still remember her father preaching to her: "One day you'll learn that courage is in the blood."

Four

OVER THE SUMMER, Nikkie had become increasingly silent. When Anne questioned Mae about it, she said the child was a friggin' retard—what did she expect?

But Nikkie wasn't the only thing that she had to worry about. Mae and Kirk's weekly arguments had begun to scare the children.

One night they heard him yelling downstairs, "You ain't nothing but a whore, girl!" Mae hadn't come home until four in the morning.

None of his ranting and raving bothered Mae. Once the kids were put to bed and Kirk had fallen asleep, she went back out.

Last month he'd caught her getting out of the car with Jimmy Cranbrook, a married man who lived in the block behind them. Mrs. Cranbrook had called their home, spoke to Kirk, and threatened to kill Mae.

Ultimately, Mae promised to end the affair.

She lied.

Kirk told her, "I'll see you in hell one day, girl!"

Even Wesley began to become withdrawn. He wanted someone to take Nikkie to see a doctor. He pleaded with Kirk, who only laughed him off when Wesley offered him the $35 that he'd managed to save.

Bentley seemed the only one oblivious to what was going on. Lost in her drawings, she colored a different world from the one they were living.

During the spring and early summer, Nikkie's seizures and Mae's supposedly secret abortions went on in their household as surely as Walter Cronkite's evening news came on.

On May 10, peace talks to end the Vietnam War began in Paris. Three weeks later, on the 5th of June, Senator Robert Kennedy, the late president Kennedy's brother, was fatally wounded by Sirhan Sirhan at a Los Angeles hotel.

On the sixteenth of October, black American athletes Tommie Smith and John Carlos gave the Black Power salute in the Olympic Games in Mexico to protest racism in the United States. Their senseless act held the country's and Anne's attention and even got a dry comment or two out of Mae: "Those guys got balls."

It wouldn't be until March 10, 1969, that James Earl Ray, Martin Luther King's killer, was jailed for ninety-nine years.

In the spring of that same year, Jacqueline Smith began a daily vigil at the Lorraine Motel. Ms. Smith was protesting the conversion of the hotel into a newly formed National Civil Rights Museum.

It wasn't until July 21, when Neil Armstrong walked on the moon, that the topic of conversation would finally die down from the King assassination.

In early September the Russell family managed to see the hit summer movie, Peter Fonda's *Easy Rider*, and eagerly awaited the beginning of the school year.

ANNE RUSSELL PUSHED her school desk back on its heels, and put her legs up on its cluttered surface. Ever since she began ninth grade, she'd lobbied for the position as the editor of their school newspaper, and had finally won it.

Her first assignment was to write an article about the NAACP, the National Association for the Advancement of Colored People. The local chapter of their organization was calling on students and teachers to wear black and boycott classes on Mondays for several weeks. Some 63,000 students and one principal, Willie W. Herenton—honored the boycotts, which accelerated the process of school desegregation, created new leadership, and integrated the Memphis Board of Education. Anne was lucky enough to get a brief interview with Mr. Herenton and incorporated it into her highly successful editorial.

Even though her schoolwork was on track, home was another matter.

Kirk had developed a passion for horses. He felt that he was born to be a cowboy, not a city worker. For the past year, since he'd gotten back to work, he threatened to sell their home and move to Millington. There he could buy a house with twenty acres and raise show horses.

Everyone in the house objected, especially Mae, who had a new male friend whom she met regularly at the Shrimp Shack a few blocks away.

At fourteen, Wesley seemed restless in school and often threatened to quit and get a full-time job. Anne persuaded him that it wasn't the right decision, yet she understood his frustrations. What worried him was the fact that Nikkie's seizures made her miss so much school. Even though Mae managed to teach Nikkie her numbers and letters with the help of *Sesame Street,* Wesley felt like it wasn't enough. He felt that she needed more interaction with other special kids like herself.

The one constant that helped keep Wesley focused were the numerous awards that Bentley received from art contests in school.

That same year, Memphis celebrated its sesquicentennial, giving its citizens a renewed appreciation of the city's history. And on the sixth of November, Americans had elected Richard Nixon as the nation's thirty-sixth president.

Even though a year and a half had passed, Anne would always believe that her father's death was the match that sparked the sanitation strike, and it took the death of Dr. King to extinguish it.

As the fall season wore on, Anne noticed that Bentley often fell asleep at night drawing at the kitchen table. Her artwork told of family atrocities so vivid in nature, Anne worried that she was too serious for a child her age.

Had their family been so cruel?

For the next year Anne dedicated herself to spending more time with Nikkie. With her father's image forever embedded in her psyche, she knew what he would expect of her.

Nineteen seventy began with talk of the Vietnam War escalating, and the loss of fathers and sons. By the end of April, the war had spread to Cambodia. On May 4, National Guardsmen at Kent State University in Ohio killed four students. Two days later, over a hundred colleges closed due to the student riots over Kent State.

No one laughed anymore. The country was in serious turmoil.

"Tears of a Clown" by the Miracles was an instant hit, as was Eddie Holman's "Hey There Lonely Girl."

A new subdivision was being built in the city. Located between Southern and Park, just east of Airways Boulevard, it was called Orange Mound. This neighborhood was the first black subdivision in Memphis built for blacks by blacks.

Bentley would listen to some of the kids at school bragging about moving into one of the new homes. Her prayers about moving into a new home, where she and Nikkie could have their own bedrooms, began to take precedence over her nightly prayers to her parents.

Uncommon in the black neighborhood, when Bentley walked home from school, was the soulful sound of a Caucasian singer named Elvis Presley. "The Wonder of You," was beginning to grow on her and put a smile on her face.

A SHORT YEAR LATER, in the late spring of 1971, Anne, at age sixteen, was a conscientious worker with an excellent work ethic. Thanks to her work at *The Defender*, she also had three years of editing experience under her belt. With her abilities as sharp as a tiger's tooth, Anne landed an interview with the *Hamilton Appeal*. She was so nervous, she nearly left the house without putting her nylons on.

Over the past two and a half years, she had accumulated dozens of editorials from school and *The Defender* about the ongoing civil rights movement and the blatant discrimination that was occurring in Memphis. Some were published in her school newspaper. But today she was striving to go mainstream when she applied for a job at the *Hamilton Appeal*.

From the look on their faces, she felt that some of the employees thought that her application was a prank. The *Appeal* was the biggest paper in Memphis and rarely hired teens. That stipulation hadn't mattered to Anne. To her surprise, her work had gotten the attention of the owner, Scott Hamilton.

The first thing that Anne noticed about Mr. Hamilton was his piercing hazel brown eyes. The second thing she noticed was that he loved the color gray. From suit to carpet to drapes, his huge office was decorated in variations of slate, charcoal, and smoke.

He told Anne that he especially enjoyed reading the editorial about her father's and his co-worker's untimely demise. She told him of her nightmares, and what it took to finally come to terms with his death and find peace. The article ended with her quest to start a scholarship in her father's name one day in the near future.

"Where on earth did you come from?" he constantly asked her. "You're like a shining star. I admire anyone who stands up for their rights."

"Thanks, Mr. Hamilton. I guess I got my grit from my dad."

"I've heard wonderful things about your father."

"From whom?"

"Sister Berry. We belong to the same church."

"That's nice. But you know what, Mr. Hamilton? Nobody seems to care about my father and Mr. O'Conner. After all, their death was one of the major factors that precipitated the sanitation strike. It's as though that horrible accident never happened. What's wrong with the people in Memphis? They don't seem to have a conscience."

"Well now, young lady, don't be so angry. Channel that energy into your work here. You're hired."

Anne was flabbergasted. "I am? When do I start? Is it in the department I asked for? Who's my boss? Will I ever report to you?" Suddenly Anne was so embarrassed she had to laugh. Scott laughed too. It was the beginning of an easy friendship.

During the first few weeks of her employment Anne worked harder than anyone at the paper, and they all knew it. It wasn't long before people began to cut their eyes at her. The unspoken questions were: Who in the hell do you think you are? Are you vying for my job?

She had few friends unless you counted Bentley. And for now, she liked it that way.

Less than nine months later, Scott Hamilton asked Anne for a date. She told him that she'd give him an answer by the following week.

"I don't give a damn that the man is rich!" Kirk argued when she asked for his opinion. "That man is old enough to be your father."

He's exactly thirty-nine years old. Their father would have been forty-nine this year, had he lived.

While Anne waited patiently for Kirk to change his mind, she and Bentley had hung new curtains and put a matching couch cover in the living room. In two weeks she planned on purchasing new spreads for the girls' bedroom. They were so patched they looked like the Scarecrow's tattered clothing on *The Wizard of Oz.*

She tried again one afternoon when he was reading the evening paper.

"Think about it, Kirk," she said, breaking a string of thread with her teeth. Her mind had already raced ahead two years to marriage. "Eventually I'll be one less mouth to feed. I know things are tight."

"I said no, and I mean it. I may be a garbage man, but I know a few things that you don't!" Kirk said, throwing down the paper and storming out of the house.

When Bentley came downstairs, Anne was crying.

"Sister, what's wrong?"

Anne hugged her. "Nothing. Everything is going to be fine." She rolled her eyes at the door. "Just fine."

BUT THE RUSSELL HOUSEHOLD WASN'T FINE. Kirk never gave in and Anne found herself becoming more and more attracted to Scott. It took all the courage that she could muster to abide by Kirk's command and fend off Scott's weekly proposals for a date for nearly a year.

"Teenyboppers" was the new slang, and Anne put Bentley in that category. She and Nikkie both loved the Jackson Five as well as the Osmond Brothers.

Wesley worked on construction during the summer months and into the fall. With Nikkie's seizures becoming a daily occurrence, he saved nearly every dime he could to find the right specialist to help her. The physician she saw now told them that Nikkie's brain would never mature past that of a five-year-old.

With the weather being so seasonably warm this fall, Bentley and Wesley took turns taking Nikkie on outside activities. Nikkie loved going to W. C. Handy Park, named for William Christopher Handy, the Father of the Blues.

However, no amount of activity could prevent Nikkie's seizures that came and went like clockwork. The last one lasted almost twenty minutes. She was in the hospital for two days and put on regular doses of Ativan.

Wesley did his daily chores of taking out the trash and mowing the grass once a week. Having matured at such an early age, he acted more like Nikkie's father than her brother. Anne worried that her young nephew wasn't interested in the slightest in girls. He never talked about them; only his two sisters mattered.

By Thanksgiving, Anne began to feel so comfortable at work that she brought Bentley along with her on the weekends.

Kirk finally gave in, and she and Scott went out on their first date. He took her to the University of Memphis's homecoming football game. People stared at them as they watched the game. Anne could almost hear the whispers that she was dating him because he was like a father figure to her. But they were so wrong. Scott was nothing like that. He was charming, funny, and sexy as all get-out. She chastised herself for fantasizing about their first night in bed.

Even though she and Scott had begun to date, he rarely spoke to her at work. The few dates they'd been on were to the movies, dinner at a posh restaurant, and then back home. He hadn't even attempted to kiss her. Anne sensed that even though Scott was all smiles, he was a very lonely man. When she asked him what happened to his wife, he said that she was killed and the killer was never found.

By Christmas, she managed to make him laugh with one of Bentley's drawings.

"That girl's got talent. Is anyone saving for her college education?"

"Not yet. Her brother and I are hoping that she'll get
a scholarship."

"I'd say it's in the bag." He winked at Anne, and she
melted like hot wax.

Five

"NO ONE UNDERSTANDS ME," Bentley wrote in her
diary. "Sure, my sister sister, Anne, tries to. But how
can I tell her that every time she's away from home her
sister and brother torment me and my brother and
sister?"

I know Anne loves us all.

But now, since Anne went to work at the newspaper, I've come to learn that Anne loves a man
she calls Scott Hamilton. She doesn't tell me this,
but I can tell. This is the first time that she's allowed Mae, who makes Nikkie sit still for hours
watching her stupid soap operas, to be in charge of
her on the weekends. I don't blame Anne. We've
had so much misery in our house lately; I'm glad
that she's finally found the time to laugh. I haven't
learned that trick yet.

Nikkie laughs. But she has no idea what she's
laughing about. I fear for my sister. Her health is

getting worse. Wesley was able to take her to the Health Department for her latest checkup. I heard them talking about lupus, as well as the mental retardation and epilepsy that we all knew about already. What exactly did lupus mean? I'll get Aunt Anne to explain it to me whenever she has the time.

I don't know what's wrong with Wesley, either. He works every odd job in our neighborhood and people have begun to nickname him "the little Jitney Jew." When he's at home, he seems to notice everything about Nikkie, but nothing about me. Does he know that I'm four and a half feet tall and wear a size 2 shoe? He kisses me now and then, but he never notices my drawings. I know he loves me. But I wish he would tell me so.

When she finished her diary entry her thoughts trailed back to Anne as they usually did. At nine years old, Bentley tried to pay attention to what was important to her Aunt Anne: the Vietnam War, civil rights, SNCC, the Student Nonviolent Coordinating Committee that she planned to join in her first year in college, and finally, her job at the *Hamilton Appeal*.

Bentley secretly watched her brother making plans to join the army. How could he leave them? Soon Anne would be gone too. Bentley believed that she could survive, but what about Nikkie? Nikkie needed Anne, Mae, and Wesley to care for her. How could Bentley take the place of three people?

Apparently, none of that mattered to her brother. The first Friday in June after Wesley completed the tenth grade, he began to pack his bags. That night he kissed her and a sleeping Nikkie good-bye, then left.

Bentley didn't know that her brother planned to send his first check home to get another telephone line installed in their room so that he could call them on a regular basis.

She also didn't realize that Kirk was about to quit his job and embark on a rodeo career. Without the combined income from Wesley and Anne, Bentley and Nikkie would surely end up in a foster home.

It took Kirk on one of his regular weekend drunken stupors to make it real for her.

"Bentley," he whispered, standing just inside her and Nikkie's bedroom, "C'mere."

Tightening the grip on her lip, she slid out of bed and glanced back at Nikkie, who was snoring lightly.

"Fix Uncle Kirk a jelly and peanut butter sandwich."

Not thinking anything was amiss, she went downstairs, wearing her panties and an old pajama top of Anne's with all of the buttons missing. While she was making the sandwich, she hadn't noticed that her uncle had gone into the bathroom.

"Bentley," he commanded, "C'mere for a minute."

Laying the butter knife down on the counter, she entered the bathroom. The tiny room was barely lit by the light from the kitchen. Looking around, she didn't spot her uncle right away.

"Is something wrong, Uncle Kirk?" she asked innocently.

Silent, dark as shame, he emerged and greeted her with an odd smile on his face.

He never bothered to answer her. Already reaching for the Vaseline on the shelf, he lowered her panties, and proceeded to swab her private parts with the thick jelly.

He began to breathe heavily, and with each breath Bentley felt a tremor of fear race down her body. She tried to speak, to tell him to stop, but the words caught in her dry throat. As if in slow motion, she watched him lower his briefs and for the first time in her life, she saw a grown man's penis.

With a startled gasp, she clamped her legs together and prayed that she would find her voice and scream.

Kirk grinned and stumbled a step backward.

"Stop it," she finally yelled and hoped that it was loud enough for someone to hear her. As quickly as she could, she snatched her panties back up and tried to push past him. When he grabbed her, she bit his hand as hard as she could. He cursed out loud, releasing his grip. Bentley managed to duck between his legs and scurry to the door. As she tried to open it, she heard him whimpering behind her.

"I'm sorry, girl."

Bentley managed to get the door open a crack before he held it with his large hand. She felt her entire body recoil with hate. She didn't feel afraid of him now. She only felt anger.

"Let me go!"

"Bentley. Wait. I won't hurt you. Uncle Kirk made a mistake. Can you forgive me, girl?"

He was looking down at her with tears in his eyes and Bentley didn't feel the slightest bit of sympathy for him. "I said, let me go."

Stepping back, he released his hand. She opened the door and quickly ran back upstairs, her heart beating wildly in her small chest.

Back in her room, she hurriedly locked the door and slipped into bed with Nikkie. Trembling, she sucked on her lip, clutched her arms around her sister, and held on for dear life. A part of her wanted to wake up Anne and tell her. But what good would that do? Her uncle would probably deny that he'd try to harm her and she knew that Mae wouldn't give her an ounce of sympathy.

No, she thought. She'd keep it to herself. Tears threatened and she let them fall, promising herself that one day she and Nikkie would escape this horrible place. One day they'd have their own home and she and her sister would watch cartoons all day long and eat as many snacks as Nikkie wanted.

Later, as she lay awake, willing herself not to start crying again, she wished for her mother. There was no one here, she felt, to comfort her. No one to lend her strength.

No, she wouldn't cry. She'd already shed enough tears. Turning over on her side, she linked her fingers with Nikkie's and glanced outside at the twinkling stars. Together, they would survive. Because she now believed that strength is born in the deep silence of a long-suffering heart—not amid joy.

Six

IN JANUARY OF 1973 an agreement to end the Vietnam War was reached in Paris. To Anne's surprise she received a long and heartfelt letter from Wesley. In it he told her that he wouldn't be coming home and he wasn't sure how to break the news to Bentley and Nikkie. He asked her if she could please find a way to tell them that he'd decided to make a career out of the army. Anne wrote back and promised him that she would.

The winter days flew swiftly by, so much in contrast to other winters when time had crept monotonously while they grew older and youth was stolen from them.

Yet years after King's death the city seemed to have lost its momentum. Amid racial divisions on nearly every issue, black and white, public and private could rarely agree on either larger goals or the programs and priorities for reaching them. Anne believed that because of such divisiveness, economic growth had nearly ceased.

In the spring, the city of Memphis began to make changes in its physical makeup. As part of the Greater Memphis Program, the business elite attempted to redress discrimination against blacks and women and bring the community together. Local leaders and the Chamber of Commerce allocated several million dollars attempting to get Memphians "to believe" in their city and try to stimulate job-creating investments from the outside.

The *Hamilton Appeal* wrote about the physical and economic changes in the downtown area that resulted in the drop of property value. Middle- and upper-class white shoppers had largely deserted downtown for the shopping malls in the suburbs. Even so, work began to try to revitalize the downtown area by the construction of the Cook Convention Center and Exhibition Hall at a cost of $31 million. It would be completed the following year.

Few people in the Memphis area cared that the Spanish artist Pablo Picasso died the second week in April. That is, unless you were Bentley Russell. She seemed to think, or so she told her aunt Anne, that she would one day be as famous.

The following month in May, the beginning of the Senate hearings in the Watergate affair began. President Nixon's nickname, Tricky Dick, would become a popular slogan.

Anne couldn't remember the *Hamilton Appeal* being so busy in all the time she had worked there. It seemed that something newsworthy was happening minute by minute. The longer she worked at the newspaper, the more inquisitive she became. She felt her relationship with Scott wasn't just personal. It was educational as well. With Scott's abundant knowledge about people, politics, and business, Anne began to imagine that her dream of racial equality in the city of Memphis would one day be possible.

Anne kept it to herself that Scott had asked her to marry him after she graduated. But she knew that she would eventually have to get Kirk's permission because she wouldn't turn eighteen until late fall. Anne dreamed nightly of moving into Scott's beautiful home that he had told her so much about.

To Anne's growing dismay, Kirk was still dreaming of the rodeo circuit. He managed to purchase a three-year-old Appaloosa, which he kept boarded in Millington. Every now and then he drove Bentley and Nikkie out to the farmhouse and let them ride her.

Shortly after winning the Homecoming Queen crown last fall, Anne's circle of friends had increased—she now had a total of five. They spoke at school and even called her at home. It was awkward not spending as much time with Bentley as she used to, but Bentley said she understood when Anne explained that she needed more friends her own age now.

Back in January, Anne as well as her friends had sent out applications to local as well as out of state colleges. By the last week in February, she had received numerous opportunities at Memphis colleges. To her classmates' disbelief, Anne had been the first student in their class to be offered a scholarship in journalism at Columbia University in New York.

Being a small-town southern girl, Anne was petrified. Thanks to her two years of working at the *Hamilton Appeal*, her skills as well as her academics were in great demand outside their small town. She'd hoped that one of her friends would help her make the right decision.

Not so. Jealousy was a bitter pill to swallow—not just at school, but at home as well. Mae told her that she should forget about college and keep the job she had. Anne didn't know whom to trust.

At the final graduation rehearsal, her friends were even crueler.

"Old Man Scott," Helen said, "hell, rumor is, he killed his wife."

"A regular old Norman Bates he is," Angela snickered.

"You're both lying," Anne countered, hoping that what they said wasn't true.

"No she ain't. I heard that Scott killed his first wife, too—her name was Lulu."

"Stop it. I don't want to hear any more," she whispered to herself. Her mind slipped away to the words of an old blues lyric by Ida Cox:

> *Takes a southern woman to sing this*
> *southern song*
> *Lord, I'm worried now, but I won't*

> *be worried long*
> *When I was downtown I wouldn't*
> *take no one's advice*
> *But I ain't going to let that same bee*
> *sting me twice*

"Uh-huh," Angela chimed in. "Her name was Leigh. And, like you, she was a really beautiful woman. The old boy was acquitted at the trial, but the young fool ended up going to an insane asylum for nearly three years."

He told me that he was vacationing abroad for three years.

Anne questioned, "Why would he kill his wife?"

"Because she whored around on him. In short she was dirty—the one unacceptable word in a southern woman's vocabulary."

"I don't believe you." *You're just envious.*

Anne heard someone whisper loud enough for her to overhear, "Let's not forget the fact that he's old enough to be her father. Naw, grandfather."

Then Anne remembered her brother's words. "The man is a bit of an eccentric, Anne. I can feel it. Marrying him would be a mistake."

She clamped her hands over her ears. *I don't believe you! Everyone's lying. Just plain lying!*

During the next few days, she tried to avoid Scott, electing to take time to think things out.

On Friday afternoon, she tearfully filled out the acceptance papers for Memphis State University. Ever since she'd talked to Scott about accepting the scholarship to Columbia University and leaving Memphis, he had been pressuring her to get married.

Her guilt made her finally give in to his seductive

charms later that night. It was quick and fast, and Anne hated every second of it. The second time, Sunday evening, was better, and Anne found herself responding to Scott's ardent lovemaking. She told herself that she shouldn't feel ashamed of the pleasure she began to feel. After all, she'd be his wife in a few weeks.

On Monday morning, her first full day home from school, she slept until noon, then took an hourlong bubble bath. She found herself caressing her body in ways that she knew that Scott would.

Funny, since they'd become intimate, she hadn't thought any more about Scott's wife. It didn't matter anyway. She knew that Scott would give her an engagement ring any day now.

When the phone rang, her heart did a back flip.

It was just past three, and Anne could hear Bentley coming in from school.

"Be ready by seven-fifteen. I've got box seats for the eight o'clock show at the Orpheum Theater."

"To see what?"

"*Cats!*"

Goodness gracious, she hated kittens and especially cats. "Okay, Scott. I'll be ready."

After she hung up, she took a good look at Bentley. At ten, she looked thirteen. Her hips and breasts were already developing much faster than most girls her age. But it was the sadness in her eyes that made Anne take a second look.

"What's wrong, Bentley?" Anne asked, taking her schoolbooks from her slender arms.

Bentley shrugged it off. "Nothing." She quickly sucked in her lip.

"Girl," Anne said, tugging at Bentley's bottom lip,

"one day soon, when you're about sixteen years old, a man is going to faint when you kiss him. I'll bet that lip of yours feels like whipped cream."

Bentley blushed.

"Mae's taken Nikkie to the doctor. He's changing her medication. Apparently Mae's concerned that Nikkie's been sleeping too much."

"That's a relief. I've been worried about her, too." Bentley smiled weakly, and then asked. "You going out tonight?"

"Yeah. Scott is taking me to the Orpheum Theater. Would you like to go? I'm sure Scott can get another ticket."

Bentley shook her head no and slid the books from Anne's arms. "I've got to finish the entries in my journal. But thanks for asking."

Something was wrong, but Anne couldn't put her finger on it. Today was one of those moments when Anne wanted to act like Bentley's mother and demand that she sit down and talk.

All during dinner, and after she dressed, Anne couldn't work up the nerve to approach her niece.

When Scott knocked on the front door, Anne kissed Bentley and Nikkie good night and told herself that she was worrying over nothing.

All through the show, Anne tried to conjure up images and events over the past school year. She fidgeted in her seat so much that Scott totally misread her body language. Taking her hand in his, he leaned over and whispered in her ear, "I'm getting the impression that you're not enjoying the show."

Anne made an impish expression and Scott laughed.

The second act had just begun when he said, "Get your purse."

Fourteen minutes later, she found herself in a luxury suite at the Peabody Hotel.

None of the opulence of the room mattered as Scott quickly took control of the situation. He led her back to the bedroom and willed her mind to forget about what her friends had said.

They sat on the edge of bed facing one another, and in seconds he kissed her forehead and gently hugged her. The barriers that once shielded her heart had finally broke and Anne came alive in his arms.

His palpitating kiss against her mouth took her breath away. Anne felt him clasping her lower lip, and casually brushing it with his tongue. Afterward, he seized her lower lip with his and pressing puissantly against it, intently began to tantalize her upper lip.

Anne felt the palm of his hands caress the soft cleft between her breasts, then fan outward to massage their fullness, until he felt her nipples harden. Her body trembled convulsively and felt the hot throbbing between her legs converge with the sound of her heart as she heard his sharp intake of breath.

Opening her eyes, desire-darkened irises followed his every movement. Lifting a hand, she touched his face, drawing her fingers along his chin and jawline, and loving the feel of his thick mustache and the texture of his smooth-shaven cheeks. She outlined his thin eyebrows and the soft tip of his nose, and then toyed with the fullness of his lips.

Scott's head slowly lowered and slanted toward Anne's lips once more. Anne opened her mouth and welcomed the kiss. His tongue tentatively traced her sensitive inner lining and she felt as if blue flames of fire were vaulting through her insides, burning her . . . incinerating her.

Finally, his kiss deepened into a passionate, demanding kiss. As ephemeral as a dream, he slowly removed her clothing, and then removed his.

Next, she felt him reach down and ever so gently caress the cavity between her slim waist and pelvic bones with his fingertips. He continued until he felt the warm lubrication excreting from her moist center.

"Scott," came her breathy cry. Without disengaging their lips, he pushed her down onto the bed and straddled her. Melting beneath his naked body, Anne wrapped her arms around his shoulders, and then daringly brushed her moist palms down his hairy chest.

Though they had made love twice before, his tenderness seemed to solidify Scott as her dream lover. He had made her feel like a woman. He was soft and tender, yet cold and calculating. She loved every inch of him. And now in his nakedness, all of his enraptured maleness confused her, and she felt a quiver of vulnerability.

As her hands caressed him, she heard him moan her name against her mouth.

"Shhh," she said guiding his hardness between her legs. She arched her body to offer him more of her. All of her wanted to be consumed by his lovemaking.

She panted as he eased himself gently inside of her.

Lifting himself up on his elbows, he eased halfway out, deliberately giving her time to feel every inch of him inside her. His hips moved persuasively as she parted her thighs a little further to envelop even more of him. She knew that she was tight and warm—her silken casing receiving him benevolently, ravenously closing around him.

Anne felt the pulsating force of his thrusts teasing

her . . . quick, slow . . . hard . . . easy . . . working up to the mountaintop, but not quite going over . . . again . . . and again . . . until . . . neither one could take the pressure any longer.

Next, with his back against the wall, he encouraged Anne to sit on his hands while he supported her buttocks. Placing her hands on his shoulders, she positioned her legs on the sides of his waist and placed him inside of her warm center. With the balls of her feet pressed against the wall, she engaged in the rhythmic movements of close union.

This was Anne's favorite position, and Scott knew it all too well.

When Anne was close to a climax, Scott slowed the pace. Anne shuddered with pleasure as his cool fingers massaged her pert nipples while he slid deliciously out of her.

"You want some more, baby?" he asked huskily. "I can tell by the way you worked your hips that you want it."

Even saying yes to this would have broken the spell, so she leaned over and sucked the tips of his brown nipples.

Scott was breathing heavily when he carefully placed Anne's right leg over his shoulder and stretched her left horizontally on the bed. She felt the tip of his member touch her vagina, and she widened it to receive him. He pushed her left leg even wider, getting their pelvises as close as heat is to fire, altering the position of the legs each time Anne climaxed.

When Scott came inside her, she felt every cataclysmic spurt. By then both their bodies glowed with pleasure like fruit when it colors. But for Anne, that was not the end. Just learning how to use her muscles adequately, she gripped him, until she felt him harden inside her once more. In seconds, his hips began to gyrate in rhythmic waves of ecstasy, each crest taking them a little higher until perception shattered in a storm of stars.

A sudden urgency gripped them, and quickly, ever so fastidiously, they climbed passion's peak once more. When they reached the summit, looming in that one glorious moment when both lovers reach the apex of pleasure at the exact moment, they vellicated with all the pomp and circumstance of Fourth of July fireworks.

Supreme bliss claimed and held them for several seconds, before they dislodged, then lay side by side. Drained, they took one final passionate look at one another. With his eyes closed, Scott smiled.

"I love, you, Anne."

"And I love you, Scott."

She pulled the sheet over them and closed her eyes.

When she awoke an hour later, Scott was looking down on her, smiling. He had slid a diamond baguette wedding band around her finger.

"Will you marry me, Anne?"

Her instant tears meant yes.

Seven

AWAKENING IN THE MIDDLE OF THE NIGHT had become a bad habit for Bentley. She found herself lying in bed, staring at the ceiling for hours before she would drift back off to sleep. Often, like tonight, she would get up and open the windows wide and inhale the sweet fresh air.

For the past year and a half, she had managed to stay out of her uncle Kirk's way. Up to this point, he still hadn't been able to look her in the eye.

Sure, he put on a front for everyone else, but they both knew the truth.

The few times he took her and Nikkie on a ride on his horses, he was silently saying that he was sorry, trying to put a smile on her face. But she never smiled. She secretly prayed that he would leave and never come back. Maybe then, Anne would forget about getting married and stay home with her and Nikkie.

Wesley wrote home frequently, but Bentley didn't tell him how things were at home. A part of her wanted to tell him the truth so that he would come and save her and Nikkie. But then she realized; it was good for someone to escape the tomb they called home. At least she could tell from the tone of his letters that he seemed happy.

What did that mean exactly, happy?

Was it what Aunt Anne felt now that she was about to be married? Didn't her aunt know how much she was going to miss her? Didn't she realize that without her sweet smile and spontaneous laughter, it was pure hell living here?

With her lip in tow, she felt the southern breezes blowing, caressing her cheek and whispering unconvincingly that everything would turn out all right.

Outside, the moon beguiled her. Silently, one by one, in the infinite meadows of the heaven, blossomed the lovely stars, the forget-me-nots of angels.

And her heart, so heavily burdened for so long, felt a brief reprieve. Maybe life did exist outside of fairy tales.

Maybe she and Nikkie were worthy enough to hold their heads up high beneath God's blue sky; maybe they weren't misfits grown from the wrong seed and planted in the wrong soil.

Eight

IT WAS KIRK WHO DECIDED that Anne should wait a year before she and Scott could marry. Until then, Anne happily made plans for their wedding the following September. Working full-time at the *Hamilton Appeal* kept Anne so busy, she forgot all about familial problems.

In August of 1974, after one year at Memphis State, and one day after Nixon resigned over the Watergate scandal, Anne discovered that she was pregnant. Her fiancé did the honorable thing and telephoned Anne's guardian. Scott told his would-be brother-in-law that he planned on marrying Anne as soon as possible. Kirk cussed him out, and then hung up in his face. It appeared that Kirk was embarrassed about the thought of canceling all of the festivities. More than 500 people had been invited to the wedding.

Anne didn't care anything about the brouhaha. She'd had morning sickness so bad since she told Scott, that she had to take a week off of work. Since then, her situation hadn't gotten much better.

A week later, in the early evening, Anne and Scott stood before the justice of the peace on Elvis Presley Boulevard. Bentley and Nikkie were Anne's attendants. Mae and Kirk refused to come.

The newlyweds honeymooned in Jamaica for two weeks. Scott treated her like a queen.

Once home, Anne moved into their historic home on 4225 Walnut Grove. Their Mediterranean-inspired 11,000-square-foot Memphis home was previously owned by Dr. Ralph Mueller in the 1920s.

Scott encouraged Anne to redecorate the house.

"I'm not sure I know how to do this type of thing adequately, Scott," Anne told her husband before he left for work one morning.

"Would you like an interior designer to help you?"

"Can we afford one?"

"Certainly." He kissed her good-bye. "I'll call Vuxebaum's Interiors today."

"Are you familiar with their work?" Anne called out. She wondered if his ex-wife had used the same designer.

"The *Appeal* just landed a huge advertising contract with his company."

Anne breathed a sigh of relief. "Okay, then." She waved good-bye and closed the door. With her back against the door, she stood there blinking in disbelief. How had she managed to be so lucky? The rotunda entry, with its marble black and gray slate floor pattern emphasizing its elliptical shape, tied together the vast cherry dual staircase that formed singularly at the base. Anne thought that her grand home looked like a *Gone with the Wind* movie set.

She sighed. What in the world had a little girl from southwest Memphis gotten herself into?

The decorator's name was Vester. They had several meetings before they came to an agreement of how to remodel the house. They settled on pastel greens and lemon yellows with matte gold as the accent color. As the work on the house began, Anne began to pack on the pounds.

By the fifth month of her pregnancy, she had gained nearly thirty pounds.

Because her dream, along with her father's, was to finish college, Scott gave in and told her that after the baby was born, she could return to Memphis State.

This was the beginning of the lies that Scott would tell her.

After Basil was born, Anne experienced her first problems with Scott.

"Go on, you heard me. Get on that scale!"

Wearily Anne stepped on the metal object in their master bathroom while Scott fidgeted with the sliding gadgets.

The scale read 160. "Scott, the baby is barely six weeks old." She sniffed back tears. "I'll lose the weight. I promise."

Scott was already on the phone calling a trainer. "Yes, that's the place—the old Mueller mansion." He gave the woman the address and ended by saying, "Seven-thirty A.M. will be fine." He hung up.

"Scott," Anne pleaded, "that's when I breast-feed Basil."

"Give him a bottle."

Even their sex life changed. Anne's prancing around in the endless peignoir sets he constantly bought for her replaced the foreplay. He became obsessed with just looking at her curvaceous body.

In four weeks she was back to a trim size 6, but was disappointed that her hips had become even more voluptuous from having the baby. Her breasts constantly leaked with breast milk, and Scott tried to pretend that he didn't enjoy sampling the creamy fluid.

During the second year of their marriage Scott announced one night that the *Hamilton Appeal* was buying the Memphis *Press-Scimitar*. It was odd because he usually didn't discuss his business with her. She merely read about the paper in the paper.

After the buyout, Scott was away from home more than usual. But he began to boast to Anne about the money that the *Appeal* was making by efficiently running both papers while using virtually the same staff. Anne wasn't told about Scott's other business interests, and the fact that there was a sister *Hamilton Appeal* in Cincinnati, Ohio.

Through the hiring of a chauffeur, cook, and a full-time maid, Anne deduced that their wealth was substantial.

While the baby slept most of the day, Anne had absolutely nothing to do but read, which had begun to bore her. Their house was a showplace but not a home. One room that she was especially proud of was the dining room. Etched glass, silver goblets, and candlesticks made an opulent table setting in the mustard yellow formal dining room. Filling the antique silver epergne was an arrangement of roses, viburnums, and lilacs that was elaborate enough to be appreciated but not too tall to prevent conversation across the table. Shannon had suggested that the same floral motif be repeated on the silk damask wallpaper. Yellow tiger-striped chairs with dark cherry lacquered legs and arms brilliantly contrasted the shiny hardwood floor. A six-foot cream-shaded chandelier completed the formal room.

Shannon did exciting things in the room, like making silver trays out of antique picture frames, and making vases out of champagne flutes.

There was special lighting and an improvised stage created by the original hand-carved mantel that made

Scott's collection of blue-and-white Chinese porcelain the center of attention in their warm living room.

The custom kitchen was fit for a chef. Endless stark white cabinets with granite countertops caught one's eye. A double stainless steel Sub-Zero refrigerator at the end of one row of the U-shaped cabinetry commanded attention. Warming ovens pulled out from hidden drawers, woks rose up from their hidden alcoves, and numerous assortments of cuisine gadgets for mixing and baking were lovingly stored in the lower cabinets. A custom seating area of ecru leather benches along the wall completed the homey atmosphere of a well-appointed kitchen.

All six bedrooms looked like pages torn out of *Architectural Digest*. And Scott and Anne's bedroom was no exception. The main appointments that Anne enjoyed in their bedroom suite were the separate closets, bathrooms, and dressing areas.

The funny thing was that after the decorating was completed, Anne had expected to entertain guests. Or just invite friends over for a cocktail. After months of waiting for Scott to broach the question, Anne asked, "Should we invite some of your friends over for dinner?"

"No."

"Why?"

"I said no, Anne."

Why in the world had they gone through such an expense to redo the house if no one would see it? She wanted to show it to the world. *Look, see what I've done. I've finally made it to the top. She wanted to shout it, especially to her brother and sister.*

No matter how good her argument, Scott wouldn't budge.

Taking care of their beautiful baby boy became her focus. She taught him to say his ABCs by the time he was thirteen months old. By fifteen months he was counting to twenty-five. This was the only time that Scott seemed happy, watching his son show off abilities that most children didn't achieve until they were two years of age.

During this period, she and Scott rarely made love. When she called home to check on her nieces and nephew, Bentley seemed withdrawn.

"Ask Uncle Kirk to bring you over. I still don't have my driver's license yet, so I can't come and pick you up."

To her growing shame, Scott had forbidden Anne to have any dealings with her family. She could have asked the chauffeur to pick up Bentley and Nikkie, but Scott would find out. The entire staff was completely loyal to him.

Before the fall semester enrollment began, Anne told Scott that she wanted to resume her studies at Memphis State. She had just taken a shower, and used her new Beautiful perfume to entice him.

"Don't I give you everything you need?"

His voice sounded so eerie, Anne was afraid.

"But you promised me, Scott, that I could go back to college after the baby was born. He's sixteen months old and walking and talking. I thought . . ." Anne immediately reached for a towel.

"I do the thinking in this house. Remember that."

"But Scott . . ." With a quick flip of his wrist, he backhanded Anne, causing her to drop the towel. She could feel his fingerprints along her cheek, and felt an instant swelling.

"Don't ever question me again."

Cold sweat crawled down her back like frightened

mice. Anne covered her naked body, trembling. She reached for her bathrobe, and after he exited the bathroom, she followed him, holding back the desire to break down and cry. *Why am I so frightened? He's my husband, for God's sake.*

"Scott . . ." she said, calling out his name softly. *I love you. Don't you love me anymore?*

"What!" he said turning around to look at her, seething. "What do you want from me now?"

Lowering her eyes, she felt an instant stab of fear. "Nothing."

Nine

DRIVE. DESIRE. DEDICATION. DETERMINATION. The four *D*'s that Bentley told herself that she and Nikkie would live by. If her goals for success were high, she felt that she had good reason.

Bentley was actively trying to stop her bad habit of sucking her lip. So far, she only did it when she was nervous.

Presently, Nikkie seemed to be content. Mae had actually taught her how to crochet doilies. Her workmanship was perfect. A relatively inexpensive hobby, Kirk reluctantly agreed to buy the needles and colored thread for his niece. With enough thread to last her until Christmas, Nikkie began crocheting the delicate disks and starching them into stiffened masterpieces with sugar water.

Even as Mae seemed to be taking a special interest in

Nikkie, Bentley, a teenager now, began to take notice of her aunt's moods.

For instance, she guessed that her aunt had recently had an abortion during the Halloween weekend. Bentley had overheard Mae and Kirk arguing that this was Mae's tenth operation and that she'd never bear any children of her own into this world if she continued this practice.

Why couldn't she use birth control pills like other women did? Bentley wondered.

At times it seemed that Kirk was bitter, especially since his dreams of being a rodeo star weren't exactly coming true. Even so, he had softened a little in the years that had gone by—he was thinking about applying for a supervisor's position at the Department of Sanitation. More blacks were being hired in that area, now that the strike was behind them.

Kirk had gotten a few raises and for the first time that Bentley could remember, he gave Mae money to spruce up the house a little.

Now their meager home had a few new items: sofa, stove, refrigerator, and even a fifteen-inch Zenith color television. While Nikkie kept busy working on a bedspread for her and Bentley, Mae was able to watch her soap operas without much interruption. Twice a week, she would meticulously clean the house and then wash and iron everyone's clothes.

Always a good cook, they never left the kitchen table hungry. It was Bentley's daily duty now to keep the kitchen clean.

Sure, the house looked nice inside, but when Bentley complained about the rats in the kitchen and bathroom, Kirk told her that the house was too old, and nothing short of building a new foundation would keep them out.

The rats in the house terrified Bentley, especially when she heard them scratching and gnawing at night. Nikkie didn't understand what they were and would sometimes take the dead rat and trap and hand it to Kirk. He would holler at her, shake his head like she was the stupidest fool in the world, then go on and repair the hole in the house. That would work temporarily, but soon the rodents would be back.

Like clockwork, twice a month, she and Nikkie would receive letters from Wesley. He never mentioned coming home. He only had good things to tell them. Most of his questions were always concerning Nikkie. Was she seeing a doctor regularly now? Had she stopped wetting the bed at night? Had Mae stopped picking on her?

Never, Bentley noticed, were there any words about his health, his mental stability. Encouraging, though, was the fact that he'd just made a Spec IV last month. With nearly a hundred more dollars a month in pay, he'd be sending more money home now to help out.

Several times when she wrote him back, she considered asking him why he couldn't be their guardian instead of Kirk. He was old enough now to move them to where he lived. But she never posed the question to her brother, possibly because she already knew the answer.

In her waking dreams she dreamed of Anne coming to get her and Nikkie and moving them into the big house that she and her family lived in. She'd only seen pictures of her son, Basil, and her husband, Scott, when Anne sent them Christmas cards. Bentley couldn't help it. She was instantly resentful.

What had happened to her sweet and loving sister sister?

Lately, the pictures and cards had stopped. Bentley hadn't heard from Anne since January.

Nikkie turned fourteen in April and Bentley became a full-fledged teenager in June. At age thirteen, her body felt like one of a woman a generation older than herself. Was that the reason why she was getting so impatient now with Anne?

She'd heard an old adage that Mae loved to recite: "You know a cat is supposed to chase the mouse. When the mouse starts chasing the cat, something is wrong!"

Bentley began to think about Anne less and less. When she did, the same questions always surfaced— didn't she know that they were still having a hard time? Didn't she care?

She wondered; did money change you so much that you forgot about your family? If it did, Bentley thought, she'd rather remain poor for the rest of her life.

During the Thanksgiving holiday, Mae, at the tender old age of twenty-five, had her thirteenth abortion. This time she nearly died. They removed half of her uterus, and, as Kirk predicted, there went the chance of her ever having any children of her own.

That realization seemed to kill something inside Mae and she became angry and distant toward everyone. As swiftly as the glance of a falling star, everything changed.

As Bentley continued to try and keep peace in the house, she began to care for Nikkie more and more. Mae, she realized, wasn't worth the price of a soda cracker. All she did now was sleep and smoke stinky Camel cigarettes.

At night the sounds of filthy rats scratching incessantly made her tiny nostrils recoil in fear. She wondered, as she lay there listening to the noises, about other girls her age. Were they still playing with dolls? Did they have sleepovers with their other friends? Did they go to the movies with their boyfriends? Did they go with their mothers and fathers to church every Sunday? Did they enjoy having girl talks with their mothers?

She wondered so much about the real world and normal-acting people her head ached.

What was this thing called life? She was taught in her eighth-grade English class that life was the jailer of the soul in this filthy prison, and its only deliverer was death. What most people call life is a journey to death and what we call death is a passport to life.

If that were true, she thought, why should people like her and Nikkie want to live? There had to be hope. Would hope be the name of her new friend?

Ten

THE CITY OF MEMPHIS was back in the news again. Federal Express, a brand-new shipping company, was garnering interest all over the nation. The founder, Fred Smith, had looked long and hard at Smyrna, Tennessee, among other airport locations. But Fred's hometown connections and the Memphis International Airport won out.

The timing was fortunate. Kimberly-Clark and Firestone were already closing up shop. From their inception, hiring 30,000 employees, Federal Express directly impacted every stratum of the Memphis economy.

And with nearly the same fanfare as Federal Express, Danny Thomas's St. Jude's Children's Research Hospital opened. St. Jude's battle against childhood diseases touched the heart of Memphians. The hospital was like the sun breaking through after a storm.

Memphis had once again surrendered the dark days of the civil rights struggle, the death of Martin Luther King, and the city's worst garbage strike.

The *Hamilton Appeal* constantly wrote about the changing demographics in Memphis. Midtown was now the in place for blacks to live. The street boundaries of midtown were Jackson, Bellvue, Park, and Godlett. It was a racially integrated area, but with a white majority. It was closer to downtown, just to its west, than the more affluent East Memphis. To the north and northwest, blacks were a majority in an area called North Memphis, and to the far south, they were in a majority ironically called Whitehaven. Besides midtown, whites predominated in the more affluent areas to the east, referred to as East Memphis. To the north was the working-class area called Frayser and to the northeast a more middle-class area, Raleigh.

Anne read the articles, but could no longer report her thoughts to the *Hamilton Appeal*. After all, she was the CEO's wife. She wasn't supposed to have an opinion. She was supposed to be sublimely happy. With a state-of-the-art computer in her home, she was learning more about less important matters such as graphics than what her father had taught her about courage.

The following year, the election of black congressman Harold Ford Sr. sent a ripple through the city of

Memphis. Some constituents said that Harold Ford owed the political machine of former mayor Crump royalty payments for casting the mold that launched his political success.

Changes were being seen and felt all over the city.

Throughout the fifties, sixties, and seventies a young man named Elvis Presley won the hearts of blacks and whites. His style was unique—here was a white boy who "sang with soul," expressing emotions freely and liberated from the conventions of American popular music. Through the years Elvis recorded a vast range of music, blues, rock, country, gospel, and even light opera. His distinctive voice appealed to people of all ages and as he matured his following grew worldwide.

On August 16, 1977, Elvis Presley died. The King of Rock and Roll's death was talked about across the nation. People all over the world who couldn't speak a word of English, and who knew nothing about the city of Memphis, were learning about Memphis and Graceland.

Elvis's death had a special effect on Bentley Russell. His rags-to-riches story had inspired her. She admired his triumphs and believed that one day she would also be able to showcase her God-given talent.

But her focus shifted from this tragic period to a more personal level. When she came home from school on Friday afternoon, she was surprised to find that Nikkie wasn't eating a snack in the kitchen like she usually did. Bentley usually arrived home at 4:00 P.M. The bus dropped Nikkie off at 3:30. Bentley was later today than usual. She'd spent the last thirty minutes talking to her teacher about the rumors surrounding Elvis's death.

By 4:40 Bentley had scoured the house inside and out and Nikkie was nowhere to be found.

"Where is she?" Bentley demanded of her aunt Mae, who had been asleep on the sofa, the volume on *The Guiding Light* soap opera turned down low.

"How in the hell should I know?" she said, warding off Bentley's shoves.

"Tell me. What did you do to her?" Bentley knew that Mae had to have done something evil to her sister while she was at school to make Nikkie leave the house.

"Get the hell out of my face, girl," Mae spat out, "you're blocking my view."

Bentley saw the cache of switches in the corner, twined together. She felt bile rising from her stomach to her throat. Immediately, she caught hold of her lip. She was certain that Mae had beaten Nikkie. Without another word Bentley ran from the house, stopping at every door to inquire about her sister.

The temperature had dropped to forty degrees that October, cold for Memphis, and Bentley worried that Nikkie had left without wearing a coat *or shoes*.

Hours later, when it was beginning to get dark, she still hadn't gotten any closer to finding her sister. When Kirk came home from work, he called the police. After giving the policeman a description of Nikkie, Bentley got a flashlight and slipped on her wool overcoat.

"It's dangerous out there, girl," Kirk yelled. "Let the police do their job."

"I can't just sit here and do nothing." She rolled her eyes at Mae. "I won't be too long."

Tears streaked her face as she walked the streets. People stared at her, and she didn't give a damn, nor offer any explanations as to why she was crying. Every now and then when she saw a friendly face, she stopped and gave them a description of Nikkie.

No one had seen her.

At eleven o'clock, she didn't know what else to do. With trepidation, Bentley stopped by a phone booth and called Anne.

"Can I speak to Anne, please?"

There was a slight hesitation before the man said, "Mrs. Hamilton is unavailable at this time."

"Please, it's very—"

Click.

Angry, and crying even harder, she dialed the number again and received the same message. This time he added, "Please don't call back again."

She fell down on the floor of the phone booth, crying with the receiver in her hand. Her shoulders heaved up and down as she desperately tried to hug away the pain. She hated Anne then. How dare she pretend to be unavailable? Was she trying to tell them that the family she had before she married Scott Hamilton didn't matter anymore?

Obviously she made her choice, Bentley thought. Feeling frustrated and cold, she stood up and hung up the phone.

During the next ninety minutes, she scoured the neighborhoods in a ten-block radius of their home. Her feet ached and her empty stomach growled like a bear that had burnt his paw. When the sun threatened to come up, she was amazed to see that the clock on the red-brick building read five minutes to six. It was time to go home.

She slept for a couple hours and ate a bowl of tomato and rice soup.

"Bentley, the police called," Kirk said, buckling his

belt and preparing to leave for work. "They said no one's seen any signs of Nikkie."

"All the nosy busybodies on the street, somebody had to have seen her. She couldn't just disappear."

"That dumb-ass girl. You know she ain't never had good sense," Mae said, coming downstairs and lighting a cigarette.

"Don't you call my sister dumb, you stupid fool. It's your fault that she's missing anyway."

"Stop it, Bentley. This ain't doing nobody—"

Bentley stood in Mae's face and pointed to the switches in the corner. "She beat Nikkie, that's why she ran away. Didn't you? Didn't you beat her?"

"Mae . . ." Kirk began.

Mae sputtered out a trail of smoke, then paused to meet Bentley's eyes. "Yeah, I whipped the stupid bitch. She scraped that plaster off that hole beneath the sink. You think I like rats running around in my kitchen? That dizzy girl is trying to let them back in!"

Tears of hatred rolled down Bentley's face. In two strides she went into the living room and got the switches. While Mae was at the sink with her back turned, Bentley came down on her back, whipping her hard and fast.

Mae whipped around, dropping the cigarette from her mouth, and grabbed the switch. Kirk, stamping out the burning cigarette, cursed and yelled at them both, then pulled the two women apart.

"I'm going to kill that heffa," Mae hollered. "Turn me aloose, Kirk!"

"Get your hands off me!" Bentley said, getting free from him.

Kirk steered Bentley upstairs, yelling over his shoulder for Mae to have the house clean and dinner cooked when he got home from work.

"Look, you get dressed for school. And for the remainder of the day, try to stay out of Mae's way and I'll make sure she does the same to you." He shook her shoulders until she stared up at him. "Do you hear me, girl?"

"Yeah, I heard you."

After he'd gone, Bentley didn't go to school. Instead she began searching empty buildings, going a few blocks further out than the day before.

No luck.

She had Wesley's telephone number to his barracks and thought to call him. But then realized, if she couldn't find Nikkie, how could he?

Still, the next day was even harder. Policemen hadn't fared any better than she did. Kirk claimed that he was too exhausted from work to look for his niece.

Nearly out of her mind, Bentley couldn't sleep, and today she couldn't manage to make herself eat.

By day three, she was back out on the streets, this time with a picture of Nikkie that was four years old.

"She looks the same," Bentley pleaded, "exactly the same, only a little heavier."

"I haven't seen her, child. I'm sorry," one person after another told her.

On day four, Bentley was numb. She had covered nearly five square miles, and imagined all kinds of horrible things happening to her sister. How could she face Wesley when he came home?

She thought back about Wesley's last letter. He seemed saddened about his friend who had died in Germany.

. . . *he had a smile, a grin really, that would disarm the devil and make the girls smile back. Yeah, that was Teddy. A man so admired by everyone that he had more girlfriends than either of us could ever dream about.*

What bothers me is that his death was so unnecessary. I can't stop thinking about him dying on a frozen, muddy hillside in a training camp in Frankfurt, Germany. Teddy thought that he was safe in that foxhole, that snow-covered hole in the ground. One malfunctioning artillery shell killed him and seven of his comrades.

Eight heroic men, who truly believed that they would live to be old men, did not make it.

In his last letter that he wrote his mom, he had written: "Mother, if I should die here, I know my God. My Bible is with me at all times . . ."

I wish my faith, Bentley, was as strong as his was. It's not. I sit here sometimes, and I ask myself: Why, dear God, did I volunteer to do this? Then I think of you and Nikkie at home, and I know why. I love you guys. Wes.

Dear God, Bentley thought, how could she explain to him what had happened to Nikkie? Without Wesley telling her so, she felt that she was responsible for Nikkie's well-being.

Just as she was about to lose all hope, someone called. They thought they saw a young girl meeting Nikkie's description downtown. Bentley jumped up, put her coat on, and headed out the door. Ten minutes later, she found her sister sitting on a bench in W. C. Handy

Park. Her clothes were dirty, and one of her shoes was missing.

"You late."

Bentley hugged and kissed her sister. "I didn't know where you were, baby." She removed her coat and covered Nikkie up. She looked so tired, Bentley thought as she hailed a nearby policeman.

"I hungry. I wanna eat."

Their tears blended together as Bentley kissed her face and hands. "I know. I'm here now. Everything's going to be fine." Bentley wiped the tears from Nikkie's face. "Trust me?"

"I love you."

It was the first time in years that she'd said it and Bentley had to force herself not to break down and cry. "I love you too, Nikkie." She pulled her close. "God knows how much I love you."

Eleven

DURING THE NEXT FEW MONTHS, Bentley kept a careful eye on Nikkie. She celebrated her sixteenth birthday on April 22.

There weren't any visible signs that Nikkie had experienced any long-term trauma while she was missing except the fact that she woke up some nights shaking Bentley and telling her that she was scared. On those nights, Bentley rocked her big sister back to sleep like she was her baby.

A few months later, Nikkie began to get better, only

waking up once every two or three weeks. But the smiles were all gone. She no longer took any interest in crocheting. The bedspread that she was working on was three-quarters finished. Even her favorite game, playing with marbles, didn't work anymore.

It was obvious to everyone that when Mae became irritated with one of her lovers, she took her anger out on Nikkie. Her latest punishment was when Nikkie made a mistake in her clothes and no one but Mae was home, she would make Nikkie keep on her urine-stained clothes and not give her her afternoon snack.

"I'm sorry, Aunt Mae," Bentley overheard Nikkie saying to her aunt one day. Bentley came in from school just in time to see Mae and Nikkie hugging one another.

Bentley was speechless. She assumed that Nikkie hated Mae.

"I know you don't mean it," Mae told Nikkie. "Sometimes Aunt Mae loses her temper. I don't mean to hurt you, child." She took Nikkie in her arms and rocked her gently. It was the first time in years that Mae had shown any kind of sympathy toward her sister.

All three began to cry. Bentley felt especially moved because she had brought home with her a large pack of *Depends* for Nikkie that would solve her wetting problems. She told Nikkie that she had to wear them all the time, pushing them down like underwear when she was able to use the bathroom on her own.

THE SUMMER OF 1978 was a scorcher. Trying to keep cool was the primary goal. Children were rarely seen playing outside. With temperatures topping 102 degrees, some of the old people were taken to the hospital for heat stroke.

At the end of an "end of the summer sale" in August, Kirk broke down and bought an air-conditioner. All four of them were now sleeping on quilts in the living room where the new unit blew full blast.

At fifteen, Bentley took up baby-sitting on weekends. Her grades at Manassas High School were above average, especially in art, where she received A+'s. Like her aunt Anne, she worked on the school newspaper. Her illustrations and caricatures of the school staff garnered her respect among her classmates.

Thanksgiving was a blessing, but when December rolled around, Bentley believed that the Christmas holiday would be a special one.

Mae allowed Nikkie and Bentley to decorate the tree that sat on two apple crates in front of the living room picture window. This year Kirk splurged and bought three strings of new lights. Since Anne had left, most of the bulbs had burnt out.

Bentley and Nikkie colored stale popcorn red and green and alternated it on five-foot strings with fresh cranberries. Mae tried to help, too. She made oversized, spicy gingerbread men and houses, and she let Nikkie sample one of each. With the new string of colored bulbs, the tree looked good, but it was obvious that something was still missing.

"We need more ornaments, Aunt Mae," Bentley suggested.

Still in good spirits on a freezing Saturday afternoon, Mae said, "You're right."

"I've got an idea," said Bentley. She ran down to the neighborhood park and gathered a grocery bag full of large pinecones and suggested to her aunt how they could decorate them.

Mae gave in and bought ornament hooks, a can of

white spray snow, Elmer's glue, and gold glitter from Wal-Mart.

They had everything they needed to make the tree sparkle. Cutting out white paper stars and snowflakes at the kitchen table, Nikkie and Bentley shared a special moment. Nikkie laughed they way she did before she'd been missing. And when they put the glue and glitter on the stars and snowflakes, and the snow and glitter on the pinecones, and put them all on the lighted tree, Nikkie beamed with pride.

Getting into the Christmas spirit, even though it was a selfish one, Kirk bought himself a new 1978 Ford pickup truck. Vanilla Mae shocked Bentley and Nikkie both by buying them matching red, white, and green Santa Claus gowns, housecoats, and house shoes.

Bentley bought Nikkie two new Sunday suits—her church clothes had gotten too tight—and her first record player. Nikkie had begun to love listening to music. For her aunt, who believed that she was a diva in distress, she purchased a shocking pink peignoir set with matching fingernail polish. Mae's eyes misted with tears. For Kirk, she caught a bargain at Wal-Mart on pocket watches that were becoming popular.

Kirk nearly spoiled all the fun when he informed all three females that his gift to them was a ride downtown in his new truck. Bentley and Nikkie had been in their bedroom listening to records and enjoying themselves. They elected to go another day. After painting her short nails and imbibing a double shot of whiskey and eggnog, Mae told Kirk that she was ready for a cruise down Beale Street.

When they left, it was a relief. Bentley cherished the rare time at home alone with her sister. She and

Nikkie drank hot cider and ate some of the gingerbread cookies from the tree. They sang songs, and
talked about missing their mother, father, and brother.
Afterward, Bentley told Nikkie about her plans to get
a full-time job and move into an apartment in two
years.

"Why you tell lies, Bentley," Nikkie said, as they sat
side by side on the sofa.

"I'm not. I intend to get a job at a newspaper. No. I
know I'll get a job at the *Hamilton Appeal.* I'm going to
enroll at Memphis State part-time, and hire a personal
nurse to care for you while I'm away."

"Don't leave me, Bentley. I'm scared all by myself."

Bentley put her arms around her sister's shoulders
and pulled her close to her heart. "Listen to me,
Nikkie. No one . . . absolutely no one is going to harm
you anymore. Things are better here now, but it doesn't
matter. You and I are going to have our own place
soon."

"What about Wesley?"

"Him too. He should be home soon and all of us
are going to live together. Doesn't that sound good?"

"Um-hm. Do you *dreams,* Bentley?" Her words felt
warm against Bentley's chest. "You know, like Aunt
Anne. She *dreamded* all the time."

Bentley stiffened. She didn't want to think about
Anne. Wasn't Christmas the time when family was supposed to show their love for one another? Where was
Anne? Just her presence alone would have been the best
gift that Bentley could ask for.

Bentley patted her sister gingerly on the back, releasing her, and then began taking loose her braids. "No, I
don't *dreams.* Dreams make you lonely for what you
don't have."

Bentley Camille Russell was a young girl who would one day develop into a very attractive woman. She'd grown two inches over the past two years, and her already long legs seemed endless. She was now five feet seven and a half inches. Her hair—she'd shed the affable Afro puff at age twelve—was now straightened and parted in the middle in a classic bob style that hung an inch past her shoulders. Never learning how to wear makeup, she decided that the looks she received from men were because of her natural beauty, and elected to not wear the Indian paint that most of the girls in her class wore.

And today, Bentley was disappointed in herself. Unconsciously, she was beginning to imitate one of her aunt Mae's bad habits—not smiling. It would be another week before she was due to go back to school and she hated to admit to herself that she missed going.

On a rare roller-skating outing during Christmas break, she noticed that several servicemen were home on leave. Some wore their uniforms. Others had on their street clothes, but every one of them had on their army boots and caps. One gentleman in particular had been checking her out all evening.

Regardless, she kept a watchful out for Nikkie, who was standing at the far end of the rink, waving at skaters as they breezed by her.

"Always and Forever" by Heatwave had just come on and people who had been sitting on the bench moments before scrambled to get on the floor with their sweethearts.

"Can't you skate backwards?" the stranger challenged.

No, she couldn't. But she wouldn't let him know. Unconsciously, she sucked in her bottom lip. Leaning to her right to make a half-circle, she whipped around and began bouncing her buttocks to a precise figure eight like she'd seen the other girls do but rarely had the nerve to try. It was like pumping the pedals on a bicycle that she had borrowed but never owned. It was also easier than she thought. Bentley smiled, secretly thanking the man for giving her the opportunity to do something that she hadn't thought that she could do.

When he skated around her again she ignored him. Happily skating backward, she felt uninhibited. All the misery from home evaded her. There was no way that this man could possibly understand all the drama that had unfolded in her life.

While she waited for Nikkie next to the concession stand, he stopped her again.

"I knew you could do it. You skated like a pro out there. If you can move like that on skates, I can't imagine how well you can dance."

"Well, I have tried it a couple of times. But I do love to dance." Bentley noticed how he licked his lips between every sentence. He was more handsome to her now than before. But it was his eyes that seemed to bore into her soul and uncover her most hidden secrets. She turned away in shame.

"Bentley?" Nikkie tapped her shoulder, handed her the change, and asked for help to open her bag of peppermint kisses.

"Excuse me for being so bold, but my name's Erik. And yours—"

"Bentley," she said, opening the bag and handing it back to Nikkie. "And this is my sister, Nikkie."

When Erik told Nikkie how pretty she was, she blushed.

"It's nice to meet you, Erik, but my sister and I are getting ready to leave."

They went to the nearest bench and took a seat. Even with all the noise around them, she could feel that he was still following her.

"The Tracks of My Tears" came on. Bentley had been waiting all evening for that record to come on. She loved skating to it. The latest dance was one that she'd perfected and she'd gotten her moves down pat. Nevertheless, she didn't want to encourage this man to skate with her, so she elected to let the song pass. There was always a next time.

Sighing, she began unlacing her skates. *Ooh that hurts.* Bentley wiggled her socked feet. Reaching down, she massaged her sore toes and then stretched them out.

"Excuse me," he said again.

Bentley frowned. "Yeah." She hadn't meant to sound so tart as she walked away from him and toward the counter to exchange the skates for her shoes.

What was wrong with her, she wondered?

"Say, I wanted to ask you if you'd be here tomorrow night."

Bentley eyed him.

"Hey, I'm not trying to be fresh. I'll only be home for another two weeks. I was merely trying to make some new friends. I'm sorry if I came on too strong." He hooked his thumbs in the back of his jeans and made a half turn to leave, then stopped. "You might know my family, the Berrys. They live on Olive Street."

Bentley did know the Berrys—more by name than by face. She did recall that her aunt Mae had mentioned the name before. There had to be a connection, she thought, as she studied him.

Erik had a beautiful smile. One thing she admired in a man was good teeth. He seemed to have good grooming habits, like most men in the service. The creases in his jeans and tan shirt were starched to the bone. Casually checking him out, she guessed that the shoe size of his black army boots was about an 11—or a 12 at most. Approximately six-foot-two, he had a roundish, bulldog pug nose and small ears. His neat crew cut was parted on the left side. Tasteful sideburns and a trim mustache gave him the polished look of a serviceman or a professional.

What bothered was his age. She guessed that he was twenty-two or so. That meant that he was a little old for her.

Oops . . . she'd nearly forgotten what he'd asked her. Oh yeah, the big family on Olive Street. "You aren't talking about —"

He nodded yes, smiling.

"Mrs. Gingy Berry—"

"Virginia," he corrected her.

"The woman who sits on the front pew of Mount Sinai Methodist Church with all eleven of her kids?" Bentley asked incredulously.

"Twelve," Erik said blushing. "I'm the oldest. But I've been gone so long, most of our neighbors seemed to have forgotten about me since I enlisted."

Wesley hadn't written since her birthday in April. Bentley was eager to find out what was happening overseas. The Vietnam War had ended five years ago, but Wesley still hadn't mentioned when he planned on returning home.

"Say, would you and your sister like a Coke?"

Nikkie nodded.

"Even though the Vietnam War was a disaster,

there's still a lot of work to be done. There are hundreds of soldiers still missing in action," he added seriously.

Bentley elected to have a 7-Up instead of a Coke. While Nikkie openly stared at Erik, they continued their conversation about the war. She knew that three years ago, Saigon fell, and the last Americans were evacuated. Wesley had been stationed in Saigon, but she never anticipated that he might be missing in action.

"Our brother, Wesley, *was* stationed in Saigon."

"That was a tough pill to swallow. I heard that some of those soldiers elected to stay there."

"What!"

"Yeah. A lot of the men have families there. Especially kids."

Bentley gave him an odd look.

"I like babies," Nikkie said, still goggling at Erik.

"Shhh, Nikkie," Bentley scolded. She checked her watch. It was nearly nine and time to put Nikkie to bed. "Well, it was a pleasure meeting you, Erik." She drained her cup and stood up. "It's time we headed home."

"Dog. Can't we stay longer, Bentley? I like him."

"No." She liked him too, but felt silly about the way her mind was playing tricks on her. She could already see him kissing her good night.

Erik stood. Her body acknowledged what he was about to say before her mind did. She became nervous. "I'm going the same way, can I give you two a lift?"

"Sure," she said, trying not to sound too eager.

On their way home, Bentley whistled the last tune that was playing before they left the roller rink. She hadn't felt this comfortable in months. As they headed home, she and Erik continued to share information about the war and finally family.

He and his mother argued at lot, he told her. It bothered him. He had hoped that joining the army would help him to mature and see things from his mom's perspective. In the six years he'd been gone, she'd borne five children. In this day and time, her excuses about childbirth prevention didn't work. Erik told her that he and his mother were about as close to each other as the U.S. was to North Vietnam. He hated going back overseas knowing that he hadn't been able to bridge the gap between them.

Bentley objected when he suggested that they stop for an ice cream cone at Baskin-Robbins, but relented when Nikkie threatened tears. Afterward, their short drive to her home on Chelsea Street was closer than she remembered. Erik was still talking nonstop when he parked in their driveway.

She noticed the instant the curtains were pulled back. Bentley wasn't certain if it was Mae or Kirk.

The moment she stepped inside the house, Kirk asked, "Who was that man that brought you two home?"

"Nobody."

Even though Kirk had never put his hands on her again, Bentley had never forgotten that night in the bathroom. And she doubted if she ever would.

"I *asked* you who the man was. I expect an answer."

"His name's Erik. He's Virginia Berry's son." She glared at him. "Now, are you satisfied?"

When he rolled his eyes, Bentley grabbed Nikkie's arm and they ran up the steps.

She and Nikkie took a bath, changed into their pajamas, and spent the next hour talking about how cute

Erik was. Bentley hadn't felt so lighthearted in years. The smile on her face felt good. And in her heart, she believed that when it was time to make her New Year's resolution, it would be one of hope.

There was hope for Wesley. He was alive and healthy.

There was hope for Nikkie. She had almost mastered holding her urine.

There was hope for Anne. That one day she would come back home and become a family the way they were before.

And maybe, if Bentley's prayers were answered, there was hope for her, too.

Twelve

IN FOUR SHORT YEARS, Anne had grown to despise her husband. In her opinion, her son, Basil, wasn't a loving child. He was self-centered and selfish just like his father. Both seemed to know how to push her buttons.

Holly, her daughter, born two years after her son, was her joy. She was extremely petite and very prissy. She wanted things just so—her frilly clothes kept neat and pretty in all her waking hours. Anne admired her little girl-soldier. Holly had a mind of her own and a will that was just as strong.

Privacy was a word that wasn't in Scott's vocabulary. On the few occasions that he let her out of his sight she savored them. At other times, she counted the minutes in the morning when he left for work.

"I love you, sweetheart," was the routine ritual, then the kiss. She felt totally immune to his kisses now, but especially the quick hug, when she dutifully said, "Have a wonderful day."

How could she feel otherwise? She was a prisoner in her own house. The housekeeper watched her every move. Though they were rich, she'd never had the pleasure of having any money in her possession. Scott either bought everything she needed or the housekeeper did. In early June he had hired a local tailor to come to their home and fit Anne for winter, summer, and spring clothing.

She was told what colors looked best on her. What type of suits and dresses to wear and which designer shoes made her wide feet look daintier.

What continued to persecute her was the fact that Scott insisted that she stop all contact with her family. She wasn't allowed to visit them or speak to them unless he supervised the calls. She was allowed to send cards only on holidays and birthdays.

With no one to discuss her feelings with, Annie cried on Nikkie's sixteenth birthday. She cried the following year, on Bentley's sixteenth. And she cried even harder last Christmas, when she had fought and begged with Scott to let her go and visit her family.

"They haven't seen the children yet," she pleaded. "Basil and Holly should know their family."

"No. Absolutely not. We've got our life and they've got theirs."

She'd cried enough tears to fill the Mississippi River, and pleaded with Scott to give her some freedom. His answer was to ignore her.

What have I done to deserve this prison you've put me in? she constantly asked herself. His answer without her verbalizing the question was, "I'm merely protecting you, Anne. You should understand that by now."

Sure. She understood that he was *crazy* and that he beat her when she made him angry.

When the holidays came this year, she was fed up. She couldn't take another day of seclusion. The day after New Year's she made an attempt to run away.

After packing a suitcase for herself and the children, she woke them up at one in the morning. Scott's plane for Cincinnati had left at eleven. It had taken years, but she finally located the stash of cash that Scott kept hidden. More than $5,000 in twenties, fifties, and hundreds were inside the kimono of a full-size geisha girl that stood on a high pedestal in the library.

With enough cash to last for a month, she took the keys, kids, a few clothes, and left. She was gone for five glorious days. On the fifth night, the police found them at a hotel in Arkansas, by the plates on the Mercedes.

Anne remembered pleading with the police to help her. She told them that her husband was crazy. They ignored her explanations. The blank looks on their faces were so matter-of-fact; they barely listened to her. It was as if Scott had already rehearsed what she'd say to them and they were prepared for any story that she might have concocted.

When they arrived back home it was 9:20 in the evening. Pungent paint fumes greeted them at the front door. The children were too tired and sleepy to notice or even care that there were workmen painting the living room. The carpeting had been removed, and a large roll of new carpeting and padding were lying against the hallway wall.

Anne noticed the frightened looks on the nursemaid's and butler's faces. Something was wrong. Suddenly, she wanted to grab her kids, turn back around, and run back out of the house.

"Get upstairs," Scott snarled. "I'll be up in a few minutes."

The nurse took Basil and Holly by the hand and Anne followed them.

"Be careful, Mrs. Hamilton," the nurse cautioned her after they'd put the children to bed.

"What happened to the living room?"

Closing the door to the spare bedroom, the nurse pulled Anne to the corner and began whispering. "He's got the entire household afraid of him. I think he's going crazy or something. For days he's been scouring the neighborhood asking people if they'd seen you or the kids. When he couldn't find you, he started tearing up the house like he'd lost his mind." She tiptoed back to the door to make sure no one was listening.

Anne sucked in her breath in horror. She could feel her hands and legs begin to shake.

"My Lord," Anne breathed and began to cry. "He's lost his mind."

"Shhh," the nurse cautioned. They heard his footsteps on the stairway.

"Some of the staff is planning on leaving," she said hurriedly. "I ain't made up my mind yet. Most employers don't pay this kind of money."

"Anne," Scott called out.

The nurse rushed out without another word.

Taking a deep breath, Anne quickly collected herself, wiping the cold tears from her eyes. Slowly opening the door, she forced a small smile and stepped out into the hall. When Anne saw his eyes jumping like popcorn, she froze. He grabbed her by the arm and half dragged her to their bedroom.

"Please, Scott. Don't hurt me. I'll never leave again. I promise."

"Too damn late for that." He yanked her body as swiftly as if it were a piece of cloth and threw her down on the bed. Removing his belt, he began to beat her mercilessly.

"Yeeeow!" she screamed.

"Shut up! Goddammit, shut the hell up, or you'll get it twice as hard."

Anne stuffed her fist in her mouth to muffle her cries while he continued to whip her. Within seconds, she could taste the blood from her teeth scraping against her knuckles, as she endured lash after lash.

He was sweating as profusely as a bull in heat when he finished. He took a seat on the bed and ordered her to take a bath, put on a silk negligee, and get into bed.

Immediately, he removed his clothing—not even bothering to take a shower. From a few feet away, she could smell that his sweat-soaked body reeked of fresh funk. When he climbed on top of her and tried to push his swollen member inside of her, he grumbled a vulgarity when he felt how dry she was. The pain she felt was excruciating when he forced himself deeper inside.

She closed her eyes and turned her head away from his kisses. Willing her mind to concentrate on another plan of escape, she tried not to focus on the pain she felt as he screwed her like a trick that had found out that his whore was a transvestite. Anger was in every thrust until he climaxed.

Feeling a breath of relief and thinking that it was over, she gritted her teeth when she felt him ease out of her, then slide his face down to her pelvic area.

When he performed oral sex on her, she thought he'd suffocated down there. Afterward, he placed her legs on his shoulders. He entered her with such brute force that she clutched the sheet and ripped it with her fingernails. Obscenities followed, calling her bitch, cunt, whore, as he quickly came. Next, he turned her on her stomach and entered her from behind. The verbal abuse continued. Almost an hour later, he was soaked from asshole to dickhole. When he fell on top of her, exhausted, she shuddered with disgust.

Anne held the vomit brewing in her stomach for as long as she could.

When she heard him snore, she pushed him off of her, went into the bathroom, locked the door, and threw up. Afterward she cried tears of vengeance. There had to be a way to get away from him. The next time she left, there would be no way he would find her.

Less than six weeks later, Anne realized that this was the night when he'd impregnated her. Even before it was born, Anne hated it.

It was a relief to Anne when, in her fourth month of pregnancy, she miscarried. Scott didn't have to worry about his wife losing weight this time. She was thin as a straw. She hadn't wanted the child in the first place and promised herself that she would commit suicide if she got pregnant again.

There had to be a way to sneak to the doctor's office and get her tubes tied. She'd heard that a woman had to be thirty before a doctor would perform this procedure, but with enough money, a doctor would forgo his ethics.

With the nursemaid's help, she located a physician, and paid him with a piece of jewelry that Scott bought her on their fifth anniversary—a diamond and pearl brooch worth at least ten times what the doctor's normal fee would have been.

Throughout the years of their marriage, the trinkets he lovingly gave her amounted to a couple million dollars. Scott had moved the stash he had kept in the geisha. It took a few more months before she found where he'd hidden it. A stickler about safes, and wall safes in particular, Scott believed that a man of his status needed to have cold cash at his disposal. Thanks to his ignorance, she found the money—this time in Basil's room, stuffed inside the rear wheel of his car bed.

She hid several thousand dollars inside her hosiery bag, knowing that one day soon she would walk out on Scott for good. It would take another six to twelve months to sell off more of her jewelry without Scott's finding out. This time she'd go to another state and have enough money to last her for a year.

Anne didn't know how Scott found out, but he did. It wasn't the jewelry that she sold, like she originally thought. It was the tubal ligation that had set him on fire.

"This is how you show your appreciation. By making a fool out of me!"

He grabbed her by the neck and threw her down on the floor. Taking off his belt, he whipped her half-clothed body. She screamed, but his fury didn't end. When she looked up, Basil was staring at her, frozen. She passed out, hearing Holly screaming her name from the nursery down the hall.

Two days later, on Sunday morning, Anne begged Scott to excuse her from church.

"I said get dressed. You *will* take my children to church and sit with your husband on our assigned seats. You *will* be ready at ten thirty A.M. You *will* have your

Bible and smile and not say anything out of the ordinary to the members of the church. Do you understand?"

Anne nodded.

Her yellow Christian Dior couture suit hung off her lithe body. Scott held Basil's hand, and Anne clutched Holly to her bosom as they walked down the center aisle of St. Peter's Baptist Church.

No matter how hard she tried, she couldn't stop the tears from building up in her eyes. She was certain that people recognized how sad she was, even through the phony smiles.

Halfway into the service, Anne reached down to retrieve Holly's purse that had fallen on the floor, and when she did, she heard a sharp intake of breath from the woman sitting beside her.

As she sat back upright, she could feel a trickle of fluid oozing from the pain she felt from her buttocks. When she looked down to check herself, she noticed a half-dollar-sized bloodstain on the hip of her suit.

"Scott," she began, tugging at the crystal beads around her neck. Her fingers shook as she tapped his knee. "Scott . . . I'm—" Clamping her hand over her quivering mouth, she willed back tears. Out of the corner of her eye, she noticed that other people were whispering and pointing at her. Not knowing exactly what to do, she jumped up, clutching Holly to her chest, and ran out of the church. With no money on her, there was no place to go but home.

She removed her stained clothing and took off the crystal beads, deciding that she would never wear them again.

Minutes later, Scott arrived.

How could she humiliate him in public? How dare she walk out in the middle of service?

The thwack of a belt drowned out the rest of his insults. She tried to train her mind to another place. The shame of being so humiliated hurt worse than the belt. There had to be a way to escape this insane abuse. There had to be an answer somewhere.

Miraculously the beating stopped. She turned over on the bed and saw Scott turning purple. He'd dropped the belt and was clutching at the bedspread. Falling to his knees, his eyes begged her to help him.

Sniffing back tears, she moved away from him.

Anne watched, as he struggled to breathe. In doing so, his body began to stiffen like a corpse's. Every now and then his feet kicked beneath him as he grasped for air. Then finally, he was still, his cold eyes staring right through her.

Anne thought he was dead, until she felt his pulse.

She called an ambulance, and then called the housekeeper. They helped him into bed and tried to comfort him until the paramedics came. Hearing all the commotion, Basil had run into the room. Instead of looking at his father, he stared at his mother through Scott's accusing eyes.

Thirteen

IN THE TWO SHORT WEEKS that Erik had been home on leave, Bentley had felt more relaxed than she ever had before. He never rushed her, never kissed her, and never pursued any sexual activity with her. They seemed to connect on a higher level, both needing someone to understand them without judgment.

Wanting to talk to a female about her feelings, Bentley decided to try to contact Anne. Maybe there was a simple explanation of why she hadn't kept in touch.

"Hello, this is Bentley Russell, Anne's niece. Can I speak to her, please?"

"Mrs. Hamilton is unavailable." Click.

A few days later, she tried again. Same reaction. She memorized the man's voice, and realized it was the butler's. After a week of trying, Bentley gave up. Erik's leave was up and he was due back in Germany in two days. He gave her a preengagement ring and she promised to wait for him.

After he left, Bentley felt guilty. *What had she done?* Only sixteen years old—how could she commit to something so serious?

He'd told her that she was the most perfect woman he'd ever met. Of course she didn't believe him. He really didn't know her that well. Two weeks wasn't enough time to get to know a person. What he wanted, she felt, was to make sure that she didn't sleep with anyone until he returned.

Their preengagement was sealed with sex.

He was very gentle. More so than she'd ever expected. He kissed her and talked to her throughout the entire act.

No matter how tender he was, Bentley couldn't get into it. She hated the feeling of him inside of her. The pain was so agonizing she could think of little else. And realizing that the crimson substance on the sheet was her proof of virginity made her feel even more disenchanted with sex. All the dreams she'd had of men and women making love were different than what she'd experienced today. And without him saying so, she knew that she'd disappointed her partner.

"I'm sorry, Erik."

"It doesn't matter, baby. I love you." He kissed her like he meant it.

And this time, Bentley relaxed and allowed him to seduce her, letting her mind concentrate on the three words that she'd never heard from a man before: "I love you." Even though she felt she could love Erik, it was too soon to tell him so.

The next morning, as she lay in a dream state fantasizing about Erik, a noise from the kitchen awakened her. She looked to her side and noticed that Nikkie was missing out of her bed. Without another thought, she skipped down the stairs.

"What are you doing?" Bentley screamed.

From where she stood, she could see Nikkie's clothed body on the floor. Kirk was straddled over her.

Looking around the room for a weapon, Bentley grabbed the rolling pin from the counter and began beating Kirk on the back. "Get off of her! You freakish bastard."

Nikkie's legs and arms were shaking as if an earthquake had passed. With the rolling pin held high above her head, she stopped. White foam was coming from the sides of Nikkie's mouth.

"Get back, girl," Kirk shouted. She could see now that he had been trying to put a spoon into her mouth. "Call an ambulance. Shit, call the police. Hurry up!"

While she dialed, Bentley screamed, "What . . . what happened?"

"I'm not sure. She ate something," Kirk said, looking over his shoulder at her. "Mae must've fell asleep on the couch and Nikkie . . . I'm guessing, Nikkie must've got into the cleaning products."

When the ambulance arrived, Nikkie's stomach

had swollen up nearly double its normal size. Her eyes were rolling around in her head and when she tried to speak, more foam spewed from her mouth. The paramedics let Bentley ride in the back of ambulance with her. She held Nikkie's hand and prayed all the way to the hospital.

"Lord, please don't let my sister die. She never hurt a soul in her life. Dear God, she's suffered so long, don't take her away from me. She's all I've got."

The doctors wouldn't let Bentley come in the emergency room until they finished with their examination.

After fifteen minutes passed, Bentley heard Nikkie scream. She ran into the room and saw her sister struggling with the nurses who were trying to hold her heavy body down on the bed. Nikkie's arms were lashing out in all directions. Bentley was used to seeing the seizures, but what startled her was how still Nikkie's legs were.

As one of the nurses steered Bentley back out of the room, Nikkie's eyes met hers for a brief moment. Instant tears choked in her throat and filled her eyes. In a matter of seconds she felt the warm hands of another nurse on her shoulder, helping her to sit down.

It took a grueling eighteen hours for all of the tests to be completed on Nikkie. Bentley and Mae stayed in the waiting room, but Kirk went home to lie down, telling them to call him when they knew something. The result of several tests showed that Nikkie had ingested rat poison. Part of her brain was damaged; she'd had a stroke and was paralyzed from the waist down. The strychnine in the rat poison had caused the paralysis.

As the doctor consulted with Bentley and Mae about

how to care for Nikkie when she returned home, Bentley barely listened. Her thoughts were of yesterday, before all this crazy stuff happened and her sister was laughing and happy to be alive. She heard the doctor mention that Medicaid would provide them with a wheelchair for Nikkie's home care. He also gave her the name of a physical therapist that Nikkie would need to start with as soon as possible. He assured her that he felt her paralysis was temporary; it could take one month or as long as a year. But as her attention was diverted to her sister sleeping peacefully with the aid of dozens of tubes attached to her large frame, she wondered how the quality of her life would be from this day forward.

THE RUSSELL HOME had to be completely changed around. Because of Nikkie's nonambulatory state, a hospital bed was set up in the living room. Kirk and a friend took the sofa and a chair upstairs in Bentley's room, to make room for Nikkie's bed and wheelchair.

In the days and weeks that followed, Nikkie rarely talked. She slept a lot and only spoke when she was spoken to. One good thing that had come out of the ordeal was the ironic fact that her seizures had dwindled down to once or twice a week.

During those awkward times, the house was so quiet that Bentley felt like a stranger. Kirk was making noises again about leaving for the rodeo, and this time, she and Mae believed him.

The Department of Social Services worked with Mae and Bentley until Nikkie was well enough to go back to school. If all went well, she'd be able to graduate next year.

Like a chameleon, Mae completely changed. She stopped her clandestine meetings with men and announced that she'd accepted a job at Tiny Tots Day Care Center. The director, Bonniejean Bolton, had been after Mae for months to take the job as the head cook for the center—they'd been using temporary help since January. Mae told her, in a tone cheerier than Bentley had heard before, that she'd be in charge of cooking for 105 preschoolers. She would have her own fifteen-inch television set to watch her soap operas, and her salary of $350 a week included breakfast and lunch. The day care center was just four blocks away, and with Mae never learning how to drive, the new job was perfect for her.

Bentley was happy for her aunt. Maybe she'd finally be able to find a husband. These days, the only time that she had left the house was to shop for groceries, and twice a year, buy clothes at Wal-Mart's summer and winter clearance sale.

In the same week, Bentley was apprised of another revelation—Kirk had quit his job. She should have been relieved, but she felt jaded when Kirk announced that he was moving to Texas. He'd landed a job on a rodeo circuit. It was all he'd ever dreamed.

Dreams? She hadn't had a decent one in weeks. Every time she looked at her sister's sleeping body she no longer believed in them.

Bentley had toyed with the idea of quitting school like Wesley did and getting a job. Then she could afford an apartment for her and Nikkie. She believed that if she and Nikkie could get a place of their own, Nikkie's mental health would improve and she would start talking again like she used to. But that was dumb, who would rent to a sixteen-year-old girl?

Maybe Anne could get it for them in her name.

In a moment of desperation, Bentley dialed Anne's number.

Please God, let her husband be gone. If I could speak with the servants, I could reason with them. Please, please, let me talk to Anne before I lose my mind.

The phone seemed to ring and ring.

If you don't answer this phone, Anne, I will never, ever, speak to you again in my life. I don't care what kind of excuse you come up with. I don't want to hear it. Bentley tugged at her bottom lip and waited.

Nothing.

I hate you, Anne.

1980

Racial Politics

at the Crossroads

Fourteen

MEMPHIS MOURNED THE DEATH of E. H. Crump. He'd been an icon in the community for decades. Both blacks and whites felt his loss. But, like one old song that was the anthem of the civil rights movement, "Keep Your Eyes on the Prize," the opening of the Harahan Bridge bought a temporary bout of jubilation to the bluff city.

1980 marked the year of Rubik's Cube, a handheld multicolored cube invented by Hungarian Erno Rubik. That same year, the rededication of the Med, the Regional Medical Center at Memphis, was held. The historic hospital held a charter dating from 1929. The Med was a teaching as well as a research hospital. More than 750 medical trainees from the University of Tennessee graduated every year. It was the top neurological team at the Med that had worked on Scott Hamilton and had made Anne believe that her husband's condition was temporary.

Having visited him daily for weeks, Anne hadn't believed that her husband's health would be normal again until today. She noticed a change in his breathing first, and then saw that he was trying to move the fingers on his right hand.

"Scott," Anne asked calmly as she leaned over him. "Scott, can you hear me?"

He blinked uncontrollably, and then his eyes fluttered open. Even though his eyes registered fear when he first looked at her, she could sense the hatred in every fiber of his being.

Anne was instantly afraid. She wasn't sure if he was going to get up and attack her or verbally abuse her. When he didn't do either, she pressed the button for the doctor at the head of the bed and took a seat. "The doctor will be in soon to explain what happened to you."

Scott's lips pressed together in an angry frown as he tried to speak. His breathing became labored from the effort and Anne tried to convince him not to get too excited until he spoke with the doctor.

"We're fortunate to have located a Dr. Braun from Texas," Anne began. "He's a specialist in brain-stem strokes."

It was the second time that fear shone in Scott's eyes. The hard lines in his face softened briefly, and the normally dormant water buckets beneath his eyes puffed out, making him look years older. To Anne's amazement, tears began to form in his eyes—pleading eyes that shed tiny tender tears.

Anne found herself crying, and patting his hand gently. "You'll be fine, Scott. It'll take time—"

"Mrs. Hamilton," the doctor interrupted. "I'd like to speak with my patient."

She gathered her purse and released her husband's motionless hand. "Certainly, Doctor. I'd like a conference with you later, if that's okay."

He checked his watch. "I should be about ten to fifteen minutes."

Scott had been in hospital for six weeks before he regained consciousness. Anne hadn't had a moment's rest since his stroke. Basil had kicked and hollered himself into a temper tantrum when she told him that he was too young to visit his father in the hospital. When Anne whipped him, he cried like the five-year-old child that he was. Up to this point, Scott had forbidden Anne to hit him. But since he was no longer home to object, she took special pleasure in spanking his spoiled butt but good.

Four days before Scott's stroke, Basil had trapped two of his gerbils in a soda pop bottle. He filled it halfway up with water and poured several capfuls of Drāno inside the bottle.

"Basil!" Anne had hollered when she heard his uncontrollable laughter. "Quiet down in there." She headed toward the irritating sound. Her mind imagined Scott in his youth, doing some indecent act that seemed funny at the time.

She found her son in the utility room by the kitchen. When Anne approached him, Basil was on the floor giggling like a hyena. A few feet away sat Holly, terrorized. Apparently, he was making her watch. Anne hadn't noticed that Scott was just a few yards away, and when she grabbed Basil by the shoulder to slap his narrow buttocks, Scott grabbed her.

"Leave that boy alone," Scott said sternly.

"But Scott. He can't be allowed to do these unconscionable things. You know this isn't the first time he's tried stupid stuff like this. I draw the line when he makes his sister sit and watch his devious acts."

"Go to your room, Basil. Holly, get upstairs." Scott picked up the bottle with the now dead gerbils and tossed it into the trash. Turning on her, he said, "He's just doing what comes natural to little boys, that's all. You don't want him to be a sissy, do you?"

"No. But I don't want him to be evil either," she screamed. Instinctively she cringed, waiting for a slap that didn't come. She relaxed and added, "And I don't want him growing up believing that he can hurt things and there'll not be a price to pay. It's wrong, Scott." He'd known what she meant.

Was Scott paying now? She wondered. When she met with the doctor, he told her what she already knew: Scott had had a brain-stem stroke. It affected his brain, as well as his spinal cord and cerebellum, which emit the nerves that project to the face and head. Her husband had had the most severe attack, which caused paralysis. His only communication was through eye movements. The doctor told her that with a lot of work, hopefully, he would improve through physical therapy.

Anne couldn't cry. She expected much worse. Anyone knowing her relationship with Scott would say that he deserved it. But the sad fact was that no one, except the servants, knew.

"He'll need a hospital bed, weekly deliveries to the house, a live-in nurse and—"

Anne tuned out the rest of his spiel. He wrote down the names of physical therapists and hospital supplies and gave her five prescriptions for the medications that a nurse would need to treat Scott at home. Recovery varied for each individual. There were miraculous cases that he recalled when the patient was back to normal in less than three months.

Please, Lord, she prayed, don't let Scott be a miracle. She focused on freedom.

Finally, she could rear her kids the way she knew they should be raised. She could fire the nosy butler and cleaning woman and keep the nurse. In her mind she made a checklist of how she would regain control of her house and life.

One thing that worried her was Scott's position at work. She had no idea how to deal with the board of directors and the vice president, Jim Walker, who had called every day since Scott's stroke.

"Jim's an asshole," said Isabell Ford, a woman who'd

called her once the news about Scott's illness made the papers. "Tell him to fuck off until you bring Scott home."

The next day, Scott's attorney, Phillip Hawkins, called. He suggested that they set up a consultation soon at her home. She could determine the time and date.

Later that same day, Isabell called again. Finally, she learned who the woman was. Isabell was on the board of directors and clued Anne in as to who was who and who had the power in the company. In a week's time Anne knew more about the *Hamilton Appeal* and all of Scott's holdings than she ever imagined. No wonder Scott had hidden nearly everything from her. He was a walking gold mine.

Anne tried not to appear shocked when Isabell told her how much Scott's salary was.

"Twenty thousand a month," Isabell said after their fifth phone call, "and that's not including bonuses and stock."

"Honey, hush," Anne breathed. Quickly calculating their house payments that she'd snuck and read in his office, Anne surmised that Scott had to have a large sum of money in the bank somewhere. "Which one could it be?" she thought to herself. There were eons of them in Memphis.

By the end of the week, she found out.

"Mrs. Hamilton," said the hesitant male voice, "you and I haven't had any dealings in the past—"

"And who are you?"

"Alan Dingle," he said in a perfunctory tone, "Mr. Hamilton's personal accountant."

Anne thought for a minute before speaking. "Mr. Dingle, I believe that we should meet."

"Please call me Alan—"

"Next Friday would be good for me. About ten in the

A.M. I believe we have some important business to discuss."

"Definitely. There are signatures that I need."

Anne exhaled. "As I said, Mr. Dingle, we'll meet on Friday. Mr. Hamilton's attorney will be at the meeting as well. Please be prompt." She hung up.

SEEING ISABELL WAS A SHOCK. When they met, Anne was nervous and regretting that she hadn't had a background check done on her. Who was this woman who knew all of Scott's business? Was she a lover? A former lover? A person who wanted to destroy him? Who?

"Hello, Anne," Isabell said, giving her a quick hug, "it's so nice to finally meet you."

"Forgive me, Isabell," she stuttered. "I don't know what to say."

Isabell shrugged it off, and began busily chatting about how beautiful Anne was, and how much the employees were going to love her.

Me?

Anne thought that Isabell was gorgeous. For a Caucasian woman, she had excellent coloring. When she spoke to Anne, her hazel eyes shocked her with their brilliance. Isabell's tiny nose, slanted eyes, full lips, and near-perfect oval face made Anne look deeper and deeper to find an imperfection. Anne assumed that the champagne-beige suit she wore was custom made, because of her huge breasts. From the edges of her wide, black synamay straw silk and organdy hat, she could see that her hair was jet black. One perfectly coiled ringlet spilled from the right side of her head. Her nails, perfume, and even her nylons made this striking woman look like a Spanish heiress.

Anne took notice that Isabell called the waiter at the Peabody Restaurant, where they were having lunch, by his first name. They waited on her like a queen. Less than fifteen minutes into the luncheon Anne felt that she had found a friend.

"I love your bag," Anne complimented. It was the newest Louis Vuitton coach purse that Anne had seen in last month's *W* magazine. She'd felt guilty about thinking about going shopping while Scott was sick, but hadn't gotten the bag out of her mind.

"Thanks."

Isabell told her as discreetly as she could that she didn't need the meager salary that she was paid for being on the board. Her father had left her a fortune, and, not wanting to be bored and rich, she held seats on five of the largest corporations in Memphis.

"I should have met you years ago," Anne began.

"That wouldn't have been possible," she stated bluntly. "Would you like for me to order the wine, or do you have a preference?"

Suddenly, Anne felt uncomfortable. "No. Order whatever you'd like." As a matter of fact, Anne had never had wine at lunch before. And after that whammy that Isabell just laid on her, she could certainly use a little cooling off about now.

After the waiter had left Isabell said, "I know about the abuse, Anne. And I'm not the only one. Employees at the *Hamilton Appeal* remember how it was with Scott's first wife. She was a little more aggressive than you, though. She came down to the paper. Showed off. Embarrassed Scott."

Anne kept silent. She didn't know this lady. She could be lying her ass off. Still, the woman did know a lot about Scott's business practices. She decided to listen and smile and make her judgments later.

Near the end of lunch, two hours later, Anne asked, "So

why are you confiding in me, Isabell? You've never met me before. What do you have to gain by befriending me?"

"Nothing in particular. I heard how pretty you were. I know that you wanted to go to college. And I've heard that you're interested in politics."

Who was this woman?

"I'm not stupid, Isabell. You want something? I have nothing to offer you. You're already rich."

Isabell signaled for the check. "Oh, but you do."

She paid the check and she and Anne walked outside. In the near brilliant sun, Anne got a better look at this woman. She seemed a little more weathered than she did inside the restaurant. Though Isabell was attractive, and had a fairly shapely body, she seemed terribly frail.

Halfway to the valet booth, Isabell dropped the bomb. "I'd like you to teach me something."

Finally, the punch line.

"I would like for you to show me how to be a black woman."

Anne hid her laughter. The woman was serious. It made no sense. In a millisecond it did. She loved a black man.

"Yes—" Isabell concluded. "I'm in love. But he claims I embarrass him. He says that I'm too white bread and that his family would never accept me."

Hiding her half-smile proved to be a bit difficult. "Excuse me, Isabell. I couldn't help it. I've never been asked to do anything like this before. And truly never expected that I would."

"I understand. I'm sorry that I bothered you." Her car arrived and she turned to walk toward it.

"Hold on, Isabell. You misunderstood me." When Isabell turned around to face her, Anne smiled. "When would you like to begin?"

A week later, Scott had been brought home, and, with a great deal of help, Anne had turned their bedroom into a virtual hospital room. On order was a new Boardmaker device that would help Scott communicate with them.

Anne decided that she and Isabell would have their first lesson at her home—they would begin in the kitchen—cooking soul food.

"The way to a black man's heart is through his stomach," Anne told Isabell as they prepared to make southern fried chicken and dressing, mustard and turnip greens, macaroni and cheese, and garlic potatoes.

While the main entree was in the oven, Anne gave Isabell a quick tour around her home. As she did so, Isabell made several helpful suggestions about the interior decorating. But what really perked Anne's interest was when Isabell told her how and when to throw her weight around the *Appeal*.

Later that evening, Anne went upstairs to read the paper to her husband. Tonight there was no mistaking the distrust that she saw in his eyes. She kissed him, as she usually did, and took a seat beside his bed. Scanning the headlines and reading out loud, she constantly looked up, judging his mood by the movement in his eyes.

Anne smiled. *So you noticed.* The happiness she felt now was openly expressed on her face and definitely in her mannerisms.

The nurse, Mrs. Features, had told her before she left to go home this weekend that Scott refused to eat breakfast or lunch. She did, however, manage to get some beef broth in him at dinnertime, but not much.

Since Scott had left the hospital, he'd begun vomiting his food at least once a day, but only when Anne was present. He was careful not to do it when the children were around. He wanted their sympathy, not their disgust. It was fairly obvious, Anne surmised, that his reasoning for regurgitating his food was directed solely at her—the sight of her made him sick.

Anne could tell from the cracked red lines in his eyes that he was getting little sleep. Her impromptu checks on him at night verified that she was right. She asked his doctor to prescribe a sleeping agent.

Just the other day Mrs. Features had said that she thought that she suspected that Scott sometimes faked his labored breathing. He was doing it now, Anne thought, as she watched him gasping for air.

Like a good wife, she took control of the situation by pressing slightly on his chest, the way the nurse had showed her, until he calmed down. Afterward, she sat back down and continued reading the paper.

Oh so badly, she wanted to tell him how she was going to run the paper. Even if he was the great-grandson of the owner, *she* was the boss-lady now.

Through Isabell she learned that the employees weren't happy with Scott's leadership. There were union problems, stockholder problems, and the lowest morale in the company's sixty-year history. She kept silent that day, though, and decided to bide her time.

During his daily physical therapy, Anne read his messages to him. It appeared that in the few short weeks since Scott's absence the company was thriving, and the stockholders couldn't be happier.

By courier, Isabell sent Anne as much information about the company and its employees as she could. Anne was supposed to study all of the information and be ready for a board meeting by the first Wednesday in August.

Just yesterday, Anne was given the power of attorney from Scott's personal attorney. She was so confused she wanted to scream! Happy, on the one hand, about finally being in control of her life and terrified of making a huge mistake on the other, she fought back the urge to break down and have a good cry. She told herself that there wasn't time for such foolishness. If she were ever going to gain the respect of Scott's employees, she had to assert herself in the same controlling manner as her husband had.

Even though the therapist told Anne that she felt Scott was fighting the therapy, he was showing some improvement in other areas that he wasn't aware of.

Out of the blue, death threats began to surface against Scott. Anne was terrified. What had he done to someone to cause him or her to want him dead?

Jim Walker was her first thought. Isabell was her second. After all, she knew more about the *Hamilton Appeal* than Anne did. Was she feeding her false information? Had Anne been so eager to learn about the company's inner workings that she accepted everything Isabell said as fact? She hadn't even bothered to verify anything that the woman had told her.

Who was the invalid now? She or Scott?

Fifteen

BENTLEY HAD READ about Anne's husband's stroke in the *Appeal*. Since Nikkie's accident last year, Bentley hadn't tried to contact Anne again. Nikkie had made progress over the past months and was now walking with the aid of a cane. Bentley had hoped that Anne would call, come by, or just send a note explaining to everyone why she'd lost contact with the family. They deserved at least that much. That hadn't happened. Not even when Nikkie graduated from school. Even though Anne lived just thirty miles away from them, it might as well have been three thousand.

Over the past year Bentley had been lucky; the annual Jobs Conference for economic growth had been key in landing her a job as a secretary at an attorney's office. Unfortunately, she hadn't been able to locate a job in the field of her choice, art. No matter, her meager weekly salary kept Nikkie full and happy with the Little Debbie snack cakes that she loved, and also afforded Bentley enough cash for her personal needs. She never liked asking Aunt Mae for money.

In January, the American hostages who were seized in Iran in 1979 arrived safely in Algiers, the first step in their journey home. The release of the remaining fifty-two hostages was deliberately delayed by Ayatollah Khomeini until the day Ronald Reagan was sworn in as the new president. Bentley was thankful that Wesley had written her that he was being reassigned to Munich, Germany. She was disappointed that he'd told her then that he wouldn't be able to make it home in time for her graduation.

And today, as Bentley sat in the auditorium, it didn't matter. This day was supposed to be one of the most memorable days of her life. Instead she felt isolated and alone.

"Congratulations, Ms. Russell," Mr. Hillman said when Bentley accepted her high school diploma and shook his outstretched hand.

"Thank you," Bentley said, forcing a smile. Unlike the students that came before her, there were no whistles or claps when her name was read.

It was ten in the morning, and already Bentley felt fatigued.

Despite the sadness in her heart she still smiled. She

hadn't expected to feel this way, but now she wished that she hadn't told Aunt Vanilla Mae not to attend the ceremony. She had no idea that it would be like this. Viewing all the families—seeing all the hugs and love shown to her other classmates—made Bentley melancholy. Even her last letter from Erik hadn't brightened her spirits.

Dear Bentley,

> *I enjoyed reading your letter. And the lovely pictures that you sent showed me that you're maturing mentally as well as physically. I've included some photos of me at the army base in Frankfurt, Germany.*

> *Please don't be mad at me for not making your graduation. I've sent you a special gift that I hope will put a smile on that pretty face of yours. I should be home by the end of August for two weeks.*

> *I received a letter from my oldest sister the other day. They're still struggling to make ends meet, as usual. I'm helping out as much as I can, but I'm also trying not to feel guilty about making monetary provisions for our future. By the way, I've just gotten word that my promotion to first sergeant is secure.*

Disappointed that he said very little about loving her and missing her had left her despondent after reading the short letter.

Her mind raced ahead to the gift. It wouldn't surprise her if he'd purchased something intimate for her, though what she would really have appreciated was a few books on the history of German art. Nevertheless,

Bentley thought, as she walked down the stage steps and took her assigned seat in the auditorium, at least he said that he had sent something to commemorate her special day.

Like most of the girls graduating, she wore white. Looking up to her right in the bleachers, she noticed that some of the mothers were holding bouquets of flowers for their daughters. Bentley pressed the scroll of paper against her chest and aimed her gaze at the opened door to the left. The scent of fresh-cut grass drifted in.

Outside the sun was shining. Meadowlarks, bluebirds, and wrens were busily chirping elaborate vocal repertoires. Spring had become summer on this twenty-sixth day of May. Bentley stared at the neatly trimmed butterfly bushes that were shaped into disks and cones, and the pale purple wisteria trees that were blooming; white and pink azaleas ran riot everywhere, and the huge row of magnolias that bore thick white bulbs were soon to flower. In the humid stillness a school of butterflies circled. Bentley could almost hear their wings flap as they fluttered by.

It was the first time in a long time that she had thought about her mother and father. And she knew that she would feel this way again when she married and when she birthed her first child.

For now, Nikkie was like her own child. She remembered scolding her last week.

"No, Nikkie, you've had enough."

"More cake. Please."

"No."

"I hungry. I hungry. Feed me now."

You're not hungry, just greedy.

Because the income level in their home had gone up since Mae began to work, Social Services no longer paid for a nurse for Nikkie. They found Benita, a pregnant eighteen-year-old who lived on the same street as they did, who agreed to baby-sit Nikkie for the going rate of $1.25 an hour. Nikkie's mood seemed to change for the better while Benita was there. But the problem was all she did was pacify her; Nikkie had gained twenty-three pounds in the past fourteen months. She now weighed 144 pounds.

"What school are you going to, Bentley?" Jim Ellis, a student who worked on the school newspaper, asked, interrupting her thoughts.

"Memphis State. I'm taking a correspondence course."

"Art major?"

"Yeah."

"That's what I thought. Well . . ." he said, giving her a low-five, "good luck."

"Yeah. Same to you."

As the ceremony ended and the graduates exited the assembly room, Bentley overheard the students reminiscing about how much fun they'd had at the senior prom. Bentley had sat home alone that night, cherishing the gold bracelet that Wesley had sent her.

A week went by and still, there wasn't another package for Bentley. Erik had told her in his letters that he'd sent something special—but the special gift must've gotten lost in the mail. Nothing from Erik Berry came, no matter how many times she drilled the postman.

But what Bentley did notice was that a late-model white Mercedes had begun following her when she went to put in her applications for a job. At first she didn't pay the person inside any attention. But when she caught the bus to the *Hamilton Appeal,* the woman got out of the car and seemed to follow her inside. Bentley saw that the woman was wearing a hat that concealed most of her face and she thought she caught the woman smiling. At that point Bentley decided to confront the woman. Just as she headed in her direction, the woman quickly stepped on the elevator and pushed the button before Bentley had a chance to get on.

Why, Bentley wondered, would a white woman be following her?

Sixteen

SHE PLACED A SPRAY of peach roses and fresh baby's breath on the grave, then turned and walked down the hill to where her silver Jaguar was parked.

Clarice Jewel Littleton had just been interred. The only relative or friend present was her granddaughter, Isabell Ford. Her grandmother would have been eighty-eight years old the day before Labor Day.

The doctors told Isabell that her grandmother had died of natural causes. But Isabell didn't believe it. She believed that her grandmother was tired. Tired of trying to convince her not to be bitter about her past.

"I understand why you're so angry, Isabell. But you've got to get past that pain. A good family name is at stake. You can't just endure that—"

"Shhh. You'll upset yourself, grandmother."

"Promise me, child. Promise me that you'll do what's right—"

She had uttered those words three days earlier, before she fell back on her pillow and expired. Isabell breathed a sigh of relief, because she knew that her promise would be one that she knew she'd never keep.

Once home, she removed her tulle violet dress, plopped the wide-brimmed straw hat on the dresser in her bedroom, and kicked her black patent leather pumps off her aching feet.

Taking a seat at the desk, she opened the diary that was a few inches from her fingertips.

Laminated on the top cover was the poem she wrote at age twelve: "My New Best Friend."

> *Today I met a great new friend*
> *Who knew me right away*
> *It was funny how she understood*
> *All I had to say*
> *She listened to my problems*
> *She listened to my dreams*
> *We talked about love and life*
> *She'd been there too it seems*
> *I never once felt judged by her*
> *She knew just how I felt*
> *She seemed to just accept me*
> *And all the problems that I'd been dealt*
> *She didn't interrupt me*
> *Or need to have her say*
> *She just listened very patiently*
> *And didn't go away*
> *I wanted her to understand*
> *How much this meant to me*
> *But as I went to hug her*
> *Something startled me*
> *I put my arms in front of me*
> *And went to pull her nearer*
> *And realized that my new best friend*
> *Was nothing but a mirror.*

She smiled to herself, as she always did when she read her old words, which were even truer now than they were back then.

Opening the bottom drawer, she removed the pile of pictures and spread them out before her.

Most were baby pictures of her and the grandparents who raised her. Isabell's granddaddy Allan had died twenty years back of heart failure. She chuckled now remembering how he loved to take her to the corner store and buy her peanuts. Isabell would let out gas before they reached home and he would laugh and laugh.

There were pictures of her mother, Melissa, and her stepfather, Joshua Hardy, an investment banker who wouldn't let Isabell live at home with them. Joshua died in a plane crash in 1969. Her mother committed suicide three months later.

And finally there was one picture of her father, a handsome young fellow of twenty-three, whom she barely remembered.

Reaching inside her purse she removed a picture of Anne that she had taken at the last board meeting. Isabell took a pair a scissors from the narrow drawer and cut out every person but the smiling face that had come to trust her.

Picking up the pen, she began to write down the next step in her plans. When she finished, she ended the entry with capital letters, I HATE YOU.

She put the pictures back in the drawer, her racing heart filled with hate. Yes, she hated them all. The grandparents who had spoiled her and given her everything she wanted except the one thing she wanted most, her mother who was weak without a man, a man who wouldn't claim her as his daughter—but more than anything . . . she wanted Anne Russell-Hamilton to suffer.

Seventeen

THERE WERE TWO DIVISIONS in the *Hamilton Appeal* newspaper—the editorial side and the business side that was comprised of reporters, editors, marketing, advertising, and circulation.

Like Scott had been, Anne was now the central force in the company, pulling everything together and making it cohesive. The top link to the corporate office was in Cincinnati. Anne planned on tackling that issue once she was secure in the Memphis office.

Jim Walker and Rupert Napier, two of the four vice presidents, told her right from the beginning that the paper would be on her mind twenty-four hours a day.

Anne assumed that Jim would break her in to the inner workings of the paper, since they'd had conversations over the past months. He didn't. When he made eye contact with Rupert, Jim excused himself from the meeting.

"You're going to work twelve- and fifteen-hour days."

"I can handle that," Anne said bravely.

Rupert continued schooling her. "Your mind will always be on the news and what's going on in the world. You'll read, talk to people, and apply it to your job."

The vice president reminded her of a little old man who was looking for his hat when it was on his head all the time.

She stifled a laugh. "And the competition?"

"Excellent question. Television news—such as *World News Tonight*—is a daily concern, because all of our customers are important. If anyone has a problem with the *Hamilton Appeal,* we want to talk to them. We want to save every customer we can. The knowledge of what's going on in the world is something that *everyone* should be involved in."

Anne was informed after a lengthy spiel that her company employed 175 photographers, editors, and artists.

There were content managers, graphics, and advertising using the *Appeal*'s news but creating the space. There were folks that were copy aides; they pulled the agates (the birth records, court records, arrests, trials, and who was fined in court, the briefs, and the scoreboards in the sports section). Anne had no clue that for as much information that came into the paper, there had to be an allotted space to put it in. Sometimes they came up short.

The employees who worked in the obituary section usually worked their way into copyediting and then a reporting job. The newspaper reporter who took interviews, then wrote the stories—had the most sought-after job.

Anne took notes when Rupert toured her around the buildings to see hands on how the reporters conducted their interviews at work, how they got their contacts on the telephone. It was a fast-paced four-Tylenol-a-day type of job.

The president, Hal Curry, wasn't as nice. Anne could feel the friction the moment they shook hands. She wasn't sure how to react to him. She felt a bit intimated, yet a step above him, because after all, she was the owner's wife and owned the majority of stock in the company. Regardless, she and Hal would meet daily and go over the administrative and budgeting items.

She also met with the managing editor, the deputy managing editor, the general manager, six directors who headed up the business office, accounting, advertisers, the business section, and personnel and production.

Production, the people who put the paper together, was another huge entity.

There was no way that Anne would remember a tenth of their names, she mused as she went into her office. Jim, Hal, and Rupert were the ones she'd start with. Per past protocol, she was to have a short meeting with them every day as well as two formal meetings per week.

Scott had maintained an open-door policy, which meant that taking care of employee matters would occupy a good deal of her time. Even though Anne hadn't worked in nine years, she relished the opportunity to get back into the newspaper business.

Although she allowed Rupert to show her the ropes of the company without interruption, Anne hadn't come to work today totally unprepared. She'd gone to the library and did some research on the newspaper industry. She remembered one item in particular:

> *By the year 2000 newspapers will be juggling priorities; fragmentation of news consumption, fragmentation of advertising investments, the advantages and disadvantages of being a mass medium, balancing the wants of the marketplace with the company's duty to provide the needs of the marketplace, a journalistic backlash against industry changes, the sheer physicality of ink-on-paper production and distribution versus the (upcoming) digital distribution, increasing profit pressure surrounding the core print product, and extension of the company's core brand into other profit centers.*

It never ceased to mystify her how analysts could project the future of any business so accurately—especially nearly twenty years from now. What was acutely obvious to her, though, was that she would have to be quickly conversant on every aspect of the business in order to get some respect.

After closing the door to her gray-on-gray office, she studied her notes briefly, and then buzzed her secretary in.

"Jennifer, could you come in here for a moment? I'd like to you to take a memo to the employees."

Fifteen hours, my butt, she thought, leaning back in the black leather recliner; she'd be here twenty if necessary.

BY THE END OF THE SECOND WEEK, Lily Fellows, in the Personnel Department, apprised her of Bentley's application for employment. Anne's name, listed as a referral, hadn't gone unnoticed.

"We told her on numerous occasions that we didn't need an artist at this time. But she insisted on being interviewed. I'm not sure how to proceed, Mrs. Hamilton."

"Move . . . ah . . ." she checked her notepad ". . . Dionne Minor to the graphic arts department and hire Ms. Russell. I've seen her comic strip. It has a fresh approach that will appeal to both our white and black readers."

"But Dionne has four years senior—"

"Just do it, Lily!"

Early Thursday afternoon Anne called the governess, Mrs. McKinney, whom she'd hired after going to work at the paper. She asked the fifty-two-year-old gem to take out a package of chicken breasts from the freezer—she'd be home in time to prepare dinner herself this evening.

Working at the *Appeal* had helped her to appreciate her home more. She enjoyed the time away from the kids and couldn't wait to tell them about her day when she came home.

On this day, Anne looked forward to going home. It would be the first time in a long time that she was able to prepare dinner for her children.

At precisely 7:35, Anne said good-bye to Mrs. McKinney and headed for the kitchen. Preparing a garlic roasted chicken salad, Campbell's vegetarian vegetable soup, and garlic bread had taken only seventeen minutes.

When she removed the garlic bread from the toaster oven, she could hear the children sitting at the dining room table, already arguing about their latest video game.

"Holly!" Anne called out. "Could you help me, honey?"

Her perky six-year-old daughter came into the kitchen, frowning.

"What's wrong, honey?"

"Oh, nothing," Holly said, picking up two plates of salad.

Unlike her brother, Holly was even-tempered. She rarely argued with Basil. She just let him have his way.

Anne followed her daughter into the dining room and ignored the fact that Basil was sitting at his father's seat at the head of the table—again.

At eight years old Basil was already a handsome young man. His wide-spaced eyes, keen nose, thick lips, and square chin were nearly identical to her brother Kirk's—a miniature Jackie Robinson. Holly, three shades darker, but with reddish-brown hair like her aunt Vanilla Mae's, looked like Basil's identical twin. The only features they had taken from their father were his high instep and hammertoes.

Once dinner was placed on the table, Anne sat down. It was Basil's turn to lead the prayer. Afterward, Anne quizzed them as she usually did about their schoolwork.

"I think we should fire Daddy's nurse," Basil interrupted.

"Why?" Anne said, looking toward the doorway and hoping the woman wouldn't come downstairs and overhear them.

"She's not helping him. All she does is watch TV all day and crochet those stupid afghans. She doesn't help him exercise his muscles twice a day like she's supposed to. The baths she gives him aren't long enough. And Daddy doesn't smell the way he used to. If Daddy could speak for himself he'd fire her."

Anne exhaled. She should have known this was coming. Mrs. Features, Scott's live-in nurse, was very efficient. She left a checklist for Anne to approve every day. There was a written report on Fridays that assessed Scott's progress. What Basil didn't like was that Mrs. Features ignored him. She didn't like his practical jokes and his incessant questions that Anne had constantly warned him about.

"How do you know what she's supposed to do?" Anne queried.

"I did a report about physical therapy in my science class. Besides, me and Daddy have our own mode of communication."

"What—"

Holly gave her mother her *he's lying* look, then rolled her eyes toward the ceiling.

"Uh-hm. We do too," he said, folding his arms on the table in front of him. "I want to know what you plan on doing about her, Mother?"

Anne didn't like the confrontational look on his face. How dare this little boy, who forgot to brush his teeth every morning until she reminded him, question her about *her* husband's welfare? "I'm very satisfied with Mrs. Features' work, Basil."

"Well, I'm not."

Basil winced, and Anne noticed a casual smile on Holly's face. Apparently, she had kicked him under the table.

"You should stay in a child's place, Basil. You're too young to understand your father's condition."

He jumped up from his seat. "I know you don't love my daddy! You never did. You're the reason why he's in that bed in the first place!"

Anne rose, clutching the soup spoon in her hand. "How dare you speak to me like that!"

"You can't deny it, can you? You hate him. Why don't you admit it?"

Anne rounded the table and grabbed Basil so fast she was shaking. She swung her right arm back and slapped him dead in the mouth.

"Don't you ever speak to me like that again!"

"Dad did." He scowled.

Anne slapped him again. This time he fell down on the floor. When he looked up at her she could tell that he was holding back tears.

"Now you get upstairs, and don't come back down until you're ready to give me a full apology!"

"Mommy," Holly said, after Basil had left, "*do* you love Daddy?"

She took her seat. "What, baby?" Her hands were shaking when she picked up the glass of ice water.

"Love Daddy."

Anne cringed. "Of course I love Daddy." But the moment she uttered those words, she knew that for all intents and purposes she didn't have an ounce of love for that man left. Was it wrong for her to hope that he wouldn't get any better?

Eighteen

WHEN BENTLEY FOUND OUT that Anne had given the "go-ahead" for hiring her, she called her up on the telephone.

"I'd like to thank you for the job, Aunt Anne."

"That isn't necessary. I know that you're more than qualified for the job."

"Well . . ." Bentley began awkwardly. She didn't know what else to say. Getting her a job still didn't fill the void left by her absence over the years. Nothing would.

"All right, then, Bentley, I'll talk to you later."

"Okay, 'bye."

She must have known, Bentley thought. They both had their own lives now. Better to keep it that way.

On the rare occasions they saw each other at work, they said hello and that was it. No phone numbers were exchanged or asked for.

Bentley told herself that the hefty salary she was offered was well deserved, and not out of familial guilt. Even so, she had to cut corners with clothing, rent, and furniture so that she could afford a secondhand van with a chair lift to cart Nikkie around.

Getting guardianship of Nikkie had been easier than Bentley anticipated. Mae signed over the papers without argument and even helped Bentley pick out an apartment that was only five miles away.

Their two-bedroom apartment had a wood-burning fireplace with a tile hearth, ceiling fans in the kitchen, two bedrooms, mirrored dining area, and two huge bay windows.

Though she didn't ask for it, Erik sent money so that she could purchase a 1978 Chrysler van in June. She and Nikkie moved into their apartment with three pieces of furniture—two beds and a couch. Fortunately, Benita from their old neighborhood was still willing to watch Nikkie while Bentley went to work.

Ten months ago, Benita gave birth to a nine-pound son. To everyone's shock, Benita gave the father custody. She saw her son twice a month and told Bentley that it was working out for both her and the baby's father.

Bentley didn't know what to say. But she did like the young girl. She was a hard worker and very dependable. Benita braided hair to supplement her income, and as long as Bentley didn't mind her customers coming to her home, Benita told her that their situation could work out indefinitely. She loved getting paid and not having to pay taxes.

When Bentley had time to herself, she'd read Erik's letters over and over again and rhapsodize on the long and fantastic future that she and he would have one day soon.

When Erik came home every six months on leave, they spent as much time doing outdoor activities with Nikkie as they did together. When Nikkie finally fell asleep, exhausted, they would silently make love, and make plans for their future.

She believed that her future with Erik was one worth waiting for. After all, how many men take the time to cater to his fiancée's handicapped sister?

IN 1982 THE MISSISSIPPI RIVER MUSEUM on Mud Island opened. The island descriptively called *Mud* was dumped on Memphis's doorstep by a ship that ran aground and stayed far too long. When it finally moved away, the ship left behind a sandbar that grew into a pile of dirt—some of the same dirt was what the public saw today. To create the riverwalk, the top of the island had to be raised eighteen feet with silt dredged from the river. On this accidental sandbar rose one of the finest architectural designs in Memphis's history.

There were two principal attractions: a model of the river, cut into the concrete pavement, and the Mud Island Museum. On the model, the river flows through at the same level as the river stage had been in Memphis on that day. Depth is shown abstractly through the use of contours. The principal cities and towns along the river were represented by plans carved in slate, while the bridge that crosses the river appeared as a stainless steel bar wide enough to walk on. Walking across the bridge and reminiscing about her future was Bentley's favorite activity on the island.

The museum was a showplace, too. But what most people enjoyed, and especially the children, was part of a riverboat that was built at actual scale. There were other buildings on the island, but they were designed to be background buildings so as to not draw attention away from the riverwalk. One day, Bentley thought, she would bring her children here to picnic and take in the cool breezes of the Mississippi River.

On the weekends, or on a hot day after work, Bentley and Nikkie would stay on the island for hours—Nikkie quietly enjoying the fresh air and Bentley carefully drawing her characters. As she wove tales of her imaginary family, the characters seemed almost real to her.

The Riverdocks, the name of her cartoon strip, debuted in the *Hamilton Appeal* in late June. The female editor claimed that her soap-opera-style strip had dramatic continuity. The strip was similar to *Apartment 3-G*, which was created in May of 1961, but told from a black perspective. Thanks to the civil rights movement, the *Appeal* was a springboard for a black comic strip.

By the first of July, Bentley had received hundreds of letters and cards. It seemed the handicapped Sasha, eighteen, was a sympathetic and beloved character for the *Appeal*'s broad audience. Sasha believed that she would one day walk again and be able to hold down a job like her sister, Abby.

Abby, twenty-two, Bentley's character, was a young woman in search of self. She struggled with getting married and leaving her handicapped sister in the hands of an unstable aunt or asking her young husband to accept the lifetime burden of her sister.

Finally, there was Lidia, the aunt who wouldn't let them address her as such in public. Lidia was an endearing character, though misunderstood, who had done devious things to Sasha and Abby. Lidia was a lonely fortyish unmarried woman who'd endured years of heartbreaks. Her quest for a husband and a family only led to one disappointment after another.

"Guess what, Miss Russell?" her editor shrieked, coming up from behind her. "The response has been overwhelming for *Riverdocks*. Circulation is up ten percent. Mrs. Hamilton is talking about giving you a raise. Can you imagine that? No one's gotten a raise this quickly before."

She'd been working ten hours a day, six days a week, and had even helped in the creative process of some of the other artists in her department. In three months her life was changing like a storm cloud in the night.

Even though Bentley had offered to find another sitter for Nikkie when she worked overtime, Benita wouldn't hear of it. She was buying a new car and could use the extra money.

On Saturday afternoon, it rained all day and spoiled the trip that Bentley had planned to Mud Island. Instead, she decided that she and Nikkie needed to spruce themselves up a bit.

Steering Nikkie to the kitchen sink, Bentley placed the shampoo, conditioner, and hairbrush on the counter, and then began loosening Nikkie's braids.

"This is going to feel great, Nikkie," Bentley said, smiling. "The girls at work showed me this new hairstyle that we're going to try today."

"No. No. I sleepy, sister. Take me back to bed."

Bentley leaned over her shoulder, smiling. "Oh no, Ms. Russell," she said, mussing her thick tresses, "we've got to get the pretty young lady ready. Benita's going to take you to see Dr. Elliott on Monday morning. And you know how much you blush when you talk to that handsome young fellow."

Nikkie snickered mischievously to herself.

Bentley pulled a chair close to the sink, and motioned for Nikkie to take a seat.

"I know what you're thinking," Bentley teased as she helped her sister relax and lay her head back against the cool bowl. After checking the temperature of the water, she wet Nikkie's hair and then applied Head and Shoulders shampoo.

"Don't hurt me. That hurt," Nikkie complained as Bentley massaged her scalp. "Stop. Please. Please."

"We've got to make you pretty, girl. I'll bet you didn't know that you've got a ton of dandruff. You know, I wish I could sing, Nikkie." Bentley said, ignoring her sister's protests. "I'd sing you a lullaby that I believe Mama would have sung to make us feel comfortable and secure."

Bentley hadn't a clue why she mentioned their mother; she hadn't thought about her in years. As hard as she tried to remember her, she still seemed a mere figment of her imagination. Someone who was never loving or caring.

When Anne spoke to her a year after her parents' death, she clearly remembered telling her young aunt that she'd forgotten her mother.

She hadn't.

At four, her memory was vivid. Her mother never hugged her children. She couldn't remember a kiss or a loving phrase. All she remembered was the constant arguing between her mother and father. She could tell that her mother was unhappy in their marriage. Why, she didn't know.

Bentley shrugged off unexpected tears as she rinsed Nikkie's hair and applied the conditioner. Nikkie seemed to sense that Bentley had something on her mind and did something that she rarely did; asked about Wesley.

"Where he?" Nikkie attempted to raise her head up and look at her.

Bentley gently guided her head back and hurriedly rinsed out the conditioner. "He'll be home one of these days. Then the three of us are going to move into a bigger place. Together, Wes and I are going to take good care of you, sweetie." Bentley wrung the water out of her hair with a strong twist of her wrist, then wrapped a towel around her head. "Wes and I are even going to shoot marbles with you—"

"Cat's-eyes."

"Yes, Nikkie. You're going to win dozens of cat's-eye marbles. And we're going to let you keep them in your shoe box."

"When? When!" her voice was splintered with pain.

"Just wait, baby. It won't be long."

She felt Nikkie's thick arms circling around her waist like she never wanted to let go. "I've got something for you," she whispered in her ear.

Bentley removed from a bag on the table three pairs of size 24X slacks and blouses that she'd bought at Lane Bryant's. There were also six pairs of underwear in pastel colors with matching brassieres.

While Nikkie looked inside the bag, she applied B & B Castor Oil and Scalp Conditioning Crème with Aloe on Nikkie's dry scalp.

"For me?" she squealed.

"Yes. For my special sister." While Nikkie fidgeted with the items in the bag, Bentley envisioned the goddess-braid-style hairdo her co-worker had showed her. "Now you sit back and let me fix your hair real pretty."

Just as she was about to part Nikkie's hair, she felt a tug on her arm. "No. Stop."

"What's wrong, Nikkie?"

Her body began to shake and convulse. Bentley had seen it dozens of times before. The seizures were starting.

"Help me, Lord," she mumbled to herself and noted the time on the clock.

By then, Nikkie's eyes were rolling around in her head like loose marbles. Drool slid out of the side of her mouth as Bentley guided Nikkie to the sofa. Helping her to lie on her side, Bentley glanced at the clock again and held her breath.

It seemed like an eternity before she calmed down. Bentley went into the medicine cabinet and retrieved the Tegretol. After giving Nikkie a dose, she helped her walk to her bedroom. Usually, the seizures left Nikkie exhausted and she would sleep at least three to four hours.

Bentley placed the bag of new clothes in the bottom

drawer by her bed, and then sat down beside her. She steepled her hands and lowered her head.

When she closed her eyes she said aloud, "You said that you wanted me to have peace." She reached out and laid her hand on her sleeping sister's shoulder. "Where is peace?"

Within yourself.

Nineteen

"IT TURNED OUT BEAUTIFULLY, ISABELL." Anne beamed. "It's like a dream come true." The two women were admiring Holly's newly decorated bedroom.

"Yeah. I believe so," Isabell said, fluffing one of the yellow cotton pillow shams on the bed. "If Holly wasn't such a wonderful little girl, I would never have loaned you my decorator. My home is already behind schedule as it is."

Holly Anne Hamilton's birthday was tomorrow, August 29. She was going to be seven years old. Her birthday present from her mom and dad was redecorating her bedroom, a room that was originally done up in frilly confection pink and white gingham.

A month ago, Isabell's decorator, Rudy, had suggested a dream theme in yellow and blue for Holly's bedroom.

Rudy had designed her room so that when Holly awakened she would see a room filled with celestial images—and one happy frog. He cut and stenciled a six-foot sun on the wall as well as a single custom-designed friendly frog hanging from a star. Anne, Isabell, and

Rudy found Italian, Spanish, French, Chinese, Russian, German, and Portuguese translations for "Good Morning Sunshine" for the freehand lettering on the sun rays. The celestial feel of the room was further enhanced with a stenciled moon and stars that had touches of silver in them.

"You know, Isabell, it kind of makes me want to do some decorating in my bedroom."

Because of Scott's condition, Anne had moved out of their master suite and had given the nurse the second master bedroom next to it. Her new bedroom was located on the opposite end of their home, right next to Basil's. That room, decorated in gray, silver, and white, was meant for a second son that she and Scott would never have. The linen was done in a dark burgundy plaid pattern that made the room feel even more masculine.

"Rudy's spoiled you already," Isabell said, removing her shoes and curling up in the cushioned window seat. "Next week I'll see about finding you someone equally as talented. Meanwhile," she said, patting the empty place beside her, "take a seat, home-girl. I'd like to talk to you for a moment."

"Honey, hush. You're getting good, girl," Anne said, giving her a high-five.

"Don't I know it." Isabell winked. "Now, let's talk about something a bit more serious."

"Scott?"

"No. Men."

"Who? Are you finally going to tell me the name of this hot black man you're in love with?"

"Not yet. I was referring to you. Scott's been ill for some time now, right?" Anne nodded. "Then what are you doing about sex?"

"That's really none of your business, Isabell." Anne shook her head. "We're friends, but I never assumed that we were *that* close."

"Chill, Anne. I'm not trying to get all up in your business. I just wanted you to know that I know somebody who'd be very discreet—"

Anne jumped up. "Hold up, honey. You've gone a little bit too damn far. I'm a married woman, Isabell, and I respect my husband, no matter what his situation."

"He's not taking care of you, girlfriend. And you're a vibrant young woman. Don't tell me you don't think about sex?"

"I never said I didn't. It just isn't . . . isn't something that I want to discuss right now. I've got responsibilities. It isn't Scott's fault that he's ill. We've been married for over nine years. That counts for something." Anne tried to think of something better to say, while Isabell stared her boldly in the eye.

"So it's gotten that bad at night, huh?"

How would you know? Anne thought.

Footsteps on the steps silenced Anne's nasty retort. A few seconds later, Holly burst into the room. Her mouth made a wide O. She dropped her baseball glove in the doorway and ran to jump on her bed.

Anne and daughter stared at one another for a moment. Here was her perfect angel, who only two months ago wouldn't be caught in jeans. And now here she was, playing first base on the church's softball team.

"Oooooh," she squealed bouncing up and down, "I love it! Thanks, Mom. Thanks, Aunt Isabell. I know you helped, too."

"You're welcome, sweetie," Isabell said, putting her shoes back on.

"Can I sleep in my room tonight, Mommy?"

"Only if you promise not to bring your friends up until tomorrow."

"Dog. I wanted Ericka to see it. I told her that it'd be finished today."

The white princess telephone rang, and Holly answered it.

When the giggles started, the two women rose to go.

"Mom . . ." Holly called just before she and Isabell reached the doorway, "Ericka's mom wants to talk to you."

"I'll see myself out," Isabell said, then stopped to whisper in her ear, "Anne . . . you never once mentioned love."

Twenty

THE BULK OF HER ENGRAVED INVITATIONS were written out to the most prominent business owners in Shelby County—the most prestigious being Fred W. Smith, the owner of FedEx.

Local dignitaries, such as judges, city councilmen, pastors, and congressman made up most of the twenty-five guests on her list.

When the incumbent mayor, Richard C. Hackett, turned down her invitation to the dinner party, Isabell extended one to the first-term-seeking superintendent of schools, Willie W. Herenton. He readily accepted, and she was pleased that the mix of black and white guests would be more even.

The event was scheduled to take place on Saturday

evening. And today, on this windy Wednesday afternoon, she was getting irritated that the decorator wouldn't be finished with the banquet room until late Thursday morning. To her displeasure, the cleaning crew and the caterers would be working right on top of one another.

Seated at her desk, Isabell glanced over at the bookcases located at the opposite end of her bedroom. Resting on pedestals was an extensive collection of nineteenth- and twentieth-century hat forms from French and American milliners. She wondered which hat would suit her needs most on Saturday night—the hostess, the campaigner, the seductress, or the matchmaker.

Opening the diary as she sat her desk, she placed a check beside a name, then picked up the telephone. As she dialed, she smiled to herself.

"Hello. This is Isabell Ford calling, Delia. I wondered—"

"Yes, Ms. Ford, the senator's in, I'll put you through."

Isabell tapped her finger beside Anne's enigmatic photo.

"Say," came Orin's pleasant voice shortly thereafter, "I've been meaning to call you."

"Sure. Tell your old friend any kind of lie."

"You know me better than that. How've you been?"

"Oh, okay, I suppose. I was wondering what your plans were for Saturday evening."

"Let me check." She could hear him flipping the pages of his appointment book, and then said, "My wife and I are attending a fund-raiser for the Ronald McDonald House. She's chairing the event."

"Can you get out of it?"

"It all depends. What's my incentive?"

"A night of hanky-panky with me."

"Hmm, sounds tempting."

"C'mon, Orin, we haven't seen each other in months," she purred. "And I know you miss me."

"Definitely."

"And don't I fulfill your wildest fantasies?" She heard him hesitate, then added, "I found what you wanted."

"The—" He stopped.

A smile curled at her lips. "Um-hm." The last time they met he told her that he wanted her to purchase a female belly with an artificial vagina. The apparatus was designed to give a man the perfect illusion of a real woman by providing him with just as sweet voluptuous sensations as the woman herself.

Outwardly, it represented a woman's abdomen, minus the legs. The secret parts, the pubis, covered with an abundance of silk hair—the labia majora, the labia minora, and the clitoris—offered themselves to a male's covetous view as temptingly rose-colored as the female love temple. The contact, supposedly, was soft, and a pneumatic tube could regulate the pressure. Furthermore, the apparatus included a lubricating mechanism, to be previously filled with a warm and oily liquid and released by pressure into the vagina at the critical moment, just as in the case of the natural female glands. This was the only apparatus that duplicated exactly the copulatory organs of a woman, and therefore, was capable of giving the perfect illusion of reality. Being readily inflatable and deflectable, the contraption could be hidden in the pocket as easily as a handkerchief or any other toilet article.

At this precise moment, she knew what his twisted mind was thinking. She could also hear him panting. "Well . . ." he said huskily.

"Well nothing. I need you to attend my dinner party on Saturday night. The man who's going to whip

Hackett's butt this fall has agreed to come." She decided to change the tempo. She knew that by now he was licking his lips with anticipation.

"Who, Willie?"

"The same."

"Hmm. I think he's a man I need to get to know."

"I believe so."

"Wait a minute, Isabell. He's not the reason you want me to come. Cut to the chase."

"Well . . . it's a little more personal. I've met someone who's having some problems. With your talents, I think you could help her . . ."

Twenty-one

IT WAS JUST AFTER EIGHT Friday morning, and Anne knew that she couldn't put it off a minute longer. She took the elevator down to the fourth floor and went into the small cubicle that was occupied by a strikingly beautiful young woman.

"Bentley?" she asked incredulously.

"Yes."

Anne extended her hand, knowing that it was too soon to expect a hug. "Why, hello. It's so good to see you."

"Yeah. Same here," Bentley said awkwardly.

"It's been about eight, nine—"

"Nine years," Bentley said flatly.

"Do you mind?" Anne asked, nodding in the direction of the chair.

"No, please. Have a seat."

"Let me start by saying, I didn't realize how beautiful you were, Bentley."

Bentley blushed. "Thanks. And you're still as pretty as ever, Aunt Anne. I thought you'd look much older. But you look exactly the same."

"Bentley . . . I think that it's important that you understand something." Her eyes were far away, her memory sharp. "I feel I should explain why I haven't been in touch. When I married Scott I thought it would benefit the entire Russell family. I made a huge error in judgment. He was selfish, self-centered, and demanded every minute of my time. I wasn't allowed to communicate with my family. Believe me, I tried. But whenever I did, he found out, and I suffered because of it." Despite her efforts her voice cracked. "I don't expect any pity or anything, just understanding."

"I didn't know, Aunt Anne. I thought that you . . ."

Anne's face pinched with sadness and her voice dropped. "Thought I was rich and too good for all of you? No. But I couldn't blame you for thinking that way."

Bentley reached out and touched her aunt's shoulder and smiled. "Let's not discuss the past. We can't change it anyway. Okay?"

"Okay. Tell me. How is Nikkie doing?"

"She's fine. Her seizures are less frequent now. She's gained a few pounds, but I feel that she's happy living with me."

"That's good news." Anne was silent for a moment, while Bentley nervously scribbled on a piece of paper. "And Wesley? Is he still in the service?"

"Yep. And he's doing okay, I guess." She paused. "But tell me, Aunt Anne. How are you doing? I read about your husband's stroke."

Anne took a few minutes to update Bentley about her husband's current condition. She left out the part about him beating her, and chose to tell her instead that Scott was doing as well as expected. The conversation took a turn for the better when Anne mentioned her two children. When she told Bentley about Holly's baseball team, and Basil's practical jokes, Bentley let out a chuckle. The innocence of her children seemed to break the barriers between them.

Anne was glad to hear that Bentley was enrolled in a correspondence class part-time. She'd recently transferred to Shelby State and hoped to receive an associate degree in art in three years.

When Anne mentioned her friend, Isabell Ford, Bentley stiffened.

"I read about the big party she's having tomorrow. Seems like all the affluent people in Memphis are invited. How about you, Aunt Anne? Are you going?"

"I haven't made up my mind yet." Anne wished that she hadn't brought Isabell's name up. Bentley cleared her throat.

Anne changed the subject. "I've been told that your strip is syndicated now."

"Yeah. I'm in thirty cities. My goal is a hundred twenty-five markets and possibly foreign countries; you know, like Charles Schulz's *Peanuts*—that strip is in seventy-five countries, twenty-six hundred newspapers, and twenty-one languages. My editor feels that we'll make the one hundred twenty-five mark in another year or so."

"That's good news."

Bentley caught Anne up to speed about the character she was working on this week—Sasha. The lovely heroine, Sasha, was handicapped and very unhappy. Rarely was she able to go outside and feel the fresh air on her face. There were little neighbor children who stopped by and brought the sad lady gifts and flowers. Wanting to do something for the children, Sasha began to knit wool gloves that she knew they would need for the winter. The trouble was that Sasha couldn't make the gloves small enough. She ended up knitting hats, which fit them perfectly.

Anne enjoyed the short segment of *Riverdocks*. But she felt relieved that she and Bentley had finally broken the ice and had a face-to-face conversation. She left Bentley's office with a promise to keep in contact.

Early the next morning Anne was awakened by the telephone. It was Isabell reminding her of the party that night. When Anne told her that she had decided to pass on the event, Isabell was a little more upset than Anne thought necessary.

As the holiday season approached, Anne realized that she hadn't heard from Isabell in weeks. She called and left messages, but Isabell hadn't returned any of her calls.

Anne decided to concentrate on family this year. She dressed up the kids in red velvet and together the three of them delivered Christmas presents to Nikkie, Bentley, and Mae on Christmas morning. It was the best Christmas that Anne remembered having since she was first married.

Almost a week after the holiday season passed, Memphis experienced a light blanket of snow. In the winter solstice, Anne looked out the library window at the icicles and their shadows hanging from the rooftops. A snow goose lifted from its shadow toward the moonlight. Too agitated to rest, Anne paced about the room, unable to feel the usual positive emotion she felt during the beginning of the new year.

No matter how concerned she was about family, she considered problems that were occurring in the city of Memphis a major part of her life as well. Editorials in the *Hamilton Appeal* were about the white flight. Hundreds of thousands of citizens were leaving the city. The majority of citizens believed that these people had left for the more progressive city of Nashville.

Race relations were ripe in the city once again. One of the most consistent themes throughout the literature on southern politics was the prominence of race. From the Civil War to Reconstruction, from Jim Crow to the civil rights periods that Anne knew so well, southern politics have long revolved in significant ways around the issue of race. One thing about southern politics, white people would cut off their nose to spite their face.

Less than two weeks later, race relations would become even more volatile.

Early on Tuesday, January 11, 1983, an armed cult group, following an apparently deranged leader named Lindberg Sanders, were holed up in a home at 2239 Shannon, near Chelsea and North Hollywood in North Memphis. When white police responded to a complaint call, the black cult members attacked; they wounded one officer and took another hostage. During the suspense filled siege, which lasted a day and a half, the sounds within the house were picked up electronically and recorded.

The incident would come to be known as the Shannon Street Massacre.

On Thursday the 13th, police raided the home. When the people inside heard the sound of the police attempting to surround the house, the group's members systematically beat Officer Robert S. Hester to death. When the tactical squad later stormed the house, it killed everyone inside, indicating that everyone inside had fiercely resisted the arrest. This tragedy was the beginning of the second round of racial politics at the crossroads.

Throughout the spring and summer months, blacks as well as whites packed up their belongings. For the first time in Memphis's history, the population declined: 620,337 persons living in Memphis, with 826,330 in Shelby County. Anne, although very busy at work at the *Appeal,* was paying attention. Blacks had become a definite majority, 54 percent inside Memphis. About 75,000 more whites moved out of the city than moved in. Anne wondered, as she made plans to attend her first class reunion, how many of her classmates had moved away from the city.

THE DOMINANT THEME in the banquet room of the Holiday Inn on Poplar Avenue was the blues. Oversized colored cardboard cutouts of shiny saxophones, player pianos, and mammoth-sized musical notes decorated the white walls. A large banner in the entryway spelled out in bold gold letters: 1973 10th Class Reunion. The excitement over the opening of B. B. King's Blues Club on Beale Street had infected the black community.

Hundreds of printed name tags were spread out on a six-foot white-clothed table.

Music boomed down the hall, but Anne couldn't recognize the tune. As she approached the front table where two women were sitting that she didn't recognize at first, Anne gave her maiden name for the first time since she and Scott married.

"Anne Russell," she said to a familiar face.

When the girl finally recognized her, she asked, "Girl,

how you doing? Remember me, I'm Lucy Adler. I sat beside you in algebra."

My, my, Anne thought. People certainly did change. She wouldn't have recognized cross-eyed Lucy, who came to class faintly smelling of urine. Some of her classmates used to joke about the pissy Adlers. Nine children lived in a two-bedroom shotgun shack near Mississippi Boulevard. Lucy now smelled of expensive perfume and she'd definitely gone to a good ophthalmologist. Her eyes were no longer crossed and she was wearing contacts.

"Ten years have done wonders, Lucy," Anne said, smiling. "You look even prettier than you did back then."

The deejay was starting a new song. Marvin Gaye's trademark music couldn't be duplicated. Anne was relieved that they weren't going to play blues all night. She didn't really care for the whiny tunes. They made her sad, and caused her to think about her unbearable marriage.

Lucy beamed. "This is great, girl. Nearly everyone's here. Wait until you see Betty Anderson, she looks like a four-hundred-pound sumo wrestler." The girl beside her nudged her leg. "She's really sensitive about it, though, so pretend not to notice."

Anne laughed. The line was beginning to grow behind her. Instinctively, she turned and looked into a pair of charming brown eyes.

"Avery Cameron," he said, while looking directly at Anne. "Why, hello, Anne."

"Hi."

Pinning her name tag on, Anne swiftly left the entryway and headed down the hall toward the music. Her heart pounded wildly at the thought of dancing with Avery. He'd tried from their freshman year until they became seniors to date her. Anne had always refused. She wondered if he was married and was as miserable as she was.

The dimly lit hall leading to the banquet room seemed to last forever. There was a couple in front of her laughing and holding hands. Anne wondered if it was another one of her classmates who might remember her. She was tempted to tap the man on the shoulder, but stopped herself. What would she say? Would the woman think that she was his old girlfriend? What would he think seeing her alone? She wished that she had someone with her that she loved. Scott? No.

Gold and blue balloons flanked the ceiling and walls and even lounged around the dance floor. Dozens of round tables that would seat eight were decorated with beautiful floral arrangements and a questionnaire that she assumed would be used during the course of the evening. On the right side of the room, a movie projector was flashing on and off with different pictures of classmates during their four years at Manassas High School.

A few couples were dancing to the tunes the deejay was playing without interruption.

Anne took a seat at an empty table. In no time, the entire room was bulging with smiling, laughing faces. She overheard someone saying, "They should have put our yearbook pictures on our name tags, otherwise, I won't be able to recognize half of the people here." She had to smile.

The next song was by a hometown artist and a huge favorite. Johnny Taylor's "I Feel Sorry," came on and the dance floor filled to capacity.

As she eavesdropped on the conversation beside her, she overheard people discussing race relations in the city of Memphis and also the subject that most people wanted to discuss: Sally Ride, the first female American astronaut. If a woman could travel to the moon, they were saying, the next target was the White House.

Anne wasn't so sure she agreed.

There was a cash bar in the far right corner of the room. Dozens of men were huddled there laughing and, Anne guessed, discussing the women there tonight. To the left, and near the women's bathroom, a group of women had converged and, Anne assumed, were doing the same thing the men were.

Anne smiled at a few familiar faces at the table in which she sat and made small talk. She turned down a few offers to dance and wondered if she'd made a mistake coming. Deciding to try and make an effort to be friendlier, Anne walked over to the bar and ordered a glass of champagne. She overheard whispers and pretended not to notice the ravenous stares she was receiving.

The event was called to order and officially began.

While Anne sipped champagne, she thought back about her last conversation with Isabell. She'd finally broken down and called Anne in early May. Things were still a little touchy between them, but Isabell seemed especially pleased when Anne told her about the reunion invitation.

"We've got to go shopping," Isabell had insisted.

"I'm not going," Anne had said flatly. "Scott is just learning how to communicate to us. It may take months for him to learn how to correctly disseminate the entire alphabet by blinking."

"What has that got to do with the reunion? Face it, Anne, you're overdue for a break."

"I don't know." Anne had peeled a potato and

dropped it into the pot of chitterlings. "Maybe I don't want to go alone."

"Look. There will be women as well as men there who've been divorced or widowed and will come alone just like you. Send in the twenty-five bucks before the deadline expires. Why should you skip one of the most important events of your youth?"

Anne couldn't think of an excuse. Truthfully, Scott didn't need her. The therapist and weekly doctor visits were handling her husband's health better than she'd expected. He was comfortable and eating well, but his breathing was still very labored. She noticed that he never seemed agitated while the children were with him. The years of being bedridden hadn't softened him toward her. Hate was written on his face, and Anne found more and more excuses to delay her morning visit.

Isabell was right—she could use a night of excitement to get away from all the stress at home. Why not have a little fun. She sure deserved it.

Together, they'd shopped for Anne's ensemble. Isabell had also convinced her to trade in the 750 SL Benz that was nearly eleven years old, and purchase a new, more sporty 1983 BMW. She'd relented and drove the Beamer for the first time tonight.

An hour into the evening, she found herself looking for Avery. When she spotted him dancing with someone she didn't remember, he smiled at her. Anne pretended not to notice.

Making small talk with the other people at her table was easy. Most of her fellow classmates remembered that she'd been crowned the homecoming queen in her senior year, but after that the conversation fell flat. She didn't disclose that her husband was Scott Hamilton, the CEO of the *Hamilton Appeal*. Living a low-keyed life had its benefits tonight, she thought.

Dinner was served, and afterward the award ceremony began.

Awards were given away for the person with the most children, the person most recently married, the couple that'd been married the longest, the classmate who was the most successful, and finally the one who'd moved the farthest away.

"We've been married twelve years," a man said, standing up. Everyone else said ten, nine, or less.

Twelve years meant they'd secretly married at sixteen. Anne listened to their storybook relationship and saw the obvious love that shone on both their faces. Anne felt an emotion she hadn't felt in years—jealousy.

After all the awards had been given out, the projector started up again for the late arrivals. Life-sized pictures of the classmates that had died saddened Anne. A feeling of remorse came over her. She hadn't been a close friend with most of them, but they were a cherished part of her past that she'd never forget. She found herself crying and reached in her purse for a tissue.

"Say, would you like to dance?" a voice from behind her asked.

Sniffing back tears, she took a deep breath and turned around, certain that it was Avery. Instead, she saw a gentleman at least twenty years older than she was. All around her, people were staring and whispering.

"I'm sorry, I was just about to leave." She started to pick up her purse, when he placed his large hand over hers and pressed against it.

Not wanting to draw any further attention to herself, she agreed to dance with him. While they slow-danced, she learned that he was escorting his sister tonight. He also told her that he was Senator Orin Matthews.

"From Nashville?" she asked a little bit too excitedly. His silence meant yes. No wonder everyone was staring at them.

It wasn't his title that flattered her. It was his incredible knowledge about the civil rights movement in Memphis fifteen years earlier. Of course, Anne's first comments were about her father's untimely death. Orin told her that he'd read about it, and had even planned on introducing a bill that would commemorate the victims that had also suffered losses during the sanitation strike.

This man had definitely gotten her attention. It had been years since she'd discussed the movement. Scott had never been interested in racial issues. Making money had always been a priority. He felt that since he was rich, he was above the color line. He wouldn't risk losing circulation by making a stand on the ongoing civil rights issues in the city. Anne felt that he was a coward. Scott ignored her arguments about people who died fighting for black men like him to become business owners. Scott didn't see it that way. And Anne finally gave up trying to make him see her point.

It was during their third dance that Anne began to feel comfortable with the senator. It was obvious that he respected Martin Luther King, Huey Newton, and Malcom X's struggles.

"So," he said, "were you a member of SNCC?"

The SNCC that had formed in 1960 was the Student Nonviolent Coordinating Committee. The organization became virtually defunct three years ago. He wondered if she was one of the few trying to get the organization started up again.

"Yes," she said worriedly.

Three dances later, Orin introduced Anne to his sister, Gwen. She didn't place her immediately. But then she remembered, she was on the Honor Society, and very quiet, as Anne had been. She asked Anne to join them at their table, which she did.

The next three hours were filled with old jokes and talk about family. Orin brought them several rounds of champagne. Everyone relaxed and enjoyed all the gaiety around them. Even though Gwen spoke candidly to Anne about her divorce, Anne merely mentioned that she was married and that her husband had recently been very sick.

She missed the knowing glances from Orin.

They exchanged pictures of their children, and talked about the usual women things—baby-sitters, shopping, and men. While they talked, Orin was approached several times by men and women. Politics was the main subject, and though she heard bits and pieces, most of what was discussed was way over her head.

Both she and Orin caught each other's eyes while they talked to others. She noticed the crowd beginning to thin and, checking her watch, realized that it was 12:45. The event ended at one.

When she rose to leave, Orin took her hand. "Allow me to walk you outside."

Just when Anne was about to accept, the deejay instructed the group, "This is the last dance, ladies and gentleman of the Class of 1973. I'd like to leave you with "Have You Seen Her," by the Chi-Lites. This song is for all you lovely ladies that blessed us with their presence tonight."

"Can I have this dance, Anne?" Raymond (Dumpy) Pullman asked. Anne reluctantly accepted the invitation. Dumpy had been pestering her for a dance for over an hour. Before her fat friend claimed her in his arms, Orin whispered in her ear. She nodded and headed out on the dance floor.

It seemed that most of the crowd stayed for the final dance. When it was over, the shuffle through the maze of laughing folks seemed endless as Anne headed toward the exit.

Once outside, the humid air blew through her hair. She could hear car doors slamming and people jangling their car keys. Standing beside her, a woman was rolling her eyes at her date, while he communicated to another woman to his left. Others were crying on each other's shoulders, saying their good-byes and exchanging telephone numbers and business cards.

Reaching inside her purse for the parking ticket, Orin signaled the valet. While they waited she thanked him for waiting for her.

"I'd like you to give me a call sometime," he said, handing her an official-looking business card.

"Orin, didn't I mention that I was married?" She blushed awkwardly.

"Anne, I don't think that Scott Hamilton, in his present condition, will have much to say about that."

Anne exhaled nervously. He knew who she was all the time. But how? He didn't even live in Memphis.

When she opened her mouth to speak the valet pulled up, screeching the tires of her new BMW. She cut her eyes at him when he handed her the keys.

"I'm sorry, Orin," she said, walking away, "that's not possible."

He followed around to the driver's side. When she was seated, he closed the door and, reaching inside, stroked her chin. "Call me." He whisked off, with Anne's mouth gaping open.

What a fool, she thought to herself, she hadn't even bothered to ask if the man was married. And, thinking back, she recalled that he hadn't offered his marital status as being single or married. Anne couldn't wait until morning to call Isabell. If anyone knew who was married to whom, she did.

Twenty-two

BASIL WENT INTO THE BATHROOM and got water from the sink to fill the small pitcher of water. Coming back into the room, he spoke softly as he wiped his father's forehead with a damp rag.

"How you doing today, Dad?"

He tried, but couldn't avoid his father's penetrating stare that had become his main mode of communication. Scott had never mastered the blinking technique.

Sniffing, he tried to hold back his tears, not wanting his father to see him breaking down inside.

"Do you need anything else?" Basil scanned the bedroom, outfitted almost exactly like a hospital room, complete with bed, monitors, tables, and trays. The nurse had just given him his bath and had changed him into a clean pair of beige pajamas. The covers were tucked tightly around his small, withering body. His motionless hands were placed across his narrow chest.

When Basil looked back at his father, his eyes looked hardened.

"Something's wrong, isn't it, Dad?"

Scott's dark eyes closed to almost a slit. He blinked once; that meant yes.

"I know. Somebody's made you mad." He leaned over the bed. "Is it that stupid nurse?"

Scott eye's widened, then blinked twice.

"No . . ." Basil scratched his head. "Who, then?" He thought for a moment.

The communication picture board was on the table across from him. There were pictures of a sun and an ice cube that signaled hot or cold. There were pictures of two heads, one with an arrow up, and one with an arrow pointing down, that meant he wanted the head of the bed rolled up or down. There were pictures for medicine, pain, food, drink, lights on or off, and a picture of body parts so that Scott could designate what part of his body was in pain.

Initially they'd begun with four large pictures, and then graduated to more than thirty. But none were of people.

Basil decided to make a poster of the people that his father knew personally. He also looked inside his father's *Black Enterprise* magazines and copied down the names of the types of people that his father would come in contact with, like doctor, secretary, attorney, board of directors, his wife, etc. That task had taken him nearly two hours.

"It's time for his medicine, Basil," the nurse said after coming into the room for the second time. "You're going to have to leave now."

Basil scrunched his mouth into a tight circle. "In a minute." He turned back to his father and pointed. "It's this one?"

Scott blinked once.

"Okay . . ." Basil scratched his head. "But what . . . never mind."

The nurse whisked the board out of his small hands. "Out, now!"

"I'm going. I'm going."

As Basil headed downstairs, he glanced back at his father's bedroom door and wondered, *what did his dad want his attorney for?*

Twenty-three

THIS *IS* THE RIGHT THING TO DO, isn't it? These words kept repeating in her mind. She shook her head, shaking the words from her thoughts. This *is* right.

She rolled over to face her lover's back. He was sitting on the opposite side of the bed, bent over, with the telephone angled between his head and shoulder. Every now and then he glanced over his shoulder at her.

Wrapping her arms around him, she dug her chin into his nude buttocks, and then kissed the tender flesh. Her eyes rolled upward when she heard him say quietly, "Yes, Mother."

Easing herself up in a sitting position, she whispered in his ear, "Get off the phone, honey."

He raised a finger to silence her, and then reached back to caress her hip. When he ended the conversation, she lay back on the bed and waited. The air was still filled with lust from moments before.

This time, instead of the tip of his tongue, he used his hands, kneading her between the legs, his knowing fingers bringing her to a paroxysm that she'd rarely known, not in all of her adult life. She could feel the faint prick of his whiskers on her swollen lips as he brought her buttocks to his mouth; heard the sound of his thick tongue lapping over and over her until she dissolved in excruciating ecstasy.

Unwilling for their lovemaking to end just yet, he reared back and allowed his enormous member to kiss her celestial womb, his thighs caressing her delicious bottom. He pressed himself in further, pushing himself in and out, flicking the tip of her clitoris with the tip of his member, and massaging her breasts, her buttocks, everywhere at once, it seemed, until she begged him to stop. As she struggled to pull him in deeper, her whole body broke out in a sweat, so that she could feel the fine spray flying as she tossed her head from side to side. Now she rolled over and stretched out full length on top of him, reaching for his toes with her own, circling his penis with a tightening grip, rotating slowly, coaxing him to come. This contact provoked such an essence of love in her womb that she felt as if they were in a bath together. Erik's fingers tugged on her hair, signaling her, as if they'd been lovers for years, until a final, exquisite shudder passed through their bodies. The feeling lingered for a few precious seconds. Never in her life had she felt such a sense of power.

Rising from the bed, she walked over to the dresser and removed his chocolate fedora hat that kissed the brim on hers and placed it on her head. She cocked the hat to the side and rolled down the brim to shadow the right side of her face. Next she put on her London Fog trench coat, tied it, picked up the umbrella lying against the chair, then turned to face him.

"You game for a few tricks?"

His lustful eyes penetrated hers. She could feel her nipples growing large, red, and appetizing. Automatically, he turned over on his stomach. She circled the bed, straddled him, and raised the umbrella. She came down on his buttocks and laid the first whack solidly across both cheeks.

"I am ashamed, and very sorry for what I've done. I expect to be punished," he said in a low voice.

Whaack! went the next stroke. A bitter grin twisted her lips, as she heard him suck in his breath. In turn, she breathed hard, her breasts throbbing with pleasure.

"Is this what you wanted?"

"Yes, yes."

For five minutes she whipped him, then suddenly a heart-rending cry split the air, like the screams of vanquished demons.

"Yes!" cried Erik, his features contorted, his arms outstretched as though he'd been crucified.

She fell forward against his chest, releasing her own pent-up pleasure. Only once before had they played out this masquerade; they had sinned against their thinly disguised love, a love which, in order to thrive, needed to face reality, while combating it at the same time with its own innate strength.

ISABELL THOUGHT ABOUT HER LOVER that night as she lay in her own bed. She wondered how much longer he'd be able to resist her.

At the same time, she wondered how much longer Anne could resist Orin's continued assault for her affection. Eight long months had passed since they first met. It had taken that long for Anne to finally agree to meet with the senator at the Pink Palace Museum.

Things weren't exactly going as planned. But if she had learned anything about Anne over the past few years, it was that she was a sucker for older, intelligent men.

Twenty-four

THE PAST YEAR had been the best that Bentley could remember. She and Anne had long talks about her relationship with Scott. Even though it seemed difficult for her to admit, she finally told Bentley about the beatings and the night that Scott had his stroke.

All this time, Bentley thought that Anne had cared nothing about them. She hadn't known that her aunt had suffered as she and Nikkie had.

Even Bentley's relationship with her Aunt Mae seemed more relaxed now. Occasionally, Mae would cook a large pot of gumbo and invite everyone over.

Nikkie began to enjoy being around her second cousins, Holly and Basil. They were good kids who clearly understood Nikkie's situation and were able to find simple things to make her laugh, like filling up water balloons and busting them in the driveway.

One hot August weekend, they all sat around in Anne's living room and watched Carl Lewis win four gold medals in the Los Angeles '84 Olympics—matching Jesse Owens's 1936 feat in Berlin.

Whenever Bentley went to Anne's home, she did the polite thing and went in to see Scott. She only stayed five minutes or so. But it seemed to please Basil that she took the time to try to get to know him a little.

With her home life finally back on track, it was no wonder that her personal life would be suffering. She and Erik began to argue about the length of time that he had agreed to stay in the army. She told him that the amount of time they spent together wasn't enough and that he had to make a decision. It was either her or the army.

Erik refused to choose. When he came home on leave Christmas Eve, Bentley decided to break it off with him. He became really defensive about how he was helping his mother and begged her to give him another chance. Knowing how important her family was to her now, Bentley reluctantly agreed to give Erik three more years.

The following year Anne helped Bentley find a day care center for Nikkie to attend so she could interact with people her age. It seemed like the perfect situation. The cost was just twenty dollars a week more than Bentley was paying Benita. But the benefits were worth it. Nikkie made crafts and went on field trips once a week. It allowed Bentley time to relax on the weekends, instead of always scrambling to find an activity for her and Nikkie.

With more time to herself, she began to create more dramatic situations for Sasha, Lidia, and Abby. Deciding they needed a face-lift, she decided to move them to a new high-rise apartment where they could interact with new colorful characters.

It had taken longer than she and her editor anticipated, but *The Riverdocks* had finally managed to secure 125 markets. And when Bentley received her diploma from Shelby State in May of 1986, she received a $6,000 a year raise. She immediately started a fund to purchase a home for her and Nikkie.

In November of that same year, Bentley and Erik watched Mike Tyson, a twenty-year-old American with a sledgehammer punch, defeat Canadian fighter Trevor Berbick in two rounds to become the youngest world heavyweight boxing champion ever.

By the time the holidays rolled around, Bentley noticed some changes in her health. She began feeling dizzy at work. Her head ached and throbbed even with the aid of several doses of Excedrin. When she experienced a ringing in her ears, she decided to see a doctor.

To her dismay, Bentley was diagnosed with high blood pressure. Her pressure was 180 over 100. The doctor prescribed thirty milligrams of Procardia and put her a diet of fruits and vegetables. He also suggested that she reduce her intake of protein and salt. Wanting to shed about eight pounds for the past year, Bentley decided to give up meat altogether. Getting Nikkie to try the vegetarian dishes was a challenge at first. But knowing that Nikkie could stand to lose about twenty pounds, Bentley tried numerous recipes until she found which ones Nikkie liked best.

In six weeks, Bentley saw the benefit of the change in diet for both her and Nikkie. The headaches weren't as frequent and the dizzy spells had completely stopped.

By June of the following year Margaret Thatcher was elected for a third term as British prime minister. Less than two weeks later Hollywood legend Fred Astaire died at age eighty-eight.

Those newsworthy occurrences merely piqued Bentley's interest as she continued to keep on top of current events and incorporate them in her comic strip.

October 19, "Black Monday," Bentley swallowed a bitter pill. Like thousands of others, she lost money on the stock market. If her calculations were correct, it would take nearly two years for her to recoup her losses. That meant that her plans to purchase a new home for her and Nikkie had to be put on hold.

* * *

To celebrate Holly's eleventh birthday, Anne suggested that all the women have their hair done. Holly insisted that before she went back to school for the fall semester, she wanted her hair cut.

It turned out that all the Russell women, including Nikkie, received a new cut and style.

Less than a week after winning the Olympic 100-meter final in the world record time of 9.79 seconds, the Canadian sprinter Ben Johnson was stripped of his gold medal and banned from representing his country. Urine tests revealed the presence of an anabolic steroid, a drug that allegedly increased strength artificially.

A few months later, George Bush was elected as the new U.S. president. He ran on a platform of no new taxes. But that would come to haunt him throughout his presidency.

Current affairs such as politics, increases in circulation, and fan mail no longer held Bentley's interest. What had begun to bother her was how lonely she'd begun to feel. Most of the girls her age were married and had children. On her next birthday, she'd be twenty-six years old. The thought of turning thirty and being unmarried terrified her.

She seemed to find peace of mind only when she was creating dialogue for her *Riverdocks* characters.

In early May, Bentley received a registered letter from a Mr. Norman Harold at D.C. Comics. The letter tracked her eight-year history of *The Riverdocks*. They highly approved of the addition of two characters, newlywed neighbors, Mia and Judd. The comic book circuit was growing fast, and the annual conventions drew thousands of fans. Mr. Harold asked if Bentley could design mock-up copies of a *Riverdocks* comic book to show at the upcoming convention.

The following day, she went to see her editor.

"I believe this is an excellent opportunity, Bentley," Miriam said, after reading the letter. "I've heard about the strong comic cults and the growing interest in comics."

"Yes. That's true," Bentley said nervously. "But I'm mainly concerned about the travel time they suggested."

Miriam leaned back in the chair and folded her hands. "Two weeks is quite a long time. However, you've got enough vacation time to cover it." She smiled. "In the past we've let other artists work at home as long as they turned in their work on schedule. If this project proves worthwhile, then we'll talk about your permanently working at home. That is unless you planned on quitting the *Appeal*?"

"Oh, no. I love my job here."

"Good. When you get a confirmed date as to when you plan on leaving for the convention, please let me know."

Three months later, production began on the twenty-two-page *Riverdocks* comic book. She'd agreed to D.C. Comics' terms: $30,000 a year. It broke down to $150 a page, with the incentive of $200 per page by the end of one year if the strip did as well as they anticipated. When she signed the contracts, Bentley received an advance of $10,000.

Working at home for the *Appeal* afforded her more time to work on the comic books that she'd grown to enjoy. Being able to create a complete story instead of the continuation of the weekly strip was a challenging endeavor, but one that she looked forward to.

Months later, when the comic books were in production, Disney approached Bentley. If the strip did well, prime-time television comics would be the next step. All she could think of from that day forward was the word *syndication.*

Reality set in before she got too carried away. How could she deal with all this fame? It was too much too soon.

A month before Erik was due to come home for good, Bentley purchased a new car, a 1989 Mitsubishi Galant, and drove by his mother's house on Olive Street. She wanted to stop in and say, "Hi, I'm Bentley, Erik's fiancée. I work at the *Hamilton Appeal.* I even have my own comic books." She wanted to show this woman that she was successful and would be an asset as Erik's wife.

In a household of twelve children, she felt there had to be a lot of love in that house. It didn't matter what Erik had said, that he and his mother hadn't gotten along in the past. Getting their relationship back on track would be one of the first priorities on her list to fix.

Not willing to wait another year for a house, she let her lease expire on her two-bedroom apartment off Poplar Avenue, and moved into a three-bedroom condo in the newest black booming area of Hickory Hill.

Since she'd been working at the *Appeal,* her yearly salary had nearly doubled. And with the added income from the comics, her savings account was starting to grow rather nicely. Using half of her savings as a down payment, she planned on purchasing a brand-new home within a year. The interest rate was low and she'd read several articles in the business section in the *Appeal* that reported that more programs for first-time home buyers were becoming available. Over the summer, she'd driven by several new subdivisions and couldn't make up her mind which one she liked best.

Six days later she received the call that she'd been waiting on for months.

"Hey, Bentley, it's me," he said, emotionless and a bit bored. "I got in this morning."

Her heart ached, wanting to see him. She needed to hear that all of her sacrifices were worthwhile. "Can you come by this evening?"

A long pause. "My mom's got me watching the kids. I'm taking my sisters and brothers shopping in the morning."

"I understand. I'll be home. Just call me, okay?"

He paused and let out a long, deep gasp, then cleared his throat. "I don't know how long that'll be. My mom's got a real estate agent lined up. She wants me to go looking for homes with her. With all these kids, she needs a bigger house real bad."

Bentley caught her bottom lip with her top teeth and sucked, forcing her to keep her comments to herself.

What about me? I need you real bad, too.

Bentley tried to be sensible. Her man was home. She knew where he was. She'd just have to wait a little longer to physically touch him.

During these times, country music was becoming more popular with a few black folks, and although Bentley wasn't a proponent of country music, the lyrics in the love songs did have a blues flavor about them. Lately, after finishing her work for the week, she found herself stopping by the record shop and purchasing tapes by Reba McEntire and Bonnie Raitt.

No wonder women loved these songs, she mused—they were real-life stories. They told of heartaches and misunderstandings.

Why haven't you come to see me, Erik?

She'd told a few people at work whom she thought

she could trust that Erik had come home and had planned on giving her an official engagement ring. Two weeks passed and not a single band or diamond was wrapped around her left ring finger.

Finally, he called and told her that he was on his way over. She was able to put Nikkie to bed early and promised her a special treat in the morning if she would be a good girl tonight.

Bentley opened the door after three knocks. "Hello," she said, falling into his arms.

"Hi." He pecked her on the cheek as perfunctorily as he would a long lost third cousin.

Looking over his shoulder, she noticed a shiny black Cadillac parked in her slot. "Hey, it's good to see you. Come on in."

Bentley proudly showed off her apartment, hinting at items that she'd recently purchased for their home—especially her new IBM computer. In one of the spare bedrooms she set up a small office with a complete workstation. It had two large easels in different heights and sizes, where she did all of her drawings. Erik seemed impressed. He hadn't followed the strip, he told her, but was proud of her accomplishments.

Sitting on the sofa, he patted her knee. "You're doing better than I expected, Bentley." He fidgeted around, trying to position himself on the couch. Bentley watched him nervously straightening his tie, looking around at the contents of her apartment, and avoiding looking her in the eye.

"Is something wrong, Erik?"

"No," he said a little too quickly. "Where's Nikkie?"

"She's asleep. Maybe you can see her the next time you come over."

Bentley didn't know what was wrong or why he seemed so restless. She looked at him and smiled, and without another word leaned over and kissed him on the mouth.

Years of being alone had matured Bentley, but it had also put a strain on their relationship. After all, he'd said only two years in the beginning. That time had dragged on to seven more years. How long was a girl supposed to wait?

Removing his shirt, he offered little resistance, though she could tell he didn't seem especially turned on.

What's wrong, baby?

After they kissed, Bentley led him back to her bedroom. Again, Erik seemed hesitant. She attributed it to his being away from her for so long.

"It's okay, baby. I know it's been a long time. But I miss you so much." As she straddled him, she was haunted by the memory of the large, arched form that she now held in her hands, magnificent, erect, hard, and unbearably hot. Pressing against it with all the softness of her body, she began removing the rest of his clothing.

She'd expected passion, possibly quick and fast, but still . . . passion.

Not so.

Tonight was different. She felt used.

"Fuck me, bitch," he whispered in her ear as he came. "Yeah, yeah, fuck me, baby. Work that ass, baby. Ooooh, Yeah. I'm coming . . . mmmmm."

Bentley watched him fall against her side like dead Louisiana moss. She was confused. He'd changed since the last time they made love.

Erik rolled over. In no time he was snoring.

As Bentley lay beside him, admiring his sculpted body, she took the time to reminisce about old times as if in a waking dream. She had in her dream no true perception of time—but a strange property of mind—for if time be true, she was also its property. When she entered into its eternal disembodied state, time would appear to her an eternity. And while the world was moving—traversing around their still restless uninhibited bodies—the infinite space around them traveled more swiftly than by real thought.

"What are you thinking, Erik? Where have you been? A part of you has left me. Why?"

Erik turned over and grunted.

With her arms folded behind her head, she blinked hard. She loved him, but she was nobody's fool. Getting an orgasm was not lovemaking. A man could satisfy himself with one of those life-sized, plastic blow-up dolls. She didn't flatter herself by thinking she'd done something special.

Days passed, and Erik had turned himself into Harry Houdini once again. Bentley didn't understand this game-playing bit.

Three weeks later, he called her, wanting to come over. Few words were spoken. They screwed. Making love was too kind a phrase. He hurt her. Pounded her as if she were a bass drum. Bentley felt mixed emotions when he decided to take the time to talk to her. She wanted to know what was going on with their relationship. But on the other hand, she didn't want to hear his excuses. She really wasn't in the mood.

"I guess you're wondering why I haven't given you a firm date for the wedding."

Bentley held back shameful tears. "Not really." She knew what was coming. He'd gotten a last fuck and was saying good-bye. "I'm not stupid, Erik. I knew weeks ago that something had changed between us."

"Um-hm."

"Excuse me," she said, feeling overwhelmingly filthy.

She took a shower, making him wait and ponder over what he would say next.

"Look. I know it's over." She buffed her lean body dry, dropped the towel, and began spraying Sea Breeze moisturizing mist on her bare skin. *Look and weep, you bastard.* She went on with her ritual acting as though she weren't naked. The words of Johnny Mathis and Denise Williams rang in her ears—*too much too little too late to ever try again.*

"Baby,"

Bentley pulled on leggings and a T-shirt. "Look, I'm not stupid. And I'm certainly not your baby. I'm just somebody you like to fuck."

"Don't."

"No, let's." She walked over to the seat farthest away from him and sat down. "When you didn't come here the weekend you came home, I knew there was a problem. You should have told me, Erik, what it was. If I had done something wrong, maybe I could have fixed it. But no, you let too much time lapse and you made me wonder. I've waited for your lying ass for nearly ten years. Been faithful to you, and was stupid enough to think you'd done the same for me." She folded her arms and shook her head. "Boy, was I a fool."

"I loved you."

"Loved?" Her eyes widened.

Bentley tossed him his clothes, which didn't make it to his open arms and fell to the floor. "You'd better leave, Erik. We don't have anything else to say to one another. Obviously you've been fucking somebody. I haven't. But I will now. And I don't expect, nor want, another complimentary fuck from you."

"Uh . . ."

"Get out, Erik."

When he left, Bentley didn't cry. Her body cringed at being used. But no tears came. She thought about what had just happened and was proud of the things that she'd said. How she was so strong and hadn't held anything back. She smiled to herself, remembering that she didn't let a tear come to her eye. She was more glad than sad now that that bastard was out of her life. Somebody must have had her in mind when they penned the old phrase: *I can do bad without bad doing me.*

Two months later, Bentley was singing the blues. The morning sickness that she'd attributed to her monthly period suddenly got worse. When she began to crave a two-inch-thick steak, she knew something was wrong. She had to be pregnant. Her first instinct was abortion. She didn't want to bring a child into this world without all the benefits and love of a two-parent family.

Continuing to work, the slant on her comics changed. The fan mail became heavier and her editor, the consummate worrywart, called Bentley into her office.

"What's happening, Bentley?" Miriam asked, "Suddenly, your comics aren't funny anymore."

She was stone cold blunt. "At the moment, I don't feel particularly funny. I'm pregnant. I've been struggling with the idea of getting rid of this baby or bringing it up alone. Then I thought, like me, most people go through transitional periods—so why not give them what they want—a little drama."

"But Bentley, we also have young readers."

Unintentionally, Bentley's tone was cocky. *"They* don't buy the papers. Their parents do."

"Still, loosen up."

Biting her lip, Bentley turned to leave.

"Bentley, I hope you keep the baby."

She kept on walking, pretending not to hear.

Twenty-five

EVEN THOUGH BASIL was only fourteen years old, Anne didn't know if she would ever trust her son again. She'd put up with his terrorizing small animals, pestering Holly, and setting fires. This time he had started a fire in the garage.

The governess had caught him, and brought him to Anne. "Why do you play with matches, Basil?" she had asked him. "Don't you realize that you could burn the house down? Along with your father in it?"

Ever since she'd taken the kids to see the movie *Batman* this year, Basil had been trying to imitate Jack Nicholson's grotesquely grinning villain, the Joker. The special effects in the $200-million-grossing film were remarkable. But it was the Joker's character that the children were impressed with and not the hero, Batman.

"I'm not that careless, Mom. I know what I'm doing." He held an empty coffee can that was all black inside.

"But why fire?" She took the can from him, shaking her head in disgust.

"Because I like to see how stuff burns. Paper burns differently than plastic does. It doesn't smell the same either. And the bugs, man . . . when I put those bugs in the fire, you should hear the crackling—"

"Basil! That is so cruel. I don't want to hear about you ever putting your hands on a match, a lighter, or anything else that can cause a fire. Do you hear me, boy?"

"Yes, Mom."

"I'll put you on a punishment and you won't be able

to leave this house until you turn eighteen. And I'm *not* playing."

Well, now it seemed her little prince had lit a fire in his father's warped mind and all hell had broken loose in the Hamilton home.

Even though he was disabled, Scott Hamilton had filed for a divorce. His attorney, Phillip Hawkins, in Shelby County court, had filed the papers. Anne had been served the day before her thirty-fourth birthday, November 1, 1989. He'd also put the newspaper up for sale and was now debating on one of several offers.

Subsequently, Anne had hired her own attorney, a woman named Jasmine Hollins. Last week a Shelby County Circuit Court judge ordered Anne Hamilton not to dispose of any of their assets except for living expenses, without permission from the court.

Presently, Scott Hamilton was in a court dispute with his estranged wife over the money he would earn from the sale of the newspaper and how it should be spent.

It was embarrassing having Scott wheeled in in a wheelchair, and blinking like an incompetent fool in front of the judge.

From what Isabell told Anne, Scott was being offered $26 million for his interest in the 122-year-old paper. Both offices, the one in Memphis and the one in Cincinnati, would be sold.

Anne contended that Scott and his lawyer were trying to cheat her out of her interest in the marital assets. She'd never signed a prenuptial agreement. He'd offered her the house and $2 million in cash, which Anne vehemently turned down.

Scott's attorney had even brought in a psychiatrist to show that Scott was competent and in his right mind.

And how much are you getting out of this deal?

Anne thought as she rolled her eyes at Phillip Hawkins.

During all of the weeks of proceedings, Holly had been a godsend. She rarely visited her father now, and had clearly drawn the battle lines with Basil. Home was hell. It reminded Anne of the days when she was at home with Kirk and Vanilla Mae.

Not even the upcoming holidays could make their house a home.

It was the first time in Anne's adult life that her Christmas wish was one of death.

DECIDING TO KEEP THE BABY was a headache. In all Bentley's life, she couldn't remember having anyone else love her other than Nikkie. Anne didn't count. The idea of becoming a mother was beginning to appeal to her. She'd acted like Nikkie's mother for years now and it would be a wonderful challenge to raise a child of her own.

Throughout her pregnancy she didn't hear a peep from Erik. His mother called her a couple of times to see how she was doing. Since they had never met, the conversations seemed forced. But the woman did seem concerned about having her first grandchild know her. She definitely wanted to be a part of the child's life.

In her first few months of pregnancy, Bentley went to see her obstetrician as scheduled, and read as many books about pregnancy and labor as she could digest. Hearing differing opinions about Dr. Spock and his baby books, she purchased publications about child rearing by other authors the bookstore worker recommended.

In her sixth month of pregnancy she tried the Lamaze classes for two months, but ended up quitting. She hated the breathing technique, and didn't believe that when the time came, it would really work.

Anne had been a godsend and offered to keep Nikkie at her house on the weekends.

Believing that she had taken all the precautions deemed necessary for an expectant mother, Bentley elected to work up until a week before the baby was due. Her co-workers gave her a surprise baby shower and asked if she would send them pictures of the baby after she or he was born.

It was a cold November night when Bentley felt her first contraction. She gasped from the acute pain—she hadn't realized that it would hurt so much. Glancing at the clock, it was two in the morning. She got up, dressed quickly, and called her doctor.

Next, she called Anne, who said she'd be there in thirty minutes. While she timed her contractions, she woke up Nikkie, who seemed to understand that something important was about to happen. After Nikkie had changed into her street clothes, Bentley retrieved the overnight bag that was already packed in the closet.

By the time Anne arrived, Bentley's contractions were four minutes apart.

It seemed to take forever to drive the eleven miles to St. Francis Hospital. When they reached the canopy at the emergency entrance, an intern was already waiting with a wheelchair.

While Anne filled out the necessary paperwork, Bentley was whisked into a hospital room. Just when the nurse was helping her change into a surgical gown, Bentley gasped. She felt a rush of water gush down between her legs, followed by a pain that took her breath away.

When her daughter was born three hours later, Bentley felt the oddest feeling. Instantly, she felt a kinship when the nurse placed the bloodied body of her healthy eight-pound, four-ounce baby daughter on her chest. And when that baby looked up at her, screaming and hollering, Bentley had tears in her eyes. The emotion she felt was fear. This child needed her. Needed her milk to nourish her. Needed her love to survive.

Motherhood. It was a strange and overpowering experience that no one had warned her of. There was a part of her that was frightened. But she rationalized that by hook or crook she'd be a decent mother.

When the nurse removed the baby, Bentley relaxed and drifted off to sleep.

"Ms. Russell," the nurse said shaking her. "You've got a visitor."

Getting her bearings, she realized that she was still in the recovery room. Grabbing the bed rail, she tried to lift herself up. When she did so, a stabbing pain, from the stitches in her womb, made her grit her teeth. She took a few deep breaths and eased herself back down on the bed.

She wondered, who could be coming to see her so soon? It was probably Anne. But would she bring Nikkie up so soon? Bentley had hoped to explain the baby to her first.

Her hopes were dashed when she saw Erik's smiling face. A woman, who Bentley assumed was his mother, was standing in the doorway, apparently too embarrassed to come and say hello.

"She's beautiful, isn't she?"

Bentley said nothing.

He came closer, as if he was going to try and hug her, but stopped. "Even though we haven't kept in touch over the past months, I know that the child is mine. I want the baby to carry my last name."

"Get out, Erik."

The syrupy smile remained on his face. She should have expected this reaction coming from a family of twelve. But she hadn't.

"Bentley, my mother is here."

"Tell her to leave. I don't want either of you goggling over my baby."

"She's mine, too, Bentley."

Too weak to argue, Bentley turned over and pretended to go to sleep. He kept talking, and she closed her eyes, feeling hot tears clouding her vision. If he didn't leave soon, she thought, she might not be able to hold them back.

The moment Bentley brought the baby home from the hospital, the phone was ringing in her apartment. Not bothering to answer it, she listened to Erik's voice as he recorded a message.

Anne helped Bentley pick out her daughter's name— Reo René Russell. Anne had also offered to stay with her for a week until Bentley could manage. But Bentley declined. Because Anne was under so much pressure from her much-publicized divorce, Bentley didn't want to put any more strain on her than was necessary. She and Nikkie would manage just fine.

But Nikkie wasn't fine. She hated hearing the baby cry. And when Reo cried for long periods of time, Nikkie became supersensitive to it. She began to cry whenever Reo cried.

When Anne and Holly came by to visit, Bentley kept her growing problems with Nikkie and the baby to herself. Anne looked defeated when she saw her. She'd lost so much weight; she didn't look like herself anymore.

Bentley had taken three months off from work to

care for Reo and to locate a good baby-sitter. She found one, a widow named Patty, fifty-nine years old and recently retired.

When Reo was two months old, Bentley received a letter from Erik's attorney. He was willing to take a blood test to determine that the child was his. The bottom line was, he wanted to pay child support and receive weekly visitation.

The blood tests proved that Erik was the father. He was given his first visitation rights when Reo was five months old. When he came to pick up his daughter, an entourage of Berrys was outside her apartment. Bentley felt as if she were burying someone when they all filed in and introduced themselves.

"Bring her back by five on Sunday," Bentley warned.

BASIL LACED UP HIS CLEATS, and then ran out to his position in left field. The coach hit a short pop fly toward him. He was eager to show off his skills to his mother and sister. He made a routine catch look difficult, falling on the ground as he made the catch. No one applauded him. He hadn't known that Anne and Holly had gone for refreshments.

The past few months had been difficult ones. His mother was barely speaking to him and even his father had become distant. When Basil had contacted his father's attorney, he had no idea that his father had planned on divorcing his mother.

Where would they live? Would his dad leave his mother any money?

He'd overheard her crying on the phone with her attorney. They'd made his mother leave her job at the newspaper. And now his mother spent most of the time in her bedroom crying.

One day, he thought, I'm going to be a professional baseball player like Barry Bonds and make my mother real rich.

BY THE SUMMER OF 1990, Jacqueline Smith was making good money panhandling at the National Civil Rights Museum. There were articles and coverage about the young woman from all over the world. Thousands of people were truly interested in how long Ms. Smith would keep her vigil. Up to this point, she'd been at the museum for more than twenty-one years and it didn't look as if she had any intention of leaving anytime soon.

Bentley wasn't interested in reading about this woman whose uncle was purported to have been the first black bus driver for the city of Memphis. No, Bentley was more concerned about things closer to home: her bubbly toddler, Reo. Presently, Reo weighed nineteen pounds and was crawling all over the apartment. She had eight teeth and was able to eat table food with her mother and aunt. Nikkie was obviously jealous of the attention that Bentley paid to Reo. It took all of Bentley's patience to try to keep peace in her house.

Bentley noticed that when Reo was eight months old she developed a habit of sticking her hand inside her diaper when she was wet. Bentley couldn't help but laugh—this child was going to be easy to potty-train. Still, Bentley couldn't share any of these treasured moments with Erik.

When the baby was asleep, Bentley missed her laughter. She would check on the baby during her lunch and breaks, but kept to her work schedule of nine to five, five days a week.

Bentley was fortunate to have located a reasonably

priced kiddie cab that took Nikkie to day care every weekday morning and brought her back home in the afternoon.

Nikkie rarely had seizures anymore. She understood how important it was for her to take her medicine. But Bentley wasn't as fortunate with her own health; her blood pressure had begun acting up again and her doctor increased her dosage of Procardia from thirty milligrams to ninety, along with five milligrams of Ziac.

On February 11, Bentley, Nikkie, and Reo, along with millions of others, watched on television as Nelson Mandela, the black political leader who was imprisoned for twenty-seven years by the South African government, was freed from Victor Verster Prison near Capetown. Bentley cheered, admiring his tenacity, and was astonished by how youthful Mr. Nelson looked.

The next morning, while Bentley was reading the paper, she saw an ad for makeovers at Goldsmith's at Oak Court Mall. The internationally famed Adrienne Arpel would be supervising the sessions this Saturday between 2 and 4 P.M.

Anne, Holly, and Basil picked up Nikkie at five. And Erik was on time as usual at six that evening to pick up Reo. Bentley felt so relieved to finally be by herself.

The next day, Bentley left the apartment by noon, stopping by the bank to withdraw enough money to buy some new clothes. She hadn't shopped for herself since Reo was born.

When she arrived at the mall at one-thirty, the line for the makeovers was fifty women deep. There was no way that all these women could be served in two hours. Bentley left the makeup area and went into the women's department. She found two suits that she liked and caught three colorful summer dresses on sale. While she shopped out in the mall for shoes, she noticed the different hairstyles that the women were wearing. Lately, Bentley's hair was parted in the middle and a single ponytail.

She didn't buy any shoes, but picked up a *Black Hair* magazine in a nearby bookstore. Leaving the mall, she headed back toward home, stopping by a black hair salon with a large Walk-ins Welcome sign in the window.

The shop, Curl Up and Dye, was filled to capacity. She thought she recognized some of the faces from her old neighborhood on Chelsea Street.

Ninety minutes later, she was placed in a chair. She'd found a simple blunt-cut hairstyle that she liked while she was waiting and showed it to the technician.

"That's a classic style," she said, snapping a blue cotton wrap around her neck. "It fits the shape of your face well. Now what about color? A deep maroon would look gorgeous on you."

Bentley shook her head no. Looking around the salon she noticed that nearly everyone's hair was tinted. "Can I see a color chart?"

In five minutes, she selected the color that she wanted. The technician removed the cotton cloak and replaced it with a clear plastic one. She was taken to the shampoo bowl, where another person shampooed and conditioned her ten-inch hair.

Twenty minutes later, she was sitting back in the chair waiting for the technician to mix the deep auburn hair color that she'd selected.

"I heard that his woman loves that baby," said a woman in the chair opposite her.

Bentley pretended not to listen. She was getting her hair colored for the first time in her life. If she was ever to attract a husband, she needed a complete makeover. Getting her a new hairdo was a start. Before she left the shop today Bentley had decided to treat herself to a full-blown salon day—hair, makeup, manicure, and pedicure.

No one at the salon knew Bentley personally. She hadn't been there before. But apparently, a lot of the patrons went to the same church as the eldest Mrs. Berry and her son Erik. "I'll bet his white whore's sterile."

It only took four minutes to learn all about Erik's business since he'd returned from the service. Bentley had had enough. She asked the woman to just cut and style her hair, electing not to have the color after all.

When she got home, she called him.

"Are you married?"

He hesitated, and then asked, "Why?"

"Is she black or white?"

"What's up with you, Bentley? Why are you so angry?"

"Is she black or white?"

"Isabell is white."

Why did that name sound so familiar?

"A white bitch! Bring my daughter home now. Otherwise, I'll call the police." They argued for several minutes. Bentley could hear Reo laughing in the background. That bitch was playing with her daughter. "I write comic strips, remember. I'm very creative. Bring my child home now or I'll have you arrested."

An hour later, Reo was cooing and extending her chubby arms toward her mother as Erik handed her and the diaper bag to Bentley.

"You underestimate me, woman. I love my daughter. Who I've chosen as my partner has nothing to do with it."

"You're not taking my daughter around that white whore."

"Isabell's my *wife.*"

Bentley paused, thinking. She'd heard that name somewhere before, but couldn't place it. Where was it? Where was it? Her mind went blank.

Just then, she felt as if the wind had been knocked out of her. She had seen this woman at the *Appeal.*

She didn't know what the connection was yet, but come Monday morning she would.

"Tell your white whore to give you a baby."

1991

We Are Coming

Twenty-six

IT WAS JUST AFTER SEVEN and Basil had had the same recurring thought since four that morning. *What had his father been trying to tell him that night?*

The word *wife* kept coming back to him. He was almost certain that that was the key to what triggered his father's final heart attack.

Had his mother done something to him and was keeping it a secret? *Wife*—somehow his mother was involved, but his heart didn't believe that she'd actually caused his death.

But then, his father had been married before; maybe he meant his first wife. He'd seen pictures of her before in the trunk in the basement that his dad had tried to keep hidden. But Basil had found their wedding pictures, taken back in 1955. Her name was Leigh, and she sort of reminded Basil of his mother; tall, with a heart-shaped face, high cheekbones, broad smile, and creamy mocha coloring that—

Footsteps coming toward his room interrupted his thoughts. He could tell by the hollow tone of the knock that it was Holly.

"What is it?" he yelled.

Stepping just inside the door she closed the door behind her. "Can we talk for a minute?"

Not this again. They'd had the same conversation last night, and Basil hadn't gotten three hours of sleep. He was irritated and didn't want to talk about it anymore.

"Holly, it's useless. I'm not going." He threw back

the covers, the top of his black-and-white-striped pajamas unbuttoned, exposing his bony chest. He left the door to the bathroom open while he washed his face and brushed his teeth.

"But Basil. You only graduate once in a lifetime. Why are you being so mean to Mom?"

"All right, you want to know the truth? I miss my father. He won't be at the stupid ceremony."

That statement was the truth, but it wasn't the only reason that he wasn't going.

Basil was one of ten black male students graduating at Christian Brothers High School. During his three years there, he hated the racial injustices that he'd endured. In his freshman year, Basil was double-promoted, and still managed to maintain a 4.1 GPA throughout his senior term. All of his classmates, and even a few white ones, agreed that he should have been chosen as the valedictorian of their class. Instead, Henry Adler, a white male with a 4.08 GPA, whose father was a city councilman and highly respected in the community, was given the honor.

So, today, he, as well as the other nine black students, were boycotting the graduation ceremony. At least they said they would.

Holly took a seat on the edge of the bed, while Basil removed a pair of khakis and a white FUBU T-shirt from his dresser drawer.

"I know about the award, Basil. A girlfriend of mine dates a guy at Christian Brothers and she told me what happened. I can't say I blame you, but I'm still thinking about Mom. She deserves to see her first child graduate."

"Mom's a survivor, she'll get over it." He sat on the bed putting on a pair of socks, and staring at his father's picture on his dresser. "Others weren't so lucky." He motioned for her to turn around while he put on his clothes. "You're too young to understand a lot of things, Holly."

"I may be fourteen, but I'm not stupid. I do know that Mom's been very unhappy. And I think she wants to start dating, but she won't because of us."

Going into his closet for a belt, he took out a black one and turned around to face Holly. "Dad's been dead for nearly a year. Mom's still young. She deserves—"

"Stop it, Basil. You say those words, but you don't mean it. You crucify her with your constant interrogations about where she's been. Who was she with? You sound just like her husband."

Holly didn't understand.

The telephone rang. Holly leaned over and noticed the number on the caller ID. "And I know about that, too." She got up and left.

"Hello," Basil said after Holly had shut the door. "I didn't think you would call."

"Can you come over?"

"Not now." He reached inside the nightstand and lit a cigarette. "My mother's planning a big bash for me this afternoon."

"I need you, Basil," she whispered in the throaty voice that he'd grown to love. "Don't be mad at me for the other night. I'll make it up to you."

He felt himself getting aroused. His lust, however, was rising furiously from his loins to his heart. He wanted her feel, her flesh. This woman made him feel like an animal before he knew he was one. The other girls his age that he screwed seemed so childish during intercourse. Always trying to appear so innocent. It was a turn-off. Not this woman; she was bold and very sensual. She wore her sexuality like a Richard Tyler suit. Only those that she allowed could penetrate it.

"You sure it's safe?"

"He left fifteen minutes ago. He's got an interview with the architect at the Civil Rights Museum. I don't expect him back until one or two."

Automatically, he reached inside his jeans and stroked himself. "I'll be there in ten minutes."

ANNE FELT THAT SHE HAD WASTED too much time crying over a man who'd lied from day one about loving her. It had taken some deep soul-searching to make a decision about what she would do with the rest of her life.

The first thing she had decided to do was to go back to school. She had gone through the admissions process at Memphis State in April and would begin summer classes in late May. Since she'd been out of school for so long, her year of credits in the 1973–74 freshman term were lost. She had to start all over again. She kept political science as her major, with a minor in English.

Next, she took a more active role in the NAACP and joined the 100 Black Women organization, and signed up for the weekly meeting of Toastmasters. Keeping busy nearly every day of the week kept her mind off of her personal problems.

And now, she had another event to celebrate. This afternoon, on the last Sunday in May, her son, Basil, had done one better. He walked across the stage, accepting his diploma, at age seventeen.

Some of the happiest moments in a mother's life were when her child secured a good job, married, and gave her a grandchild—but topping the list was her child's high-school graduation. It gave parents the secure feeling that they'd done what they were put on earth for in the eyes of God.

Her daughter, Holly, had been given the task of organizing a late-afternoon brunch to celebrate the occasion. Because of Basil's growing love for horses, he had chosen the Kentucky Derby as the theme for his party.

Polished silver urns filled with long-stemmed red roses were positioned throughout the first floor. Anne could hear Holly in the dining room, changing the table settings, and sounding like Anne as she argued with the caterers.

At fourteen, Holly stood five foot nine—an inch taller than her brother. A thick thirteen-inch pixied mane of layered hair that was parted in the center framed her bronze-colored oval face. A petite size 6, she always wore a fresh smile on her face.

To Anne's increasing admiration, Holly was as mature as most eighteen-year-olds. Anne attributed her innate talent of understanding life to when Scott died. He'd been successful in selling the paper to a subsidiary of the Gannett Newspaper Corporation for $26 million, but had a massive heart attack and expired two months before their divorce was finalized.

Not surprising to Anne was the fact that Scott had changed his will and left the bulk of his money in trust to their children. They would each inherit $2 million apiece when they turned twenty-five and another $3 million when they turned thirty. Over $10 million went to pay off Scott's debts from other failed investments. Holly and Basil would inherit their home if Anne either died or remarried. Anne was left the car, stocks and bonds worth $5 million, and roughly $2.5 million in cash.

Basil had taken Scott's death harder than anyone. He

was so depressed afterward, blaming himself for his father's heart attack, that Anne took him to see a therapist. It was not until recently that she felt Basil stopped feeling guilty. Holly had insisted that it was a woman who had come into her brother's life that brought about the change. Anne didn't care who was responsible— Basil was cured. Her son was pulling far less dramatic practical jokes on his sister; he'd poured dishwashing liquid in Holly's parrots' water bowl. The colorful creatures, Chess and Checkers, burped up bubbles for days, and Anne couldn't have been happier.

While Holly nursed her pets, she announced to her mother that she intended to become a veterinarian and left no room for discussion. Presently she had a toy poodle named Deirdre, two parrots, and a Siamese cat named Scotty. The time that she took caring for each of them was endearing. Anne was convinced now that her daughter would make a great animal doctor.

Disappointment came back to tug at Basil's psyche once more last fall when his future in baseball came to a screeching halt. Their personal physician had discovered that Basil had a heart murmur. His plans to attend the University of Tennessee and become one of the famed Vols' power hitters nearly crucified him.

To Anne's delight, in late January, Basil applied to five black universities with the intent of pursuing a degree in accounting. It was Holly who had finally told Anne which one he'd selected.

"Are you saying that you've changed your mind about going to Morehouse College?" Anne asked her son, who was resting on the loveseat in the library.

He shrugged his shoulders.

Anne studied her son. He could be perceived as handsome. With her and Scott's combined looks, Basil was an attractive young man. At five-eight he wasn't very tall, but made up for his height with an overabundance of self-confidence. He wore his short dark brown hair brushed to the back. His baby-soft beard and mustache gave him a sexy, playful kind of appeal, yet the expression in his wide-spaced eyes was unabashedly friendly.

"You should know, Basil, that I don't expect you to lay around this house for a year doing nothing. If you don't plan on attending school, you're going to have to get a job."

She and Basil had never discussed the large sum of his money that his father had left him and his sister, but Anne believed that he had formalized some kind of plan in his mind of how he would spend his inheritance.

"Don't pressure me, Mom." Basil got up and walked to the window—his hands were fists in his pockets. Shrugging his shoulders, he continued his defiant, smug pose that was intent on telling his mother to leave him alone, but without voicing the words.

Less than thirty-five feet away, a hired staff of five was busily setting up extra tables and chairs in the dining room. Anne could smell the apple cobbler baking in the oven and the aroma of beef tenderloin with Henry Bain sauce seasoning the fragrant air. The strawberry-cheese horseshoe mold had been prepared this morning. The menu included mushrooms in sour cream, roasted vegetables with fresh sage, baby hot browns, shrimp bourbon, curried chicken pâté, and Kentucky Derby tartlets.

As far as Anne knew, Basil didn't have a date. Maybe that was what was bothering him tonight.

The clock on the mantel struck four. In two hours the guests would arrive and Anne knew she would have to leave her son soon and get dressed. But he seemed so depressed today that she wasn't sure how to reach him.

Just last week, she'd purchased a 1991 silver Volvo for his graduation present. It was still in the driveway with a huge blue ribbon attached from front to rear bumper. He hadn't even bothered to start the engine.

When the doorbell rang, Anne left the room to open the door and showed the deejays where they could set up their equipment.

"Mom," Holly called out. "I'm going upstairs to get ready."

"Okay. I'll be along in a few minutes." Anne went back to the library and wasn't surprised that Basil had left.

Looking out the side window, she noticed that the Volvo was gone. Knowing her son and his impromptu mood swings, she wondered if he'd even come back for the party.

Upstairs, Anne clipped on her second pearl earring. She fanned nervous sweat from her upper lip with the white cardboard insert from the package of nude brown panty hose.

Ten minutes later, Anne, wearing a pale pink ankle-length skirt and tunic top, knocked on Holly's door.

"I'll be out in a minute, Mom." When she did, Anne tried to be discreet in her comments. Holly looked absolutely radiant in her fuchsia and orange print slack suit, but her choice of makeup, that made her look as if she were of voting age, didn't please Anne in the slightest.

On their way downstairs, the doorbell rang. When the maid hurried to answer it, she and Holly exchanged glances—this was the first time they'd entertained in their home. Anne promised herself, for Holly's sake, it wouldn't be the last.

When the door opened, Anne couldn't believe her

eyes. "Hey, there, sister girl." Her handsome brother Kirk greeted her in his entire rodeo regalia—black leather vest, blue jeans, denim shirt, and a black ten-gallon cowboy hat.

"Honey, hush. Kirk!" she said, hurrying down the stairs, "I didn't think you'd make it. Goodness. It's so good to see you."

Hugs were exchanged. Looking around, he whistled. "Say, girl, I didn't realize that you were living this good. What a house!"

Anne's smile was bittersweet. It had taken Scott's death before Anne actually felt comfortable inviting her family to her home.

The main entrance hall was decorated with a collection of Japanese artifacts, original art, life-sized Greek statues, and inviting cushioned chairs that conveyed the message that whether or not you chose to sit, you were welcome to linger and admire.

"And who's this fine young lady?" Kirk asked, winking at his niece.

Holly extended her hand. "I'm Holly."

Anne noticed that Holly was giving her uncle that "please don't give me that I-haven't-seen-you-in-years routine" look.

"Say, Holly," he said, after giving her a quick kiss on the cheek, "could you show your uncle Kirk where the bathrooms are?"

"Sure. Afterwards, I'll show you around the house."

It was a quarter to six and already Anne could hear the sound of car doors slamming in the driveway. There were always people who felt they needed to arrive early.

"Time, Love and Tenderness" was playing in the background. Someone yelled, "Turn up the volume!"

Anne watched her daughter's easy conversation with

her uncle as they headed down the hall. "Excuse me, Mrs. Hamilton," the chef interrupted, "we need you in the kitchen. It'll only take a moment."

Ten minutes later dozens of teenage guests had arrived. Anne tried to contain her growing fear that Basil wouldn't show up.

A table was set up for gifts and cards on the patio. The table was nearly full when Anne noticed Bentley placing a card on top of the pile. She was holding her feisty toddler, who was trying to kick herself out of Bentley's arms.

"Bentley." She hurried toward her and gave her a kiss and hug. "I'm so glad you came. You look as pretty as ever." Removing the baby from her arms, she fondled the toddler's cheeks. "Honey, hush. Isn't she precious?"

"Thanks, Aunt Anne," Bentley said proudly. She wiped her daughter's runny nose as Reo squirmed in Anne's arms. "She wants to get down."

When Anne put the chubby baby down, she took off running.

"She's not used to so much open space," Bentley said, following after her. "She probably thinks she's at a playground."

"I thought you were bringing Nikkie," Anne said.

"She's at home sick with a cold. A neighbor is watching her—" She noticed her child trying to remove the umbrellas from the stand. "Come back here, Reo. No. No, baby. Don't touch that. Bad baby."

To Anne's delight the party was going better than she expected. Everyone seemed to be having fun.

Basil finally showed up around six-thirty and rescued his uncle Kirk from Holly. Anne overheard them discussing the 117th Kentucky Derby winner, Strike the Gold, while shrimp toast, sweet and sour pork, deviled eggs, and caramel-toffee bombe hors d'oeuvres were being served. Nonalcoholic mint jubilees were passed around on trays and the easy atmosphere of the party was well under way.

Anne let the young people determine the tempo of the party, while she and Bentley stole an empty corner in the living room and chatted. During their pleasant conversation Reo kept sneezing and soon began to cry. Holly tried to console her, and when she couldn't, handed her back to her mother.

"Can I lay her down somewhere?" Bentley asked, "I think she's sleepy. She's not used to being around so many people."

"Sure, follow me." Anne got up and walked to the circular stairway.

The three women went upstairs to Anne's room.

Cream drapes hung on both sides of the open window. Wind blew in, making the tropical plants in each corner sway back and forth. The room was full of great period pieces like a Louis XVI screen and nineteenth-century Barbedienne urns that served as lamps. The silk upholstery on the twin Louis XV bergers would never go out of style. The antique canopied king-sized bed, done up in plush English linens, was made of cherrywood, as were the dresser, night stands, and armoire. In every crevice of the large room was the smell of Anne's Opium perfume and summer spice potpourri.

While Bentley rocked Reo to sleep, she told Anne how jealous Nikkie was over Reo. She had to come up with clever ways to keep them separated and keep peace in the house.

As Anne listened to Bentley talk, she wondered why she and Bentley never talked about men. For some reason it seemed to be a forbidden subject. For instance,

Anne wanted to ask Bentley if she was dating anyone, but she wasn't sure if Bentley would think she was being nosy or ask her the same question. It was sad, though, Anne thought, that none of the Russell women had found a good man.

"By the way, Anne, I love what you've done to the house. It's fabulous."

Holly filled Bentley in on all the decorating that she and her mother had done over the past year. Anne had completely remodeled the master suite, foyer, and living room after Scott passed.

The telephone rang. "It's for you, Holly." Anne handed her the phone and smiled. Her boyfriend of six months was on the line. They'd been feuding for days and Anne knew that Holly was hoping that he'd come tonight.

"Mom," Holly gushed after hanging up the receiver, "that was Allan. He's waiting for me downstairs."

Anne warned, "Don't you leave this house without telling me where you're going." It wasn't that Anne disapproved of Allan. What she didn't like was the fact that he was four years older than Holly and way too serious. Allan monopolized all of her time and reminded her of Scott.

After she'd gone, Bentley said, "Holly's a beauty, Anne. And so mature for her age."

"Thanks. She's such a good kid. We're best friends."

Bentley looked away so that Anne wouldn't see the hurt in her eyes. When she did so, her slight movement awakened Reo. She sneezed and began to cry again.

"Anne, can you hand me that bottle of cough medicine out of the diaper bag, please?" Anne could see Reo loved taking the grape-flavored medicine. It seemed like so many years ago that her children were infants. She missed holding them in her arms, rocking them to sleep. Even though she and Scott had problems, he had always been a good father to his children. Anne wondered how Bentley was managing to care for Reo and Nikkie all alone.

"How long has she had a cold?"

"A little over a week. The doctor said she should be fine in a few days." Bentley looked down at her child, and lovingly stroked her hair. "I found the perfect sitter. She treats Reo like her own granddaughter. I don't know how she caught this cold—unless she caught it from someone at her dad's house."

"Who, Erik?"

"Yes. Of course . . ." she stopped. "You know he's married."

"Yes, I heard rumors before I left the *Appeal*. But to tell you the truth, I'm not too familiar with Erik. I remember his mother, but not him."

"He's nobody special." When Reo began snoring lightly, Bentley laid her face down, in the middle of the bed.

They tiptoed out the room and left the door cracked open an inch or so.

"I finally remembered who his wife, Isabell Ford, was," Bentley began. She followed Anne to the stairway. "I'd seen her at the *Appeal* on a few occasions walking around with her nose in the air like she was one of the head honchos."

"She's pretty well off, Bentley."

"I know that. But I can't figure out what she saw in Erik. He's not *that* good-looking."

Anne had been pondering that same question for months. When Isabell married Erik, she'd stopped all communication with Anne. Their relationship had begun to deteriorate a few years back when Senator Matthews hinted that he and Isabell were very good friends. Putting two and two together, Anne concluded that during the time that she and the senator had kept in contact with one another, the arrangement had been all Isabell's doing. Now the only thing that Anne knew was that Erik had moved into Isabell's home in Germantown, and since that time, Isabell's face or name hadn't graced the society pages in the local magazines or the *Appeal.*

The thought of Isabell's being married to Bentley's ex-fiancé didn't sit well with Anne. Somehow, she knew that this wasn't just a coincidence. Her thoughts were interrupted by her daughter's presence.

"Mom, is it okay if we let everybody eat outside? Most of Basil's guests are out back shooting hoops. I was thinking that we could get some quilts and make it like a picnic of sorts."

Holly's friend Ericka, who idolized Holly and tried to imitate every aspect of her personality, said, "Yeah, Mrs. Hamilton, I can help Holly get things organized. You know, get everybody to form two lines and serve him- or herself."

Anne looked at Bentley, who was nodding that she thought it was a good idea, too.

With over forty people in the house, Anne gave in. A comfortable seventy-eight degrees outside, it was a beautiful day for the informal setting that Holly and Ericka suggested.

The guests traipsed off in small groups, as the two girls passed out blankets and quilts. Afterward, Anne, Kirk, and Bentley found themselves sitting in the dining room alone. Kirk discussed how his career was building in the rodeo circuit. He'd been to Las Vegas, Texas, and

Colorado, and looked forward to coming back to Memphis one day. While he spoke, Anne noticed how uncomfortable Bentley seemed.

Immediately after dinner, Bentley excused herself to check on the baby. A few minutes later, she came downstairs carrying a still-sleeping Reo and diaper bag.

"I've got to go, Aunt Anne," Bentley said to Anne, who was standing with Kirk at the bottom of the stairs. "Reo's got a fever."

She promised Anne that she and Nikkie and Reo would be back as soon as Reo was feeling better. Bentley hugged Anne, said good-bye to Kirk and left.

"Kirk," Anne said to her brother, who stood behind her as she waved good-bye to Bentley, "something isn't right."

Twenty-seven

"MY BABY ISN'T BREATHING!" Bentley screamed at the emergency room nurse. "Help me. Please."

While the doctors worked on Reo, Bentley sat in the nondescript cubicle at St. Francis Hospital and filled out the numerous papers that said that she had insurance coverage and would be responsible for the bill.

Before she finished a nurse came up to her and asked, "Are you Ms. Russell?" Bentley held her breath as she nodded yes. "The doctor needs to see you right away."

For her child's sake, Bentley tried to remain calm as she followed the nurse back to emergency room 3.

An eternity passed before the doctor came into the room. He held a manila envelope in his hand.

"Doctor?" Bentley began.

"Just a moment." He removed the X rays, studied them under the light for a few minutes, and then said, "It appears that your daughter has double pneumonia in both lungs."

From the other side of the curtain, Bentley heard a child scream. "Where's my baby? What have you done with her?"

"She's in good hands, Ms. Russell. We're in the process of transferring her to LeBonheur Children's Hospital. A helicopter is in route now."

"What? Is Reo going to die?"

Calmly the doctor patted her on the shoulder. "We're doing all that we can. We don't have the facilities here at St. Francis to care for your daughter adequately."

Bentley couldn't remember the flight to LeBonheur. Reo was in critical condition and had lapsed into a co-malike state. Less than thirty minutes later Reo was put on a respirator.

More tests were taken, and Bentley was left alone for a while. She considered calling Erik and changed her mind. When she called Anne, she quickly volunteered to pick up Nikkie from the neighbor's house and take her home with her.

Throughout that day and the next the nurses allowed Bentley to stay in the intensive care room with Reo, where she prayed until her words became hoarse. The transparent look on her daughter's face sent her heart out of rhythm.

"Listen to me, Reo," she said, placing Reo's tiny hands in hers, "you're not going to believe all the fun we're going to have when you come home." Bentley wiped back a tear. "Winnie the Pooh misses you, baby. And remember that tabby cat on that Purina cat chow commercial that you liked? Mommy's going to buy you one when you come home, too."

The doctor had told Bentley that Reo's heart rate went up whenever she talked to her. Obviously she recognized her voice, and it especially got stronger when Bentley held her hands. Reo's responding to Bentley the way that she did made the doctor feel fairly sure that she didn't have any brain damage.

"Ms. Russell," the doctor said, cautiously awakening her from a short nap, "there's been a further development in your daughter's prognosis. A heart specialist was called in and he's positive now that your daughter has a hole in her lung that may require surgery."

Bentley lost it. She broke down screaming and crying and needed to be sedated. How in the world could her little baby, who only weighed twenty-four pounds, withstand surgery?

How could *she* handle it?

With trepidation, she called Erik. He arrived at the hospital twenty minutes later.

"You should have called me days ago," Erik seethed. "I could have been here with her. She knows that I'm her daddy and I love her. What if she had—" The tears came, and Bentley turned away in shame. He couldn't possibly love Reo as much as she did.

That same night, Reo took a turn for the worse. She had trouble breathing and her blood pressure went up.

"My associates believe that your daughter is having seizures or strokes."

Bentley fell back on the chair, lifeless—a vision of Nikkie's last seizure flashed before her. She barely heard the doctor telling them that Reo required sixteen chest tubes and that scar tissue was now building in her lungs.

"The right lung has no healthy tissue at all. But at this point she would not survive a lung transplant."

Bentley didn't know how she got on her knees. She vaguely remembered praying to God that He could take her life if He spared her child's.

The doctor's words were optimistic when he said, "She's still on life support and may be on it for a long time."

It was then that Bentley heard Erik weeping.

Twenty-eight

ONE OF THE MORE STIMULATING aspects of being a woman in her position was meeting the board members on a personal level. The men seemed businesslike at first, and later, upon learning of her numerous connections throughout Memphis, as well as Nashville, viewed Isabell's presence on their board as that of a prestigious member. Even the women, after she'd lavished them with expensive gifts, never stopped grinning in her face, telling Isabell everything that she needed to know about any individual she might be concerned about.

It was at her last board meeting at the *Hamilton Appeal* that she learned about Bentley's problems with her comic strip. She was told that the sales were way down on last month's *Riverdocks* comic book and the feedback they were getting from her daily strip was less than positive.

Isabell moved quickly. She contacted Bentley's editor

and let her know how disappointed the board was with Ms. Russell's work. She planted the seed that they were looking for fresh talent—something completely different from the *Riverdocks* strip.

Damn fool, she thought about her husband. He worked so hard trying to please her. He had no idea that the only purpose he served was destroying two women's lives. When his daughter was born, Isabell hadn't anticipated that she would one day care for the child as much as she did.

And now that the child was at home recuperating, it wouldn't be long before Isabell could put the next phase of her plan into play.

DURING THE WEEKS that Bentley was convalescing with Reo, she juggled caring for Nikkie with her duties as a mother. She ignored the signs that signaled her blood pressure had flared up again.

When she saw the doctor, he increased her medication to ten milligrams of Ziac and warned her that the stress she was under trying to care for both her child and sister was wearing her down. He suggested that she hire a live-in nurse until her health improved.

Unwilling to give in to what she felt was weakness, Bentley continued to go to the hospital every day, work at her job, and care for her sister.

This year, Bentley hadn't looked forward to the holiday season. The people she worked with seemed to be in such good spirits—shopping and laughing like they didn't have a care in the world. But her heart was heavy. Nothing was less in her power than her heart, and far from commanding it, she was forced to obey it.

There could be no gift that she could receive that would be as precious to her as Reo's full recovery.

On New Year's Eve night Bentley went to church for the first time in years. When New Year's Day began, Bentley, along with Anne and her two children, was on her knees saying prayers and making resolutions.

In the ensuing days, major changes began to take place in the city of Memphis. Willie W. Herenton was sworn in as Memphis's first black mayor. The $63-million stainless-steel Pyramid downtown opened with a sold-out Judds concert. The National Civil Rights museum, open for five months, had been well received by the Memphis community.

It would take nearly sixty days before Reo was able to come home. When she did, Bentley was faced with another problem. Nikkie seemed to resent more than ever the attention Bentley gave to her daughter.

As the weeks passed, the strain of running her household became nearly unbearable. Bentley's headaches claimed her at all times of the day. The medication the doctor prescribed no longer relieved the tension.

Working and drawing used to relax her and brighten her spirits. But now her work merely added to the strain she felt from trying to be the perfect mother, the perfect sister. Her desire to make her daughter, sister, publisher, and two editors happy was becoming more of a challenge as each day crept by.

Unable to sleep more than one or two hours a night, she worked until the words became unfocused. Feeling like a living zombie, the truth was something she couldn't admit to a living soul—she was extremely unhappy.

She also hated to admit to herself that she was lonely. Of course she loved her daughter and sister, but it took the lonely nights to remind her that a part of her wasn't being fulfilled. She missed a man's touch. Hearing his caring voice. Knowing that she had someone to talk to who understood her.

The guilt she felt thinking about something so selfish when the two people she loved most in the world needed her so badly nearly tore her apart.

In mid-January, Bentley received a letter from Wesley. The letter came the day after General Norman Schwarzkopf launched an air attack, Operation Desert Storm, bombing strategic Iraqi troops and targets. But the air attacks weren't enough to stop Saddam Hussein, the Iraqi president. So on February 24, the U.S. and allies sent tanks into Iraq and Kuwait. Much of the Iraqi army fled. The war on the ground lasted only one hundred hours. Bentley received another letter on February 29. Two days after President Bush declared the end of the war, Hussein's army surrendered and was driven out of Kuwait. Wesley was supposed to be one of the next troops sent to Kuwait. Thanks to the efforts of Chairman of the Joint Chiefs of Staff Colin Powell, it was no longer necessary. He ended his letter by saying that if he ever had a son he'd name him Colin.

The warmth of the coming spring wasn't lost on Bentley. She noticed that the buds that formed on the magnolia trees in her yard had actually formed in autumn and winter, but the spring warmth and moisture brought swelling and visibility—especially as the buds now cracked, revealing hints of pink and white.

Reo turned two on May 19. And just as Bentley had promised, she took her daughter to the pet shop, and together they chose a newborn kitty that Bentley named Tip Top.

Nikkie seemed to dislike Tip Top, so Bentley kept the kitty out of her way when she came home from day care.

Nikkie usually wanted to eat a snack cake, then take a nap until dinner. Reo would already be asleep, and Bentley took this time alone to clean up the apartment and get dinner ready.

Tonight she had planned on making pasta primavera. She'd made the dish a dozen times or so, but for some reason couldn't remember the recipe. Looking through her files in the kitchen, she spotted the old card, skimmed it, and went to get the fresh asparagus and broccoli out of the refrigerator.

She went to the sink and began snapping off the ends of the asparagus. When she started to remove the skin, the telephone rang, startling her.

"Bentley, it's me, Erik. I'm running a little late today."

What? Was it Friday already?

"Uh-huh, Erik. Sure."

"I'll be there around seven. Bentley, could you please pack an extra dress for Reo? My mother wants to take her to a christening tomorrow afternoon."

"Look, Mommy," Reo said coming into the kitchen, dragging a roll of toilet paper behind her. Poor Tip Top was drenched with water. Wet pieces of paper were plastered all over his small body.

" 'Bye, Erik." She slammed the phone down.

Wiping her wet hands on a dish towel, she was stopped short by a second call.

"Hello?"

"A-1 Collision. Your car is ready, Ms. Russell. You can pick it up anytime."

My car. What the hell was he talking about?

Bentley hung up the phone and tried to think when she had taken her car in. Ruminating gave her an instant headache. Leaning back against the counter, she stared at her daughter, too exhausted to stop her from running around the room and making a white mess with yards of tissue paper.

Something was wrong. Going over to check the calendar on the kitchen wall, she saw, in her handwriting, Friday, pick up car from A-1 Collision. But for the life of her, she couldn't remember why she'd taken it in.

When Erik arrived, Bentley didn't have anything ready. He pushed past her and packed his daughter's bag himself.

Tip Top's litter box was ripe, and needed changing, and she hadn't noticed the smell until now.

"I don't know what's wrong with you." He looked down at her dirty shirt and wrinkled jeans. She wore no makeup and her hair wasn't brushed. The ingredients for the pasta dish were still lying on the counter. Cereal bowls from this morning's breakfast were on the table. To make matters worse, Reo's toys were strewn all over the room.

"Maybe you should think about seeing somebody."

Maybe you could give me the number of a friend, she thought when she closed the door behind him.

That night she didn't finish cooking dinner. She called Domino's for pizza, which was one of Nikkie's favorites. The next morning, she called a sitter to keep an eye on Nikkie while she picked up her car and then shopped for groceries.

Trying to make sense out of everything that was happening right now was hard for her. She knew that she needed some rest. Yes, sleep, that's what she needed, and everything would be okay.

Exhausted, she shopped at Kroger's, picking up only the bare necessities. Reluctantly, she stopped at the pharmacy and picked up a bottle of over-the-counter sleeping pills. To her shock, when she headed for the produce section, Kirk's sneering face followed her. A few minutes later, as she selected the paper products, she still couldn't shun his naked image. As she headed for the checkout counter, people walking past her glanced back at her in an odd way. She had no idea why.

When she managed to fall asleep that night, she awoke minutes later, sweating profusely. Nightmares of Nikkie being in a nursing home made her shiver with guilt.

Splitting headaches kept her in her pajamas until Reo returned home on Sunday evening. Nikkie was a sweetheart and didn't complain about the chunky soup she ate for two days.

On Monday, Bentley missed her deadline for the monthly comic strip and was given two more weeks to complete the project. During the days that followed, Bentley became even more confused and fatigued. She thought that she'd received a letter stating that she'd gotten a raise. In reality she'd received a letter telling her that if she didn't send in a letter from her physician stating that she was under his care and unable to perform her duties, her employment would be terminated.

The sleeping pills seemed to work in reverse. On Wednesday morning the neighbors knocked on her door. A woman told her that the baby had been screaming for hours.

To Bentley, her life to this point had the feel of a carnival with nothing but Ferris wheels inside going round and round like a nonstop clock. Everywhere she turned, she felt off-balance, dizzy, and sick to her stomach, with an incessant sense of anxiety.

There were no adequate words to describe how frightened she was. She couldn't make sense of time.

Couldn't force herself to bathe or eat. Each time she moved an arm, a leg, her head, she felt incredible fatigue.

Her mind felt jumbled. On the one hand, it told her to watch the baby, make sure Nikkie was fed and had her bath. But it was the other voice that scared her. That told her that she couldn't help the baby or Nikkie. And then the images began to taunt her. She kept seeing Nikkie's death after eating the rat poison. Imagined that Reo had died of pneumonia at the hospital. Over and over again their deaths pervaded her mind, telling her that she was to blame.

Later that night, Nikkie coming out of the room and going into the kitchen was a blur in her mind. Bentley thought she heard noises, but couldn't react to them. Smelled something burning on the stove but couldn't make any sense of it.

Smoke burned her eyes and seconds later she heard someone pounding on the front door. Ignoring it, she curled up into a little ball, wanting to be invisible. There was no grounding, nothing solid or secure to her existence. Even her own body no longer obeyed the commands from a brain that was on fire with fever.

There was no energy or fight left in her. She sat on that sofa, numb to the core. She couldn't conjure up any more tears, think of a reason to walk or talk. The mere fact that she was breathing told her that she was alive.

She could hear louder noises outside the front door. Then she heard a loud thud. Someone was breaking down the door. In a matter of minutes they were in. She vaguely remembered seeing someone put out the fire on the stove. Nikkie was taken out of the house, followed by a man rushing Reo out the door seconds later.

Someone was shaking her. "Miss. Please come with us. We're here to help you."

Help.

As if in a fog, Bentley didn't remember anything after that.

How many days passed, she had no clue. She mumbled in her sleep, "My baby, please help my baby."

"Ms. Russell," a voice said. "Ms. Russell, I'm Dr. Savage. You're a very sick young lady."

"My baby. Nikkie. Got to help . . . my babies."

Dr. Savage patted her hand gently. "They're both fine, Miss. Now let's concentrate on getting you better. You're the one who needs help."

Twenty-nine

BLACKS IN THE CITY of Memphis were in a state of jubilation. William Jefferson Clinton had defeated his Republican opponent, President George Bush. The talk around town was all about how much soul Bill had. He played a saxophone and loved the blues. A Democrat hadn't been in office in twelve years. The poor people, it seemed, were finally going to get some relief. It was even rumored that he'd gotten a black girl pregnant. A picture of a young black boy about age six, who bore a striking resemblance to the president, was on the front page of the *National Enquirer*.

But it was more than politics that took Anne away

from Memphis for the weekend. She needed a break.

Since Bentley had her breakdown, Anne took over her responsibilities with Nikkie. Erik had assured her that he would care for Reo. They made plans to talk weekly.

Bentley's doctor had no clue as to how long Bentley's recovery would take. They were taking it one day at a time. Anne packed up Nikkie's clothes, moved her into the spare bedroom, and made arrangements for her to attend a day care center nearby.

At first it was difficult to make Nikkie understand that Bentley would be gone for a while. She cried a lot, and wet on herself a few times before Anne was able to reassure her that she would take care of her.

Weeks turned into months and there was no change in Bentley's condition. Most of the time she wouldn't talk or eat. The doctor suggested to Anne that it would be better if she didn't come and visit her niece until she made some kind of progress. Right now she had no idea of what was happening to her.

And so at age thirty-seven, Anne was back to being a caregiver again. She'd forgotten how many times they had to remind Nikkie to brush her teeth. Put her clothes on. Put her pajamas away. Straighten up her bed. She'd forgotten how much time it took to care for someone who was so dependent on you.

By the end of the third month, Anne was exhausted. When she finished her homework, she went to bed at 8:30 P.M. right along with Nikkie. It was a relief when Holly told Anne that she enjoyed having Nikkie live with them. She baby-sat without any complaints whenever Anne needed her to. But what was especially nice was when Nikkie found a friend. Her name was Asha. And she and Nikkie would call each other every evening after dinner and talk about Asha's new boyfriend.

This weekend she'd done as Holly suggested—took some time out for herself. She planned a weekend excursion to Nashville for the annual NAACP convention.

For the past year, Anne had been an active member of the NAACP. Every fourth Sunday she would meet with a group of over 100 men and women at Mt. Olive C.M.E. Church on 538 Linden.

During the Christmas holiday, she had met Dr. Benjamin Hooks and his wife, Frances. Dr. Hooks and his wife had been affiliated with the NAACP and were members of the Civil Rights Museum as well. Anne and Frances seemed to have a lot in common. And it was Mrs. Hooks who persuaded Anne to join the board of the National Civil Rights Museum.

And now, with a weekend of seminars and luncheons looming in front of her, she welcomed the opportunity to share intellectual conversations with other men and women close to her own age.

What had been unexpected was meeting a widower. His name was Dusty Baker and everyone joked about it. He even looked a little bit like the San Francisco Giants manager.

"Say . . ." he read her name tag—"Anne," Dusty said when they were on a break, "I'm Dusty. What do you say about having dinner with me when this session is over?"

"No thanks," was her immediate answer. "I usually dine alone in my room."

"That's no fun. C'mon. We could eat a good meal and I could tell you a few jokes. You look like you could use a good laugh."

Anne was put out. Had she seemed that unfriendly? Sure, she had a lot on her mind, but anyone that wasn't close to her wouldn't know. Or did it show?

"Uh, I don't know, Dusty." She glanced around the

banquet room corridor. There were several women she felt were better looking than she was. Why had he picked her? "I'm kinda tired. I think I better pass."

Then he did something odd. He picked up her hand, patted it gently, and then let it go. "I'm not being fresh. You just look like you needed someone to talk to. And talking ain't never hurt nobody."

There was a sparkle in his eyes that impressed her. He looked so happy and confident standing there smiling at her.

Anne blushed. "Okay, then."

"I'll meet you at Michaelangelo's at six-thirty, then."

Their friendship had begun that easily. At dinner he told her jokes like he'd promised. Some of them Anne had heard before, but she laughed anyway. She found out that he'd been widowed for five years and had two teenage daughters close to Holly's age.

His situation was similar to Anne's, and his girls had coaxed him into joining the NAACP so that he could get out more. He told Anne that he had a good life and didn't want to complicate his life with a relationship right now. He was a people person, enjoyed making people laugh, and owned a novelty shop.

Anne told him that she worked puzzles and would come by sometime to see his store, but in truth, she felt that she wouldn't see him again. It was funny, she thought, how much information you could reveal to a stranger, knowing that you wouldn't see him again.

Over a glass of white wine, Anne relaxed and told Dusty about her feelings about her niece's state of mind in the mental institution. No one in their family had been ill before. She wasn't sure how her niece was going to come out of this. Right now it didn't look good. Bentley refused to let anyone see her.

"Give her time. She'll be fine, Anne."

"I'm not so sure, Dusty. I've got a bad feeling about this."

Then he said something to comfort her that she'd never forget.

"It's in sickness, Anne, that we most feel the need of that sympathy which shows how much we are dependent upon one another for our comfort, and even necessities. This disease, opening our eyes to the realities of life, is an indirect blessing."

Thirty

SEASONS CHANGED, but Bentley's condition remained the same. She didn't feel the blessings of Thanksgiving, nor did she comprehend the abundance of love that was shared during the Christmas holidays.

For the first time, little Reo Russell opened her gifts without the help of her mother.

Bentley was tired. Dead tired. She felt so fatigued she didn't want to talk. She just wanted to sleep. Day and night. She didn't want to think or to worry about babies, deadlines, and dinner. She wanted to think about nothing. Just nothing at all.

As months sped by, Erik's attorney was busy drawing up documents. Because of the amount of time that had lapsed, and Bentley's psychological condition, Erik had grounds for neglect. It was a mere formality when the judge gave Erik temporary custody of his daughter.

Thirty-one

OVER THE YEARS there had been numerous complaints of police brutality and excessive force being used in the Memphis police department. Profiling, in particular. The concern was genuine, yet no one did anything about it. Basil was well aware of the problem, but couldn't get a local politician to listen to his constant complaints.

Harold Ford Jr. had been elected to Congress. The famed Ford family would come to play an important part in politics in Memphis. Thus far, they'd had numerous legal and financial problems, some of which ended in indictments. Some Memphians loved the Fords—others hated their power.

Another serious issue that Basil didn't agree with was the opening of the casinos in Tunica. Basil, like other taxpayers, felt that the city of Memphis was losing out on millions of dollars that could have been made if Memphians had voted for the casinos instead of letting the state of Mississippi capitalize on it.

A local professor had written an article that claimed that the states had stopped regulating the industry and instead promoted its interests. The professor published an article, "The Luck Business," which examined the government's coziness with gambling interests. The professor stated that politicians eager to maintain gambling tax revenue now had a conflict of interest: They couldn't protect the public if it required reining in the cash cow.

The professor said that states increasingly reliant on that revenue, like Mississippi, had moved from a regulatory to a promotional "predatory" role. Once the government took on a promotional role, he stated, who's to look out for citizens? The professor also noted that Mississippi's regulatory body was "rightfully proud" of its role in stimulating economic development while at the same time fining wrongdoers and monitoring casino activities.

Basil realized that the professor's study held some truth. But regardless, nothing would make him stop frequenting the casinos each time he came home on vacation. The excitement of winning felt like an orgasm.

Through his friend David Ramsey, who had a father who worked in the capitol building in Nashville, Basil learned of another cash cow—the lucrative day care center business in the state of Tennessee. Millions of dollars could be made. David told Basil that if he could come up with $50,000 they could pool their money and buy a half dozen low-income houses and open a chain of centers.

It took a ton of convincing, citing how much his centers would help the community and help out the less fortunate, before his mother acquiesced and agreed to loan him the money for him and David to start up a nonprofit business.

ON MAY 10, 1994, Nelson Mandela was inaugurated as the first black leader of South Africa. In his speech, Mandela gave much praise to F. W. de Klerk, the last white president, who abandoned apartheid and released Mandela and other political prisoners so that the "rainbow nation" could take its place among free and democratic states.

By the end of the month, Basil had completed his junior year at Morehouse College. This time he didn't register for fall classes. He was tired of school. His goal was to become a multimillionaire by the time he turned thirty. The only problem was that he knew going to college wasn't the ticket to his getting there.

In late July David and Basil were called up to Senator Matthews's office. Basil tried not to appear nervous, but in truth, with $5 million in his trust, he felt nearly as important as the senator.

"Mr. Hamilton," the senator said, extending his hand, "it's a pleasure to meet you."

Though Basil was flattered by the personal contact, he wondered why the senator had chosen to open up to him. Through Isabell, Basil had heard a lot of weird things about the man. His sexual habits were beginning to be the brunt of jokes in some circles.

Once the senator had outlined the short-term windfalls with the insurance and broker companies, Basil was even more receptive to the day care business. What he didn't like was the fact that the senator suggested that he and David marry as soon as possible. It would look better if the heads of a multimillion-dollar corporation were grounded family men. They were also told that they would have to go back and get their college degrees. It wouldn't take long for them to receive a bachelor's degree in business administration—one year for Basil and two for David.

Getting enrolled in Memphis State was easy. Finding a woman to share his life with was another matter, though for David, it was simple. He married his childhood sweetheart, Wilma. The only woman that Basil cared about was already married.

Pressured by David, Basil finally found a woman. Bette was a sophomore at Shelby State College and majoring in sociology. For three months he catered to her every whim. He sent her flowers on a regular basis, and made her feel that she was the kind of woman he'd always dreamed about. By September, she was deeply in love with him. He proposed and she readily accepted.

Besides sex, the one thing they had in common was gambling. Bette loved going to the casinos. What he didn't like about her was the way she tried to hide her drinking problem. With that in mind, and at least two weekly visits with his woman, he could put up with her.

"Bette," he said one evening after they'd left Tunica, "let's do it."

"Do what, Basil?"

"Get married. Tonight."

Driving his Volvo ninety miles an hour and heading toward Memphis, he said, "We could be on a plane to Las Vegas and be there in three hours. You can get married any time of day or night in Vegas."

"I don't know. Our parents would be upset."

"Why ask them? We're adults. How long are we going to let them run our lives? C'mon, Bette. Let's do it!"

Reaching over, he eased his right hand beneath her orange corduroy miniskirt until he felt the cloth blocking her triangle of love. Easing the elastic back, he inserted his finger between the lips of her vagina. From the corner of his eye he could see that she was enjoying his fondling. As he continued to drive up Highway 61, he probed deeper and sped up his strokes. The further he plunged, the more delicate his caress, the more languishing her eyes became. Her soft mouth unclosed itself, and her bosoms, firm and soft as velvet, became distended, and her nipples, he knew, were growing large, dusky burgundy, and appetizing. He watched her arms growing weaker, and her angelic legs opening themselves in a voluptuous manner.

"Basil," she whispered, wriggling her hips forward toward his probing finger.

"We could have a helluva honeymoon. Think about it." He increased the pressure, and movement of his finger. "Are you game?" She was close to an orgasm and he knew that at this moment she would promise him anything.

"Yes! Yes!" she screamed as Basil brought her to a climax, "anything you say, baby."

Weak bitch.

THREE DAYS LATER, the newlyweds returned to Memphis. Basil had called his mother from the airport and let her know that he was on his way home. After he parked his Volvo in the driveway, he opened the back door with his key and went into the kitchen.

Anne was at the sink preparing coffee. When she turned around, Basil didn't remembered ever seeing his mother look so pretty before.

"Hi Mom, this is my new wife, Bette."

"Honey, hush. Why hello, there! This is an unexpected but pleasant surprise." She took a moment to hug her new daughter-in-law and then called Holly downstairs. While the two young women talked in the living room, Anne tapped her son on the shoulder.

"Basil. I need to speak with you for a moment." When she asked Bette to excuse them, Basil knew that the conversation was about Bentley.

His mother took Basil into the library and closed the door. She told him how important it was to let Bentley know that they all supported her. Bentley still hadn't made any progress worth noting. Each day she went through the motions of eating and sleeping, but after nearly a year, she still wouldn't talk to anyone.

The last time Anne saw her, she'd lost ten pounds.

When Basil agreed to see his cousin next week, his mother was relieved. She brought him up to date on Nikkie's adjustment living with them now, before the conversation turned back around to his recent marriage.

"I'm not so sure if I like this sudden wedding or not. Usually when people marry this quickly, they've got something to hide. Is Bette pregnant?"

"Gosh no, Mom."

"Was she homeless?"

"Stop kidding around. Her parents live out in Cordova. She's a woman I've been dating for a few months. A couple of days ago, we just decided to fly to Vegas and get hitched. It's not any more complicated than that. You know I've never been a skirt chaser, Mom. I'm twenty years old—old enough to settle down. And I really love this girl. Bette's got a lot of good qualities. You'll see."

"Well, I hope so." He kissed his mother on the cheek. "And Mom, we're both planning on finishing college. We don't anticipate having any children until then."

"Now that's good to hear."

"C'mon now," he said, leading her back into the living room, "she's going to think that you don't like her."

His mother and sister gushed and fawned over his wife like an adoptive daughter. While they all got acquainted, Basil went upstairs and made a call.

"Nothing's changed. Can I see you tonight?" In their three years of being together, he had never asked her if she would leave her husband.

"Where?"

"The Graceland Inn Hotel. Ten o'clock." They knew that with both of them being married now, the stimulation would be titillating.

"No. Never mind. I've got a better idea. What about the bridge?"

"Which one?

"The Harahan Bridge. It just opened. I've never made love beneath a bridge with hundreds of cars rolling over me."

"The excitement—"

"Would be overwhelming."

"I agree." It had been ages since he saw her and his heart ached to touch her hot flesh again, to see, smell, to kiss, and suck and fuck her delicious cunt, and give her all the pleasure that she could stand. " Make it nine, then."

Thirty-two

THE FLOWERY SCENT of summer wafted by the warm south wind hinted at renewed life. Echoes of footsteps drifted down the street from the few people out walking. Against the crystal blue sky, green-tinged branches swayed gently.

Anne parked her car in front of 2334 St. Paul Street. To her surprise, over the past twenty years the neighborhood had undergone a complete face-lift. Gone were most of the shotgun houses that were so prevalent in the sixties.

Grabbing her purse and keys, she was stopped short. Devastating pains seared down the right side of her body. The keys shook in her hand, while she waited for the moment to pass.

"Get it together, girl," she told herself out loud. Exiting the car, she felt a growing stiffness in her hip.

Anne walked up the narrow walkway to the side door. Stepping up on the porch, Anne looked around. It was as if no one lived there. There were no chairs or plants or welcome rug.

After she'd knocked twice, she heard footsteps, then saw the instant glare from the porch light.

"Hello, Mrs. Berry," Anne said after the elderly woman opened the door. "My name is Anne Russell. My father used to live in this neighborhood years ago."

The woman studied her for a moment, then said, "I know who you are. Come on in."

Mrs. Berry's hair was as silvery as a song; her smooth face and endearing smile made Anne wish that she'd had a grandmother.

What Anne had thought would be a short visit turned out to be a heartwarming one. After accepting a cup of hot lemon tea, Mrs. Berry gave Anne a history lesson about all the people in the neighborhood who had either died or moved away over the last thirty years. She knew every family and every child who lived in each household.

When Mrs. Berry began to talk about Anne's father, Walter, Anne didn't notice the tears. She remembered most of the details about the fatal accident, and even knew the date when Anne's brother Stuart and his wife were killed.

A flash of anger showed in Mrs. Berry's wise eyes. "You were too young to know what was happening, Anne. The racism back then was unbearable. Even so, we were a proud community and did what we could for one another." Mrs. Berry's face softened a little. "Before he died, your father used to come over here and fix my roof when it was leaking. He would repair my stove and refrigerator when I didn't think they would run another day. Yes, Lord, Walter Russell was a good man. He refused to take a dime from me." Above them, she could hear the monotonous sound of rap music being turned up. "That's Janie. The last one." She exhaled. "Being divorced with twelve children was difficult back then. My boys did what they could to earn money, but without the help of men like your father, we probably would have starved to death."

When Mrs. Berry finally got around to talking about her son, Erik, and Bentley, she seemed saddened.

"Erik loved her. I know he did. Even before the baby was born, all he talked about was marrying her when he came home."

"What happened to change his mind?"

"That scandalous white woman. She polluted his mind with money." She looked over to the coffee table next to her chair. There was half a pack of Winston cigarettes. She grabbed the box and slid one out. "Do you mind?"

"No. This is your home."

She flicked the lighter, and as the flame caught the cigarette, she took a nice long drag before speaking. "Before Erik left for the service in 1975, I was a very unhappy woman." She exhaled. "My husband had left me three months before my eighth baby was born. The washing machine had broken and my two eldest daughters and myself had rubbed our hands raw washing clothes."

"And my father? He wasn't able to help you out?"

She studied Anne before she took another drag from her cigarette. "No. I'd had a relationship with a coworker of Walter's. Walter heard about it, and casually mentioned it to me. Mind you, it was only to feed my children. But Walter seemed to have less respect for me then and I couldn't bear to explain to him how much it took for me to have relations with a man that I cared less than a dead roach about." Anne wondered if her father had the same idea in mind but his friend beat him to it.

"I can just about guess what you're thinking." She flicked an ash into the glass ashtray. "No, your father and I weren't intimate. He was a gentleman, and a damned good friend."

"But you couldn't explain to him—"

With the cigarette secure in the corner of her mouth, she checked her smoke-stained fingernails. "I've got some pride. Your father had enough responsibility taking care of his own children, and grandchildren. I couldn't continue accepting favors from him." Removing the cigarette, she let the ashes fall into the ashtray, then leaned back in the chair, crossing her legs. There was a long run up the front of her stockings, but she didn't seem to notice it. "Besides, the septic tank had filled up and we'd been going to the bathroom in a bucket for months. I was sick of it. Sick of making excuses why the kids couldn't have any company." She took one last puff and ground the cigarette out hard in the ashtray. "So, I did what I had to do."

"Honey, hush. Most women in your situation would have done the same thing, Mrs. Berry."

"My, my. I guess I've been wrong about you, Anne. I thought you were living the life of glory with a rich husband and looking down on us poor folks who had tainted pasts. It just goes to show you that I'm not the only one in this world that's been abused."

Why had she said that? Did she know about Scott's first wife, too?

Anne thought back on her turbulent years with Scott.

Inwardly, she flushed with embarrassment. Her inner turmoil so acute, it was as if someone was pulling out her guts with their bare hands.

"Still, Mrs. Berry, I totally understand what you were going through."

"Erik didn't. He came home early from school one day and saw something that he shouldn't have seen."

No amount of explanations could control her son's anger toward her, she told Anne. Within a week's time, he'd quit school and left for the army. She wrote him letters trying to explain, but he never answered any of them.

When Erik came home on leave nearly five years later, he'd begun to change. For some reason, he felt guilty about abandoning her and the kids and began giving them large sums of money. With eleven other children under eighteen years of age, she told Anne that she would have been a fool to turn down the money.

"Later, after he was discharged, he started giving me even more money—upwards of a thousand dollars a month. Said he wanted to buy me a bigger house."

"This one?"

"Yes. At the time, I didn't know where Erik was getting the money. I thought he'd saved it from his earnings in the service."

"So he married this woman for her money?"

"Not by his account. He told me he loved her." She sported a wry smile. "I never questioned him. But I tell you; I knew I was right about the entire situation the moment Erik's daughter was born. He adored that child. When he brought her over on the weekends, I could see the sadness in his face."

"What about the child's mother? Did you know who she was?"

"I didn't at first. But after she had the baby, one of my

daughters told me that she was Walter's granddaughter. I'd seen her at the hospital when Reo was born, but we've never formerly met."

"And your son's wife?"

"I've only seen her once—at the wedding reception. I believe she thinks she's too good to come over here. I really don't think she has much use for black people. To this day, none of us have ever been invited to their home. It seems that Erik is a man that she decided to dress up and show off to her white friends," she said with a heavy sigh. "*His* family don't matter."

"Do you know anything about her family?"

"Sure. She's a Ford. Ms. Isabell Ford. That's her name. I still can't bring myself to call her a Berry."

Anne left Mrs. Berry's house with more information than she could have gleaned from Erik or Bentley. What confused her was the fact that Mrs. Berry believed that Erik truly loved Bentley. But what was abundantly obvious was the fact that Isabell was obsessed about Reo. Mrs. Berry said that Isabell treated that baby like it was her own.

Like it was her own.

That was it. Isabell wanted a black child. All this time, Anne wondered why Isabell wanted to learn black people's ways, but she never attributed it to being a black child's mother.

Why had she done this?

LESS THAN A WEEK LATER, she would find out some of the answers to her questions. Mrs. Berry had given Anne Erik's number and when she called, he agreed to see her on Saturday morning.

"I made the worst mistake of my life, Anne," Erik told her while looking out of the mullioned windows of the library. Soft edges, moderately worn rust wool carpeting, and wood with a gentle patina of age lent history to the room. Like the books in Erik's well-stocked library, they surrounded Anne with stories waiting to be told. The room was filled with priceless Asian and Indonesian antiques, each piece as individual as their owners.

Isabell had taken Reo shopping for a fall wardrobe that Erik claimed she didn't need.

"Last year, I found out from one of the artists who used to work with Bentley that she was having problems getting her assignments in on time."

Anne appraised the handsome young man, dressed in Georgio Armani's finest trousers and silk shirt. "Hold up, Erik. If you suspected that she was in trouble—"

"I wanted to see her first. Talk to her." His eyes turned from hers.

"And why didn't you—go and see her?" She wondered if Isabell had discouraged it. "Never mind. Tell me Erik, do you have any feelings for her?"

"I . . . um, I'm not sure. Don't judge me too harshly, Anne. You don't know me that well."

"I don't know what I expected from you, Erik. When I spoke to your mother—"

"You've been by my mother's house?"

"Yes. I felt it was necessary to see her *first*. You know, before I saw you."

He smiled. "My mother talks too much, Anne. I'm not sure what she told you, but I'm certain you left knowing that she's never cared for my wife."

"That's none of my business. My concern is the welfare of my niece and her child."

"Under the circumstances, Reo is a very well-adjusted child. She's in an excellent preschool—"

"Excuse me, Erik. But what about her mental stability? Are you telling me that she doesn't ask about her real mother?"

"Of course."

"And what do you tell her?"

"That her mother has been very sick."

"That's very commendable of you," she snarled.

"And what prompted this visit from you now?"

"I feel that Reo's old enough now to spend some time with her family. I wanted to ask your permission to come and get her once a month."

Taking a seat in the leather-winged armchair, he hesitated before he spoke. "I'm not sure how my wife would feel about it."

"What does she have to do with me seeing my niece's child?"

"Isabell is in the process of becoming Reo's legal mother."

Just then Reo came whirling in, while Isabell deposited the colorful Laura Ashley bags on a chintz-skirted table in the foyer. A shadow of recognition passed over Isabell's face as she slowly came toward them.

"Daddy," Reo said, running to jump on his lap and rubbing her eyes, "I'm tired. Mommy said I have to try on my clothes for you. Do I—" She stopped and stared at Anne. "Who's she?"

Tall for a four-year-old, but still wearing the innocence of a precocious toddler, Reo mirrored Erik's physical features and Bentley's compassionate brown eyes.

"Why, I'm your aunt Anne, Reo. I haven't seen you since you were a little baby." Reo smiled and let out a small giggle. Anne studied Reo up and down. Her dress was nothing like the ones that she and Holly had selected when she was her age. This dress looked far more grown-up. And even her permed hair seemed a bit straighter than normal. In Anne's opinion it appeared as if Isabell was trying to turn Reo into a little white child. Even in the dim light Anne noticed the sparkling diamonds on Isabell's ears, neck, and wrists before she realized that mother and daughter wore the exact same dresses. In Anne's opinion, it was inexcusable the way Erik had let Isabell dominate his daughter's life. Her curt look from Reo to Erik let him know how she felt.

Bending down to hug his daughter, he kept a protective arm around her shoulder when he asked, "Okay, missy, we both know the routine. What do you say to our company?"

With the grace of a child who'd gone to charm school, Reo came over to where Anne sat and said, "It's so nice to meet you, Aunt Anne." She glanced over her shoulder back at Isabell, and getting her nod of approval, added, "Please excuse me, I have to change for dinner."

After she left the room, Isabell pasted a fake smile on her immaculate face. "Hello, Anne." After kissing her husband on the cheek, she stood beside him, resting her hand on his shoulder. "It's a pleasure to see you again."

Erik looked confused. "You two know each other?"

"Yes. I was on the board of directors at the *Hamilton Appeal* before it was sold. We met back then."

Without understanding all the circumstances, Anne had never been clear about the buyout of the *Hamilton Appeal*. Scott's attorney as well as Isabell assured her that it was in the best interest of their client, if the deal went through. She had accepted and banked the millions in profit.

"How've you been, Isabell? You look great."

"I'm well. Thanks." She seemed to float to the window as if she was unable to be touched. She lowered the balloon shades, blocking out part of the sunlight, and took a seat on the ivory-fringed sofa. "My family and I don't have any complaints." She stretched a smile across her overly powdered face. "What brings you to our home?"

"My niece, you know, Reo's *mother.*"

"I'm her mother." Isabell glanced at Erik, who went to mix a drink. He offered one to Anne, which she declined. "The adoption is nearly complete."

She was positive that if Bentley had all her faculties, she would stop Erik and Isabell from going through with this selfish act. Not knowing the legalities, Anne decided to let it drop. After she found out a few more details she'd have another talk with Erik, without the presence of his wife. She rose to leave.

"Oh, dear me," Isabell said, faking concern, "I was so sorry to hear about your husband's death, Anne. It must have been a terrible time for you." She turned away from the window and faced Anne. "It seems that your family has had more than its share of tragedies."

"I agree." The telephone saved Anne from saying something nasty. After Erik answered it, he nodded toward Isabell.

"Excuse, me, Anne."

"I'd better go." She turned to leave and heard Erik's footsteps close behind her.

This was all a little too perfect for Anne. The entire situation smelled of crisis. Perfect child, dutiful husband, rich wife—it reeked of inner turmoil.

When he opened the front door, she turned and asked him, "I don't mean to be so bold, but I believe I've known Isabell a little longer and a little better than you do. She's not the friend I thought I knew back then. Something's changed her." Anne wanted to add, *How could you take Bentley's child away and allow this hypocrite to raise her?*

"We've all changed."

Thirty-three

SICKNESS AND DISEASE are in weak minds the sources of melancholy; but that which is painful to the body may be profitable to the soul. Sickness, the mother of modesty, puts us in mind of our mortality, and while we drive on heedlessly in the full career of worldly pomp and jollity, kindly brings us to a proper sense of our duty and destiny.

Bentley knew she wasn't well. And she knew she wasn't crazy.

When Bentley thought about Reo, her mind went on automatic pilot. When she thought about Nikkie, she felt numb. She would often backtrack to the night of the fire, and realize that she couldn't re-create what had happened. It was during those troubled times that she willed herself to just hold on.

Hold on for Reo's sake.
Hold on for Nikkie's sake.
Hold on for *her* sake.

Thirty-four

"SO YOU'RE NOT SPEAKING to me again today, huh?"

Nikkie shook her head no.

They were in Nikkie's room. Anne had tried for the third time to get her to come downstairs for breakfast.

"Not even if I promise to take you over to Asha's house?"

"No. I'm not happy, Aunt Anne. I'm going to miss my friend."

Anne thought about Dusty. Her friend had called her last night. They'd talked about her childhood and growing up poor until one in the morning.

Nikkie had been upset with Anne since Friday afternoon. Her friend Asha was moving into a group home on Monday. Nikkie wanted to move in with her. When Anne told her no, Nikkie refused to speak to Anne.

However, just this morning, Anne was on the telephone with Asha's mother, Nellie. It appeared that Asha had been on the waiting list for Shelby Residential and Vocational Services, SRVS. Her application had just been approved for the residential facility.

Nellie gave Anne the admissions director's name and number. When Anne called, Ms. Mellons was extremely friendly. She asked Anne to come down and visit the facility.

"We've been here since 1965, Mrs. Hamilton. We serve over twelve hundred developmentally disabled citizens a year."

"I've never heard of SRVS."

"A lot of people haven't," Ms. Mellons said as she gave Anne a tour of the huge facility.

Located at 4599 Knight Arnold, the complex was approximately thirty miles from Anne's home. The admissions director told Anne that there were several other locations around the city as well. At this location, group homes for six people as well as homes for single and double occupancy were available. A fully staffed community center provided arts and crafts from eight to four. If the person wanted to work, there were job coaches hired by the state of Tennessee to help them perform their tasks until they learned to do them themselves. SRVS had a contract with FedEx, American Greeting Cards, Troll Books, and Yardley products. There were two facilities on the complex that housed companies where work was done on a production line in a sort of factorylike atmosphere.

"People think that the people who live here are unhappy," Ms. Mellons began. "They're not. They like nice clothes. They like to shop and go to movies. And they especially like to go to the Pyramid to see those wrestling matches."

"Are you kidding?"

"No. It's the biggest night of entertainment here besides the weekly dance."

"Well, now. I'm very impressed. I had no idea that my niece could live a normal life like this."

"Hold on, Mrs. Hamilton. I don't want you to think it's that easy for your niece to get into our facility. There's a very long waiting list."

"I've heard. If I can, I'd like to put my niece's name on the list. But first, I'd like to bring her down here and see if she'd like it."

"That can be arranged. Come in my office, and I'll let

you know when one of the staff members can schedule an appointment."

As Anne drove back home, she worried about Bentley's approval. Would she want her sister living in a place like this?

When she spoke with Mae about it, she thought it was a good idea. Holly and Basil agreed, too. After all, Nikkie was nearly thirty years old. She deserved to have a full life just like everybody else.

It was just over a week before SRVS could accommodate a walk-through with her and Nikkie. Anne brought with her the copy of Nikkie's IQ test from Manassas High School. One of SRVS requirements was that the occupant had to have an IQ of 70 or below. When everything was settled, Anne shook hands with the staff member, who promised to call as soon as a room was available.

Anne hadn't seen Nikkie so happy in years. She actually had tears in her eyes when they drove away from the facility.

All Anne could do was pray that Bentley was coherent enough to give her permission by the time Nikkie's name came up for occupancy. Which day would come up first was anybody's guess.

FOR THE NEXT FEW MONTHS, Anne considered what she would do next year after she graduated.

Basil's unsolicited suggestion was the booming day care business. At first Anne had been skeptical of Basil's and his friend David's day care business. But in just over a year, their nonprofit corporation, Children's Castle Academy, had received more than $2 million from the state during their last fiscal year. Basil bragged that he and David's salaries were in the lower six-figure income bracket. When Anne questioned Basil about the exorbitant pay, he assured her that it was all legal.

It wasn't a bad idea.

"You could come and work for me, Mom," Basil had teased her one afternoon when she and he were home alone.

"Doing what?"

"Becoming the executive director of Hamilton's Children and Family Services. We're going into the broker business."

"Why?"

"Because it's a big moneymaker. The government is going to pay my company millions a year to administer aspects of subsidized day care in Shelby County. All we have to do is place poor children in subsidized day care facilities. . . . Matter of fact, I was thinking, Mom, that you *could* become a partner. I've found a building on Airways Street that I plan on purchasing, but I'm short about forty grand."

"I could spare that much," Anne offered, "but I'd like to remain a silent partner. A director of a day care center doesn't work—"

"It's a brokerage firm, Mom," Basil corrected, "and I need to get everything up and rolling in thirty days, otherwise I'll lose the contract."

"Hmm," Anne said, getting her thoughts together. She had read something about a day care broker who was being sued for fraud. And now Basil said he *had* the contract, and hadn't even bid on it. Apparently Basil had some connections that she wasn't aware of. "I'll have the money for you tomorrow. But Basil—"

"I know. It's business, Mom. I'll have my attorney get the contracts ready and it'll be a seventy-thirty deal. Does that seem fair to you?"

"I like sixty-forty better." If this venture were as successful as Basil's day care business, Anne wouldn't have to touch her savings.

"My, my, you're getting greedy. Okay, it's a done deal."

That quick transaction transpired in March and Anne was set to receive her first payment by the end of May.

And now, the first official weekend of summer vacation, Children's Castle had just opened up two new centers.

On this particular day Anne found herself in the house all alone. Nikkie was spending the weekend with Asha, and Holly was spending the night with a friend. It was Basil who suggested that the three grown-ups go out on the town and celebrate tonight. The casinos in Sam's Town were Basil's first choice. Natalie Cole was performing. When the show was over, Anne spotted her son and daughter-in-law at the blackjack table. Basil was betting $2,000 a hand.

Even while Bette tried to cover up Basil's activities with her animated conversation, Anne could tell that Basil was hooked by the serious look on his face. And since the couple was still living in her home, she also learned that Basil was not hooked on Bette. His constant slipping out at night hadn't gone unnoticed.

It also didn't take long for Anne to discover Bette's weakness—bourbon. The petite young woman who wore her hair permed, parted on the side, and less than an inch long looked like a sixteen year old. She reminded Anne of Jada Pinkette, a young woman whom she didn't consider pretty, but was extremely cute. It would take another ten years, Anne believed, before Bette would begin to look her age. That was, unless the liquor caught up with her first.

Anne never mentioned to Bette that she knew about her addiction to alcohol—if she or Basil didn't bring it up, she wouldn't either, although she wanted to. But Anne knew, and she was certain that Holly knew too, that Bette began drinking at five in the afternoon, right after she finished her job as director over the ten child care centers. All the mints and mouthwash she constantly used couldn't camouflage the strong scent of alcohol. Before nine in the evening, Bette was usually passed out and unavailable for phone calls.

Another woman could call their home for Basil, and Bette would never know.

Holly had hinted to her mother who the other woman was, but Anne stopped her short of telling. She didn't want to know. And she didn't want to believe that her son was capable of adultery. Presently, Anne had more important things on her mind.

"Hello, Mae, this is Anne. I haven't heard from you lately. Are you feeling all right?"

"Yes, I'm making it okay."

"Good. Now tell the truth. Have you signed up for those driver's education classes yet?"

"No. But I will."

"It's not that I mind driving over there to see you, Mae. But it would be nice if you could come and visit Holly and me every once in a while."

"You're so right. I'm going to go to that driving school and buy me a car just like I been telling you I would. You'll see."

After she hung up, Anne smiled to herself. It was funny how terrified Mae was of driving a car. Both Anne and Holly had offered to teach her on weekends, but Mae wouldn't hear of it. She wanted to do it on her own.

Anne understood her point. She'd be forty this fall.

She realized at this point in her life, family meant everything. Anne made it a priority to write Kirk and send him pictures of her children on a regular basis. She also made a point of writing Wesley once a month. It didn't matter that he didn't write her as often. She knew that he would be glad to hear about Nikkie's progress toward independence.

The only downside to writing her nephew was telling him about Bentley. It was difficult to tell him how little change there was in Bentley's condition. The last time Anne saw her niece, Bentley didn't seem to recognize her.

Her doctor told Anne to have patience. His only concern was that Bentley wasn't getting any worse. With that in mind, Anne made the decision to terminate the lease on Bentley's apartment. She and Basil packed up her things and put them in storage. They parked her Galant in Anne's driveway. Seeing Bentley's car parked there every day when Anne left for school was hard for her to get used to. Not wanting to dump all of her personal problems on her daughter, she enjoyed confiding in Dusty.

Their long-distance friendship was a godsend for Anne. They'd talk once or twice a week—usually about their daughters. Like typical teenagers, one or all three of them would be going through a crisis.

Dusty never failed to invite her to come up to Nashville and see his store. Anne kidded that one day she'd surprise him and just show up. But a part of her didn't want to spoil their friendship. She felt the miles between them kept away the pressure of anything serious happening between them, and right now she preferred it that way.

The following year both Anne and her daughter graduated—Anne from Memphis State University, and Holly from Germantown High School. Together, she and

Holly picked out a blue Audi for Holly's graduation gift.

Holly had received several academic scholarship offers, but she accepted the offer from the University of Tennessee in Knoxville. In three weeks, tryouts would begin for UT's softball team, and Holly planned to beat out the competition for her usual position at first base.

Twenty-one days wasn't enough time to get used to the idea that Anne would be losing her best friend. They'd been so close—like sisters. When she and Bentley had told each other that they were sister sisters, it was different. She and Holly were of the same blood, thought, and spirit. Not having a mother to use as an example, Anne knew that she depended too much on her child. Fortunately, Holly never complained. They'd shared so much over the years—especially when Holly was old enough to understand how unhappy Anne was in her marriage to her father.

And to this day, Anne regretted not having participated in sports. If she had not worked on the newspaper during her high-school years, she would have chosen the exact sports that Holly did—softball and volleyball. Several trophies lined the library shelves, ranging from age eight to eighteen. It saddened Anne that Scott hadn't been present when she received any of them.

When this year's season ended, Holly had told her mother, "After I graduate from UT, I'm never going to be far from softball. I'm hoping that I'll be able to coach a girl's high-school team."

"I thought becoming a veterinarian was your dream."

Holly had hugged her mother and kissed her on the forehead. "It is. And I can do both. But I also have other dreams, Mom." Taking her mother's hand in hers, she wiggled her left ring finger. "You can probably guess what one of them is?"

The thought of Holly getting married as young as Basil did worried her. Call her sentimental, but she wanted her daughter to have the storybook wedding that she should have had. And that included waiting until she was twenty-five and mature enough to handle a man who might not be suitable for her.

A week later, Anne was relieved when Holly broke up with her boyfriend of six months. Like her mother, Holly had always been attracted to older men. This one, however, had lied about divorcing his wife. And when Holly found out from a friend that he had two small children as well, she wouldn't return his phone calls.

Right after graduation, Holly had put an ad in the *Hamilton Appeal* to give away all of her pets. Scotty and Deirdre, the Siamese cat and toy poodle, were the first to go. When Chess and Checkers were about to leave one sunny afternoon, they chirped Anne's and Holly's names in unison. Anne cried. She'd taken their company for granted and just now realized how much she'd miss them.

The following day, an unexpected call came from Ms. Mellons. A vacancy was available. Nikkie could wait until fall for the Bartlett location closest to Anne or accept the group home where Nikkie's friend Asha lived. Of course Nikkie chose to move to the Knight Arnold location.

Since Bentley wasn't available to make the legal decisions for Nikkie, a meeting was set up with a social worker, an instructor, Nikkie's physician, and Ms. Mellons to discuss Nikkie's needs and wants. Anne was so proud of Nikkie when she told them that she wanted a place of her own with her own job and money. She wanted to be independent like her friend Asha. Everyone smiled when Nikkie added that Asha even had a boyfriend.

Holly helped Anne move Nikkie's things into her new home. It was truly unbelievable. The staff had been wonderful in assuring Anne that they would make Nikkie's transition to her new surroundings as smooth as possible. Ms. Mellons had secured a position for Nikkie where they made greeting cards. Her friend Asha was already employed there.

The staff at SRVS was very loyal to the occupants. There were individuals hired by the state to prepare daily dinners and also to take them shopping. Though everything they needed was on the grounds, there were buses available to take them to their doctors' appointments, hairdressers, and sightseeing tours around the city.

The first week Nikkie called home every day. Anne wasn't sure if she understood that Bentley would be away for a while, but still and all, Nikkie seemed to have enough sense to know that it was time to move on with her life. And Anne couldn't blame her. She was learning more about herself, life, and people, than she or Bentley could possibly have taught her.

Six days later, Holly went through the same motions as Nikkie, packing, getting rid of clothes she no longer wanted, and constantly telling her mother how much she loved her.

That night Basil ordered pizza and popped open a bottle of Dom Pérignon from their little-used bar. Bette, Anne, Holly, and Basil sipped on champagne and went through the dozens of photo albums that Anne had accumulated over the years.

At eleven, Holly announced that she had to go to bed. When Holly hugged Anne good night, Anne was certain that she felt tears.

By midnight, Anne had cleaned up the mess in the family room and gone up to her room. After taking a long shower, she turned on the television set. She surfed the channels and couldn't find anything that piqued her interest.

At one, she picked up the phone to dial Dusty and changed her mind. Instead, she decided to get up. She went into Holly's room and watched her sleeping. Holly slept on her stomach as she always did, with the music playing low on the radio a mere six inches from her face.

Two large suitcases and a trunk that were left open for a final inspection were in front of the closet. Beside it stood the three-story Victorian dollhouse that they'd purchased when she was eight years old and still looked as though she'd played with it the night before. It was years of beautiful memories between a mother and daughter that Holly had said that she wanted to share with her own daughter one day.

At five in the morning, Anne heard a knock on her bedroom door. Glancing at the clock, she jumped up and put on her robe. She'd intended to be up by three.

"Why didn't you wake me, Holly?" she said, following her down the steps.

"Because I knew how you'd react, Mom."

Tears were already forming in her eyes. Wiping her eyes with the sleeve of her robe, she tried to hide them from her daughter. "At least let me fix you a decent breakfast. I can make your favorite. Blueberry pancakes."

They were in the kitchen now, and Holly picked up her purse and keys that were lying on the counter. "Thanks, Mom. But I've already had a bagel and a glass of juice."

"Holly . . ."

"I know, Mom," she said hugging her. "I'll miss you too."

Anne waved good-bye to her daughter as she backed

her blue Audi out of the driveway. She hollered from the street that she'd call her this afternoon.

Anne was brokenhearted. Holly was the one person in her life from whom she received constant love without any strings attached. How could she live without her?

Thirty-five

ON THE FIRST OF AUGUST, Basil and Bette had finally moved into their first home in Hickory Hill. Anne worried that after four years of marriage, Bette still hadn't gotten pregnant. She'd obtained a degree in sociology and seemed to be absorbed with pleasing Basil. And pleasing Basil meant adding one or two more centers a year to their day care business. They'd put all the day cares in Bette's maiden name last year so that his broker business wouldn't be a conflict of interest.

Anne wasn't told the reasons why David and Basil decided to part ways, other than the fact that David was opening his own chain of day care centers, Hungry Minds Learning Academy, in the midtown area.

Basil told his mother that there was no end to the amount of money that he could make. He felt that by the time he turned twenty-five, he'd already be a multimillionaire and wouldn't need the money left to him by his father.

Regardless, Basil was spending money like he had millions right now. He and Bette owned light and dark 750 sport Mercedeses, and Basil was even talking about buying a forty-foot yacht. Whenever they went out to dinner, Basil insisted upon paying. The wad of bills in his pocket seemed inappropriate and childish to Anne.

Apparently, to Bette, whatever Basil did was cool with her. Even above her daughter-in-law's expensive cologne, Anne could smell the bourbon. She would study Bette, who was doing her best not to fall asleep at the table. Every item that she wore, down to her nylons, had designer labels. Visiting their contemporary home revealed more of the same. Ralph Lauren was evident from entrance to exit. No matter how expensive the artwork and sculpture that Bette showed off to her mother-in-law, their home seemed cold and void of love.

FOR THE FIRST TIME in Anne's adult life, she was alone. Her 11,000-square-foot home that was normally cheerful and homey was now like a haunted house. With Holly, no pets, and Nikkie's absence, there was no one there to breathe life into the home. Even the walls seemed to miss the reflection of their limitless laughter.

Anne tried going out to social events that most people in her position attended. But she found herself bored—resenting the forced conversations and false pretenses of appearing happy. In truth, she was lonely. There was nothing more she could do for Nikkie or Bentley. She told herself that they both were in capable hands.

Reading the *Hamilton Appeal* daily was still a habit of Anne's. She also looked forward to reading Billy Graham's column. His spiritual comments made her feel less lonely. She believed that beginning her day with the Lord first and foremost on her mind was what she'd been taught to do as a child.

For some uncanny reason she began reading her horoscope. Scorpios were supposed to make changes soon. It seemed that every time she read her horoscope, it talked about relocating. Nashville, of course, was her first thought.

When she called Dusty and told him about her plans to move to Nashville, he seemed excited for her.

"Don't get the wrong idea. I'm enjoying being single." But even as she said the words, she knew they weren't true.

By the first week in October Anne had packed up all of her clothes and personal items and was ready to move. She'd contacted a hotel in Nashville about living accommodations and couldn't wait to leave.

Mae hated to see her go, but understood that Anne was at a crossroads in her life. It was time she found out what she was supposed to do in this world.

Before she left Memphis, Anne and Mae went to see Nikkie, who was still learning her way around the complex, and had made several more friends. Mae promised that she would call Nikkie periodically to let her know that family was still close by.

Bentley was a different matter. Anne felt guilty when she spoke to her doctor and told him of her plans to relocate. She purchased a beeper and told the doctor to contact her day or night if there was any change in Bentley's condition. Anne believed that when Bentley did get well enough to come home, she would elect to come with Anne to the big city and start over again, too.

On a cool Monday morning, with a U-haul truck attached to the back of her BMW, she headed east for Nashville. When she was in Nashville last year at the NAACP convention, she stayed inside the hotel and hadn't bothered to check out the residential or business areas like some of the other members had. This time would be different.

When she arrived, Anne took up temporary residence at the Four Seasons Hotel in downtown Nashville. While they were married, she and Scott rarely strayed from home any longer than one night at a time, so the luxury of living in a suite was a welcome change.

The realtor who sold Basil and Bette their home recommended one of her associates at Real Estate One in Nashville to Anne. The woman's name was Edna Hall.

Mrs. Hall was very patient with Anne. She'd even, on occasion, pick up Holly to house-hunt with them. Fortunately for Anne, Mrs. Hall had a very considerate husband, because the real estate agent spent four out of seven days a week with Anne. When they weren't looking at homes, Edna was taking her to see some of the wonderful sites in the city. There was the charming district in historic downtown Franklin, where Anne shopped for new bed linens—the Belle Meade Plantation, the Grand Old Opry, The Imaginarium—an interactive experience for children that was designed to stimulate discovery and imagination. She enjoyed exploring the themed areas, including a dinosaur room, rain forest, art studio, outer space, theatre, pirate ship, aquarium, supermarket, fire station, hospital, and toddler room. When they left, Anne told Edna that one day she'd bring her grandchildren back to visit this place, or maybe she'd come back again all by herself, she'd had so much fun.

One afternoon they stopped for fresh seafood at Lowell's Oyster Bar on Market Street, and then purchased an imported case of ale at the Market Street Brewery. Edna purchased more clothes at Dangerous Threads than Anne did.

What really sold Anne on Nashville was the Par-

thenon. Nashville had the world's only full-size repro-
duction of the famous Greek temple. The Parthenon was
located in Centennial Park in midtown. The museum
featured Athena, who at forty-two feet was the tallest
indoor sculpture in the Western world. The exhibit left
Anne breathless.

October and November flew by. It was a time when
there was a shorter supply of available homes on the
market. After the Thanksgiving holiday, Edna suggested
that Anne and Holly take the General Jackson Show-
boat Cruise. The $12 million, four-deck paddle wheeler
offered midday and evening theme cruises. Anne and
Holly elected to take the two-and-a-half-hour holiday
evening cruise. It was a brisk sixty-nine degrees as
mother and daughter sat side by side, snuggling in their
wool coats outside on the balcony, where a three-course
sit-down rib dinner was served along with a Broadway-
style stage show, musical revue, and entertainment.

It was two days after this wonderful adventure that
Anne found the perfect home in the historic district of
Brentwood—Franklin, the town that Holly had first
suggested, was the neighboring city. Located on Old
Hickory Boulevard, the 2,500-square-foot antebellum
home had an oriental garden and lap pool. Through
Edna's persistence, Anne was able to move into her
home a week before Christmas.

In the midst of moving, Anne noticed that she was
having difficulty completing sentences, and having
problems swallowing. She attributed it to the strains
of relocating until, waking up one morning, she was
shocked to find that the entire left half of her body
felt stiff and rigid. Afraid that she'd had a ministroke,
she immediately called her personal physician, Cleve-
land Fisher, in Memphis. He suggested that she see

Dr. Freeman at Vanderbilt University Medical Center.

Three weeks later she had finished a thirty-minute-long consultation with the elderly physician.

"Do you have any idea what the problem is, Dr. Freeman?"

"Not without a thorough examination. Look, Anne, you're a young woman. Your last complete physical was less than a year ago. As you may remember, the results of the tests were all negative. All of your vital signs seem to be fine."

"But—"

"Stop worrying. You'll get wrinkles on that pretty face. Now calm down and call Dr. Iverson. Ask him to send me a copy of his findings."

Writing the physician's name down, she made an appointment with Dr. Iverson and fought the urge to give into self-pity. Staying busy would keep her mind off of her health until she was able to get her condition confirmed.

After interviewing several construction companies, she hired Johnson's Construction Company, a father-and-son firm, to remodel the hundred-year-old home. White on white walls and black granite was the central theme in the home. Every room would be basic black and white with splashes of aqua, yellow, and lime green accents throughout. Her Brentwood home was a total departure from the conservative furnishings in her Germantown home, and would cost more than $10,000 to refurbish; to Anne it was worth every penny.

Buying a home of her own gave her a feeling of independence. The money left to her from Scott was barely touched.

Although her investments were bringing in over

$10,000 a month, she barely spent $6,000 on her personal and living expenses.

After speaking with Basil, she let him know that she had no intentions of living the life of a socialite. She wanted to earn her own living, like her father would have wanted her to.

" I know a man who may be able to help you." Basil seemed evasive, building her up, and enjoying hearing her constant Who is he?

"I'm getting too old for games, son."

"Be at the capitol building, Room 223, at 9:15 A.M. on Monday morning. And the appointment is with J. D. Lowe. Call me after the interview."

By ten o'clock the following morning, Anne was being led into the senator's private office. She hadn't seen Orin in years. Did her son know that they'd met before?

Thirty-six

ANNE SUPPOSED she felt like Bentley did, when she was given the job at the capitol building—if it weren't for Basil's connections with the senator, she wouldn't stand a chance of landing the position. After the interview, she felt that she wasn't exactly qualified for the position of publicity coordinator. But Mr. Lowe seemed especially impressed by the fact that Anne had held the job as chief executive officer at the *Hamilton Appeal*.

Mr. Lowe was the assistant to Senator Matthews. Although she rarely saw the senator, she learned from the gossip in the office within a week's time that the senator was very married. Regardless, she was beginning to learn more about politics than she ever imagined. Scheduling the senator's appointments and keeping track of his hectic schedule intrigued her. Learning firsthand about the latest bills that were currently on the table in the legislature sounded better than the juiciest romance novel. Still, she enjoyed the quiet times when Holly came home on the weekends. They discussed the last game of the season to Auburn and the mistakes that were made. Next year, UT would bring home the trophy, Holly promised.

All Anne wanted was to see her daughter on a regular basis. The competition for a bigger trophy never mattered. Unlike Anne, Holly had a hoard of friends. Of them, three were special; there was Ericka, her friend back in Memphis, who followed Holly to UT, and up until age fifteen, wore Holly's shoes that were two sizes larger than her own. Then there was Quinn, nearly six feet tall, on the volleyball team with Holly, who told nonstop jokes. Finally there was Sela. Sela reminded Anne a little bit of herself; she was always talking about civil rights issues, worked on the school newspaper, was the captain of the debate team, and planned on joining the Peace Corps after she finished college.

Every Saturday they went to the movies, and usually stopped by the Opry Mills Mall to shop. Occasionally, Holly had a date on Saturday evenings. On Sunday, they worked puzzles and cooked dinner together afterward.

When Holly left on Sunday evening, it was hard for Anne to get used to being alone again. Turning on her old Marvin Gaye CD, she went to the spare bedroom closet and removed from the top shelf her latest set of impressionist puzzles by Max Lieberman. Known for his use of subjects drawn from the simple life, Max was one of Anne's favorite artists. She'd recently completed the *Orphanage at Amsterdam* labyrinth.

Less than twenty minutes into the brainteaser, her hands began trembling. She ignored it at first, but the problem continued. Chastising herself for not following up on her initial visit with Dr. Iverson, she made a mental note to call his office in the morning. Taking a shower and getting into bed, she noticed a slight rigidity settling in on her left side. It was the second time this month that she'd felt this acute change.

The following morning she got to work early and telephoned her doctor. Luckily, they'd had a cancellation today. The receptionist asked Anne if she could come in that afternoon.

"Would noon be okay? I've just started a new job."

"Certainly. But please be on time, Mrs. Russell. Otherwise, I can't guarantee that you'll be out of here in an hour."

The wind was knocked out of her three hours later.

"Our tests conclude that you're in the first stages of Parkinson's disease," the doctor said a little too morbidly.

"I don't know what that is, Doctor." She felt relieved. At least it wasn't a stroke. "I was really worried, though—"

"Mrs. Russell. This is very serious. Are you aware of the long-term effects of Parkinson's?"

She smiled briefly. "No. But it's only a disease. And most diseases are curable, aren't they?"

"Not this one."

Her heart felt as if it had been trampled on. What in the hell was he talking about? "Dr. Iverson—"

"Let me explain, Ms. Russell. Maybe then you'll get an understanding about what we're dealing with."

What we? You mean me. What *I'm* dealing with.

For the next forty minutes Dr. Iverson described the symptoms, prognosis, and research that was currently being conducted on this crippling disease. He told her that this disease was rare in people her age. It had affected people like Billy Graham, Muhammad Ali, and Attorney General Janet Reno. Parkinson's was a degenerative illness, in which the death of certain brain cells caused a progressive loss of muscle control, leading eventually to paralysis and death. The symptoms included poor coordination, disequilibrium in balance, visual-spatial impairments, the loss of the ability to do familiar and purposeful movements, limb dystonia (abnormal muscle postures), hesitant and halting speech, and difficulty swallowing.

"I have to be honest, Anne." Finally, he was calling her by her first name. "There's no known remedy for Parkinson's. It's incurable. However, it is highly treatable, even at fairly advanced stages."

"But Dr. Iverson, I'm only forty-two years old. You said that this problem occurred in people around age sixty."

"I did. But there are always rare cases. Patients that don't fit the norm—"

Anne screamed. She clamped her hands over her ears and yelled as loudly as she could. The receptionist came in and the doctor shooed her off.

"Please, feel free to get a second, third, or even fourth opinion, Anne." He handed her a tissue, and came around to hold her hands. "When you get the results, please come back to see me. I'll try to help you as much as I can."

"Isn't there any type of medication?"

"Several drugs are available." Anne cringed at the thought of drugs. She'd barely taken a half dozen drinks in her life, let alone drugs. And now she needed some type of dope to help her live. "Levodopa was approved by the FDA—"

"And what will that do, Doctor?"

"This drug can mask the symptoms for five years or more by boosting production of dopamine. Side effects worsen with prolonged use."

"My God!"

"There is also a drug called pramipexole. This drug helps a patient's ability to dress themselves. Patients have also noticed improvement in their motor skills. Pramipexole works especially well in African Americans."

Well thank God for my black blood.

Anne thought back about Scott's desire to dress her. What a hoot. Was he laughing at her in hell? What had she done to deserve this?

Death, Dr. Iverson said, usually occurs within six to ten years. Death and blackness was all that Anne could think about as she returned back to work—death, when death was like sleep and sleep, everyone knew, shuts down our lids.

Would she open them one morning and find herself in another place?

In six to ten years, Holly could possibly be married. And Basil, would he and Bette have children in that time frame? Would she live to see any of her grandchildren call her name? Would she be married again by then? Would she ever see Niagara Falls?—a place that she always dreamed of going to. What about life insurance? Did she need any more? Would they refuse to increase it? Make her take a physical and raise her rates to exorbitant prices? Or would she resort to lying and then believe the lies herself?

A zillion thoughts penetrated her mind. Nothing mattered now except her family. And she wondered what would become of them. Kirk was roaming the country trying to find himself. Mae was living like a recluse, thinking mostly about herself. Wesley was halfway around the world, in search of normalcy. Basil would sacrifice his soul to become rich. And Holly . . . Holly was so innocent and trusting, she was destined to get her heart broken. How could her family exist without her?

Riding the elevator down to the main floor, she studied the men and women standing beside her. All of them appeared to be ordinary human beings like her.

Closing her eyes, she imagined that if God put everyone in a room separately, by themselves, where they could speak the absolute truth about themselves, people might realize how common everyone's needs were. That disappointment, hunger, love, and hatred were the same, universally, wherever we find them.

But dying—that was the one thing that a person did all alone.

As she exited the elevator, she remembered her dream last night.

Scott had scowled at her from the edge of their bed, while tapping a belt against his knee. Bentley had come up behind her as if she were going to choke her, but instead, removed a pocketknife from her purse and started stabbing Anne in her shoulders, arms, and heart. Pain shot to her brain. She opened her mouth to scream, but no sound came out. Her legs gave way and she barely felt herself fall to the floor. Scott came toward her, hunched over, and on bended knee, began beating her with the belt. His hard thrusts caused welts, and they bled quickly. Soon her body was covered with streams of deep blue blood. Closing her eyes, she gave in to the pain and her body began to cool. For a split second she wondered, was this the moment after her death?

She had awakened, trembling—cold as the ocean floor, but sweating and crying large tears. Getting her bearings, she panned her bedroom, trying to focus on objects near and dear to her. Silver-framed pictures of Holly and Basil on the nightstand beside her had appeared as ethereal as a cloud of smoke.

The elevator door opened and she walked out into the cold parking lot garage. For a second she forgot where she parked.

"Oh yeah, it's next to a black Chrysler minivan," she said to herself, remembering.

Once outside the parking lot, dried leaves from the past season curled and blew across the hood of her car. The ripe smell of fresh mulch that covered the base of the evergreens for spring planting filled the air. Peeking beneath a mound of dry leaves, she could see the shoes of a man, then the outline of the rest of his body. How long had he been lying there? She wondered.

That night while she lay in bed, the triumphs and tragedies that she'd begun to manufacture for herself wouldn't allow her to get any sleep. It seemed as if each impatient hour marched by with clocks without hands.

Early one Saturday afternoon, Anne decided that she wouldn't spend another second feeling sorry for herself. Dusty had given her the location of his store on Second Avenue, but she'd been walking for blocks and still hadn't spotted it. Stopping at the next corner, she asked an elderly gentleman if he knew where the novelty store was. Four doors down, right next to the Salvation Army, hung the neon sign of Dusty's Novelty Shop.

At ten-thirty in the morning, the store was crowded. It took awhile for her to finally spot Dusty. She hadn't seen him in over a year, but from where she stood he looked the same.

At forty-four, Dusty was in exceptional shape. Tall, dark-skinned, and dark-eyed, he stood out in the crowd. His hair was cut short with a neat part on the side. A simple attire of khakis and polo shirt, unbuttoned, perhaps to expose the ruffles of black hair on his broad chest, fit as if on a store mannequin.

He had greeted Anne with colorful modulations of a voice trained to charm. His perfect hands were long-fingered, deft.

No matter what their age, Dusty nodded respectfully at each patron who frequented his store.

Anne watched as Dusty stocked the books and magazines as carefully as if he were handling Venetian lace. He took money as if it were a bouquet of baby's breath, and returned change as if it were a glass of cristal.

Anne later learned that for her he held a special smile. The rhythm of the friendly faces at his store drew her back again and again, even when she didn't need to purchase more puzzles.

On one occasion, when they were in the store alone, Dusty told her one of his most guarded secrets—that he was a kid at heart, and had played every game that he stocked.

Customers periodically interrupted their discussion, which lasted for several minutes. That day, Anne left without making a purchase, but had the time and place of her first date—eight o'clock Saturday night.

Anne had second thoughts up until it was time for her to meet Dusty at his store. Their first outing consisted of going to an arcade and playing Tekken Tag. They drank sodas and ate popcorn until Anne felt nauseated.

"Are you ready to go, Anne?" Dusty asked, studying her face intently. "You don't look so well."

Trying to camouflage her illness was becoming an art form. "Honey, hush. Are you kidding?" Anne said in a teasing tone. She stood up straight as a spear to look like she was still alive and kicking. "I've still got a pocketful of quarters left," she teased. Dusty was ahead three games to her two.

"Yeah. And my name is on every one of them." Anne watched Dusty reach inside his pockets for more cash. "I'm not leaving until I've won all of your money. And it looks like I won't be here long."

Anne smiled as he elbowed her in the side. "Didn't you know that I was just toying with you, girl? Since you're getting so cocky—no more freebies for you. Now watch this!"

Dusty beat her so badly, he teased her all the way home. That night was the first time he kissed her on the mouth. Previously he'd kissed her on the forehead or the cheek, and once even touching the corner of her mouth, but this time . . . he kissed her.

It was a kiss unlike any she had felt before. It was as if the sun had orbited the moon, and the stars came down from the sky and melted, making a river of silver milk. With his right hand curved around her waist, he pulled her closer to him. First his forehead, then his nose, touched hers. "Anne," he whispered. He urged her chin upward and she felt his soft lips briefly touch hers once more and then pull back. He took a breath and slowly placed his lips against hers. His left arm curved around her shoulder, pulling her even closer in to him. Anne felt her body arching up to his when she felt the tender penetration of his tongue inside her mouth. Ever so gently he grazed the moist lining, taking the time, she felt, to read her body language, before continuing.

There was a full moon out that gave his face an ethereal glowing silver tint. The breathless sky hung with humid summer heat.

Anne responded in ways that shocked her. Her hips pressed against his, and for a brief moment she wasn't ashamed of her boldness, especially when she felt him push ever so subtly back against her.

Kissing was the closet thing to screwing, her brother constantly said, and Anne felt herself pulling back. "Mmmn, Dusty. I've had a wonderful time tonight."

"Anne . . ."

She removed the keys from her purse, fumbling with her house key. "Don't, Dusty. I'm not ready for that kind of commitment yet."

His tender eyes said that he understood. "So, I'll call you tomorrow?"

"I look forward to it."

She was inside now, and could finally breathe. But what a feeling. She wanted to share it with Holly. But looking at the clock and realizing the late hour, she decided to postpone it until tomorrow.

Surely, there was still time for tomorrow.

STEPPARENT ADOPTIONS weren't as uncommon as they used to be, Steve Mitchell, Erik and Isabell Berry's attorney, had told them months earlier.

"You don't even need a signature if the state has terminated the birth mother's parental rights."

The state of Tennessee declared that if a woman couldn't take care of her child in three years, it would terminate their parental rights. With Isabell's insistence, social services had been notified when Bentley had her breakdown. The social worker had told the Berrys that they had apprised Ms. Russell that she was in jeopardy of neglecting her child by not abiding by the visitation laws.

It didn't matter that Bentley didn't understand a word that she'd said—she was told.

Immediately afterward, Isabell petitioned the probate court for a stepparent adoption. It had taken nearly six months for the waiting period to expire and to finally get legal custody of Reo.

Reo's name was changed to Reo René Berry, instead of Reo René Russell.

Erik had gone along with the entire ordeal up until the day of the court hearing. He remained silent most of the time and didn't voice his discontent. It merely showed in his face.

But what could he do? Reo cared for Isabell. She'd been calling her Mother for over two years now. Maybe he was worried about his marriage, and how the loss of two mothers would affect his daughter.

He needn't worry, Isabell thought. He was one of the four vice presidents at the *Hamilton Appeal;* with his wife's continued support, he'd be made president in a few short years. Then she would make her move, and only *then* would he have to worry about being the ex–Mrs. Ford.

And her dear Basil, he was still serving his purpose. They didn't see each other as often—Basil's gambling habit was beginning to compete with his need for her erotic sex games. Her latest folly was a challenge for her boy toy. A man called Theophrastus had seventy orgasms in twenty-four hours and had set a record in 1910. This would be done with the aid of a dozen young women. Basil fantasized about breaking the record. And she planned on keeping him thinking that way. His Children's Castle Day Care Centers would be key in the implementation of her future plans.

BASIL TOOK THE MATCHES out of his back pocket and began to dig in his other for his Newports. The feel of a gun barrel nuzzled him in his back. The matches in his hand fell to the floor.

"No more stalling, Basil. The boss said to take you out if you don't have his money."

Basil got down on his knees. "Please, Samson. You know me. I've always paid in the past."

"Doesn't matter. Fifty Gs ain't food stamps." Samson nudged his back with the pistol again.

"Please," Basil begged once more, "I can have the money tonight. My mother's got the money in trust. I have hundreds of thousands of dollars. But she has to contact the attorney to draw up the paperwork." He was feeling more confident now and got up off of his knees. He knew if he told the guy he was worth millions, he'd never see daylight again. "Look, I'll cut you in for another ten percent if you give me until Saturday night."

"Uh-huh, Basil. *I* could be dead by then."

Basil scrambled to think. This 300-pound fool was right, he'd be offed if he didn't produce the fifty Gs. Why should he sacrifice his life for him? "Thirty percent, Samson. That's fifteen Gs for me—"

"I can count."

"Give me until eleven o'clock."

Samson hesitated. "You got an insurance policy on your wife?"

"Yeah. But don't go there, bro, I'm gonna take care of you." Basil began to sweat. Over the years, Bette had grown on him. No, he still wasn't deeply in love with her. But she'd become his habit. He could depend on her.

Even in her drunken stupor, she kept the house clean, took care of the books at the Children's Castle, and managed to stay a petite size 6. Her presence was like a model's when they entertained. All he had to do was keep her supplied with Martell and Altoids and she performed like a Stepford wife.

The only thing that Basil hadn't counted on was that Bette was secretly keeping an account of his comings and goings at night.

But his affair with Isabell wasn't his only problem. Over the past twelve months, he'd mortgaged their home to the hilt. There was no other choice but to call his mother—just in case.

Reaching deep in his pockets, he fumbled for his last ten quarters that he'd used to play the slot machine, and deposited eight of them into the pay phone.

"Hey, honey. It's good to hear from you," his mother told him.

"This isn't a pleasure call, Mom. I've got deep troubles." He covered the mouthpiece with his hand so that she couldn't hear the background noise.

"Money problems?"

"How'd you know?"

"What other kinds are there?" she said in a voice that sounded foreign to him. "How can I help you, Basil?"

"Dad's trust."

Anne didn't have to tell Basil that he had another three years before he would be able to draw his money down. Things had to be tight in order for him to ask her for it now.

"How much do you need?"

"A hundred and fifty thousand."

"Whew. That's a hunk. May I ask what the money's for?"

Basil stumbled. Jingling the quarters in and out of his pockets, his small body shook like a crackhead's. "It's sort of personal—I really need it, Mom."

Anne could tell by the way he stuttered his s's, like he did when he was a child, that he was in trouble. "I can get you the money within a week."

"No, Mom. I need it in three days."

"Son—"

"Listen. I didn't want to tell you, but I might as well get it off of my chest. Bette doesn't know that I've mortgaged the house with the casinos. They've got my marker for a hundred thousand. I owe the bookies another fifty grand, plus interest."

"Basil—"

"I already know what you're going to say. Yes, I know I need help. But please don't lecture me now. Mom, these people are going to hurt me if I don't come up with their money."

Anne wanted to tell Basil that his gambling was worse than Bette's alcohol addiction, and worse yet if you could least afford it. The way he and Bette lived, it was no wonder that he didn't have any savings.

Nothing mattered now. Her son was in trouble and the money was just a phone call away.

"I'm sure I can get the money to you in forty-eight hours."

"Thanks."

But Basil underestimated Bette. She was ready for him when he came home.

"It half killed me, but I went along with your whorish ass because I loved you. I did all that I could to be a good wife and keep you happy. Now all that shit is over. I won't be your fool any longer."

"Baby—"

"Fuck you." Bette's suitcase was laid open on the bed and her back was turned to him as she continued to open up her dresser drawers and deposit the items in the luggage. "I know about your bitch. I've always known about her. What I expected was some respect. I couldn't even get that. I tried to be the best wife that I could be. Now, I got bookies calling my home telling me that my husband owes them thousands of dollars." When she turned her head to look back at him, he could see that her right eye was still red from the tears she'd shed before he came home. "They said that I could cut the debt in half if I would fuck June Bug—the head of the mob in Memphis. When I refused, they came over here."

Turning around to face him, she showed Basil her blackened left eye, and the wounds on her chest. "They raped me, Basil!"

"What!"

"They came in here this morning, while you were I don't know the fuck where, and raped me. Three of them."

Basil dropped to his knees.

How had this happened?

Suddenly none of the money mattered. He wanted revenge.

"I'm gone. You can keep the car, the house, the clothes, and the money." She gathered her suitcase together, stuffing the toiletries back inside. "I ain't had a drink all day." She blinked and a pool of tears rained out of her eyes. "All I ever wanted was for you to love and respect me. You never have, Basil. I've been lying to myself for years. But I can't lie no more."

Basil sat on the bed too numb to move. Every word she said was true. He had no idea that one day she would be sober enough to act on her feelings.

Thirty-seven

"YOU'RE NOTHING BUT A CONNIVING BITCH," Basil told Isabell. "You sit here with your sex games and think I'm some kind of fool."

"Basil, don't," she pleaded, reaching out for him.

He slapped her hand away. "Yeah, I heard about it. I got friends in courthouses just like you do. And I don't appreciate being told that some white bitch has gone and adopted my cousin's daughter!"

"You forget. I'm married to her father."

"Yeah, and what the fuck was that fool thinking? That's who I need to talk to. That dumb son of a bitch."

Isabell clutched the sheet around her naked body and headed for the bathroom. Basil stopped her, yanking her arm back hard. "Don't."

He slapped her face with the back of his hand. "I never want to see your ass again."

She ran into the bathroom and locked the door.

"You'll live to regret this, Basil," she yelled.

"Blah, blah, blah. You're nothing but an old white bitch. You think I'm scared of you? I got friends that will off you for the price of a watermelon."

When she heard him pick up his car keys and then slam the motel door shut behind him, she looked into the mirror and smiled.

"You'd better be afraid, Basil. This is only the beginning of your worst nightmare."

* * *

DREAMS—A WORLD OF THE DEAD in the hues of life. Day or night, Anne couldn't make the horrible apparitions stop ruminating in her mind. Each night, she worked on puzzles until her eyelids were so heavy with sleep that she couldn't keep them open another second. She wanted to sleep and not dream. Sometimes it worked, oftentimes it didn't.

At the office, she found herself daydreaming about her children's future. What would become of Bette, of whom she'd grown so fond? She was an innocent soul who loved her son without question. The drinking didn't matter. Anne knew that if she delved deeper, she would find a hidden sorrow in her past that led her to find solace in the addictive fluid.

But what she truly feared was Bentley's state of mind. Each time she called to check on her, the doctor told her that there had been no change.

Time began to move backward and forward and she couldn't control it. Anne wondered when she would be able to believe in dreams again.

One night she stayed awake all night thinking about her father. She'd always planned on making him proud of her. What could she do with so little time left? It came to her as easily as thank-you.

She remembered hearing from age thirteen to eighteen that her father's death was no accident. She and Kirk were unable to find an attorney to handle a wrongful death suit against the city of Memphis. With little money, they finally dropped the lawsuit. Surviving week to week became their number-one priority.

But now her situation was different. She had money. Though her deceased husband might not have agreed that she'd earned it, Anne felt that she had.

While she worked at the capitol building, she'd heard

about a civil rights coalition, the National Civil Rights Consortium, that had begun in April of this year, 1996. The organization was just two months old and focused on three areas: providing assistance and guidance to individuals and groups in other states who were interested in pursuing antipreference legislation or a ballot initiative in their state; advocating the elimination of racial and gender preferences in federal programs and polices; and providing assistance for low-income citizens of California who were experiencing racial discrimination at their place of employment.

Not sure as to what she planned on doing, Anne looked up the organization first on the Internet. Liking what she read about the group, she then put in a call to the National Civil Rights Consortium in San Fernando Valley, California. Presently, there wasn't an organization in Tennessee—only in Washington, D.C., Florida, and California.

While she spoke with representative Todd Caleb, she was mesmerized by their position on civil rights.

"We take a neoconservative approach to civil rights. We want the civil rights movement to get back to what Dr. King espoused in the sixties—equal treatment and equal protection under the law.

"Civil rights have evolved into a movement that didn't push equal treatment but preferential treatment. The National Civil Rights Consortium, NCRC, is a grassroots organization that is four thousand strong. Our chairman is Grey Dalton and Chris Rhodes is our vice chairman. NCRC has been pretty active these past two months—we opened centers in Florida and Washington, D.C., last month, and we are already being called to set up this type of organization in other states."

"Can I start up an NCRC group in Memphis?" Anne asked.

"Yes. We can always use more contacts. If there is a group of people who want to push for these reforms in the state legislature, city council, courts, and in their community, we're all for it. We represent minorities in all walks of life. All a volunteer needs is a desire to effect change and that all people should be treated equally. Individuals who belong in our organization can't wait for the pendulum to swing the other way. We believe that the time should be now.

"Affirmative action is still necessary in this day, especially in some cases where there is still a pattern of discrimination. We plan on including more individuals who don't fit a profile. We're contacting people in rural areas, white, black or Hispanic who are trapped in run-down schools, who are fighting the blight of crime. We shouldn't limit ourselves or resort to racial stereotypes and take a color-blind approach. By practicing what we preach, we'll make a difference. And unless we take the model approach, we're sending mixed messages to our children."

This man talked so fast, he barely took a breath. Anne learned that the organization was funded by individual grants, donations, and foundations. They received operating grants throughout the year.

Todd also believed that by the next census, in the state of California alone, the minority would probably be a majority.

He told her that in the State of Michigan, two high-profile lawsuits in federal courts were filed by the Washington, D.C.–based organization for individual rights. The case involved the undergraduate and graduate schools at the University of Michigan. U of M directly challenged the use of race as a factor in the admissions process. Through legal means and a footnote by Texas, Louisiana, and Mississippi, they were governed by a 1996 decision called *Hopwood v. Texas,* that was decided by the Fifth Circuit Court of Appeals. That court ruled that race could not be used as a factor in the admissions process—effectively repudiating the landmark 1978 decision known as *Bakke v. University of California Regents.* That case by the U.S. Supreme Court said that race could be one of many factors (the other said that race could never be).

There was a patchwork of legal laws and precedents and different layers of federal and state courts that came up with different rules. Difficult decisions were made all the time, ending preferences once and for all, making it basically inevitable that these cases would be resolved rather quickly.

"The NAACP and NCRC don't see eye to eye on a lot of issues, so we don't have a lot of affiliation with them. However, our chairmen are on good terms with all of the civil rights leaders."

Anne was relieved when she heard Todd say that NCRC hadn't totally severed all ties with the NAACP. She had no intention of discontinuing her membership in what she felt was a historic and worthy organization.

The following week she enrolled in Vanderbilt University Law School, paid the $22,000 tuition, and quit her job. The first semester began on January 6, 1997. If all went as planned, in three years, after hours of reading and memorizing, she'd walk across the stage for the first time in her adult life with a degree of Doctor of Jurisprudence. Specializing in civil rights law would, she felt, help her achieve a singular peace that she hadn't felt since she was a teenager.

The challenge of attaining a second degree helped her

to put her illness in perspective. She had to believe that through hell and high water, she'd live long enough to achieve her goal.

Anne did as Dr. Iverson had suggested; she'd gotten three more opinions. All came to the same conclusion— she had Parkinson's. Their findings varied on how much time she had left. That was good and bad news.

On August 4, a Frenchwoman by the name of Jeanne Calment died at the age of 122. It saddened Anne that the woman lost her life, but it gave Anne hope that maybe she could beat this disease and live a long and prosperous life, too.

Like so many others, Anne mourned the death of Princess Diana. When she was killed on the thirty-first of August, Anne was driving back to Memphis after having spent the afternoon checking on Bentley and Nikkie. She'd been so tired trying to make the three-hour trip up and back in one day, she'd fallen asleep at the wheel, but fortunately was awakened by a truck driver's horn.

In September, news of the saintly Mother Teresa's death saddened Anne. Two of the most important women in the world had lost their lives. What had she done in her lifetime, she wondered, to be remembered with such high regard?

The initial ten years she was given to live, had been whittled down to eight, six, or even five years. And now, with as little anger as she could muster, she vowed to make every day of her life have meaning. Because she knew better than most that our yesterdays follow us; they constitute our life, and they give us character and give force and meaning to our present deeds.

MICHAEL JORDAN SHOCKED AMERICA in January of 1998 by announcing his retirement from the Chicago

Bulls. In the spring the disaster movie *Titanic* won eleven academy awards.

On September 21, 1998, the three-time gold medalist Florence Griffith Joyner died at the age of thirty-eight. The twenty-first was also the day the first videotapes of President Clinton's testimony about his affair with Monica Lewinsky were aired. Twelve days earlier, Mark McGwire of the St. Louis Cardinals hit his sixty-second home run, breaking the record set by Roger Maris of the New York Yankees in 1961.

There seemed to be numerous topics of conversations for Anne and Dusty to discuss this year other than Parkinson's disease, which she still couldn't bring herself to talk about with Dusty.

WITH ANNE BEING CONSUMED with studying, seeing less of her daughter didn't hurt as much as it once did. She still remained friends with her old realtor, Edna, who was helping her with her new hobby, collecting masks.

Anne's family room was decorated with dozens of masks. There were masks that had been worn by bank robbers, mortal men and women who had metamorphosed into gods during religious ceremonies, several hand-carved African masks, a bronze Roman second-century mask, and a simple stone burial mask from c. 100 B.C. from Guerrero that Anne was told covered the face of a ruler or a religious figure. She even had a replica of an A.D. 1200–1519 mosaic-covered human skull that was believed to depict Tezcatlipoca, the Aztec gold god linked to evil.

This latest hobby, besides her inevitable puzzles, helped Anne keep her illness in perspective. So far, her medication was working as well as could be expected. At times she had problems holding her books; when she did, she stopped, took a rest, then tried again thirty minutes later. On other occasions her body would freeze. She would sit there, and talk to herself—literally telling her body that it was now okay for her to move.

Anne was stubborn as well as optimistic. She believed that there might be a breakthrough cure at any time. Regardless of when or how, she had her studies to contend with.

Her worst class was tort law, which everyone in her class, including Anne, hated. Torts were wrongful acts that resulted in injury to another's person, property, or reputation for which the injured party is entitled to seek compensation. One of the hottest cases in the state of Tennessee right now was *Linwood v. Wal-Mart Discount Cities*.

Anne's elective was a legal writing class, which dealt with conducting legal research on a topic and analyzing a specific statute. Having been given a fact pattern to determine what to do in a particular statute and other case laws, it proved to be an exciting challenge for Anne. She looked forward to her legal writing class and excelled in it.

When Anne was in her second year of study, she was disappointed that she hadn't made the dean's list. After receiving a C− on her third exam, she posted her name on the bulletin board for a study buddy. The professor had casually mentioned that most of his students found it helpful if they worked with another student or group to help memorize the endless laws and criminal procedures. It didn't take long to find two other students who were having the same types of problems—Joy Falls and Hilda Ladd.

This year they put on mock trials, taking the position of the judge or defense attorney representing a dog owner who was accused of negligence when a neighbor's child had been bitten. Witnesses would have to be brought in, and Holly and her friends readily agreed.

Children were also brought into their class to be interviewed as well as physicians and scientists. Their professor told them that cross-examining expert witnesses was different from cross-examining everyday people.

At the end of the semester, Anne had to do the full-blown trial herself. It would be considered as the exam. The exam was how well you prepared and delivered the case for that trial.

For her final exam Anne decided that her mock trial would be a wrongful death lawsuit. She brought in two nurses, a surgeon, and a psychiatrist. Having gathered the necessary facts about a young girl who died of an illegal lobotomy recently in Nashville, Anne compiled tons of research on the mental institution as well as the physician who performed the surgery. Confident that she'd done a thorough job defending the deceased, Anne felt that she had an excellent chance for conviction.

Her final grade in this trial was an A–.

She and Dusty celebrated. It was the first time that she admitted to herself how much she'd grown to care about him.

Was she wrong not to tell him the truth about her?

Thirty-eight

BASIL HAD KEPT HIS GAMBLING HABITS to a minimum but managed to win when he did gamble, occasionally bringing home large sums. He'd even begun to pay back some of the money he'd borrowed from his trust fund. But Anne could tell from his calls how much he missed Bette—she'd been gone over a year.

Bette would call on occasion and let him know that she was doing fine. She was working in an undisclosed state at a federal court building as a social worker for abused children. She didn't tell him she'd filed for a divorce until he was served with the papers. It was the first time that Anne had heard real sorrow in her son's voice.

It was then that Basil decided to sell Bette's 750 SL Mercedes. He paid cash for a smaller car, a three-year-old blue Audi, to use as a second vehicle.

Every month or so Anne would see Basil when he came through Nashville to go to the Vols football game at the University of Tennessee in Knoxville. Throughout the months of September, October, and November, there were eleven games a season. Six or seven were home games. No matter how tight Basil's schedule was, he hadn't missed a home game since he moved back home in '94. Going to the games was also a time when Basil, as he told Anne, could check on his sister, who insisted that she wasn't lonely being up there by herself.

With a man like Dusty in her life, Anne didn't have time to think about being lonely. Dusty was either calling her or coming over to her home. She felt like a liar, knowing that their relationship could never go anywhere. But for the life of her, she didn't have the heart to tell him.

Mae was doing better than expected. She'd paid off the mortgage last year and was finally taking driving lessons and planned on buying a car for her forty-eighth birthday in September.

To her delight, Holly had finally found someone special, but wasn't ready to introduce him to Anne just yet.

As the seasons passed, Anne took time off to study by the Cumberland River where she, Holly, and Edna had

had their wonderful holiday cruises. She envied the river for meandering to places that she knew that she would never live to see.

Since early summer her most discomforting symptom was a twitch in her left pinkie. But by mid-August, her whole arm was shaking violently. Dr. Iverson changed her medication to Sinemet, an oral medication that combined Levodopa, L-dopa for short, with a buffering agent called carbodopa. It steadied her so well, Anne wondered if she had imagined the latest symptom. The side effects were agonizing hallucinations. She'd have visions in the night, anything from large animals to dead people. The L-dopa also wore off quickly, causing her to medicate herself more frequently.

She'd learned the hard way that sometimes the side effects could be worse than the disease itself.

Last month Anne had experienced her first fall, two blocks from Dusty's store. He'd taken her to the hospital and helped her back home. A week later, she fell and re-broke her nose. Just yesterday, she fell flat on her face on the kitchen floor, and this time was too embarrassed to go to the emergency room.

While she was in class, and working diligently at her studies, most of the time she didn't notice when her head and body would shake, but others staring at her made her make adjustments. Trying not to feel sorry for herself was a daily struggle.

One day, when Anne was having another humbling experience, Holly decided to drop by. While she was cramming for final exams, she and Holly hadn't seen one another in over a month.

"Hey, Mom," Holly yelled out. She had let herself into the house and upon hearing the running water in the kitchen headed in that direction.

Anne was in the kitchen brewing a cup of Earl Grey tea. They hugged, and Anne immediately noticed the fullness in her daughter's middle section.

Stepping back she asked, "Are you overweight or pregnant?"

"I'm pregnant, Mom." Anne followed her daughter back into the foyer and watched as she waved to the man sitting out in the car to come in. "And what's wrong with your nose?"

"Nothing," Anne said defensively. "Holly . . ."

"Don't worry, Mom. I'll explain everything in a minute."

Anne watched the unmistakable expression of love beaming across her daughter's face as the man came toward them. She knew immediately that her dreams of having a big wedding for her daughter wouldn't happen in this lifetime.

"Hi," he said, standing just outside the doorway.

"Mom, this is Daniel Hamilton. My husband."

"So . . . you're a Hamilton, too."

"Don't worry, Mom," Holly said under her breath, "he's not related to Dad's family."

"Hello, Mrs. Hamilton—everyone calls me Dan."

"Hi, Dan," she said, extending her hand, "And I'm Anne. Come on inside. We've got a lot to catch up on."

Dan was an inch or so shorter than Holly. He was stout with a thick goatee and possibly ten years older than Holly, but attractive in a Morgan Freeman kind of way.

During their weekend stay, Anne got to know her son-in-law well. Dan reminded Anne of her father. He was quiet, but Anne could sense an inner strength about him. From the way he doted on his wife, Anne could also tell that he truly cared about Holly.

Dan was an adopted child, and had severed ties with

his adopted family after learning that they'd lied about adopting him. He blamed them in part, and himself also, for not reading the signs about being adopted. Like most adopted children, he didn't look anything like his parents, aunts, uncles, or cousins. His male cousins always seemed to be whispering or snickering something behind his back. By the time he got his driver's license he knew why.

"I've been searching for my birth mother since I turned twenty and could afford to pay for an investigator myself."

Anne didn't pity her son-in-law as he told her of the unsuccessful turn of events over the years that he'd experienced while trying to find his mother—she admired and respected him.

Her son-in-law had an easygoing disposition and was very easy to talk to. Her mind raced ahead to when she would introduce him to Dusty. She was certain that they'd hit it off great.

Seated at the game table in the family room, they continued to get to know each other while working on a 2,000-piece puzzle.

While Holly studied the unfolding scene, Dan told Anne about his career as a computer consultant. Five years ago, he and a partner opened a firm—a year later they came to a crossroads about future growth. Subsequently, Dan bought him out. Now he owned four stores in Knoxville. But his initial investment in Microsoft stock was where he had earned most of his money. He told her that he was teased while in college about having long pockets and short arms. When Holly left the table to make iced tea, he whispered to her how much he had invested. Anne was blown away.

"Good grief, Dan, that's unbelievable."

"No. It's part luck and part of the Lord's plan. In his heart, a man plans his course, but the Lord determines his steps. Holly and I plan to have three more children. Just in case they don't receive scholarships, I'll need this money to pay for their education. I'd love for each of them to go on to get their doctorate degree."

Her instincts told her that Daniel's endearing spiel wasn't just a choirboy act. In Anne's opinion, it appeared that Holly had lucked out the first time around with a good man who cared about her and was also religious.

Anne had thought about introducing Holly to Dusty on their next visit. She and he had grown so close over a short period of time it alarmed her. Still, they hadn't gone beyond the kissing stage and she assumed that he was waiting for her signal—one that, she felt, to be honest, might not ever come.

Holly came back from the kitchen beaming. The baby was kicking, stretching out his foot, and Holly wanted her mom to see.

"Look at him, Mom. He's showing off today."

Dan rushed to her side and removed the tray of drinks and set them down on the table.

"I hope it's a girl," Anne said, accepting a drink from Dan. She thought about Holly's old dollhouse, still packed away in her house in Memphis, which she would love to pass on to her granddaughter.

"Me, too," Dan agreed. He clicked glasses with Anne while Holly took a seat on the sofa.

"No. I want a boy. A Dan junior. I don't care how old-fashioned juniors are," Holly said, moving to sit beside her husband.

Anne didn't notice that her shoulder and head had begun to shake.

"Mrs.—Anne," Dan asked, "is something wrong?" His eyes rested on her shoulder.

Turning away from Holly's accusing eyes made her blush with guilt. Automatically, her hand flew to her head. She could feel her pinkie finger starting to twitch and hurriedly balled her hand into a tight fist. "My goodness, no." She stood up quickly, trying not to look as nervous as she felt. "Will you two excuse me for a moment?"

Hurrying to the bathroom, she ingested 4.5 milligrams of pramipexole, and put a thin coat of makeup on her sweaty face. It finally dawned on her that she'd been so comfortable chatting with her new son-in-law that she'd forgotten to take her second dose of medication today. Bracing herself on the edge of the sink, she closed her eyes, willing the tremors to get under control.

Telling Holly about her disease would be a mistake, Anne thought. Seeing her daughter so radiantly happy made her heart swell with pride. She hoped that God would be merciful so that she could be healthy enough to witness the birth of her first grandchild.

Thirty-nine

BENTLEY HAD NO KNOWLEDGE of how much time had passed. She came to realize by listening to those around her that she was at Western Mental Health Hospital in Bolivar, Tennessee.

I'm not in heaven. I'm in a mental hospital.

She also had a vague understanding that the center was run with the help of the social services and adjunct therapists. She'd received clothing, meals, and had had several sessions with a doctor whose name she kept forgetting.

Initially, they'd put her on twenty milligrams of Prozac twice a day, two milligrams of Risperdal at bedtime along with two capsules of B-dryl.

Bentley was so doped up, she couldn't remember if she wanted to die or fight to live. The daily struggle weakened her.

Time crystallized. Each moment, as it passed, was like the meeting place of two eternities. And what Bentley valued next to eternity was time—the time to heal—the time to pray.

As the days ticked by, Bentley was beginning to write her name, remembering bits and pieces of her past. No one seemed to notice. It became increasingly obvious to her that the hospital's primary motivation was to keep their patients busy from six in the morning until six at night and out of danger of harming themselves.

She was just beginning to memorize the routine: breakfast at 6:45 A.M., lunch at 11:45 A.M., and dinner at 4:45 P.M. At 8:30 in the morning the women in her unit, which was long-term, would have group therapy. Afterwards, the nurse would educate the women on personal hygiene and check to see if they'd cleaned themselves correctly. This was particularly hard for Bentley.

Afterward, they could play bingo, watch television, play volleyball or basketball, or even swim. Once a week they had a field trip, usually into town. And one evening a week a dance would be held and supervised by all the staff. This was when the women could mingle with the men.

Unless you were sick, a patient wasn't allowed to go back into their room until after dinner. But they did allow a short nap after lunch, if the patient felt they needed one.

Usually Bentley would watch television in the recreation center. No one bothered her. At times, periods of lucidity would occur and Bentley would try to communicate with a nurse.

"Help me. My baby." She stopped short, then added, "She needs help." Bentley didn't realize that she was crying uncontrollably.

But it was the looks from the nurses that hurt worse—that sympathetic blank stare. Or a thinly disguised blank stare that said, "She's hallucinating."

When she met with her doctor at their monthly meeting, Bentley told him that the Prozac wasn't working. She felt terrible periods of anxiety and felt even more depressed. She told him that she was constantly constipated, her breasts were leaking milk, and her memory loss was erratic. And even though they hadn't shared the numbers with her, she was experiencing dizzy spells and believed that her blood pressure was high again. Regardless, no one would listen to her. Without totally comprehending why, she retreated into a shell, suffering in silence, telling herself that she couldn't trust anybody.

The medication remained the same until Bentley was able to say complete sentences. She would ask about her baby. Most of the time she couldn't remember her name. She would just say, "baby."

The tension she felt trying to figure out how to leave the hospital and retrieve her child was overwhelming. During those moments her head began to itch and burn. The only relief she felt was when she began tugging at, then pulling out, the hairs, one by one. The gratification that she felt at that senseless act was indescribable.

Daily, she fought the nurses who drugged her—electing to be alone and do the one thing that gave her satisfaction.

She had visions of Reo calling out to her, hurt. Underscored were Nikkie's cries to make Reo stop crying. Bentley couldn't stand the pressure of trying to please them both. She screamed when the pain became too great.

Another shot. Another dose of Prozac was the answer.

She couldn't be sure how long she'd been walking around like a half-crazed zombie. All she knew was that most of the pain in her head left once she received medication.

On one occasion Bentley blacked out. When she woke up her wrists were bandaged. She was told that she had cut her wrists with a piece of glass. At that point she vaguely remembered hearing the doctor mention Anne's name. But by then half of her hair was gone.

A few days later she remembered hearing a different voice.

"Hello, Bentley. I'm Dr. Waters. I've been reviewing your case and—"

"My baby—"

"I know," the doctor said. "You've got a daughter named Reo. I'm here to help you get your health back on track so that you can see your daughter again."

Bentley broke down crying. Though these people thought they were helping her, they really weren't. How could she make them understand?

"We've got a slight problem, Bentley. You've managed to hide an impulse control disorder—"

"What?" But Bentley knew immediately what he was referring to.

Dr. Waters walked around his desk and removed the bobby pins from her bun, then handed her a small mirror from his desk drawer.

Too embarrassed to look, Bentley clamped the mirror shut and handed it back to him. "I don't mean to do it." She began repinning her hair, and avoiding the doctor's eyes.

"I know. I've treated very few patients who have trichotillomania. But I do know that people with your condition can't resist the temptation to harm themselves and feel a relief or release of tension afterward."

"Yeah—after, Dr. Waters," she said, trying to smile. "I feel a certain degree of satisfaction, unlike anything that I've ever felt before."

"To a degree I understand what you're saying . . . how you're feeling. But this has to stop. There are several approaches that we can take. We'll discuss treatment at the next session."

"Whatever you say, Doctor." Bentley didn't realize that her hand had automatically gone up to her hair. "Yet, I'm afraid. What if I can't stop?" Immediately, she clasped her bottom lip, massaging it with her tongue.

Dr. Waters carefully removed Bentley's hand. "We'll take it one step at a time. It won't be easy, Bentley. But I believe I can help you."

The next day Bentley's medication was changed from Prozac to 100 milligrams of Zoloft during the day and ten milligrams of Zyprexa at night. She was also allowed to move from the dorm, where there were four beds, to a semiprivate room with two beds.

Presently, she had the room all to herself and she relished the privacy. In less than two weeks, Bentley felt a slight change. And for the first time that she could remember, she managed to read the entire newspaper.

Forty

ON DECEMBER 31, ninety minutes before midnight, Holly Hamilton went into labor. Six minutes before her child would have been given dozens of gifts as the first New Year's baby of 1999, Holly delivered her son. Daniel Earl Hamilton Jr. weighed in at eight pounds and nine ounces.

Basil was celebrating the new year alone at home when he received a call from his mother around eleven at night. Without a second thought, he jumped in his Audi and drove the six and a half hours to Knoxville.

In five months Basil would turn twenty-five, and it was hard for him to believe that the one thing that could have made him happy was to have a child of his own—especially a son. In five months he would receive the first payment of $3 million from his trust, minus what he still owed, and the thought of it didn't make him as happy as feeling the joy he felt while looking at his nephew.

"I think he looks like me, Dan," Basil kidded. He and Dan stood outside the glass nursery admiring his new-born baby. One of the nurses had thoughtfully pushed the waist-high Plexiglas cart up so close to the window that Basil could see the blue veins in his tiny hands.

"I don't want to hurt your feelings, but he's Holly all over. Look at that sharp nose and wide, round face. He's even got red hair like hers! And his hands—"

"Damn, Dan," Basil said fondly, "you've checked out every inch of this kid."

"Hey, I'm proud of him. I wanted a girl all along—

one that resembled Holly or even your mother. But now, standing here looking at my son who looks exactly like the woman I love, I couldn't have been more blessed. God is good, man."

His mother had been in the room with Holly the entire time and Basil had seen her for only a brief moment before he left to go back home to Memphis. It hurt him that he and Bette could have had two children by now. After eighteen months, he still had no idea where she was. They were legally divorced nearly a year ago. Since she left, he'd had numerous affairs and had even thought he cared about one woman until he accidentally found out she was addicted to cocaine.

As he drove home, he was infused with the need to gamble—to experience that indescribable feeling of winning. Without any sleep, Basil drove straight through to Robertsville. It was New Year's Day and even though there was very little traffic, the casino was packed.

He drank very little while he gambled, electing to keep his mind focused on what he was doing. All the free liquor that the casino offered, in his opinion, was there for the fools who didn't care about losing their money.

During the ten hours Basil was at Sam's Town, he won five grand. Each night of that first week in January he took the seventy-minute drive back down to the casino. By week's end, Basil was broke and the mortgage company gave him thirty days to catch up with his house notes; otherwise the property would be foreclosed.

His initial partner, David, had done well since they opened the centers, but Basil had heard through the grapevine that David was heavily into drugs. His runners told him that David's habit of heroin exceeded a thousand dollars a day. Basil calculated David's and his wife's salary—nearly $375,000 annually. But he reasoned that regardless of what they were able to steal from their day care's food program, there was no way he could get that type of cash unless he was dealing.

Besides the drugs, David's centers, Hungry Minds Learning Academy, were also in trouble. Two children had died within two weeks of one another after being left in the center's van. The deaths had been reported all over the nation. Because of the inexcusable negligence of the alleged crime by the day care workers, the state had threatened to take David's license.

David was unfazed when they met at The Blues City Café the following week. Both knew what each other's reasons for coming were. Within five minutes of their meeting, David had confided in Basil about the counterfeit money scheme that was being put together and that promised to be a huge moneymaker.

After placing their order with the waitress, they got down to business.

"Holy shit!" Basil whispered loudly. "Can I get in on it?"

"You got any cash?"

"Maybe a few thousand?"

"Be specific."

"Fifteen hundred," Basil said weakly. He knew nothing about this type of business, but didn't want to miss an opportunity to make a quick buck. "I can get my hands on another ten grand in a week."

"Better make it twenty, Basil. Otherwise, we can't deal." David reached inside his pocket, pulling out a toothpick and inserting it in the side of his mouth. "Man, I got a computer wizard working for me that's awesome."

"Wow, man, I imagined a laser-type printer of some sort."

David removed his billfold and handed Basil a fake hundred-dollar bill and a real one.

"Can you tell which one is real?" David asked, then inserted the toothpick between the large gap in his bottom front teeth.

The waitress served their order in piping hot miniature black cast-iron skillets.

The barbecued shrimp diverted Basil's attention for a split second. Shit, he missed Bette's cooking. Most of the time he was in too much of a hurry to stop and get decent food like the dish that was placed before him now.

Basil took a quick bite, wiped his hands, and studied the two bills front and back. "This one's fake," Basil stated matter-of-factly.

"You're absolutely correct," David said.

Basil frowned. How in the world were they going to make money if he could pick out the fake one so easily?

He almost didn't see it when David placed another hundred next to the two already on the table. "What you saw was last year's model. Now that we've got new computers, we've developed nearly a perfect match that's virtually impossible to detect."

After mixing up all three bills, David laid them back down. This time Basil picked the wrong one.

"*Damn,*" Basil said in a near whisper, "I think you've got something all right."

By the time they finished lunch, David outlined how much they could make each month. It was a great proposition, but what Basil didn't like was the fact that he had to set up part of the organization inside one of his centers.

Which one? Bette would've known.

David outlined how the process was set up at one of his day care centers. The code words to his main man were "baking the bread."

Besides printing the money, Basil would be responsible for exchanging the fake cash into real money to bookies who would call on him every week. Typically the counterfeit money was bought from anywhere from 20 to 50 percent of face value.

A few weeks later, Basil had the hook up. He wheeled and dealed the money like a consummate professional. The money was coming in on a regular basis, nearly $12,000 a month. And during that time Basil's gambling habit had escalated along with it. During this short period, Basil made sure that he was stone cold sober, but felt drunk on the music of his own mission to be a financial success. In what seemed like a couple of heartbeats, Basil hit a streak of bad luck and found himself back in trouble—he was being squeezed by the casino's collection department. He owed them $65,000.

In less than two weeks, Basil dropped eighteen pounds. He didn't know where to turn. Gambling was more than a deception now. Keeping the bookies at bay with the counterfeit money stimulated him. He had to be very careful not to give them all counterfeit cash. The fifty-fifty split seemed to be working okay.

They could wait another week, he told himself.

On the opposite side of town another person couldn't wait to continue her vow of vengeance.

Isabell Ford Berry and her husband, Erik, sat in a closed hearing with Circuit Court Judge Hubert O'Donnell.

They'd filed a lawsuit in June against Hamilton's Children and Family Services, contending that they were subject to the Tennessee Open Records Act.

Isabell spoke first. "The *Hamilton Appeal* is seeking access to financial records of the past fiscal year detailing how Hamilton's Children and Family Services spent the millions of dollars they received from the state.

"I believe that those records, because it's nonprofit, are state property and should be open for public inspection."

Isabell smiled a smug smile. She watched Erik fidgeting in his seat, obviously uncomfortable about being there.

Besides the *Hamilton Appeal,* a civil suit had been filed by some competing day care centers accusing Hamilton's of racketeering and conspiring with state Senator Orin Matthews and others to steer taxpayer-sponsored children to favored centers.

Isabell also knew that a grand jury had been investigating subsidized day care in Memphis since last fall. Federal prosecutors had served the Department of Human Services with at least two subpoenas seeking details on broker contracts and day care centers linked to Hamilton's Children and Family Services employees and officials.

But Isabell's threat that she'd made to Basil wouldn't come quite so easily. At least not right now.

Judge O'Donnell told them that he would delay enforcement of his order to give Hamilton's a chance to appeal.

On the five o'clock news, Isabell watched as Basil, standing outside his brokerage firm along with his attorney, Sam Mitchell, said to the reporters:

"We are confident that we can make a great case in the Court of Appeals. What has been lost in the shuffle is that Hamilton's Children and Family Services provides good customer service. They are doing an excellent job under their contract. And I want to make sure that that message gets out."

"Bullshit." Isabell smirked. "Just you wait, Basil Hamilton. I've got some dirt on you and your pal that you'll never be able to wash off."

Forty-one

GOD PLANTS FEAR IN THE SOUL as truly as he plants hope or courage. It is a kind of bell or gong, which rings the mind into quick life and avoidance on the approach of danger—it is the soul's signal for rallying.

Realization of all the time that had passed scared the shit out of Bentley. She couldn't fathom how other people had gone on with their lives and hers stood still.

At night, alone in her room, she would pace the floor, trying to figure how she'd gotten herself into this predicament. Back and forth she would walk and think, until the evening nurse gave her a Valium to calm her down. Her anxiety and fears might seem irrational to others, but to her they felt real. Being locked up in this place made her feel claustrophobic. Panicky. When the dam of anxiety finally broke, she cried and cried until she had nothing left.

She didn't want to be in this stupid hospital, listening to doctors tell her that she'd been a really sick young woman. She knew that already. What she needed was her child. To be around Nikkie and Anne and all the other things that she was beginning to miss so much.

The following morning a new psychiatrist came to see her. She told Bentley that she would be her doctor until she was well enough to go home. After all this time with the other doctor, it offended her that she would have to share her most intimate thoughts with a stranger again. Bentley struggled to be polite, but cried her way through most of the session.

That went on for weeks until the doctor finally had had it with her.

"Self-pity never cured anyone," Dr. Madsen began.

"I'm sorry. I just can't seem to get it together."

Dr. Madsen leaned back in her chair and flipped through the pages of her chart. "You've been here a very long time, Ms. Russell. I think it's time that you worked with us so that we can help you get back home to your family."

"But, I am trying—"

"No. You're not. What I'd like you to do is be honest with me. Tell me again what happened the day you got sick."

"But I've told you. I can't remember it very clearly."

"Yes you can. Let's start with the baby screaming. Now take a moment and go back to that night before the fire started."

Her first reaction was to cry. But she'd done that for months now. She felt needy and small, like the dust of the earth. A part of her felt safe with the doctor, but angry at her determination to make Bentley relive that night. Slowly, Bentley closed her eyes and saw Reo's face.

"My baby started crying. No, screaming. I wanted to get up and get her, but I couldn't make myself move. I just sat there. She screamed louder and the longer I sat there, the quieter her screams became. I heard my sister, Nikkie, calling me from her room. I don't know why, but I didn't answer her. I just sat there. For how long I don't know. I was exhausted. Physically and mentally. I couldn't believe how tired I felt. I just wanted to go to sleep and rest. Then I heard someone pounding on the door."

"The fire department?"

"Yes. I think so. I smelled smoke. And then I heard the screaming again." Bentley started hugging herself. Bending over, she pushed her hands up over her ears. "I wanted the screaming to stop." Suddenly Bentley was quiet. The horror of what she meant was written on her face.

"And did the screaming stop, Bentley?"

"Yes. But when it did, I stopped breathing."

Forty-two

IN THE SPRING OF 1999, Holly had completed the requirements of undergraduate study at Tennessee State University. Because she had four more years of school and internship at Knoxville Veterinarian School, she elected not to have a graduation party. Instead, Anne treated her daughter with a two-week trip to Japan along with her husband.

At first, Holly wanted to take the baby with them. Anne insisted that she could care for her four-month-old grandson without any trouble.

When Holly returned from Japan, she had a part-time job waiting for her. She would work as an assistant veterinarian at Berclair Animal Hospital in Franklin, Tennessee—just south of Nashville.

On July 19, news of John F. Kennedy Jr., his wife, and sister-in-law missing, along with their plane, was the topic of conversation.

It seemed that every employee who worked for Basil was talking about the Kennedy curse—all the tragedy that the Kennedy family had been through.

Basil didn't believe in jinxes. If that were true, the Hamiltons had certainly had their fair share of bad luck, as had, remembering his mother's accounts of the woes of her youth, the Russell family.

For that reason, Basil felt that his luck at the casinos had to turn around soon. His losing streak at the craps table couldn't continue too much longer. To his discontent, Basil dug deeper into his pockets, and for two solid months bet heavier than he had since his mother pulled his nuts out of the fire the last time.

When school started in the fall, attendance at the day care centers went way up, and the big money started rolling in again. Hamilton's Children and Family Services were bringing in the largest amount of cash. At this rate it would total over $2 million a year and was also causing Basil the most headaches. Like the other eleven brokers in the state of Tennessee, his firm was also supposed to monitor the attendance at day care centers and supply an accurate head count to ensure that the state didn't overpay for a child's care.

And now, two other brokers were complaining that there was foul play involved when Hamilton's was awarded the contract. Rumor was going around that Senator Matthews, who headed the state Department of Human Services, had ties with Hamilton's brokerage firm.

Though Basil believed that none of this could be proven, he couldn't stop the upcoming audit by the grand jury, nor could he halt the constant lies he was forced to tell his mother about the legitimacy of their business venture.

By month's end, exhausted and nearly broke, Basil decided to stop spending his money in Robertsville and chose instead to gamble only in Tunica. After all, someone from Robertsville had raped his wife. It took one night of losing another three grand to know that Tunica wasn't the answer either. He also realized that he didn't have any other choice; he had to sell the house. It was stupid to hold on to it; Bette wasn't ever coming back. And with the added pressure of the lawsuit from his father's old newspaper, Basil could barely think straight.

Forty-three

SHORTLY AFTER NINE-THIRTY on a particularly pleasant Monday morning, Isabell stopped by a bank that was twenty-eight miles from her home branch. She promptly withdrew a great deal of cash. Next, she drove to another bank in the neighboring city and purchased a cashier's check, then went shopping.

Two weeks later, Isabell waited for Erik to leave for work before she set her plan in motion. She oiled her skin with a special pigment that made her look like a Creole woman. Then she applied heavy makeup and placed a newly purchased curly brunet wig over her black tresses. She wore an inexpensive blouse and skirt from Sears, as well as bargain-basement shoes and purse. Two hours later, she parked her car at the Mall of Memphis and called a taxi to drive her to the Exxon gas station at Park and Poplar where she was due to meet Crocus.

During the thirty-minute drive she thought about her husband. He worked so hard trying to please her.

Once the taxi dropped her off, Isabell scanned the parking lot for the red Lincoln Navigator. When she spotted it, she went directly to the driver's side and knocked on the tinted window. "Crocus?" she asked.

"Yeah. Get in."

Isabell walked around to the passenger side and got in. "Do we have an agreement?"

"Do you have the cash?"

Isabell removed the cashier's check for $25,000 from her purse and handed it to him. "It's the exact amount that we discussed."

"When do you want this done?"

"As soon as possible."

Leaning a bit to his right, he showed her a piece of paper with a name on it. "And you're certain this is the person?"

Isabell nodded yes.

"Then it's done."

"Thank you."

She got out of the truck and went to the pay phone and called a taxi. While she waited, she opened her purse and scratched another name off her list.

The taxi arrived fifteen minutes later. As Isabell rode toward the Mall of Memphis, she didn't notice the red Navigator following her.

After locating her white Mercedes-Benz, she paid the driver, and then got into her car. She was suddenly aware of a new burst of energy. When she started the motor she felt a kinetic sensation travel from her hands to her toes. It was a stimulating feeling to know that money could buy one anything.

But the price, she knew, could rise the next time she called him. Isabell envisioned her victim's pitiful face and smiled. She was certain now that there *wouldn't* be a next time.

Forty-four

BASIL RECEIVED HIS FIRST OFFER for his home nine days later. On day fifteen, after negotiating with their respective realtors, Basil signed a purchase agreement for $212,000 to Mr. and Mrs. Dale Milton—$10,000 less than his asking price.

When the time came for him to pay off his mortgage and the casinos, he'd be lucky to have $8,000 left. Not wanting to move out of the Hickory Hill area, he found an apartment six blocks away.

On a rainy Saturday morning, Basil got up early and began the dreaded task of packing. He planned on doing a room a day, so that by the following Saturday everything would be ready for the moving van.

Starting with the attic, he brought down several boxes that were filled with Bette's and his college textbooks. The boxes had never been unpacked and he immediately stacked them in the garage.

He began to sweat after he'd hauled down the last of nine garment boxes full of old clothes that should have been taken to the Salvation Army. He worked through lunch and planned on having the attic swept out by six. At four he took a rest. Only a pair of discarded lamps and two black plastic bags were left.

He placed the lamps by the curb for anyone who wanted them and headed back upstairs. When he opened the larger bag and looked inside, he noticed Bette's winter coats and jackets that she'd neglected to take when she left. The other bag held her boots in various styles and colors. He was halfway down the steps with a bag in each hand when the telephone rang. By then it was a quarter to five, and his first thought was Bette. It would be just his luck for her to wait until now to say that she wanted to come back home.

He quickly grabbed the telephone and was surprised when he heard his sister's voice on the line.

"Hey Basil, it's me, Holly. Dan and I are a few miles away and we wanted to stop by before we headed back to Knoxville. Are you busy?"

She meant did he have any female company. "No, sis. I'm not doing anything special." He tossed an empty cigarette package in the trash.

After he hung up he picked up the plastic bags that held Bette's things and took them out to the garage. When he heard a car pull up in the driveway, he pushed the remote on the wall.

While Holly unhooked the baby from the car seat, Dan came over and shook his hand the way he always did.

"Good to see you, man."

"Yeah, you too."

"Whew." Dan blew out a breath looking at the stack of taped boxes stacked up against the sidewall. "So I guess you're in the process of moving."

"Yep. I told the new owners I'd be out by next Saturday." The baby wailed and Basil headed for the driveway to help his sister. "Hey there, little fellow," he said, kissing his nephew and grabbing the diaper bag.

"What about me?" Holly said, tapping her cheek. Basil kissed her and followed her and Dan back inside the house.

Basil asked his sister and brother-in-law to forgive his mess in the living room. Large and small empty cardboard boxes filled half of the room.

"Are y'all hungry?" Basil asked.

"No, but the baby is. Dan, hand me Junior's bottle out of the diaper bag, will you?"

"Have you heard from Mom?" Basil asked, removing the roll of bubble wrap off the sofa so that Holly and the baby could sit down.

"Not since Wednesday. She was studying for an exam yesterday." Holly took the bottle from Dan and handed it to Junior's eagerly awaiting hands. "You know, I should call her."

Basil brought Holly the cordless phone, and Dan went to look in the refrigerator. "What do you have cold to drink?"

"Nothing. But you know what, I could use a Bud. How about you?"

Holly rolled her eyes at Dan while she dialed the number, then cautioned her husband, "Remember, you're driving home, honey."

Dan blushed and said, "Just one then, Basil."

"Bud, Busch or Miller's?" Basil asked, as he reached for his car keys on the dining room table.

"Miller's."

He winked at his sister. "I'll be right back."

It was good to see Holly and Dan, Basil thought as he backed his Audi out of the driveway. When they were together, they seemed problem free—how he and Bette were in the beginning. Basil almost missed the turn at the light, there were so many things on his mind.

He thought back to the circumstances of last year. The Lady Luck casino's records showed that he had signed a marker for $25,000 of the $45,000 limit that the casino had afforded him in a twenty-four-hour period. Lady Luck casino had taken him to Shelby County General Sessions Court and obtained a judgment against him in December of 1998.

Basil had appeared and won on April 19, 1999, when Circuit Court Judge Lucius Biltmore ruled that Tennessee courts didn't recognize debts incurred through credit gambling.

Basil had been lucky.

Early in Mississippi's history of regulating the casino and just a year after the first one opened in Tunica County in 1993, District Attorney Abraham Miller of Gulfport asked the Mississippi Attorney General's Office for guidance. Miller asked for an opinion: Could those who didn't pay casino markers be prosecuted under the state's bad-check statute? The answer was a qualified "no."

Allowing Lady Luck to photocopy his National Bank of Commerce Visa card and submitting an unsigned blank check number 1976 drawn on First Tennessee Bank had been indeed lucky for Basil.

Because credit extension is legal in Mississippi, it might appear an unusual argument. And it would be— in a Mississippi courtroom.

But credit gambling wasn't permitted in Tennessee, and judgment was being sought in a Tennessee courtroom. In the future, although it would be more expensive, lawyers will sue in Mississippi and have their judgments registered in Tennessee using the U.S. Constitution's "full faith and credit" clause.

Senator Orin Matthews had kept Basil abreast of the fine line of legalities of lawsuits that the casinos were currently involved in. When the markers were not honored, the creditor casinos had to sue to get their money back.

Again, Basil had been lucky. But the senator had warned him—any more troubles with the casinos and he couldn't guarantee that he would be so fortunate.

When Basil arrived back home, the house looked just as it did before, but Holly's and Dan's blue Audi was missing from the driveway. He guzzled down the last of the Bud he had drunk on the way back home and placed the can back inside the bag.

Basil walked up to the porch steps, a six-pack of beer and a carton of Newports under each arm. He located the right key, and then swung open the door. "I'm ba—" He stopped in midsentence. The baby lay on the floor covered in blood. Basil rubbed his eyes. *Damn, am I that drunk? I must be seeing things.* He opened his eyes and the scene was the same. The screams that now came from the baby's mouth made things more dramatic. Then he saw Holly on her back on the kitchen floor. Her clothes were thick with blood. Her shirt was ripped many times. He could see that she had been stabbed all over her body. Her eyes and mouth were frozen open. Basil couldn't think—he couldn't move—he couldn't cry. What should he do? He shook his head, still unbelieving. He dropped his purchases, and then ran to the middle of the kitchen floor and checked his sister's pulse. Nothing. Next he hurried over to where the baby was and fell to his knees. The baby's screams sounded like an emergency siren as he peeled off his bloody clothes. He went into the living room and laid the baby down on the couch and went to get a towel. Walking through the kitchen he stepped over puddles of blood.

It was like a horror scene in a *Friday the 13th* movie. Browned blood was splashed over the front of the refrigerator. Bloodied handprints were smeared over the countertops. Footprints led up to the phone on the wall where the receiver hung dangling. The sound of the dial tone beeping was annoying. He picked up the phone and slammed it down on the hook. It was obvious that Holly had struggled and fought for her life.

With the baby in tow, who was still hollering as if he

knew exactly what had happened, Basil managed to get the towels from the pantry in the hallway and then hurried back to Holly. Her body lay in the doorway between the family room and kitchen. He bent down and covered her with the towels. When he stood up he felt dizzy. His head was aching and he felt as if he would fall to the ground. It was as if his mind was a carousel going in circles. He knew his sister's death was entirely his fault.

He wished the baby would stop screaming!

"I gotta call! I gotta call someone to help!" But he froze. He couldn't move again. His stomach ached and his legs felt as if they would buckle under him. He began to feel weaker and fell to his knees once more. The house seemed to spin around him. *I gotta get some help. Why am I just sitting here?* He finally dialed 911. When he did, it was the first time that he'd thought about his brother-in-law.

Where was he? Certainly he couldn't have done this!

By the time the police arrived Basil had been over every inch of his home and there was no sign of Dan.

He answered the officer's questions as best he could, and then made the dreaded call to his mother.

"Mom . . ." his voice broke.

"Hello, son."

"Mom—"

"What is it? Tell me what's wrong, Basil!"

Basil broke down crying. Before he managed to say, "She's gone, Mom," tears filled his eyes when he heard her scream.

The following day a picture of Dan ran in the local papers. Anne offered a $50,000 reward to the kidnappers for his safe return.

Three excruciating days passed.

Knowing that his mother was hurting, Basil was too

scared to tell her what he thought had happened. He'd gotten away without paying the gambling debt, but had been too cocky to pay the loan sharks. Basil learned through a contact of David's that the hit men thought that Holly and Dan were Basil and Bette. Basil had always told everyone, especially the people at the centers, that Bette was home recuperating from breast cancer and wouldn't be back to work for some time. Holly and Dan fit the description, especially with the exact car parked in the driveway.

The following evening, when the preparations had been made for Holly's funeral, the police found Dan's handcuffed body in a field in Desoto County, Mississippi. His head was wrapped in duct tape with a plastic bag tied over it.

The closed funeral was a blur. Basil was tempted to smoke some crack, seeing his mother under so much duress.

Although he now felt that his mother blamed him, Basil believed that she wouldn't totally alienate herself from him. He was all that she had left and he knew that she knew that he hadn't caused his sister's and brother-in-law's deaths intentionally.

A month and a half later, the police still hadn't found Holly and Dan's killers.

Basil was brought up on charges for passing counterfeit money the following month—a rap that he wasn't certain he'd win. It didn't matter, though. He'd lost three of the most important elements in his life—the respect of his mother and the loss of his sister and her husband.

He wasn't the least bit surprised when his mother told him of her plans to move back home to Memphis. He didn't agree with her motives. But ever since his father died, when his mother made up her mind to do something, nothing other than God could stop her.

2000

At the River
I Stand

Forty-five

TO ANNE, the meaning of death was as evasive as silence. She hadn't met anyone as of yet who could define it. Physical pain plagued her in a kaleidoscope of symptoms. No amount of medication prescribed by her doctor could suppress the pain.

Nearly every week since Holly's funeral, her friends Quinn, Sela, and Ericka had called to check on Anne. They sent her sweet notes in the mail and truly helped Anne get through some tough moments.

The saving grace for Anne was when Dr. Savage called Anne and told her the good news about Bentley. She was finally making progress. If Anne was agreeable, she could come and see her niece as early as December 15.

Anne immediately called Mae and told her about Bentley's improved condition. They decided that they would visit her together. Anne could only speculate on how long it would be before Nikkie would be allowed to see her sister.

A week before Anne petitioned the court for custody of Daniel, her attorney had apprised her of Holly and Dan's will. Anne learned that both had even drawn up a living will in case they survived an accident or illness and were unable to make cognizant decisions for themselves. Holly's will named Anne as executor of her estate. To her surprise, Dan had written nearly the same exact clause in his will. Little Dan Jr., as well as all of their earthly belongings, would go to Anne Russell Hamilton.

After leaving her attorney's office and hugging her handsome, sleeping grandson, she knew that her love was a selfish one. She decided to try to find her grand-baby's other grandparents as well so that they could share their love with little Dan Jr. also.

From time to time she would forget that Holly was gone—attempting to pick up the phone to dial her number just to see how she was doing, and then, while holding the receiver in her hand, reality sank in—Holly was gone for good. This time she wasn't leaving to go on a vacation in Japan or going on a business trip. No, not this time, Anne thought.

Burying Scott ten years ago had left her numb, and somewhat unemotional because her love for him had died years earlier. During the years of his nonambulatory state, hate had become a very exciting emotion. The hatred she felt for him at times warmed her; at other times she thought that she was going to die from it. She had hated Scott so, the hatred was in the very air she breathed, the food she ate.

After he filed for the divorce, her last words to him were "I despise you so much, I'd kill myself if I could take you down with me."

And her father's death? It still seemed like it happened yesterday and that her daughter had followed in the same breath.

Casualties from the civil rights movement, the Vietnam War, and the Persian Gulf War seemed so distant, yet as symbolic as dying waves where life was small and where death was no longer exquisite. Were their grieving families' hell as unending as she felt hers would be?

And now, just over four weeks later, with the baby at the sitter's house, Anne parked her car, rode the monorail over to Mud Island, and then took a moment of reprieve on the banks of the Mississippi River. She admired the Hernando de Soto Bridge strung like a harp between the two states, Tennessee and Arkansas—the signs hanging over the bridge that said "Arkansas, home of President Bill Clinton"—the riverboats carrying tourists down the river to view all of the beautiful sights of Memphis.

Did they know that the river carried the salt of her bitter tears? Did these laughing, smiling people know that her heart was broken in half? *Which one of you wonders why tears stand in my eyes?*

Anne watched the lights on the riverboat fade into the distant shadows of the water. She picked up her purse from the landing and tossed a quarter over the rail, making a silent wish.

As she traveled back across the river, Anne's every thought, breath, vision, was of her loving daughter. The pain kept right on coming no matter how many antidepressants the doctor had prescribed for her. Even the sounds of Daniel's innocent coos couldn't quell the empty ache that throbbed inside her heart.

Still, the welfare of her son and grandson had to be her main priority now.

Anne stepped off the railed vehicle and into the cold, quiet parking lot. The few people that were on the car with her seemed to make little noise when they walked toward their cars. She found her car with little trouble. Unlocking her door, she paused, staring at her reflection in the car window. She could see tears developing in her reddened eyes. She blinked. Lately, she'd been able to hold her tears in check.

Getting into her car and wiping away the tears, she tried to focus on the tasks that lay ahead of her. Task number one was applying for a nonprofit status for NCRC. Basil had suggested to his mother that she contact the Business Development Center on Beale Street; they would help her fill out all of the forms.

Next, she had a hoard of makeup exams at Vanderbilt Law School before she would graduate in January. And finding a permanent babysitter for Dan Jr., she knew, would be a challenge.

In just over two months, Daniel was walking, recognized her voice, and had come to reach for her like Holly did when she was a baby.

At times, loneliness crept around her as if it were a ghost in disguise. As she headed for home, she thought back to the night that she'd finally given in to Dusty.

It had been two days after Holly's funeral. They were sitting on the sofa in her living room. He had reached over to wipe the tears from her face and then his face slanted across hers in the softest of kisses. A kiss filled with passion, a promise of passion to come. But Anne, starved for a man's touch, wound her arms around his neck; his hand caressed the side of her buttocks. As she crushed her breasts against his chest, desire hardened Dusty's body. His lips softly pressured hers open, and he kissed her gently for a while, first nibbling around her mouth, and then massaging the fullness of her lips with his hot tongue.

When she innocently lay back against the cushion and felt him moving on top of her, she had arched her hips against the protruding evidence of his arousal. With a shudder of sheer ecstasy, her tongue entered the soft interior of his mouth. Both of his hands slipped to her buttocks, and he arched, bringing her even closer to him. Anne pressed closer, the most intimate cavity of her body warming moistly as she swiveled her hips.

Finally, he had lifted his head and gazed into her passion-ravaged face.

Anne's eyes were glowing with awakened desire, dreamy with the innocence of love. Her bruised, swollen, and pouting lips begged to be kissed again and again. Her breathing heightened and her palm slid from his neck, to his chest, and down to the waistband of his pants.

"Not here," he whispered, his hand halting hers. "I want our first time to be special."

She lifted herself up and silently guided him upstairs to her bedroom. They undressed without speaking and when they met in the darkness at the edge of the bed, she looked into eyes that sparkled with liquid love.

Dusty smiled and wrapped his arms around her, swiftly guiding her down on the bed. Eagerly, she positioned herself to receive him. He lowered his head and his mouth closed around her already taut nipple, as his hands explored and caressed her hot skin.

In no hurry, he moved his lips over hers again and again, then settled into a deep, demanding kiss. Her hand joined the assault of her body as his lips sank deeper and deeper into hers. When she thrust her breast into his palm, she felt him planting his other hand on the side of her body.

Abruptly, he released his mouth from hers. "Anne, I . . ." he said, looking down at her.

When her passionate eyes challenged his, she felt him deliberately yet gently penetrate her labyrinthine depths. And when she felt his hips gyrate ever so gently forward, she convulsed with desire, locking her arms around his back.

He kissed the sweat on her lips, and she relaxed as he

began to move within her and stir up a cauldron of lust. Deeper went his thrusts as he wrapped his body around hers. She rose to meet him, slipping her hands down the incline of his spine, and over the deep dimples in his lower back. Then, cupping his hips in her hands, she felt him quiver as her finger traced the sensitive contours of his buttocks.

He gasped with pleasure and began stimulating her breasts as he increased the tempo of his thrusts.

Her emotions spilled over, and she was lost in the wonderful bliss of lovemaking. She had thoughts, but none she could voice; she had feelings but was all feeling. In seconds, she exploded. She was split into a zillion pieces. She was everywhere; she was everything.

Then she felt Dusty tense and felt his member in the sheath of her insides even more powerfully than before.

Quickly, he eased himself out of her and effortlessly turned to lie on his left side, placing Anne on her right. Their legs stretched out one against the other, they telescoped their bodies as deeply as they could. She felt the tip of his hardness against the crevice of her buttocks, and then felt him slowly ease himself back inside of her. He moved his left hand across her hip, sliding his hands between her opened thighs, and inserted his finger at the edge of her opening. Her hips rotated back against his probing finger, rhythmically choreographing their love ballet to an indefinable beat as ephemeral as dreams.

When finally they neared the pinnacle of sexual satisfaction together, they entered the doorway of heaven, heartbeat to heartbeat, shuddering with relief with each pulse of pleasure.

Afterward, Dusty fluffed the pillows, put his arms behind his head, and lay there sweetly smiling. They turned their heads toward each other at the same moment and just smiled, and kept on smiling. Minutes later, Anne lay in Dusty's arms for what seemed like hours. They fell asleep, dozing, then waking, and finally lying quietly in a dreamlike state.

As Anne lay on her side thinking, she became aware of Dusty's prolonged stare. So many things were troubling her, she didn't know if she should burden him with her problems or not.

"You seem tense, Anne. Is there something you want to talk about?"

"I keep seeing her. The way she looked as a toddler."

"Your daughter?"

She nodded yes. "It's like . . . like she's running from something. She's screaming and crying my name. I look around and I see a dog chasing her. I run after her, trying to save her, and I fall." Anne clamped her hands over her eyes to block the vision.

"Babe," he said embracing her, "it's okay. You go right ahead and cry."

"She needs me, Dusty."

"Everybody needs somebody. I need you, Anne."

Forty-six

"MOMMY," REO ASKED after she'd helped Isabell decorate the Christmas tree, "when is my other mommy coming by to see me?"

Isabell's mouth flew open. A look of disgust was pasted on her face like a mask.

"After all I've done for you. Why, I can't believe this. I buy your every desire for Christmas and birthdays and this is the respect that you show me? I wouldn't bust my butt trying to please you if I didn't love you so much, baby."

When she saw the tears in Reo's eyes, she decided to take a softer approach. "Besides, I'm your mother now. Forget about that other woman. She doesn't care anything about you. If she did, she'd be here today instead of me!"

Erik jumped up. "Isabell. You're way out of line!" He grabbed his daughter by the shoulders and kissed her tears. "Go upstairs, sweetheart. I'll be up later."

After she'd gone, Erik said, "You shouldn't have done that."

"It's the truth." Isabell went to the bar and mixed a martini. "This is not some kind of Let's Pretend game. I'm legally the child's mother, and don't you ever forget it."

"It may say so on paper, but you won't truly be a mother until your ass bleeds like Bentley's did. And don't you ever forget that!"

"I'VE MISSED YOU SO MUCH, BENTLEY. And God knows how much I love you, girl."

"And I love you, too, Aunt Anne." Bentley hugged her aunt, not wanting to let go. Her aunt Mae had started crying the moment they arrived.

They spent nearly an hour talking about Nikkie and how well she loved living in her new apartment. What blew her away was the fact that Nikkie could hold down a job. It was a triumph within itself. Bentley never would have imagined that she could.

When Anne told Bentley about Reo's adoption, Bentley forced herself not to cry. She'd known that Erik would care for her, but she never figured that he would allow his wife to adopt their daughter.

Anne told Bentley that she hoped to pass the bar in a few months, and maybe by then, they could try to contest the adoption.

It was worth a try, Bentley thought. When she was released, she'd do whatever it took to get custody of her daughter back.

A week later, Dr. Madsen had finally convinced Bentley to attend her department's weekly dance. Tonight was the third consecutive Thursday. The first two times that she'd came, Bentley was shocked by the number of people that turned out. Everyone seemed to know her name.

Thursday night was the only occasion that the male and female inmates could see one another. The entire staff was on hand to supervise, allowing little if any opportunity for intimate encounters.

There was a table with punch and snacks set up to her left. A male nurse, in charge of the music selections, sat on an elevated platform at the far end of the recreation room. Patients stood around the platform, requesting their choices for the next record, which he promptly wrote down.

Tonight, Bentley had on a yellow flowered print cotton dress. Her hair, which had nearly grown back on the sides, was styled in a mass of Shirley Temple curls.

When she looked to her left, her heart gave a little jump. The same boyish-looking young man, who had stared at her the last time she came, was staring at her now.

He was of average height, black-haired with chiseled

features and a dimple in his chin. He had large violet blue eyes, fringed with thick dark lashes and brows that nearly touched in the center. Neatly trimmed sideburns and a goatee gave him a rugged look. His naturally dark skin made Bentley assume that he was Italian. He stood out from most of the pasty-looking male patients, who had turned pale from their long stay in the hospital.

When he waved at Bentley, she blushed, and then smiled. A tune by the Rolling Stones had just finished and the new selection was a ballad by the late Frank Sinatra.

The dance floor quickly filled with couples trying to learn how to dance or so-called pros who looked like they were born dancing. There were women dancing with men, men with men, and women with women. It didn't matter which.

With the center being nearly split with blacks and whites, it wasn't unusual to dance with white men. And when the dark-haired man approached her, Bentley accepted.

They exchanged names—his was Corky Bedaglia—but he said little else until the second record began and Bentley tried to pull away.

"Don't leave yet. Please," he said, grinning and showing off his beautiful dimples.

"Well . . . okay." Bentley couldn't believe her actions. She hadn't been around a man in so long, she felt awkward. When she worked at the Hamilton Appeal she'd never paid any attention to the men who tried to come on to her. And now, here she was in a mental institution and blushing like a girl twenty years younger than her thirty-six years.

As they danced the dozens of other people in the

room began to seem like wallpaper. She and Corky laughed and began to relax with one another in a matter of minutes. Bentley was amazed at how easily Corky got her to talking. She'd been so closemouthed for so long, she'd nearly forgotten to be self-conscious about her hair. As close as he held her, she was certain that he'd noticed by now.

Their friendship began that night and progressed in the following days as though it were the most natural thing in the world.

After they'd known each other for two weeks, Corky opened up about himself more than Bentley knew that she ever would.

At thirty-two years old, Corky considered himself a veteran executive. After graduating from Shelby State in 1989 he landed a job as a computer programmer at Intel in northern California. He continued his schooling at San Jose State and received a master's degree in the same field. In '91 he was hired at IBM making $35,000 more a year.

The Silicon Valley phenomenon was just beginning. IBM put him on the fast track, and by 1997 Corky's salary topped $310,000. He lived in a subdivision with other professionals where the homes ranged from $600,000 to $2 million. In '98 the bottom began to fall out. Companies began laying people off as well as firing employees in his field.

By early 1998 hundreds of computer technicians couldn't find employment, and ended up homeless. Corky was one of them. He lost his home, car, portfolio, and all of the money in his 401k account. Six months later he was broke—and forced to move back home to his parents' house in Memphis. His father criticized him until he couldn't stand it anymore. He had a nervous breakdown, and ended up in Western in July of this year.

She remembered the odd twitch on his face when he confessed to her that he'd had a breakdown. She couldn't help but wonder if there was anything else wrong with him. He seemed perfectly sane now.

Presently, Bentley's spirits were high and she began making progress with Dr. Madsen. With a little coaxing she finally opened up about her hostile feelings about Kirk, Anne, her aunt Mae, and Wesley. They decided to leave the subject of Reo alone until Bentley felt comfortable about discussing it again.

Two weeks later, Bentley and Corky—his legal name, he finally told her, was Corvin—met by the water fountain. He handed her a handwritten note that he asked her to read later when she was back in her room.

Corky could dance exceptionally well for a white boy, Bentley thought. Though they did no certain dance in particular, moving your hips in a certain way and keeping in time with the music, no matter how you chose to move your arms and legs, showed that you had some dancing abilities.

By now most of the staff knew that she and Corky had become good friends and commented on how well they danced together.

When she returned to her room that night, her roommate was already asleep. She breathed a sigh of relief when turning on the light didn't awaken her.

Opening the sheet of paper, "Guidance" was written on the top. It went on by saying:

> When I meditated on the word guidance, I kept seeing "dance" at the end of the word. I remember reading that doing God's will is a lot like dancing.

*When two people try to lead, nothing feels right.
The movement doesn't flow with the music, and
everything is quite uncomfortable and jerky.
When one person relaxes and lets the other lead,
both bodies begin to flow with the music. One
gives gentle clues, perhaps with a nudge of their
shoulder, or by pressing their hips together, moving beautifully. The dance takes surrender, willing-
ness, and attentiveness from one person and gentle
guidance and skill from the other. My eyes drew
back to the word guidance. When I saw "G" I
thought of God, followed by "u" and "I" dance.
It was an epiphany of sorts for me and states what
God means to me. As I lowered my head, I became
willing to trust that I would get guidance about
my life. For once in my life I became willing to let
God take the lead.*

Bentley felt a twinge of jealousy. Corky was getting
better. He'd made a conscious effort to put God in his
life and let him show him the way out of the institution.

Why couldn't she make that kind of commitment?

Forty-seven

BASIL LIFTED THE TONGS from the patio table, removed the turkey from the deep fryer, and sat it inside
the roasting pan. The pungent aroma permeated the
humid air and soon his neighbors above him were

coming out on their balconies to see what was going on.

"Man, Basil, can you spare a wing or a leg?" the neighbor to his right called out.

Basil took a long drag from his cigarette and flicked the butt over the balcony. "No can do, bro. I've got to take this entire bird over to a friend's house tonight. They're expecting twenty folks for dinner tomorrow and you ain't invited."

The telephone rang. Basil turned off the fryer, put the lid back on top, picked up the roaster, and rushed inside his apartment to grab the phone by the third ring.

"Hello. Happy holiday."

"Hey," Basil said, knowing immediately who it was. His telephone call from Senator Matthews was a week later than usual.

"Where are you spending New Year's Day?"

"Over at David's. And you?"

"My wife is having a few people over." The senator went on to brag about the huge affair that he and his wife were putting on at their home. A band was even scheduled to perform.

Yeah, yeah, yeah. And how much is all of this costing?

"You've got to have me and David come down soon—"

"Hrrrmph," The senator cut him off like he usually did when he thought Basil was starting to get personal. They had a business arrangement and that's all they had. "There's talk of an upcoming audit. The day care lobbyists and a House subcommittee are trying to pass a law to have day care centers audited twice a year. I don't think anything will come of it, but just in case, get your books in order."

"Will do, Orin."

"By the way, my war chest is getting a little light. I expect a larger donation next month."

Basil scowled into the dead phone and wondered if he would ever get this asshole off of his back.

Forty-eight

IT WAS NINE ON MONDAY MORNING when Anne called Edna and put the house and its entire contents on the market. Closing up her accounts and business in Nashville had taken only a week. She then called back to Memphis so that Basil could open the home for the cleaning service. Fortunately, the only utility that she'd turned off was the telephone, and that task she took care of herself.

On January 7 she received her degree from Vanderbilt. Not attending the ceremony hadn't bothered her a bit.

Originally, she'd intended to take the state bar exam in February. But she knew that with so much on her mind, she might flunk it. In the meantime she'd get in all the needed studying and take a prebar course that she'd heard some of her classmates talking about.

Memphis had changed since Anne left. The hot spot in town was the Crescent Club in Germantown. Affluent blacks in the community held their wedding receptions and special events at the predominately white banquet hall. The cost ranged from $400 to $5,000.

Anne also learned that blacks from Somalia and Sudan were now buying filling stations all around the city. Even Vietnamese people were buying businesses in the Bluff City.

By the sixteenth of January, she was back in her old home. This time she didn't need to find a sitter for Daniel. She would take him to the Children's Castle day care center on Poplar, just eight miles from her home.

After she'd been back in Memphis two weeks, she called to make an appointment to see her old physician, Dr. Fisher. To her discouragement, he'd had an emergency situation and had to leave town. He wouldn't be back for an additional two weeks.

During that time she began a campaign to stop the senseless killings by drug dealers. She drafted a bill and sent it in to Senator Matthews.

With the help of her ex-coworker at the capitol, she located a lobbyist to push the bill in the House.

Next, Anne met with Della Guinn, a member of the Southern Poverty Law Center, whose headquarters were in Montgomery, Alabama. When Della showed Anne pictures of the civil rights memorial, she wished that her father's name had been included. Before they parted, Anne promised Della that she would visit the center the following summer.

Up to this point, Anne had merely talked about helping the civil rights struggle. Now she planned on doing something about it.

She contacted Congressman Ford's office in Memphis and made an appointment. She wasn't able to meet with the congressman personally, but had a wonderful meeting with one of his top aides. He too didn't understand why there wasn't a national civil rights consortium in the mid-South, where essentially the entire struggle began. With Anne's recent degree from Vanderbilt she was assured that she would get the congressman's support if she were to head up this type of organization in Memphis.

To Anne's delight, on her third week back home, Mae caught a taxi and came by to see her sister and greatnephew.

Even though she and Mae had a wonderful reunion, Anne kept the status of her illness to herself.

Mae bragged about the seniority she had on her job, and even hinted about buying a car so that she could come by more often. To her embarrassment, Mae had flunked the written test three times before finally getting her driver's license last month.

But what Mae brought with her stunned Anne. Mae had purchased a copy of Ernest C. Withers's book, *Pictures Tell the Story*. Mr. Withers's book incorporated pictures from the Emmett Till murder, to blues and jazz performers, to the black baseball players of the Diamond League, the Montgomery Bus Boycott, the Little Rock Central High School and Tennessee school desegregation, and the sad deaths of Medgar Evers and Dr. Martin Luther King. Mr. Withers took the first photograph at the Lorraine Hotel the night that Dr. King died. His photographs appeared in *Life* magazine, in *U.S. News & World Report,* and the April 1968 condensed version of *Reader's Digest.* Mr. Withers was also one of the first black policemen in the city of Memphis back in 1957. One of his eight children, Derrick, who was deceased, had been a state legislator and businessman. In 1997 a street was named after him—Derrick "Teddy" Withers Parkway.

It seemed that Mr. Withers still had a photography studio on Beale Street. At eighty-one years old, he was sought all over the country for his knowledge about the civil rights era. Anne made a mental note to make an appointment with Mr. Withers to have some of Holly's and Basil's younger pictures restored.

That night, when Anne fell asleep, visions of Dan and Holly smiling at her seemed so real that she felt as if she had physically touched them.

Anne had been given six or eight years to live, but what if the doctors were wrong? What if she lived just three? Daniel would only be four by then. Who would take care of him? She couldn't bear the thought of foster care or adoption agencies that wouldn't know how much this child was loved.

And Basil? Would he take Daniel? Anne wouldn't bet on it.

With those thoughts in mind, she contacted a private detective and had them look into Daniel's adoption. Under the circumstances, the detective located the woman in a matter of weeks.

"I've finally found Mr. Hamilton's birth mother, Mrs. Russell. Her name is Jennifer Lowe and she lives in Olive Branch, Mississippi."

"Is she married?" Anne's heart skipped a beat.

"Divorced. She has two grown daughters. I'm trying to convince her to see you and Daniel Jr. Presently, she isn't amenable to it."

She did, however, agree to a telephone conversation. Anne learned that Daniel's birth resulted from a horrible rape. Jennifer felt nothing for the child.

"How can I love a child that was conceived out of hate?"

"Still," Anne begged, "he was an innocent child. He

never knew the circumstances of his birth. And God knows that he never will."

"I'm sorry." Anne could hear her draw in a breath. "I feel nothing. Absolutely nothing for that man or his child. Please don't contact me again. I seriously doubt that my feelings will ever change."

The phone went dead.

Giving up for Anne would be like not believing that there would be a cure for Parkinson's one day. Nor did she believe that Jennifer Lowe could continue to turn her heart away from her blood kin.

Daniel Jr. was an extension of the Lowes' bloodline. He had to matter to her. Even if Daniel Sr. never knew her love, Jennifer could do the right thing and get to know her grandson. Anne had to believe that people changed. Time changed them. Especially when they came to realize that their existence in the great beyond bordered on their deeds *this side of eternity*.

BECAUSE OF ANNE'S UNTIRING EFFORTS in Nashville, she was asked to join the International Women of Hope. Anne declined, but offered to help them in their cause when she could. Their challenge was to ask Anne to be the keynote speaker the following March for Women's History Month.

Anne hadn't told Dusty before she left that she was moving back to her old home. She wasn't sure how he would take it. Her decision had been so spontaneous there never seemed to be enough time to explain it right.

But time was her enemy. And she knew that there would never be enough time for either of them.

Six weeks after she'd moved back to Memphis and a mere three days before the bar exam, she received a package. It was from Dusty.

The wrapping was from a store she'd only read about in the newspaper—Trousseau's. Inside were two sets of Aubade lingerie, with embroidered panties that Anne knew sold for upward of a hundred dollars. Short gowns by Fernando Sanchez, Hanro from Switzerland, Freya from England, Le Mystère from Spain, Karen Newsburger, Claire Pettibone, Halston, Anne Klein, as well as Flora Nikrooz and Natori were inside the box.

The Halston gown and robe ensemble included umber dyes on a robe whose lining repeated the carefully placed print of the gown. The workmanship on the lingerie was so fine, Anne thought, as she appraised the items, that they could almost be worn wrong side out.

Discreetly placed in the bottom section of the box was a host of massage oils and powder called Kama Sutra. Honey Dust was enclosed along with a pretty brush made of feathers.

Inside, the note read, "I have these same exact items. Every night I put one beside me on my pillow and think of you. Please, darling, call me. Three hours is merely a heartbeat away. I need to be with you."

Anne felt as if she'd been swept off her feet. She hadn't been so flattered in years.

When she called him that night, Dusty told her that he'd be there by noon the next day.

That morning, she dropped Daniel off at the center and went to the hair salon for a quick beauty treatment. She was back home by eleven and anxiously waiting for her man to arrive.

When he arrived, he hugged and kissed her and told her that he wasn't mad that she hadn't told him that she was moving. They would work out everything later.

Anne felt relieved, but still felt uncomfortable about her medical situation. How would she ever make him understand why she had done what she'd done without telling him about her illness?

Over coffee and a Danish she told him how she and Daniel were adapting to living back in Memphis. He told her how his business was booming. She told him about her plans to open a law office in her old neighborhood. He told her how much he missed her. She told him how much she missed him. He told her how much he missed her again.

Together, they picked up the baby and had a simple dinner at home. That night they didn't made love, nor the next night. Anne hadn't even bothered to ask him how long he was staying.

On the third night, they made passionate love, and Anne was glad that they'd waited. She cared for him with all of her strength. She wondered where it had come from, this new strength? Her body felt like the water in a river that had gone dry. Absolute power flowed into her arms and legs as she lay in his loving arms. For a little while they slept in complete tranquility. And then she'd awaken to feel him caressing her hips and buttocks and they would begin again, their breaths and bodies in sync to the rhythm of unadulterated sex.

Their nights were full and their days were even more special.

Dusty enjoyed being around the baby. They would take Daniel to the grocery store with them and to the movies. People would often comment how beautiful their family was. Anne hid her tears.

During the ten days that he stayed, Dusty was as attentive as a newlywed, and it hurt Anne deeply on Sunday evening when he told her that he had to drive back to Nashville.

"I'm living in a vacuum, Anne," Dusty had told her. "Would you mind giving me a reason why you won't agree to marry me? You know there's no one for me but you."

Anne chose her words carefully. "I'm scared, Dusty. I've trusted other people to take care of me all of my life." She laughed. "Things have changed. I've finally learned some hard lessons in becoming an independent woman."

She told him about her involvement in the NCRC and the SPLC. He was behind her 100 percent and volunteered to help her in any way that he could.

"Stop fighting me," he said in a tone she hadn't heard him use before. "We both know that I'm nothing like the husband you told me about. I never knew your father, but I'd be hard pressed to think that any man that cared about you deeply would hurt you."

"Dusty—"

"Let me finish. I can't say I've shared your pain. I know that you've lost a father, husband, and daughter. I know that your niece is experiencing mental problems that you weren't previously aware of. And that your other niece is mentally challenged." He blew out a fragment of air. "Most people would be overwhelmed, Anne."

"I never asked—"

"Please, baby, let me finish." He had stood up from the chair and walked over to her. He dropped to one knee as he began. "Before I met you, I thought I was happy. I had a successful business, ate at the best restaurants in the city, and donated time to helping the less fortunate in my community." He exhaled. "I'm human, Anne. I've had affairs, but none that mattered, because the sex was all I wanted. I believed that no one could compare to what I felt about my wife, Jean. She was my lover, friend, companion, and inspiration. We shared more than most couples. With something so perfect there had to be a downside— cancer."

"You don't have to share this with me, Dusty."

"Oh, but I do. Because I want you to know how special you are."

"Believe me. I'm not special. I'm no more than a game on your hot sheet that would be forgotten in the next thirty days."

"You're underestimating yourself, Anne. That could never happen!"

What he told her afterward her hurt and helped her in the same breath—he was putting his business and home up for sale.

How could she tell this man that she wouldn't live long enough to fulfill his dreams?

Forty-nine

FOR EVERY MENTALLY IMPAIRED PERSON who finally finds the road to recovery, there's usually a love story behind the healing. Bentley was no exception. She and Corky were extremely close.

On Anne's last visit, she had confided in Bentley how much she was in love with Dusty. Bentley wanted to tell Anne about Corky but felt that it was much too soon.

She'd been honest with Dr. Madsen about her relationship with Corky, though. And because she'd opened up so much and was willing to face her fears, she had finally progressed to the point that she would be able to go home soon.

It was late March and the temperature was a comfortable seventy-two degrees. As the soil warmed, daffodils, narcissus, snowdrops, and bluebells filled the flowerbeds on the institution's 100-acre grounds. White and purple iris blooms popped out from clumps of fanned swordlike foliage. Pink, red, and white azaleas looked like blotches of watercolors dabbled across the landscape. Numerous dogwoods graced the air with starry blooms.

A tarnished dream on a tarnished chain, time keeps changing come sunshine or rain, Bentley thought to herself as she headed outside the building. For the first time since she'd come, she began to appreciate the beauty of the century-old institution. Places like this, she knew, served as windows through which one could see the past and get a glimpse of one's heritage.

As she walked through the grounds, Bentley tickled the leaves of a branch of fiery quince and silently thanked God that she no longer needed to take the antidepressant medications that the doctor had prescribed.

She imagined Nikkie's smiling face, playing hide-and-seek and peeping from behind a tree trunk. It was a beguiling image of her and the garden's past.

Halfway to the guest area where there were several tables, chairs, and benches set up under a huge cottonwood tree, she saw Anne in a pale blue linen dress waiting for her with a bouquet of wildflowers.

When Bentley reached her, they hugged and sat beside one another on the white metal patio bench. "Here," she said handing her the flowers, "these are for you."

"Thanks, they're lovely."

"You don't know how much I worried about letting Nikkie move out on her own," Anne eagerly began. "I hoped that you didn't think that I didn't want to be bothered with her." Her eyes, misted with tears of honesty, made Bentley look away.

"No. Aunt Anne, if it weren't for you, I probably would have never found out that a place existed for people like Nikkie. Thanks to you, she's truly found her own happiness." She fondled the flowers and inhaled their sweet breath. "Now, tell me. We haven't talked about Holly. How are you coping with her death?"

"It's tough. And most of the time I can't believe that it's happened. But I've got to face facts for Daniel's sake."

When she mentioned that her grandson was walking now, Bentley thought back to when Reo was just a toddler.

Bentley wanted to ask Anne when was the last time she saw Reo. Did she look like Erik? How tall was she? What school did she attend?

"We've come so far, Bentley. I don't know if we'll ever be able to call ourselves a family again. But I'd like to begin by asking you to come and live with Daniel and me when you're released."

Bentley was devastated. She hadn't expected that Anne would suggest that she move into her home. Truth was, she rather liked the idea of being around a baby again.

"Aunt Anne, I'd love to come and live with you. The doctor said that I should be released sometime next month." *And two months later, I'll be thirty-seven years old.*

"Perfect."

"I've nearly forgotten to tell you one more important thing."

"What's that, dear?"

"I love you so much."

Fifty

A FEDERAL GRAND JURY was exploring possible fraud and abuse in Tennessee's taxpayer-funded day care program. Documents subpoenaed in the secret probe reflected the grand jury's interest in how the state decided to award the lucrative child-care broker contract in Shelby County. Hamilton's Children and Family Services had held that contract for five years, allowing it to serve as gatekeeper to low-income families seeking subsidized day care. Recently, at least eight current and former state officials had testified before the grand jury, including Florence Johnson.

Florence Johnson was the Department of Human Services commissioner. She was a close friend with Senator Matthews, and through him, Basil had met the sassy single female last year over the Christmas holiday.

An intelligent woman, her ego blown up bigger than the boxer Butter Bean through her powerful position as

DHS commissioner, she had won the respect of Governor Sundquist and the Finance and Administration commissioner. What they didn't know was that Florence was desperate for a man cocky enough to put her in her place. Basil fit that role perfectly.

Basil called her when he felt like it and made the cunt come and see him twice as often as he took the time to drive up and see her. She seemed to enjoy the fact that he juggled other women to see her. She even admired the way he could tell a smooth lie, and took special pleasure in their two- and three-hour sex sessions even better. Thanks to Isabell, Basil had learned the art of seduction and seldom used it unless it was absolutely necessary.

Last week, a press conference was held at the capitol building. Citing an ongoing investigation, Ms. Johnson declined to answer any questions about a recent meeting with Senator Matthews the week before or the senator's involvement in the selection process of the broker contract.

The annual contract to Hamilton's brokerage company had now grown to $3 million annually. Thanks to Florence, who essentially had the authority to do virtually what she wanted when it came to awarding day care contracts, Basil had nothing to worry about.

Less than twenty miles away, Anne Russell-Hamilton had nothing to worry her pretty head about either. Dusty Baker was about to take control of her life.

It had happened one afternoon in late April. Anne had driven to Nashville to meet with Debbie Hazley, the lobbyist for Holly's bill, and spend a lust-filled night with Dusty. She'd taken her bath and while toweling off, slipped on the wet tiles and fell to the floor. Severe hand tremors made her unable to pull herself up. Uncontrollable shakes followed. She didn't panic. She just lay patiently waiting for it to stop. She'd taken her medication an hour earlier and she believed that the tremors would relent in a few minutes. Lying there nude and freezing for over a half hour, she cursed herself, then yelled for Dusty.

Wrapping her in a housecoat, he massaged her shoulder and arms until he was sure that heat was restored in her body. As quickly as she could, she told him about the Parkinson's. Throughout that time, the tremors didn't stop. Dusty dressed her hurriedly, then immediately drove her to Baptist Memorial Hospital. She was kept overnight. Her doctor arrived the following morning. It was then that she received the heartbreaking news.

"I'd suggest surgery." Dr. Fisher recommended a type of brain surgery known as a thalamotomy. It was a serious but very simple procedure that would relieve her of the tremors. He told her that surgeries of this type were done all the time.

To her astonishment, Dusty objected. He felt that what she needed in her life was faith, not some licensed quack who'd ordained himself as a living god.

Anne hadn't been to church in years. Dusty had harped about her interlude from God since she'd met him. A committed Christian, he went to mass and confession every Sunday and willingly gave a tenth of his earnings.

"Are you happy, Anne?" he asked her after the doctor had left.

"Yes. I think so."

He pulled the chair up closer to the bed. "Let me tell you something about being happy. It don't compare to joy. I've got joy, darling. Because I know that only Christ can give true meaning to my life. I've got joy in knowing that Christ helps me every day to deal with life's disappointments and heartaches. He helps me find inner strength to change my life and to do what's right. And finally, in John 10:10, he says: 'I have come that they may have life, and have it to the full.' God doesn't want you to suffer, Anne. He only wants you to believe in Him."

Anne swallowed hard as tears filled her eyes. Spasms of her old faith robbed her of her ability to speak.

"Won't you open your heart to him today? By a simple prayer of faith, confess your sins and ask him to come into your life."

"I'm sorry, Dusty, I don't know if I can find the courage," Anne said, turning her face from him.

"Have the courage to marry me, Anne. I'll take care of you. I'll make the decisions about your health and your grandson. You don't have to do nothing but love me."

"Dusty . . . I want so much to . . ."

"Baby, didn't you know that love is never having to say *I want*. Our marriage is not about you and me, you *or* me—it's about us. The Lord has told me that it's my job to care for you, provide for you. Our father has delegated that job to me as long as I'm on this earth. We can beat this disease with God's love. You have to have faith, Anne. And with faith, the Lord gives us hope this side of eternity—the hope of eternal life, when all of our problems and heartaches will be over. Never forget; the eyes of the Lord are on those . . . whose hope is in his unfailing love."

He touched her then, and like the moment when they first met, his fingers felt like flowers. He prayed over her until she cried, lifted up her hands, and asked for for-giveness.

Afterward, Dusty claimed that she'd witnessed her first miracle. If she'd trust him, she'd witness another. And in the next fifteen days she did. Dusty contacted Basil and asked him to pick up the baby from the neighbor's house and keep him at his place until he and Anne came back home in two weeks.

Next, Dusty convinced Anne to take the pre-Cana classes that were necessary to marry a person of the Catholic faith. Normally a four-week process, Dusty convinced the priest to conduct theirs in two. These classes would enable both people to respect the sacrament of marriage and also to help them to understand the expectations that they had of one another.

When they received the blessing from the bishop at his church, Dusty applied for their marriage license. He then took Anne to get a passport. While they waited for the necessary paperwork, he bought Anne a beautiful wedding dress and rented a tuxedo. The following morning he took his bride-to-be downtown to the courthouse and with the blessings of his two daughters, Dusty and Anne agreed to take one another as man and wife.

It took all the faith that Anne could muster to agree to Dusty's idea of a honeymoon.

They consummated their wedding night in a quaint hotel near Lourdes, in southern France. Anne could scarcely believe that she hadn't felt the slightest hint of a tremor coming on. The next morning they traveled to the grotto of Massabielle, where Our Lady appeared eighteen times to Bernadette Soubirous, a young peasant girl. Pope Pius XI declared Bernadette a saint on December 8, 1933, Dusty told Anne. Tomorrow, April 16, marked the day of her birth in Heaven.

That night before they went to bed, Anne thought about Scott. He had taken her to church each and every Sunday during their marriage, but she honestly believed that he was an atheist. She'd never seen him pray or read one page of the Bible. His presence in church was all for show.

Not Dusty. He believed in God. He also believed in miracles. Even as she was beginning to trust her husband, she felt compelled to ask him a question.

"Why didn't you pray for a miracle to save your wife?"

"She was killed in a car accident. I didn't have the opportunity. Besides, God was saving my miracle for you."

He went on to tell Anne, while he held her lovingly in his arms, that miracles were not a substitute for faith.

That night she heard him repeating the prayer: "Eternal Father, I offer You the Body and Blood, Soul and Divinity, of Your dearly beloved Son, Our Lord Jesus Christ, in atonement for our sins and those of the whole world; for the sake of His sorrowful Passion, have mercy on us and the whole world."

That next morning after they dressed, Anne's feelings were unfamiliar; she felt especially calm. Automatically, she braced her body for the tremors that she was certain would come, and then chastised herself. Dusty had told her that she needed to have faith. With every fiber of her soul she willed her mind to shun her negative thoughts and believe that she would be cured.

Reaching inside her overnight bag, she removed the crystal beads that she hadn't worn in years. She sat in front of the mirror admiring the beauty of them. And she promised herself that she would wear her mother's beads to church every Sunday, just like she used to, for she believed that God could not put hope into a small soul.

Very quietly Dusty had tiptoed behind her and kissed her on the back of her neck. "I love you, Anne."

Before she could respond, the phone rang. It was Anne's sister, Mae.

"Are you happy?"

"Absolutely." She turned around and kissed her husband on the lips and then signaled for him to give her a minute. Anne had promised Dusty that she wouldn't tell any of her family members about her illness. "And how about you? Have you been over to see my grandson yet?"

"Mm-hm. He's doing real well. Don't you worry about nothing back home. Basil and me are taking care of everything like it should be. We've been over to see Nikkie and she's doing just fine. And guess what?"

"You know I don't like surprises, Mae."

"It's not like that. I wanted to tell you that I've got a fellow, Charlie Mickens. He's a little older than me, about sixty. I met him at the car dealership."

"Did you buy a car yet?"

"Naw. I don't get my license till next week. But . . . don't let me forget. I got a call from Bentley, she told me to tell you hello."

"Hmm. Looks like the Russell family is finally getting their act together."

"You better believe it. 'Bye now. Give that husband of yours a big kiss for me."

Anne touched her beads again and smiled. "I miss you, Mae."

"You too, girl. 'Bye."

Forty-five minutes later, Dusty and Anne, along with dozens of others, headed for the Our Lady of Lourdes shrine in Nevers, France. They went inside the main chapel of the Convent of St. Gildard and prayed. Less than four feet away was the famous stream where hundreds of other pilgrims knelt. Dusty laid a bouquet of flowers at the foot of the shrine, and together, he and Anne lit a candle.

Around the shrine were the words inscribed of the great promise made to Bernadette at Lourdes by the Most Blessed Virgin, and fulfilled by Her: *I do not promise that you will be happy in this world, only in the next.*

Kneeling before the shrine, Anne removed the rosary beads from around her neck and held them in her hands. Dusty knelt down beside her. And when he began to pray, she echoed his words . . . "Eternal Father, I offer you the Body and Blood, Soul and Divinity, of Your dearly beloved Son . . ."

Fifty-one

TODAY WAS THE TWENTY-FIRST DAY OF APRIL—Bentley's lucky day. This morning she stood in the front office signing several release forms. She'd been cleared by Dr. Madsen to leave the hospital. She had signed the release forms yesterday and asked Bentley to promise her that she'd stay in treatment.

"I promise, Doctor."

"And stay the mature adult that I've come to know and respect. Don't allow yourself to regress. The pain is in the past. The stress of taking care of two needy people is behind you. By keeping your mind focused on your future, you can distance yourself from the deeply recorded messages of the trauma you experienced before your breakdown."

"You're a hundred percent correct, Doctor."

"Do you need a referral? Or do you have a psychiatrist that you'd be comfortable seeing as an outpatient?" Bentley shook her head no, and Dr. Madsen scribbled down the name of one of her associates who had a practice in downtown Memphis.

"Remember, there is no tag attached to your case. You can come out and make the follow-through if you feel strong enough. However, if you plan on continuing your medication, I'd like to make sure that you don't relapse."

"I don't need the medication. I haven't taken it in over a month. Besides dealing with the high blood pressure, I'm perfectly fine."

Dr. Madsen went on to tell her that she believed that she wasn't a threat to herself or others. And that she really appreciated how hard she'd worked these past months.

"Thank you." Tears were brimming at the corners of her eyes.

"You've done very well these past few months. And if we didn't feel that you could cope, we wouldn't be letting you out. But know that if things become complicated and this plan is not working out, please give me a call and we can work something else out."

Bentley thanked her again. In eight months, Dr. Madsen had become the loving, nurturing mother figure that

Bentley had never experienced before. Bentley had to watch herself from becoming too dependent on her, and hopefully it had worked.

"And if you ever need me, you're welcome to come back here for outpatient care at any time."

"Thank you, Dr. Madsen, but I think I'll stick with the doctor that you recommended."

She smiled and shook Bentley's hand. "Now you get on out of here and clean out your room. I don't ever want to see you in a place like this again."

And now, after finishing with the mounds of paperwork, the nurse told her that she was free to go. Bentley's heart skipped a beat. She felt nervous and energized at the same time.

Trying to keep her daughter's inevitable meeting in perspective, she considered the idea of seeing a social worker first.

She wasn't sure if Anne would think that she was being irrational, but she wanted to do the right thing.

When Bentley looked out the front window, she saw Anne waving to her from the parking lot. Bentley had said good-bye last night to the night shift staff and took a few minutes now to say good-bye to the day shift and thank every nurse who worked in her unit.

With happy tears in her eyes, she picked up her small bag and opened the door. As she walked through, she tried to capture the strength she felt when she talked with the doctor last night, but faltered.

Instead, she felt trepidation. Suddenly, she was scared that she wouldn't make it. Who would give her a job once they learned she'd been in a mental institution?

Taking a seat in the car, she leaned her head back and

was silent. She felt Anne's eyes on her and didn't know what to say.

"Bentley . . . I'm here for you, honey," Anne began. Tenderly, she uncurled Bentley's fingers from her side, and then took her hands in hers. Bentley loved the warmth of her touch, the strength and protection that her clasp seemed to promise.

Bentley couldn't seem to find the words, but Anne's gentle voice and the sincere look in her eyes told Bentley that she understood how she was feeling. Looking back over her shoulder at the building that had been her home for so long, she felt the dam to her emotions give and tears were not far away. When she moved her hand, Anne's grip tightened and refused to let go.

"Go ahead, Bentley. It'll be all right."

Bentley brought her arms up and hugged her aunt. She pressed her face against her chest and began to cry. Immediately she felt a sweet relief as her aunt held her close, whispering words of comfort to her.

After a few moments, Bentley sniffed and said, "I'm okay. Really I am. I didn't know that I'd feel like this."

Pushing back, Bentley released her arms and, exhaling deeply, laid her head back against the seat. "I'm strong. I'm blessed. And I can make it."

Anne handed Bentley a tissue and she blew her nose. "Better?"

Bentley nodded. A surge of relief filled her as she turned up the volume on the radio.

"Let's go, Aunt Anne."

Seventy-five minutes later they arrived at Anne's house. Anne showed Bentley her room. It was a large room, filled with family pictures; there were several of

Holly and Daniel. Bentley had already made up her mind that she would take it one day at a time.

But first she had to see her sister. She wasn't sure how she would explain to Nikkie how sick she was or why she'd been away so long. But when she saw her beautiful sister the following afternoon, she found that explanations weren't necessary.

"Bentley! I'm so glad you're home. I missed you." Nikkie hugged Bentley so tight her heart skipped a beat.

"Now stand back. I want to look at you." Bentley checked out every breath of Nikkie's body. She'd cut her hair real short, had on lipstick and blush, and wore a stylish three-piece ivory pantsuit that showed off her trimmed figure. "What happened to you? You look beautiful, sweetheart."

Nikkie explained her new life to Bentley. She had a job she enjoyed. Went shopping once a month with friends she worked with. Participated in the numerous activities that the complex offered and had even learned how to prepare meals using the microwave. But what really blew Bentley away was how confident Nikkie looked. It was something that she knew she would have to get used to. Her big sister had finally grown up. And thanks to Anne, she was finally in the right type of environment where she could live and excel with other people like herself.

As each day passed, Bentley was astonished by how close she and Anne had become. They talked about their past, their mistakes, and hopes for their future.

It was just a week later, when Bentley refused to accept a loan from Anne, that they had their first argument. Anne wanted to help Bentley until she secured a decent job and got back on her feet. It didn't matter that Bentley still had money in the bank. Anne was financially secure and could afford it. Nor did she expect Bentley to pay her back for the monthly expenses she paid while Bentley was in the hospital. They could settle all of that at another time. Right now she needed transportation and a job. Bentley's Galant had been sitting so long, it needed new tires and, she guessed, a tune-up.

It took a little coaxing, but with Dusty's help, Anne was able to convince Bentley that getting her life back on track was more important than any amount of money.

However, Bentley was told that it would take more money to repair her Galant than it was worth. After receiving a couple of hundred dollars from the salvage yard, Dusty and Anne helped Bentley select a 1995 Sable at the used car dealership where Mae's friend Charlie Mickens worked.

By 7:45 the next morning, Bentley, dressed in a new outfit that she and Anne had picked out from Steinmart, left for an appointment at the employment agency.

Dusty had been up since six. He'd already cut the grass and edged the lawn when Anne watched Bentley back out of the driveway. It was a tedious job that used to take the gardener two hours to complete and had taken Dusty only one. Anne had to admit, she loved having a man around the house. Anything that Dusty thought needed fixing inside or outside of the house, he was more than happy to oblige. The only thing that her husband couldn't seem to do was work on cars.

His ineptness was a small joke between her and Bentley.

By 9:30, Anne had fed Daniel, bathed and dressed

him, and then dropped him off at the day care center. She and Dusty were expecting a realtor to stop by their home at twelve.

Until then, Anne took a seat on the patio chair fanning flies on the front porch and watching Dusty work. Unlike herself, he loved Memphis's tradition of displaying flags on the front of one's home for the holidays. He'd purchased a colorful flag for Memorial Day, and had the ladder, drill, and bolts out to attach the flag holder to the top of the left front pillar.

Looking down from the ladder, he spoke loud enough for her to hear him. Pride filled his voice when he told her about his eldest daughter, Aretha, who was about to receive her master's degree in fine arts next month. She wanted to teach school at Fisk University. And the "baby," Yolanda, who was managing the store while he was away, was studying photography at a vocational school.

Anne watched his mouth while he talked, smiled when he smiled, nodding her head yes every now and then. She thought about Daniel at the center and mused that he was probably taking a nap about now.

Feeling a little sleepy herself, her thoughts drifted to last night's dream.

She and Holly were at the shopping mall. As she stopped to look in a display window at a lingerie store, she noticed in the reflection that her daughter's tiny little body was missing.

Manipulating her way through the maze of people walking up and down the aisles, she trained her eyes for a young female in a yellow-and-white-checked dress. She half ran through the crowd asking people: "Have you seen a little girl in a yellow dress?"

No one spoke to her and she continued to run. She

ended up at the front entrance. Just as she stepped outside the door, she saw a man forcing Holly into the car and then getting inside. Holly's tearful face was pushed against the window, screaming for her mother. The car sped off and Anne's heart lurched.

"Anne?" Dusty said, shaking her shoulder. "You were screaming."

"Oh, I'm sorry."

"Your hands are shaking, babe."

Anne didn't understand. Why was she having these types of dreams about Holly? It didn't make sense to her.

Promptly at noon, the realtor arrived. Dusty told him about his plans to purchase a novelty store in the Germantown area. Per their telephone call, the realtor had printed out a few prospects and was ready to make an appointment for Dusty to look at the properties this evening.

Dusty was so excited about seeing the stores later that day that he didn't bother to interrogate Anne about her daydream. She felt a surge of relief. How could she explain something that she didn't understand herself?

The following week, May 19 marked Basil Hamilton's twenty-fifth birthday. Scott's attorney met with Anne and Basil the day before to sign the documents and begin the process of drafting the check for the first installment of his inheritance.

Anne planned a small get-together with Basil, Dusty, Mae, Bentley, and Nikkie. Basil had requested chocolate cake and chocolate ice cream.

When Anne and Basil were alone in the kitchen, she jokingly mentioned that he should pay off all of his gambling debts.

But Basil wasn't joking when he told his mother that the money was already spent.

The six adults, along with Daniel, watched old videos of Basil and Holly when they were children from age one to fifteen.

When the videos ended Basil excused himself and followed Bentley into the kitchen.

She'd brought the empty bowl of potato chips back with her and was refilling it.

"So, do you have a job yet?"

"No. I've got several interviews lined up, though. Don't worry about me, Basil. I'm doing just fine."

Reaching inside the refrigerator, he removed a cold Budweiser. "Listen. I ain't the one to make excuses or no shit like that. What I need is a manager at my Whitehaven center. That bitchin' woman quit on me last week. After all the money I paid—"

"C'mon, Basil." She threw the empty chip bag in the trash. "You don't have to—"

"Pay attention, Bentley. I've noticed how comfortable you are with little Daniel. Most of the kids at the center are six weeks to a year old. I need someone who really loves kids and has a lot of patience. The Whitehaven center is one of my biggest locations. And I thought that—"

She went over to him and hugged him. "Thanks, Basil."

He guzzled down half the beer and took a chip from the bowl. "Look, you be at the center on Monday morning. I'll walk you through the daily routine, and if you're satisfied with the job and the salary, you can start on Tuesday."

Bentley stuffed two crisp chips in her mouth, and smiled. "I'll be there. And thanks again, cuz."

Fifty-two

OVER THE SUMMER, Bentley taught Anne how to make
a few of the vegetarian dishes that were good for her
diet. Anne worried that even though the psychiatrist
that she saw once a month was helping Bentley mentally,
she was forced to accept the fact that she'd have high
blood pressure for the rest of her life.

On a more positive note, Bentley had gotten good
news. Her old editor, Miriam, from the *Hamilton Appeal* forwarded a registered letter to Bentley. It seemed
that Norman Harold from D.C. Comics had a proposal for Bentley. If she could write a screenplay for
Riverdocks by the first of the year, Jada Pinkett's production company was interested in making the movie.
Jada wanted to play the part of Abby. She loved the
character.

Anne worried that Bentley was putting too much
stress on herself again. She worked forty to fifty hours a
week at the day care center, drove out to see Nikkie
every week, and every minute she could spare, worked
on new episodes of her comic strip. Now she was working on a screenplay as well.

Of course Bentley didn't listen. She took her medication regularly and kept right on working.

In the first week of September, the *Hamilton Appeal*
reported daily atrocities at the city's day care centers.
Anne couldn't believe how such a lucrative business
just a few years back could suddenly turn so ugly. Children were being mistreated and the parents were de-

manding that the day care centers be held responsible. Anne couldn't blame them, but she felt that the *Hamilton Appeal* was especially biased against the black centers.

This morning's *Hamilton Appeal* headlined a story about Senator Orin Matthews's former assistant, Terry Tipton. An ongoing three-year investigation revealed that the senator was implicated in a $3 million grant program that provided legal help for custody battles.

Tipton also contradicted previous government witnesses, and admitted that he had lied to reporters more than two years earlier, when the news broke that political insiders were set to profit from the no-bid, no-guidelines grant program.

As Anne read on, she couldn't believe it. It seemed that Tipton, two former colleagues, and Senator Matthews were accused of conspiring to design the program as a "cash cow" that would funnel money to the alleged conspirators without requiring much work.

The article concluded by saying that the three men had received a $30,000 payment thus far, and were due to receive nearly $15,000 monthly for two years.

The doorbell rang and Anne set the paper down next to a pile of law books that she'd just finished skimming through. The bar exam was in two weeks, and she was trying to do as her teacher had warned: "Don't try to memorize every little thing because with such a volume of information, it's virtually impossible to remember it all." He went on to tell the class that remembering one key word would trigger an onslaught of memory. He also gave the class suggestions as to how to best answer multiple choice, math, and essay questions. He had given Anne so much advice that she didn't know what to listen to. Because the tests were all standardized, the important thing to remember was that a person's test-taking skills were the most important factor.

The doorbell rang for the second time before Anne jumped up from the table.

"Mama," Daniel squealed while pounding the spoon in his half-empty bowl of oatmeal.

She wiped his face, and helped him out of the high chair as the doorbell chimed once more. "C'mon, you can go too."

Daniel followed her to the front door, and then held on to her legs, peeking between them as Basil came inside and swooped him up in his arms.

"Say, big fellow." He tickled his protruding tummy.

"Careful," Anne warned, and began heading back toward the kitchen, "he just ate."

"Gosh, Mom, this is such a cute little boy." Basil lifted Daniel up on his shoulders and Daniel giggled with glee.

"I know." She tried to keep the sadness from her voice. "Holly and Dan would be real proud of him." She cleaned off the high chair, and then refilled her cup of coffee.

"None for me, Mom." He sat Daniel down in his playpen, handed him a toy airplane, and then asked, "Where's Dusty?"

"Out with a realtor looking for the right location for his new store. What brings you over this early in the morning?"

"Problems." He sat down at the kitchen table. "The *Hamilton Appeal* is at it again."

"I know, I've been reading about it nearly every day."

"It seems that they pulled the audit report of Children's Services for the fiscal year that ended June 30, 1999. They've already got a separate lawsuit against us that is also gaining momentum."

"You never mentioned a lawsuit before. Why is the *Appeal* so interested in your centers?"

"Since Children's Services is a nonprofit organization, our books are open for public inspection. It seems that the auditing firm Mellon and Company, who audits our books, has warned the *Appeal* that there's a number of financial transactions involving our ex–executive director Sue Hawkins and her relatives."

"You said ex, didn't you?"

"Yeah. I fired her. I found out that she was clipping me every chance that she got." He toyed with the place mat. "It seems that a number of her transactions are questionable for business purposes. There are three items that Mellon has flagged—the fact that Sue paid an unnamed relative $49,000 in professional fees the last fiscal year and $44,000 in 1998. Also in dispute is a cost of $37,559 for rental and charter services provided by a business associated with a local church. The audit says that one of our board members, who I believe is Sue's uncle, is the pastor of the church. And lastly, investing $275,000 in the stock of Memphis Third Community Bank—a start-up business." Basil smiled. "Now that's my doing."

"A bank, Basil? What on earth were you thinking?"

"I think it's good business sense to have one's money in their own bank. We're required by the state to keep large amounts of cash in a single account."

Anne got up to check on the baby, who'd gotten

bored playing with his toys and was trying to climb out of the playpen. "So how does this affect our nonprofit status?" She filled the baby cup, sitting on the counter, full of apple juice, and handed it to Daniel.

"If the IRS determines that monies were spent for the benefit of the individuals involved and didn't contribute to the charitable purpose for which the company was founded, there's going to be a problem. But the smoke signals that the *Appeal* is trying to send to the IRS might not work. Presently, the IRS is participating in a wide-ranging grand jury probe of all the subsidized day cares in the city. However, the feds won't give any details about the investigation."

"Whew, I just got my approval letter from the IRS for the NCRC company that I'm hoping to open this fall. I had no idea that I'd be opening myself up to so much scrutiny."

"I think what you're proposing is a little different. Case in point—I paid Sue a salary of $155,000 last year. How much are your employees expecting to get compensated?"

"Nothing." She finished her coffee. "All four of the attorneys will work on a volunteer basis."

"Uh-huh. You're just the type of organization the IRS loves. You're legitimate."

"And is that a bad thing?" She got up to put her empty coffee cup in the sink.

"No. But I don't know how you expect to make any money."

"Everything isn't always about money, Basil. I'm providing a necessary service—"

"That your dad sitting up there in heaven is going to be awfully proud of. I know the story, Mom."

"Son, I . . ." She stopped. She hadn't called him that in a while. "I know you know the day care business inside and out, but I never agreed to anything illegal. And if that's the case—"

"Calm down, Mom," he said, getting up from the table. "I've got everything taken care of. I just didn't want you reading about this stuff in the papers and not hear the real deal from me." He walked over to Daniel's playpen and nudged him on the foot. He'd dropped the cup and had fallen asleep. "Kiss the little fellow for me when he wakes up, will you?"

As Anne followed him back to the foyer, the phone rang.

"It's for you." Anne handed him the cordless phone and left the room to take the baby to the nursery.

When Anne came back downstairs, Basil handed her the phone.

"It's Bentley, she wants to speak to you." He kissed her good-bye and left.

"Hello, Bentley."

"Hi. Do you have a minute?"

"Yeah, I just put the baby to bed."

"Good. I couldn't wait until I got home. I'm a little upset."

"About what?"

"Erik. He and Isabell have decided to send Reo to summer camp in Florida. It's for four weeks. She won't be back until the middle of July. I realize that I no longer have custody, Aunt Anne. But don't you think I should get to visit my own daughter? I think Isabell did this on purpose so that she could keep her from me."

"That's a tough one. I'm not sure what your rights are in this kind of situation. You told me that Isabell had legally adopted Reo, but where does that leave you?"

"I'm mystified myself. I went to see an attorney on my lunch hour. I'm hoping that I can take the case to probate court so that I can get regular visitation."

"I think you're doing the right thing, Bentley. If you need a character witness, I hope that you know that you can count on Dusty and me. And I'm sure that Basil would want to, too."

"Thanks, Aunt Anne. And there's something else. It's about Erik. He wants to see me."

"What for?"

"He told me that he's thinking about filing for a divorce. I know. I know. It's kind of stupid of me to hope for something like this, but I'm really confused about how I'm feeling right now."

"What about Corky?"

"I care about him. But I hadn't thought about the race thing until I got back home. It's bound to be a problem. I don't know what to do. I do know that I don't want to be alone anymore."

"Don't put too much pressure on yourself, honey."

"Yeah, I guess you're right . . . Uh-oh, Aunt Anne, that's my other line, I've gotta go. 'Bye."

WHILE READING THE NEWSPAPER on Saturday morning, Dusty cut out an article and handed it to his wife. The article was about a workshop called Dreams: An Inner Resource that was being held at the Memphis College of Art in midtown.

Anne finally admitted to Dusty that she had been having one bad dream after another, ever since they came back home from their honeymoon.

When Dusty showed her the article Anne was skeptical. She called the school and got some information about the workshop. Dr. Mary Shubert was conducting the class. Fortunately for Anne, there was one spot left for next week's class.

She gave the student her credit card number and enrolled in the class.

The first class held on Thursday was Dreams as a Creative Resource and on Saturday, Tapping into Inner Resources.

Dr. Shubert began by telling the class that from this day forward, she wanted them to keep a journal of their dreams.

"Even if you get up in the middle of the night and have to use the bathroom, I want you to take a moment and record in your journal what you've dreamed thus far. It's very important."

Within the first fifteen minutes Anne learned that dreams were a way of staying in touch with our instinctive spiritual side. They help us to grasp the ungraspable, and help us to understand those deeply spiritual questions that most people ask at some point in their lives.

She learned that dreams grow out of the dreamer's unconscious and life experiences. She was told that the famous Carl Jung believed that dreams were an undisguised message from the unconscious, but coded in symbols that only the dreamer could understand. Anne felt that there had to be some kind of symbolic reason why she kept having dreams about Holly.

Dr. Shubert told the class that evidence showed that our dreams show us that there is a world beyond ourselves—that there is an invisible world to which we can connect, that dreams are an avenue to that place, and that inside all of us there are two voices, strengths and weaknesses, control and creativity. Dreams bridge the opposites. Dreams are always a projection of our own thoughts. They were the doorways to the emotional state of our minds.

"We don't turn off our minds when we go to sleep. Life is continual even when we're asleep. Women," the doctor said, "dream more about emotion. I believe that the dream acts like an emotional thermostat that determines our mood when we wake up."

Anne learned about Sigmund Freud and his dream technique. He published the book *The Interpretation of Dreams* in 1900. He proposed dreams as the most direct channel to the human unconscious. Freud believed that some of his patient's physical symptoms were painful experiences repressed in their childhood or forbidden sexual desires. He believed that by decoding dreams, he could help his patients face their hidden feelings and perhaps be cured.

By the end of the first night, Anne discussed her dreams in a group setting. She received several theories about what they meant. Most believed that Holly was trying to tell her something.

On the second and final night, they discussed the dream series and recurring dreams: Identifying Patterns and Working with Characters and Symbols.

When Anne returned home that evening, she felt as if she were floating on a cloud. She actually looked forward to falling sleep and dreaming.

"Would you consider keeping a journal, Dusty?" Anne asked as they were preparing for bed.

"Sure. I think it'll make interesting conversation."

She got into bed and glanced at the opened journal that was lying on the night stand. "I think if we both talked about what was on our subconscious minds, we could learn more about each other in a few months than we would in a lifetime."

"That's a wonderful thought." He kissed her and turned off the light.

"Did you know that one-third of our life is spent sleeping? We should try to understand that important part of our life."

"My mother once told me," Dusty said, reaching over to snuggle closer to his wife, "that dreams are metaphors in motion."

"Smart woman."

"I agree." He passed his hand over the crown of her head and kissed her hair. "I love you, Anne."

"And I love you. Sweet dreams, Dusty."

BENTLEY WAITED ANXIOUSLY for Erik's black Lincoln to park in the slot five cars down from hers.

She stood by the entrance of the Children's Museum, and watched as Erik, holding Reo's hand, walked toward her.

Would Reo still remember her? How would she explain where she'd been so long?

It felt a little strained, but Reo immediately came to her and gave her a quick hug. "Hi, Mommalee." She handed Bentley a small gift.

Why didn't I think to bring her one? "Hi, sweetie. Thanks for the gift. You look beautiful." At eleven years old, Reo was just a head shorter than Bentley. She wore her hair in a single ponytail with bangs that curled perfectly just above her brow. Dressed in a white eyelet lace dress, she had on white sandals and held a small white patent leather purse in her gloved right hand.

"Hello, Bentley," Erik said, extending his hand.

She shook it and said, "Hi. I've already got the tick-
ets. Let's go on in." Bentley tried not to stare at Erik,
who looked so handsome in a casual charcoal brown
business suit. He seemed taller than she remembered.

As they walked down the aisles of the museum, Bentley listened as Reo talked about her recent camping trip.
She went horseback riding, canoeing, fishing, and rode
for miles on bike trails. Her scout troop put on a play
and Reo won the part to play the Fairy Godmother in
The Wizard of Oz. But the best fun of all, Reo told her,
was the art classes. They spent half a day making can-
dles—the best one she'd gift-wrapped for Bentley today.
She made several charcoal drawings that her dad had
hung in his office and even brought home a few tie-dyed
T-shirts.

Children chasing other children bumped into them
as Erik read the signs in front of the exhibits. They saw
loving parents huddled in groups; some watching and
some helping the children get play money from the
bank so that they could shop in the miniature city. The
eleven galleries, which included a dentist office, police
station, and architectural site, where children learn
how to build a house from start to finish, fascinated
Reo.

They entered the grocery store, with a produce section and pharmacy, and where kids could touch and select groceries. Reo's selections were scanned and she
even received coupons. Since the exhibit opened in
1990, the grocery store was the museum's most popular
display.

A small chubby boy with long blond hair ran toward his father, who, with arms open, had bent
down on one knee. His mother stood in front of them
snapping pictures. All three turned around when

they heard the giggles from their newborn in the stroller.

Again, Bentley chastised herself for being so clueless—why hadn't she thought to buy a disposable camera?

Erik told Bentley, while they waited for Reo to use the bathroom, how anxious Reo was to come today.

"This place," he said, forming his arms in a wide circle, "is what a child's life should be like—a fantasy. It's how a child's hopes and dreams are formed."

"I agree, Erik." But what about Isabell? she thought. They both knew that she was against Reo's meeting with her today. Isabell was also way off base, Bentley thought, if she planned on keeping her from seeing her own daughter.

When Reo came out the restroom, they headed for the Times Square exhibit, where the children could explore clocks and time zones.

Afterward, they went to the snack bar and Erik bought ice cream cones for everyone.

For the next thirty minutes they checked out the remainder of the exhibits. When it was time to go, Bentley hugged her daughter and fought back tears.

"Can I see you again, soon, Mommalee?"

Bentley turned to Erik, who was nodding yes.

She had so many regrets. There was so much of Reo's childhood that she'd forgotten. So many things that she could never share with her, like teaching her her ABC's, how to count and how to say her prayers.

Do you pray about me, Reo?

Give it time, Bentley thought as she was getting in her car. If she could keep her head clear, there will be nothing that Isabell could do to poison her child against her.

Fifty-three

SEX, LIES, AND VIDEO CARE was the subject of conversation at Basil's Mt. Moriah day care center. Imogene Cleaves, the woman Basil had been living with since January, had a troubled teenage son, Horace. Without Basil's permission, Imogene let her son make a little cash on the side working at the small center.

Tonight, when he and Imogene came home from a profitable night in Tunica, twenty-three messages were left on their machine. Eighteen were hang-ups and in three minutes Basil learned why.

He picked up the third ring.

"Hey, man, I've been trying to contact you all night."

"Who in the hell is this?" Basil didn't recognize the man's voice.

"It doesn't matter. I got something to show you. It's real hot. I could sell a couple of copies of this shit and make a fucking fortune."

"I'm going to hang up now," Basil said in an angry, controlled tone, and did just that.

"Basil?" Imogene called out from the bedroom. "Who's on the phone?"

The phone rang again. He hesitantly answered it. "Hello."

"Don't hang up on me again, fool. I ain't bullshitting with you."

He covered the phone with his hand. "Nothing important, babe. Fix me a drink and I'll be right there." Removing his hand, he said, "Look, brother—"

"Cut the shit, I said, and listen. I got a tape. I can shut your entire business down. Meet me in fifteen minutes at Porky's Barbecue on Perkins Street. I'll be in the blue Honda near the telephone booth." He hung up.

Not even bothering to tell his woman what was happening, Basil left the house and headed for Porky's.

When he arrived, there were two blue Hondas—one light and one dark. He was certain that it wasn't a coincidence. He parked his beige Mercedes six car lengths away. After removing the .38 Special from the glove compartment, he shoved it halfway down the back waistband of his black jeans and headed toward the vehicles.

The light one was occupied by a man and woman eating their meal. The dark one was empty. Basil strutted around to the driver side of the dark blue Honda and knocked on the tinted window. A man lying down in the backseat instantly rose up.

Not frightened in the least, he expected as much, and kept his right hand close to the handle of the pistol. As Basil scanned a fifty-foot radius of the vehicle, he heard the clicking of the door lock, then a man saying, "Get in."

No names were exchanged when Basil took a seat in the back. With his buttocks resting against the door and his body slightly angled toward the man, he did his best to hold his temper in check.

Even though the youth's face was half hidden by a black skullcap pulled low nearly covering his eyes, Basil memorized every nuance in his face and body. If he had to pick the man out in a line-up, he believed that he could do so in a matrix minute.

Under the most uncomfortable conditions in the

backseat, Basil watched the fuzzy scene on a nine-inch television and cheap VCR that was placed in the space between them.

"What's it going to cost me?" Basil asked after reviewing the tape.

"Ten grand."

"Fuck you." He started to get out of the car.

"Five."

Angry and madder than a disturbed queen bee, he spat out. "I *said,* fuck you."

"Six," the man said.

"What?"

"No copies. I promise you."

Outside the car now, Basil slammed the door. He heard the man roll down the window.

"Every step you take, bro, is another grand. I'd advise you to stop now."

Angered, Basil stopped and turned around. "You must think I'm a fool, boy." He could tell that the young man wasn't more than seventeen years old. Eighteen was a stretch.

"You're a fool, bro, if you don't take this deal. Seven Gs." He turned up the volume of the video so that Basil could hear it even though his back was turned.

The hairs on Basil's back rose and froze. He knew that he had no other choice. "Wait. I'll see what I can do."

Immediately the youth jumped out of the car and caught up with Basil, who was walking toward his car. Basil opened the trunk and removed a briefcase. He counted out the money that was 90 percent counterfeit and handed it to him.

"I got to warn you, boy," he said, after accepting the videotape, "I ain't never killed nobody before, but I guarantee you, if I hear or see about this tape anywhere in any shape or form, you're a dead man."

Fuming by the time he made it home, he stormed into the bedroom. "Pack your shit," he screamed at Imogene.

"What the hell—"

Basil began pulling out and emptying drawers on the bed. Imogene screamed and cursed a cauldron of filthy words at him, but Basil didn't pay attention to them. When she tried to stop him from removing her clothes from the closet, he knocked her out of the way.

Fortunately, Imogene's son had always lived with her sister, and Basil had only met the boy five or six times during their nine-month liaison. However, on the few occasions that he did come in contact with him, he could tell that the boy was sneaky and instantly disliked him.

Opening three suitcases in the closet, he began to cram them with her things. In a few swift strokes, he filled them and then clamped them shut. Speechless, she stared at him wide-eyed.

"I told you not to let that boy work at the center. Because you didn't listen, your son has cost me money."

"Please, baby," she begged, "tell me what's wrong. We can work this out."

"Naw, naw. It's over." He lifted the suitcases and headed for the back door. Halfway there, she clawed at his back and clothes, stopping when she felt the gun.

"Yeah, baby. It's like that." Turning around, fire seemed to jump like firecrackers from his eyes. "Horace has abused a ten-year-old girl at the center. Every freaky minute is on videotape." He pushed her off him, disgusted. "I told you to keep that boy away from those kids. Especially the girls."

Imogene fell to her knees, crying.

Basil didn't feel an ounce of sympathy. She'd been paid well, and her worn-out pussy wasn't that good anyway. "Get up, bitch!"

All the pleading and crying didn't matter. Basil dragged her outside, and opened the front door of her white Pontiac Grand Am with his set of keys. He then tossed all three cases on the passenger seat, and forced her into the driver's side.

He ignored her sniffling and crying and said in the coldest tone he could muster, "If I see that boy, I'm going to kill him. He better find another town to live in. Know, girl, that I ain't playing."

Back in the house, he rested his back against the closed door, closed his eyes, and exhaled.

The last thing that he needed, he thought, as he poured himself a double shot of Absolut, was more negative publicity at his centers.

Over the past year, the *Hamilton Appeal* had been bombarded with articles about day care centers all over the city: "Two Children Die in Vans from Heat Exhaustion"; "An Eighteen-Month-Old Child Left in the Center After Closing"; "Day Care Owner, Driving Van, Arrested and Booked on a DUI, After Running Red Light"; "Nine-Month-Old Baby Burned by Hot Water from Bottle Warmers—Received Second-Degree Burns." Of all the accusations, few were proven and none were related to sexual misconduct.

Basil cringed. His kids were well supervised. Even so, he knew that after the press got wind of the fact that he was single, and living with the boy's mother, they would picture him as a participant or maybe the instigator.

He could see the headlines of the paper now:

"Teenage Day Care Worker Guilty of Fondling Ten-Year-Old Girl at Memphis Center."

There was no way that the young blackmailer would keep his word. But the seven grand did buy him a little time. With a little luck, he could get things in place to diffuse the situation and save losing his license.

Basil picked up the phone and dialed the 615 area code.

But Basil's troubles weren't over. The following day, federal agents arrested David Ramsey, Basil's longtime college mate and ex-partner.

When Basil came to work the next morning, Bentley could tell that he was upset. By now, she knew his schedule. He spent approximately twenty to thirty minutes a day at each of his fifteen centers. But today, Basil had been at the Whitehaven center for over an hour and it didn't look like he was ready to leave anytime soon. "Are you adjusting here okay?" Basil asked, taking a seat in front of her.

"Yeah, fine." She set aside the file of a foster family's application for five of their eight children to be placed in the Shelby County system.

Bentley tried not to appear nervous. Her job was simple. She screened the applicants after Delilah, the office assistant manager, to make sure that they were eligible for government assistance. Listening to their heart-warming stories had helped Bentley to put her personal problems in perspective. These people were desperate. They had very little money and subsisted primarily on jobs that barely met their weekly needs.

"I wanted to let you know how much I appreciate your taking this job. It wasn't just a handout. I really needed—"

The phone rang.

It was the receptionist looking for Basil. Bentley hadn't known that his pager had been turned off. She handed him the phone.

"Yeah. I'm Basil Hamilton. What!"

Bentley watched a myriad of expressions cross his face. "Why, that lowlife motherfucker!" He jumped up from the chair. "Look, I don't know nothing about none of that bullshit. David's lying his ass off!"

The conversation went on for another three minutes. Bentley tried to keep herself busy, but she'd concluded that there was something fishy going on with Basil and his ex-partner, David Ramsey.

When Basil hung up, he told Bentley, "I'll check you later," then left.

After Basil abruptly left, Bentley turned on the noon news. Apparently, David Ramsey was arrested because an undercover cop had discovered evidence of counterfeiting at his day care center.

"Over the course of two months, undercover officers bought more than $57,000 in counterfeit money from David Ramsey."

The counterfeit bills were among the items listed seized during the search of the day care center on Wednesday by U.S. Magistrate Wilma Altman, who authorized the search warrant.

The phone rang again, and Bentley answered it. This time it was for her.

"Hey, girl. It's me."

"Corky?"

"The same."

"I'm out and about. Your aunt Anne gave me your work number. I couldn't wait until you got home."

"It's so good to hear your voice. The letters have been beautiful, but still, it's not the same."

"I know."

"Tell me, where are you?"

"At my parents' home. But just until Monday. I've got the keys to my new place."

"How?"

"Ingenuity. I'm just five miles from where you're staying. I've got an apartment at Germantown Pointe Apartments. My address is 3499 Pointe Place. Can you stop by one day this week?"

"Count on it."

"I'll see you then."

When Bentley hung up the phone she continued working on her foster family file and listening to the top stories on the noon news.

"His nickname was Dollar. And federal agents say that he was literally making money—he called it 'baking the bread'—with state-of-the-art computer equipment at Hungry Minds Learning Academy."

Over the course of three months, undercover officers bought more than $50,000 in counterfeit money from LaKiesha Matheson.

When the U.S. Secret Service agents and Shelby County sheriff's deputies descended on Hungry Minds, they found 180 counterfeit $100 bills. Some of the funny money was printed on only one side. Agents also confiscated computers, disks, scanners, and color printers from the office in the day care center.

Bentley was no dummy. She'd seen certain individuals coming into their place of business, bogarting the computer equipment as if they owned it.

Something wasn't right. Basil wasn't the businessman that he professed to be. And she knew, half crazy or not, what "illegal sources of activity" meant.

* * *

THOUGH THEY WERE ON OPPOSITE SIDES of the spectrum, Isabell Ford Berry couldn't have agreed with Bentley more. Something just wasn't right. She and Erik hadn't made love in over a month. Trusting her instincts, she'd had him followed. The meeting with Erik, Reo, and Bentley at the Children's Museum hadn't eluded her sharp duo of private investigators.

She'd specifically told Erik that she didn't want her daughter interacting with Bentley. As her legal mother, Isabell felt that she had some rights in determining whom her child could associate with.

Bentley had her chance and blew it. She'd lost custody and the law was on Isabell's side. There was absolutely nothing that Bentley could do to get Reo back.

Erik had better be careful, she thought. If he crossed her, he'd be at the courthouse fighting for bimonthly visitation rights himself.

"ARE YOU NERVOUS?" Hilda asked Anne as she positioned the black cap on top of her curly tresses.

"Not really. I'm looking forward to getting this over with."

It had taken a second try before Anne passed the bar exam. But it hadn't bothered her. At least half of her classmates didn't pass it on the first go-around either. And today, on this windy day in November, Anne Baker and two of her old school chums from Nashville participated, along with over two hundred others, in the swearing-in ceremony for practicing attorneys in the state of Tennessee.

The two-hour ritual took place in the Foggleman Center of the University of Memphis campus. All five supreme court justices for the State of Tennessee were in attendance. The Chief Justice presided over the service.

After all the attendees received their certificates, they raised their right hands and took the formal oath—affirming that they would be good attorneys.

Anne left the university that day on cloud nine. Her husband, grandson, son, sister, and nieces all came to see her receive her law license.

When it was over, all seven had gone out to celebrate afterward at the new Red Birds stadium in downtown Memphis. The Red Birds were playing at home against the Nashville Sound.

The following Friday, Bentley took sixty of her day care students to the Shelby Farms Showcase Arena in Germantown, Tennessee, to see the sixth annual Bill Pickett Invitational Rodeo.

The rodeo was dedicated to all the black cowboys and cowgirls of the past who helped shape the West and those of today who help keep the spirit of the West alive.

"See the clown, Ms. Russell," one of the children shouted as they headed for their seats.

A heavyset man done up in a red plaid shirt, red suspenders, and huge blue jeans large enough for a cow welcomed the crowd into the stadium. The strong smell of horses made Bentley's nostrils flare open. It was a smell that was unique for the inner city kids—different but not offensive.

Fresh dirt covered the arena floor. After each event, a huge man, driving a tractor and pulling a rake, would smooth the dirt for the next event. The clowns were continuous entertainment. They also helped the cowboys by distracting the bulls as they dismounted or were bucked off.

Most of the crowd was dressed in razor-sharp starched jeans, cowboy shirt, vest, hat, and boots. Even the tiniest toddlers donned a western wardrobe.

Bentley turned her attention to a small child who was tugging at her shirt.

"I see him, Brandon," she said smiling. "Now c'mon children, we have to get seated." Turning to look behind her, she waved at the four volunteer women who had elected to help her with the field trip.

The sound of the horses' hooves knocking against the fresh dirt was exciting. At the far end of the arena was a hoard of steers seemingly murmuring "Moo moo," as if on cue.

"Ladies and gentlemen, boys and girls, welcome Mr. Peanut," the announcer said. The clown who was already in the middle of the arena bowed, pulled a microphone from the depths of his jeans, and began to tell rodeo jokes.

Laughter was heard all around the stadium. Bentley managed a small smile when she saw all of her kids having such a good time.

Next came an eleven-year-old-boy, Rooster Avalon, riding two horses while standing up and stepping from one horse to another. Turning around backward, he did butterflies with the rope.

"Doesn't it look very, very easy?" the announcer said.

The children were speechless as Rooster lit the torches and circled the track to ride his horses through the blazing fire.

The children held their breath.

Rooster made it!

Bareback riding was the next event, followed by the roping competition, which the children got really excited about.

The cowboys carried two pieces of rope about twenty-eight feet long. The first cowboy roped the calf in 12.2 seconds. When the second cowboy fell off his horse and missed the calf, the children laughed and giggled.

The announcer interrupted the melee. "Here's Bubba Williams, all the way from Dallas, Texas. Bubba's a second-generation cowboy. His dad is Bulldog Billy Williams.

"All the calves are drawn for the cowboys prior to the performances," Bentley heard the announcer say.

Her mind drifted off, but her eyes were acutely trained on the children. In the few months that she'd been home from the hospital, she'd completed the first draft of the screenplay. Secretly, she was afraid that if Jada rejected her work, she wouldn't be able to secure another production company to buy it. Bentley figured that by January, she'd have at least three more drafts of the screenplay finished, and only when she felt absolutely sure that she couldn't improve upon it anymore would she send it in. On a positive note, Dusty told her that her comic books were still selling at his store in Nashville. It seemed she'd developed a cult following.

"Ms. Russell?" said four-year-old Iris, tugging at her sleeve, "I have to go to the bathroom."

"Okay, baby," she said, taking her small hand in hers. Standing up she asked, "Does anyone else have to go to the bathroom?" Three more girls and one boy said yes. "Follow me."

As they headed down the rail toward the steps, she looked up in the packed bleachers and smiled when she saw that the other fifty-five children were still mesmerized by the ongoing performances.

"That's one, two, and a Huey!" the announcer screamed as a cowboy jumped from his horse, tied the steer's two hind legs and pulled it into his chest in twelve seconds flat. He'd made the best time yet.

When the five children had finished using the lavatory and washed their hands, they eagerly headed back to the action.

"I want all the kids aged ten and under to go into the arena!" the announcer screamed. "Right now. C'mon now."

The children she was escorting back to their seats were the closest to the ring, so they ran to the first open gate and rushed inside. To Bentley, it looked as if a million little kids were causing a miniature stampede.

The now familiar voice said, "All the kids get ahold of the fence, and wait for a moment." At that point a herd of calves were brought into the arena.

Bentley leaned over the rail and kept an eye on her kids. She easily recognized them, with blue ribbons attached to their shirts. She relaxed, took a deep breath, and hooked her thumbs in the back of her jeans. She'd begun to enjoy herself, too.

It was so funny, Bentley thought, as she watched all the little kids huddled around the arena. Dozens of the young boys were dressed in cowboy gear from head to toe. But the loud giggles and screams from the girls let everyone know that they weren't to be counted out either.

"Boys and girls, we've got three prizes to give away. There are three blue ribbons attached to the calves' tails. Whoever manages to take off any of the ribbons will win a pair of custom-made cowboy boots."

The kids screamed as the calves were released from the corral.

Bentley's heart was beating faster than her thoughts. What if the animals hurt the kids? What if one of them fell and was trampled? What would she say to their mother? Father? For a minute, Bentley was frightened, but after seeing how much fun the other children who were already running inside the ring were having, that thought disappeared like smoke. She was just about to put a stick of spearmint gum in her mouth when a hairy hand clamped over her right shoulder.

"Hello, Bentley."

She froze. No one else could have that voice.

"I'd like to speak with you for a moment."

Even above the scent of the horses, she could smell his scent. Turning around, she looked him in the eye. "No." Bentley tried not to look disappointed when the children returned. None of the kids in her group had managed to get one of the blue ribbons.

Grabbing her arm, he said, "I'm not going nowhere until I talk to you."

Bentley noticed the four volunteers helping the children back into the bleachers and into their seats.

"It's time that I told you how sorry I am."

Bentley turned away, unbelieving.

He showed her his business card that read Riding for Jesus on one side and Have Bible Will Travel on the back.

Kirk went on to tell her that he was saved and filled with the Holy Ghost. He was now the pastor of Riding for Jesus Cowboy Church. To date, he had over 100 members. His church was one of thirty interdenominational cowboy churches across the country.

"Maybe one day, I can forgive you. But not now . . ." She began to walk back toward where the children were sitting.

She could hear the announcer saying, "Here's the 1998 champion steer wrestler, Chris Quinn from Beaumont—he's always got a smile on his face."

"Wait! Hear me out," Kirk pleaded.

"I understand why you feel the way you do, Kirk. Most people's conscience starts to kill them at some point."

He grabbed her hand, and then released it when she flinched. "Just know that you're in my prayers. One day, if it's the will of God, maybe you can find it in your heart to forgive me. That's the prayer that I've always prayed. With the Lord's help, people can change. I have." He blushed. "I turned fifty a few months back. Got married. My wife is expecting our first child this summer."

Bentley looked up at him. For a split second he was the man she admired when she was a child. So life did move on. She wondered if he had suffered in his personal life as she had. Even after having become a Christian, she asked herself, had he reaped what he sowed?

"I'm happy for you, Kirk." She couldn't bring herself to say *Uncle*. "Maybe I'll see you back on the circuit the next time you're in town."

The music from "Wild Wild West" was being broadcast all over the speakers.

A cowboy with a dummy and twin Colt .45s strapped to his hips was being introduced in the center of the ring.

"I'm faster than Jim West."

"Kirk . . ." she stopped, wondering what to say that would let him know that she was at least trying. Still uncertain about her choice of words, she turned her attention back to the skit. In the center ring was a black Jim West who was supposed to be a robot. Smoke came out of its back, and then the dummy went through the motions of a choreographed moonwalk around the perimeter of the ring.

The kids' laughter nearly drowned out her thoughts. Just then a singing black cowboy took the microphone and rode into the center of the arena. Riding around the stadium, he sang a gospel tune, "Trust Me Lord." Both Bentley and Kirk were silent until he finished.

When he did, Bentley had tears in her eyes. She hadn't been to church or heard a gospel song in a long time. The old spiritual moved her more than she thought it would. Wiping her eyes, she kept her back to Kirk, and said, "I've got to go!"

In the background the female cowgirls were being introduced. They were about to compete in the "Barrel-racing contest." Whoever finished the course with the fastest time won.

"Here's the cowgirl April Waters, she's the reigning champion—"

Bentley had heard enough. She walked back to the bleachers where her students sat and said, "Time to go, kids."

"Dog. I don't wanna go." A wave of complaints echoed from the kids.

"Sorry, kids. But if we don't get out of here now, we'll be stampeded when everyone stands to leave." She pasted a smile across her face and waved a brown bag in front of them. "I've got a candy bar for the first five kids that get five more kids to hold their hands."

She could hear the announcer reading off the winner's scores on the public address system. Some of the cowgirls had posted times in previous rodeo meets as they entered the ring.

"Here is the cowgirl that is the reigning champion. She has to beat the time of 17.64."

When the cowgirl finished her jaunt around the ring, the announcer said, "She tapped the barrel, folks, but it didn't fall!"

Loud clapping and cheers were heard all over the stadium.

"Her time is 17.09!" She's the sister-in-law of her trainer, cowboy Kirk Russell."

Bentley didn't bother to look back. She thought that if she did, she might turn into a pillar of salt or most likely a brick.

Fifty-four

BENTLEY FELT AS IF SHE'D HAD ENOUGH drama in her life to last at least until the New Year. Seeing Kirk had ruffled her feathers and had spawned a two-hour heart-to-heart talk with Anne.

It was a blessing in disguise to hear Anne give Bentley her thoughts about Kirk. She understood his need for forgiveness and told her niece that she didn't blame her for telling him that she still hadn't forgiven him as of yet.

"After all, our childhood hurts carry on to adulthood, and very few people could honestly say that they'd been able to purge themselves of all of the problems of their youth. It would be a lifetime struggle."

When she told Bentley that she was having trouble trying to decide how she would treat Kirk the next time she saw him, Bentley was moved. She attributed Anne's compassion to her being a devout Catholic. Since she'd lived at their home, Anne and Dusty never missed mass and confession unless one of them was sick. Bentley noticed that when they came home, Anne seemed to wear an ethereal afterglow. She seemed so happy and carefree. And Dusty had treated Bentley with every courtesy. He even tried to work on her car when the thermostat went out.

But on the personal front, Erik had dropped a whammy on her. He called her at work early Thursday morning to tell her that he and Isabell had quarreled. She'd found out about the meeting with Reo at the museum.

"We had it out last night. I'll leave out the horrible details. I'm not sure if she was lying about what she told me or not. But I do know that she's crazy. Or lost her mind . . . whatever. Regardless, I don't trust her around Reo."

"And how is Reo doing?"

"She's great. A little confused about why her mother is acting so strangely. But I've done the best that I could. I've tried to reassure her that Isabell is having some problems right now."

"I don't know what to say, Erik."

"Just know that I don't know exactly what's going to happen myself. I do know that my job at the *Hamilton Appeal* is history. I've resigned and applied for employment at other companies. I do have my years in the service as a truck driver. If the employment situation doesn't work out, I'm considering heading up my own trucking company."

"And how is Isabell taking all of this?"

"She's threatened to kill herself. Kill me. Kill everybody."

"What!"

"It's nothing but a front. That woman can act her ass off," he said tiredly. "I've known for years that Isabell has had a lover. I could never find out who the man was, probably because I didn't want to know." He sighed. "But when I mentioned a legal separation, she told me who it was—Basil."

"She's lying."

"No, I think she's telling the truth. She seems to have some kind of vendetta against the Russell family. At this point, I don't have the slightest idea why."

Bentley felt that Erik knew a lot more than he was telling her.

"Why are you telling me all of this, Erik?"

"Selfish reasons." He told her that he'd had a heart-to-heart talk with his mother. They'd never been so honest with each other before.

"I don't understand."

"Bentley, I want to apologize to you for what I did to you years ago. I am not going to tell you that I would cut off my arm or my leg if it would change things. I am not going to bullshit you with any lame excuses. I respect you too much for that. I'm sorry, and you deserve an explanation.

"Years ago when I first saw you and Nikkie at the skating rink, I wanted you then and I never stopped wanting you. Loving you. My marriage to Isabell was a mistake. The biggest mistake I could have made in two lifetimes. At the time I started going out with Isabell I was young and impressed with driving her new cars. She had a ton of money and didn't mind spending it on me. She bought me expensive clothes, shoes, and all kinds of jewelry. It blew my mind. You know where I came from. How poor we were and how my mother had to scratch and scrape just to put food on the table. I thought being with Isabell was a chance to escape that sort of life, and also be able to help my family.

"I was wrong. Oh, was I wrong.

"I found out some hard truths right after we got married. She refused to take me with her when she went out and wouldn't let me know where she was going. There were mysterious phone calls at all times of the night. I knew that she was having an affair with another man. It bothered me at first, but then I figured it was God paying me back for the dirty deed that I'd done to you. Plus, I was too ashamed to admit that I'd made a mistake. So I stayed. It didn't take all these things happening to me for me to realize how much I loved you. I always knew that, I just made a dumb childish mistake. Bentley, I'm truly sorry."

Is that why we didn't make it? Because I was so weak to you? A long sigh of regret escaped from her lips.

Erik went on to tell her, in a roundabout and unhurtful way, about their daughter's intense need for love.

"Despite the reasons why we married, Reo had begun to care for Isabell. She had begun to think of her as a surrogate mother. It wouldn't have been fair to Reo to take her away from a mother again."

"I don't care how much that woman cares for my daughter. The thought of Reo calling her *Mother* makes me ill."

"Try to understand, Bentley. Reo barely remembered you. When another woman shows a child so much love and gives her everything she wants, it's no wonder the child is going to care for her. And as I said, Isabell really does love Reo. It's not an act."

"So what do you expect me to do about this situation, Erik? Just sit back and be thankful that some white woman was nice to my daughter?"

"No. I can't tell you what to do. I only know what I'd do if I were in your position."

What do you know about me, Erik? I'm not the same woman you fell in love with at the skating rink twenty years ago. I jeopardized the safety of my child and sister. I've lost my mind, my job, and my home. I won't make these same mistakes again.

"You'll be hearing from my attorney, Erik."

Fifty-five

ANNE WASN'T SURE WHAT SHE SHOULD DO. On one hand she understood her husband's dilemma. He wanted to hire two people to run a mail-order business from the 5,500 square feet of space that Anne wasn't using in the basement. But Dusty told her that he didn't feel right remodeling the space with Basil's name still on the deed.

His suggestion was to buy out Basil's percentage of the property.

Since Anne had gone to work in September at her new NCRC office, Dusty offered to baby-sit Daniel.

He even cooked dinner on the days she came home late. He was spoiling her so badly, Anne didn't feel right refusing him anything he asked. And what he was asking her to do now was what she felt a real man would do.

Anne picked up the phone and paged her son. Trying to gather her thoughts, she still hadn't figured out when she'd say to him when he rang her back.

"Yeah, Mom."

"Basil . . . I was calling to see if you could stop by soon. I have something to ask you."

"Mom. You know I've got all this counterfeit mess going on right now. Come on out with it. What's on your mind?"

"It's the house. You know that your father left you and Holly a percentage of it."

"Uh-huh. Look, Mom. I don't want it. I realize that you and Dusty have got a good thing going on. I can add up two and two."

"But I didn't—"

"You know, Mom, I didn't graduate with a 4.0 for nothing. If I hadn't been so overwhelmed with this stuff from the IRS, I would have taken care of it after you and Dusty got married. What I'm saying is that I'm willing to take my name off the deed. I never wanted any part of that house anyway."

"I don't believe it. But Basil, I was willing to give you my interest in your business as a trade-off."

"Not necessary, Mom."

"Oh, but it is. I'll have my attorney draw up the papers. I've made a good deal of money from the day care business and I want to use that money to invest in Dusty's hobby shop. He's got a proven track record from his business dealings in Nashville."

"Your reasons still aren't necessary, Mom. I never felt good about what Dad did anyway. As I said, I never wanted any part of that house. It has too many unpleasant memories."

"Basil . . . thank you."

"There again, Mom. I'm glad that you're happy. You deserve it."

"Thanks, Son."

And this time, she meant it. Basil had never seemed so caring and mature as he did now. How could she let her son know that she'd finally forgiven him for Holly's death?

ON FRIDAY, NOVEMBER 17, Baptist Memorial Hospital ended eighty-eight years at the Medical Center's epicenter when the last patients were wheeled out of the facility.

The hospital had a long history. In 1935 Baptist was the first in the mid-South to offer physical therapy. In 1955, it was one of the first hospitals in the nation to install air-conditioning. In 1968, on February 1, Lisa Marie Presley was born to Elvis and Priscilla. On August 16, 1977, Elvis Presley was pronounced dead in Baptist's emergency department. In 1978 a flash flood combined with a lightning strike crippled pumps in the city's sewer system and flooded the Medical Center. Water again disrupted the hospital's life in 1994 in the form of ice. In 1997, St. Joseph merged with Baptist Hospital. In July of 2000 the proposal to merge the Regional Medical Center and UT Bowld floundered, setting the tone for the ultimate closing of the hospital this November.

Anne had told Bentley that she believed that closing the downtown facility was an injustice for blacks living in the downtown area. Anne and her newly formed legal staff planned to investigate the closing and to see what she, along with other inner-city and county officials, could do about getting the historical facility reopened in the near future.

College basketball was big in the city of Memphis. And the first regular season game of the Memphis Tigers was highly anticipated. The Pyramid, which held 20,000 seats, was sold out. The new Tigers coach, John Callipari, was to face off against his old mentor, John Chaney of Temple University.

The highly anticipated event was televised and Corky had invited Bentley over to his place to watch the game with him.

Bentley didn't have the heart to tell Corky that she hated sports. She complimented him on his quaint little apartment and made herself comfortable on the living-room sofa.

She thought back on the conversation that she'd had with her attorney yesterday.

"I'm sorry, Ms. Russell. But Mr. and Mrs. Berry are the legal parents of Reo Berry. They have the right to decline visitation, even if the child is your blood daughter."

Bentley tried two other attorneys, who told her virtually the same thing. Her rights as Reo's mother were terminated when she was in the mental institution. There was absolutely nothing that she could do about it unless the adopted parents would be willing to work out some kind of visitation for her and Reo.

Just this morning, Erik had called her with the bad news—Isabell refused to cooperate. Bentley wasn't surprised. Sure, she was disappointed, but she knew that she had to stay positive and not get stressed about things that she couldn't control.

The entire country was in an uproar about the presidential election. Bentley hadn't heard of so much mass confusion in politics since she was hired at the *Appeal*. Personally, she didn't care if Bush or Gore won. Her priorities were somewhere else. Maintaining peace of mind was part of the reason why she had accepted this invitation with Corky tonight.

During halftime Corky cooked butterfly shrimp and french fries and opened a bag of Caesar salad mix.

Bentley tried to contain her boredom after they finished dinner and cleaned up the kitchen. It seemed like the basketball game would never end. She tried to amuse herself by checking out interesting things in the apartment, but since he'd just moved in, there wasn't much to look at.

During the third and fourth quarter Bentley noticed that Corky's eye had begun to stray. She caught him staring at her and couldn't help but blush. Being honest with herself, she felt that they would become intimate tonight, but if it didn't happen she wouldn't force it. A part of her wanted to know if he could satisfy her. She hadn't had sex in so long, she wasn't sure if she could last two hours or two minutes.

Near the end of the fourth quarter, the Tigers were behind. Corky pulled Bentley closer to him on the sofa and kissed her. She responded and watched his intense blue eyes roguishly rake over her body. He began to caress her face, neck, shoulder, and finally her breasts. She heard him gasp when he felt her nipples harden under his touch. Corky moved closer, his mouth now demanding and hard on hers.

She pulled back, pushing him away from her and sat up, dizzy and trembling.

"Don't you want me?" he asked, leaning his head back against the sofa.

"I thought I did. But I'm not sure."

He smiled at her, and then cradled her in his arms. "Don't be afraid of me. I won't hurt you."

Bending down he kissed her fully on the lips, a kiss filled with passion. But it was a passion softened now by tenderness.

She relaxed and gave in to his kisses, allowing him to undress her slowly, as she watched him greedily admiring every inch of her.

When the game ended, neither she nor Corky noticed that the Tigers lost to Temple 62–67.

She enjoyed the vehemence with which Corky seduced her—the urgency that verged on violence. His head lowered and his mouth closed over hers. He seemed oblivious to her trepidation.

Her breasts, already pert in anticipation, hardened surprisingly quickly. She thought—if it's my body he wants, here it is—ready to rumble.

His round, repetitive strokes were like a massage, not quite sexual, but hypnotically sensuous.

How things had changed, she thought. Here she was, all streamlined curves, dimples, and tender black skin, and all of her flesh wanted and even lusted for all of his attentive groping.

He was going to come quickly, she surmised. Obviously, he wasn't adept at delaying gratification. The deep heat in her breasts and inner legs demanded a necessary fulfillment. As she felt his fingers trail down to play teasingly in her triangle of black curls, she imagined her mind in a far place where only feeling mattered and consciousness of difference didn't.

The warm feeling of his hardening member heightened her awareness, but altered it, temporarily. There was a tremble running through her body now like a radio not quite turned off. Nothing other than a man's penis could rub against her pubic area and excite her in the same way.

Bentley lowered her hand and fingered herself, closed her eyes, and thought of Corky's mouth opening and closing on her nipples. She imagined that his mouth had closed around her toes and ears. She imagined that sex would be great if it could be tasted and heard as well as felt.

In her heightened state, Bentley thought about orgasming in colors and smells. She imagined the unimaginable, because that was what coupling was all about.

When she came, along with him, she screamed. And for a moment it sounded like someone else, outside of herself. But when he embraced her and whispered her name, she knew that the time was now, in his apartment, in his place.

It was this moment that she realized that Erik's credit had run out. There was something about the newness of sex. The freshness of no problems—no connectedness—only pure unadulterated lovemaking.

Feeling as if her entire body were glowing, she folded into his inviting arms and slept the sleep of peace.

Fifty-six

BASIL WAS AT HIS WITS' END. He promised himself after Holly's death that his businesses would be completely legitimate. He would get rid of the counterfeit money, clean up all the centers, and hire competent workers.

He decided to make the changes six months too late.

To date, there was a bill before Governor Don Sundquist that would give the state power to conduct financial audits of private companies that contract to perform government services. The bill moved quickly but quietly through the General Assembly following disclosures that Shelby County's child care broker, Hamilton's Children and Family Services, had objected to a state audit requested by federal prosecutors.

The measure, which won unanimous approval in the House and Senate fourteen days after it was introduced, would allow the state Comptroller's Office to audit the books and records of contractors that receive 50 percent or more of their funding from the state.

The bill added fresh fuel to Tennessee's emerging debate over the public's right to monitor privatization of government services, stating in one potentially controversial passage that its provisions would apply retroactively to 1992.

The measure was sent to Sundquist, who later signed it.

The bill was introduced on behalf of the Comptroller's Office, which attempted this year to examine records documenting how Hamilton's Children and Family Services spent millions of dollars from the state in the 1990s to help poor families find subsidized day care in Shelby County.

State auditors sought Hamilton's financial records in conjunction with a federal grand jury investigation but began questioning their legal authority to audit the nonprofit organization after a confrontation with state Senator Orin Matthews.

The bill didn't mention Hamilton by name but stated "some entities" under contract with the state "have questioned the authority of the comptroller of the treasury to examine . . . records . . . necessary to ensure that public funds are expended in accordance with the public purpose for which they were extended."

BASIL HAD HAD HIS SHARE OF PROBLEMS. Just the month before, his so-called secret lover, Florence Johnson, had dropped a bombshell on him. She no longer wished to be in his company and their former business arrangement was about to come to an end. She didn't tell him how or why, but by her next press conference, he knew most of the answers.

"The state will stop using brokers to administer its subsidized day care program," said Human Services Commissioner Florence Johnson. "It will end by the middle of next year."

It was obvious that the intended target was Hamilton, whose brokerage was accused of "steering" subsidy payments to child care centers in which its officials had financial interests.

Ms. Johnson's decision required no legislative action.

She also won support for legislation that would allow her department to adopt new "emergency rules" lowering adult-to-child ratios, strengthen training requirements, and limit the amount of time day care children spent in transit daily.

What bothered Basil about all of this was the fact that Florence admitted that the state wouldn't be able to perform the broker tasks cheaper than Hamilton's did.

So he received a 35 percent profit margin—did that make him a criminal? No—but that's not how the *Hamilton Appeal* saw it. Their lawyers were awaiting a decision in the judicial district to have a judge appointed to hear the case.

BASIL WAS FULL OF VENOM as he drove the repaired Children's Castle van back to its Whitehaven location. Less than a quarter mile from the center, he was pulled over.

"What's the problem, Officer?" Basil asked, rolling down the window.

"You were driving fifty miles an hour in a thirty-five-mile-an-hour zone. Can I see your driver's license and registration, please?"

"But Officer, I wasn't speeding. You must've made some kind of mistake."

The mistake was made when Basil spoke.

"Could you step outside the vehicle, sir," the officer said cryptically.

It was then that Basil stuffed a pint of Absolut vodka beneath the driver's seat, which would be found later.

The van was searched. The open bottle of liquor, along with three fake hundred-dollar bills that had fallen out of his slacks, was found.

Anne was at her new office, patiently going over what was to be her first case when she received a call from Dusty—her son was in jail.

It took $100,000 cash to bail Basil out.

Three days later Anne went back to the bank to withdraw enough money for last-minute Christmas shopping.

"I'm sorry, Mrs. Baker, but there's a problem with your account," the teller told Anne.

"I can't understand what the problem could be. Could you check the account number again, please?"

Five minutes later she was being led to the manager's office. It seemed that the Internal Revenue Service had put a freeze on all of her accounts.

Unable to contact Basil, she immediately called her attorney. He told her that he'd get back to her before the day ended.

ISABELL COULDN'T HAVE BEEN MORE PLEASED. The story would run on the front page of the *Hamilton Appeal* tomorrow: "Ex-Publisher's Wife Silent Partner in Counterfeit Day Care Ring."

In the heat of passion, Basil had made the unfortunate mistake of telling Isabell that his mother had invested in his business. Isabell had sat on the bit of information until just the right moment. She knew that sooner or later an opportunity would present itself, and now was the time.

"HELLO, MIRIAM. It's Bentley Russell."

"Why, hello, Bentley. It's a pleasure to hear from you. How've you been?"

"Oh, so-so. I was calling to congratulate you on Bill Lacey's award."

Bill Lacey was the editorial cartoonist at the *Hamilton Appeal*. On Saturday, the Atlanta professional chapter of the Society of Professional Journalists at the fiftieth annual Green Eyeshade Awards banquet honored him. Bill received the first-place award in editorial cartoons for "Dying in Day Care," a biting commentary on state-subsidized care in Memphis. Working one-on-one in the day care field these past few months, Bentley could certainly relate to what he'd written about. She felt that he'd been right on target with his ironic depiction of what most people in the city believed to be an insult to the working community.

"Thanks, Bentley. I felt that Bill should have won, too. Like you, he's got a great talent."

"I appreciate the compliment, Miriam." She sucked in her pride and asked, "What's the status on the *Priscilla* strip? I heard that it's been canceled."

"Yep. As of next week."

Go on, ask her. "Is there any chance that the *Appeal* might consider replacing it with *The Riverdocks*? In case you don't know, it's being made into a feature film next year."

Miriam cleared her throat. "I'm sorry, Bentley. If it was up to me you would have been back here the moment you got out of the hospital. We're still getting letters about your strip."

"Well, then who's preventing me from making a comeback?"

"I'm not at liberty to say."

Isabell. It had to be her. Erik had told her that Isabell secretly owned the company, but she wasn't to tell Anne. It might cause some legal problems.

"I understand, Miriam. And thanks for your support. Take care. 'Bye."

Bentley had the oddest feeling when she hung up the phone. There was something strange about Isabell that she couldn't put her finger on. She remembered her aunt Anne telling her that she and Isabell used to be friends. How long ago had that been? Wasn't it too much of a coincidence that Isabell had had dealings with Anne, Basil, and herself?

Bentley didn't know that Erik had done exactly as he'd promised he would. He quit his job at the *Appeal,* filed for a divorce, and moved himself and his daughter into their own apartment.

ISABELL MOVED QUICKLY. She'd lost Erik and she didn't care. What she did care about was Reo. She was certain that Erik had tried to turn Reo against her and had filled her head with all kind of lies.

She hadn't meant for things to turn out this way, but they had. And now that meant her plans had to change too.

This morning, she'd secretly withdrawn a majority of her holdings from First Security National Bank and had it forwarded to a bank in Switzerland. She contacted her accountant and requested that he liquidate her assets, including her shares in the *Hamilton Appeal.*

Next, Isabell called Crocus and gave him the directives that she wanted carried out as soon as possible. It was time to close the chapter on Anne Russell-Baker.

Everything was in place. Three days before Christmas, she and Reo would have disappeared from the face of the earth.

She hadn't counted on the wisdom of an eleven-year-old child.

"I don't want to go, Mommy."

Isabell tried to hide the urgency in her voice. "Why not, sweetheart? We're only going to be gone a few days. I've got your gifts all wrapped up and ready for you to open up."

"No. I want to stay with my daddy."

"C'mon, sweetheart. Your daddy says that it's okay to come with me now. Now, come on. I've got your suitcase already packed in the car."

Telling her that her suitcases had been packed was a mistake and Isabell instantly realized it. "Don't worry about a thing, baby. Mommy has taken care of everything."

Isabell reached out for Reo and she pulled back. Isabell could see Erik in the shadows just a few feet away.

"Erik, tell her that it's okay to come with me." Her voice was desperate. "I'll bring her back on Sunday night."

Erik's words barely registered, Isabell was so focused on hurrying to get away. She heard his final request: "Go on, baby."

"No," Reo said adamantly.

Her world seemed to be crumbling around her. Isabell fell on her knees crying. For the first time in years, her tears were real. To this day, Isabell couldn't believe how much she loved Erik's daughter. She actually wanted to be a good mother to her. Why couldn't Reo accept that? After all, Isabell had been the only person in her life, other than Erik, that she could count on. And Isabell had given Reo everything. Especially her love. Didn't that matter most of all?

"No. I don't want to go with you," Reo said, turning and running back into the house.

"Erik, tell her," Isabell pleaded.

No response.

Erik closed the door in her face as Isabell fell to her knees crying and pleading.

When neighbors started coming into the apartment complex and staring at her, Isabell composed herself and left. By then it was eight o'clock.

Isabell told herself that she'd come back and get Reo. There was no way that she would leave the country without her. Maybe if she waited until later that afternoon, when Erik left for work, she'd have a better chance of convincing Reo to leave with her.

Didn't anybody understand that Reo had been the one most perfect thing that she'd done in her life?

Fifty-seven

THE HOUSE WAS ALL LIT UP inside and out with beautiful Christmas decorations. Dusty said that he didn't care how high the electric bill would be, he intended to make their house look spectacular this year.

Anne couldn't get into the Christmas spirit this year. Her son was facing a possible prison sentence and her accounts were still frozen. Even though Dusty had given her money to shop for Christmas, she still couldn't manage a sincere smile for her wonderful husband.

"I've got a surprise for you, babycakes," Dusty told Anne when she came home from work. "Read this. Tell me later what your thoughts are."

He handed her the Appeal section from that day's *Hamilton Appeal*. She didn't notice the small article that told about Crocus McFadden having been arrested for murder. What she read was "Woman Arises from 16-Year Sleep" under the huge picture of a woman hugging her daughters.

It was a miracle.

A beloved mother of four had arisen from a coma. Her name was Felicia "Happi" White Bull of New Mexico. Following childbirth in 1984, Happi went into a coma. Sixteen years later, a nurse had arbitrarily given her a shot of the flu drug Amantadine. She arose from the deep sleep almost immediately.

"My mom's awake," said the sixteen-year-old, and the tears began falling, the article said.

The caption read, "Living but not alive."

Was that how she felt?

Anne couldn't tell Dusty how apprehensive she was about her medication. It was true that she hadn't taken any medicine since they were married. But she wasn't as optimistic about it as he was.

A miracle? Certainly it was too soon to know. Yet she hoped and prayed that her case would be one.

The following day was Christmas Eve. When she and Bentley went to pick up Nikkie, she had bought presents for everyone, even her aunt Mae.

Mae drove over later that day with a pheasant and spicy raspberry sauce already cooked. Anne ordered a twenty-four-pound ham, cooked a potful of string beans and potatoes, whipped up a pan of creamy macaroni and cheese and a batch of homemade crescent rolls, and prepared seven mouth-watering desserts. The women stayed up until two, talking over old times and getting a kick out of Nikkie telling them about her boyfriend, Ike.

On Christmas morning, she helped Daniel open each

one of his two dozen gifts. Anne didn't care that Dusty said that she'd spoiled him. In Anne's mind, it was her grandson's second Christmas without his mother and she intended to make it special.

Basil stopped by with gifts for everyone, but declined to stay for dinner. Anne could tell that he wasn't in a good mood. He reeked of stale alcohol when she kissed him, but decided not to nag him about it. After all, it was the holiday.

Later that day, Dusty's two daughters and their husbands showed up unexpectedly. Dusty went bazookas about his new granddaughter, Asia.

Daniel, beginning to say a few words now, talked to the three-month-old baby, and made everybody laugh.

Before they headed to bed that night, Dusty's daughter Aretha sang the Christmas carol "O Holy Night." Her voice was so beautiful everyone was brought to tears. But Anne was crying about something else, Happi White Bull. She met Dusty's eyes, and he made the connection.

She had to be a miracle, too.

Fifty-eight

ANNE TRIED TO SCREAM but no sound came out. Her eyes opened abruptly and she found herself staring into darkness. Turning over on her right, she noticed that Dusty was sleeping peacefully.

She'd dreamed that she was lying in a puddle of

blood. Her hand was reaching for something, but she couldn't make out what it was. She could hear someone running from the room, and then she heard a baby's scream. Trying to crawl her way to the baby, she stopped. There were dozens of babies crying out to her. They lifted their arms, begging to be picked up. All of them looked the same to her. That's what was horrible. They all looked like Daniel, but they weren't. Anne knew that she must recognize her own grandbaby, she had to. Then she saw him, in a cagelike baby bed against the wall.

Trying to rub the image out of her mind, she got up and retrieved her journal, went into the living room, and wrote down everything that she remembered about the dream. When she finished, and tried to analyze what she'd written, she realized that she'd put herself in Holly's place when she'd died on Basil's kitchen floor.

Anne worried that her dreams were getting out of hand. She wondered if she should see a psychiatrist. By now Holly had aged to twenty-four years old in her dreams and had just given birth to Daniel.

After rereading her entry in the journal, she went to check on Daniel. He was lying on his back, sleeping peacefully and smiling as if he held a special secret.

On her way out of the room, she noticed that the night-light on the chest of drawers was flickering on and off. When she approached it, it died. She fiddled with it for a few seconds, and when it wouldn't come back on, she made a mental note to replace it before she headed back to her bedroom.

Dusty was half sitting up when she came back to bed.

"Something wrong, babycakes?" he asked, pulling her body close to his.

"No. I'm fine. Now go back to sleep."

In less than five minutes the onslaught of a drenching rain lulled her to a semiconscious state. As always, she thought of Holly. Her beautiful daughter was standing in Anne's doorway and holding one of her old doll babies in her hand.

"Come on, Mommy. Let's go."

"Where?" Anne asked.

"Shhhh. You'll wake Dusty. C'mon. Come with me."

Anne got up from the bed and followed her daughter down the hallway to Holly's old room. Her bedroom was aglow with lights when they entered it. The glare nearly blinded Anne as she watched Holly take a seat on the floor in front of her Victorian dollhouse.

"What's all this, Holly?" Anne asked. Every one of Holly's dolls and their clothing were spread out on the floor.

"My friends, Mother. You remember them, don't you?"

Of course she did. She and Holly had named all of her dolls and had taken pleasure in selecting each one of their outfits. "Sure I do. Say, what's Emily doing with this winter outfit on, it's summertime."

"Sit down and play with me, Mother."

Anne smiled and sat across from her daughter. For what seemed like hours, she and Holly rearranged the furniture in the dollhouse and made up a scenario where the eldest daughter of the family was getting married. They dressed Emily in a beautiful wedding gown and put the groom in a black tuxedo. Anne played the part of the groom and Holly played the part of the bride.

When the wedding was over, Anne cried happy tears.

"See, Mother, you did get to see me get married, didn't you?"

"What?"

"It's what you always wanted, wasn't it?"

When she looked up, Holly stood before her in the exact wedding dress that Emily had on. An ethereal glow was all around her.

"Holly . . . baby . . . are you dead?"

"Yes, Mother."

"But . . ."

"I'm okay, Mom. I just came to be with you until you got used to the idea."

Anne closed her eyes. When she opened them, Holly was gone. Finally, there was closure.

The following morning, Anne felt a sublime peace. She put in a call to Dr. Shubert at the Memphis College of Art. After Anne told her what had happened the night before, Dr. Shubert told her that she believed that she had been trying to rescue Holly from the tragic situation when she was killed.

"You really can't rescue someone who's already dead, Anne."

She ended the conversation by telling Anne that if she could release the emotions psychologically and begin to feel the healing in her heart, she could finally get some relief. Otherwise the night life of her imagination would run rampant in her heart for an eternity.

The next night, Anne didn't dream, nor did she the night after, and she knew that the doctor had been right. She felt as if a burden had been lifted from her. And it was then that Anne finally came to terms with Holly's death and put her daughter's soul to rest in her heart.

* * *

THANKS TO *THE DEFENDER* NEWSPAPER, The National Civil Rights Consortium was getting good press. Anne was disappointed that the *Hamilton Appeal* didn't print the stories about the cases that her organization was tackling. In the short duration they'd been open, her company had already made an impact on the black community.

Most of their cases dealt with the elimination of racial and gender preferences in federal programs, but they were also working on individual discrimination lawsuits.

But as of today, Anne put the affirmative action case she was working on on the back burner until she dealt with a more pressing issue—her son.

Inside her modest building located on Lauderdale Street at the corner of Madison, Anne held her breath and handed over the telephone receiver.

Basil, sitting directly across from her, nodded his head a defeated yes.

"It's a deal, Oscar," Anne said. She hung up the phone and asked her son, "Are you sure?"

"Do I have a choice?"

It was less than an hour later when Anne and Basil got into her 2000 silver and white 750 Mercedes and drove around West Memphis looking for David Ramsey. Supposedly, David held the key that would ultimately set her son free.

While they drove, Basil reiterated to his mother the conversation that he and David had had dozens of times: "Do you think that uppity Negro can put something over on old David? I don't think so. I got something that will nail him good. The brotha' don't know who he's messing with, Basil. I got him, and I got him good."

They stopped on every corner where Anne wouldn't normally dream of parking her car. Junkies and prostitutes populated the streets. And unless you knew somebody who knew somebody, you were considered a cop or one that was undercover. Regardless, these desperate people trusted no one.

"I heard that David Ramsey was staying here," Basil said to a dirty junkie outside a party store on Vance Street.

The man looked at Basil like he was crazy.

"If you see him, dude, tell him that his friend Basil Hamilton is looking for him. It's important."

Anne kept silent as they drove around seemingly in circles, searching for a cracked-out young man who used to command respect and drove these streets in a chrome-plated gold BMW. But past history didn't matter here. There were a lot of old heroes who used to command thousands of dollars, and who were now reduced to being just another good storyteller.

At three o'clock, when the junkies were beginning to wake up for their evening fix, Basil got a break. Dave was just seen two blocks over trying to sell a trunkload of Shaquille O'Neal T-shirts.

It wasn't necessary to say that the Lakers World Championship shirts were either stolen or knock-offs. Just the location was enough to get a rise out of Basil. They were minutes away from repudiation.

"There he is, Mom," Basil hollered once they turned the corner on South Third Street.

They pulled up to the curb and Basil cautiously signaled Dave that everything was cool and to come over to the car. Anne held her breath when Dave jumped into the backseat. He smelled like rotten eggs. When he smiled and said hello to her, his teeth looked as if they hadn't been brushed in months.

Basil cut to the chase—he needed some concrete information on the senator. Basil had times, dates, and places, but nothing substantial to link him to the kickbacks.

Dave smiled, showing his yellow teeth. "I got something for ya. But it's going to cost ya."

First, they had to get Dave a fix. Thirty minutes later, he was acting like a normal human being and ready to talk.

"My wife's holding the evidence. I haven't seen her in months. But if I waved some money—"

Anne removed two crisp $100 bills from her purse. "Will this do for starters, Dave? We're really running short of time."

Dave's eyes lit up as bright as stars in winter. "This is what dreams are made of, Mrs. B. Now just give me until tomorrow afternoon. I'll have something for ya by then. You can bet on that."

Basil and Anne argued all the way back to the center. Anne didn't feel that Dave could be trusted. She felt he would get high with the money and look to blackmail them with a more substantial payment. Basil didn't agree. He felt that Dave still had a few principles left.

It turned out that Dave had a tape of the senator's initial conversation with Basil and Dave back in 1993. The conversation was accidentally recorded on his answering machine. If they could make it worth her while, his ex-wife, Wilma, would hand over the tape.

It was not said up front, but Basil knew that Wilma was hitting the pipe harder than Dave was. It was primarily why the two of them couldn't come up with a plan to cash in on the tape thus far—both were too high to think things out rationally.

The next day, grudgingly, Anne handed over ten $100 bills.

"Don't mess with my mom's money, Dave. This shit ain't counterfeit!"

Fifty-nine

MIDNIGHT FOUND ANNE ALL ALONE in the family room, her eyes trained on the west wall, slowly taking in one mask at a time. She studied the hand-carved African masks, and then her gaze settled on the mosaic-covered human skull of Tezcatlipoca—the Aztec gold god linked to evil. Inadvertently, she shuddered. It appeared as if Basil's head and face had replaced that of the god.

Has Basil done something so terrible in his short life that he won't be forgiven?

This morning her heart had been so hopeful for the future. She'd read in the *Appeal* of Mayor Herenton's hopes for the city of Memphis on this New Year's Day. He'd held a prayer breakfast at the Peabody Hotel. Mayor Herenton told the crowd that Memphis would see continued economic and job growth, tax base expansion, downtown development, and neighborhood revitalization in 2001 and beyond.

"Economically, we continue to be a strong southern metropolis." Paraphrasing Psalm 127 in the Bible, he said, "Except the Lord keepeth watch over the city, they labor in vain.

"I believe He is keeping watch over the city of Memphis."

Herenton predicted another record year for local capital investments, adding that more than $1 billion in public and private funds was being invested in downtown developments alone.

He highlighted major investments by St. Jude's Children's Research Hospital and International Paper Company. He also praised Northwest Airlines, which operates a hub at Memphis International Airport and was the city's dominant passenger carrier.

The mayor counted a net gain of more than 10,000 jobs in the city and noted that wages and income continued to rise.

"For the first time in our history, the per-capita income in Memphis exceeds the national average."

He pointed out that *Inc.* magazine ranked the city eighth out of fifty for starting and expanding businesses. But what got everyone's attention was talk about a new rail system.

"Every great city in the world has a great transportation system. We just cannot continue to depend on the automobile.

"We just celebrated a $59 million grant from the federal government to begin the first segment of our regional light rail system to the Medical Center. The rail system would connect the Medical Center and Overton Square."

Herenton envisioned a rebirth for many of the city's neighborhoods, including Whitehaven, Frayser, Raleigh, Klondyke, South Memphis, and many others.

"We need more inner-city developers to build more

affordable housing in the inner city. There's nothing wrong with the inner city, we just need to give people hope."

Anne had hope for the city. But as she read on, she came across another disturbing article about the city of Memphis. It was in the Faith Matters section of the *Appeal*.

David Waters wrote about the mayor's message of the Lord keeping watch over the city. Mr. Waters wondered if we were going to use Bible verses as a measure, how would we rate in the *Biblical Places Rated Almanac*.

According to Jeremiah, Isaiah, Amos, and other prophets, God was most concerned for the poor, weak, and marginalized. In fact, nothing seemed to anger God more than our abuse or neglect of those who are poor, sick, elderly, widowed, fatherless, or in prison.

Anne immediately thought of David Ramsey.

Mr. Waters went on to state that Memphis's biggest hospital had a cross on the door but no patients inside, having closed because caring for the poor wasn't cost-effective.

Many of the mentally ill were getting about $17 a day on which to live while our city council members were getting $75 a day just to spend on food when they travel.

Hundreds of Memphis's mentally ill neighbors were not getting the treatment they needed. As a result, they were wandering the streets or wasting away in jail. The jail was controlled by gangs and filled with mentally ill prisoners who would be safer, healthier, and better supervised on the streets.

Hundreds of Memphis's poor and disabled elderly

were being kept in deficient and expensive nursing homes. Meanwhile the state cut funds that would have allowed many to be cared for at home.

Mr. Waters went on to state that Memphis received four stars in the new movie *Cast Away*, starring Tom Hanks and our own FedEx Corporation.

But he reiterated, "Instead of profit margins, maybe it's time that Memphis checked its prophet margins. Instead of watching *Cast Away*, maybe we should watch how we treat the castaways among us."

Anne agreed.

She'd cast her vote for president for Vice President Gore last November and he'd lost to George W. Bush. It appeared that the state of Florida was unwinnable to Gore under any circumstances.

It was unfortunate that the Supreme Court didn't believe in one man, one vote.

Anne thought once more about the Bible verse that the mayor paraphrased from Psalm 127: "Except the Lord keepeth watch over the city, they labor in vain."

Reluctantly, Anne stole a quick glance up at Tezcatlipoca.

Will Basil fall prey to the same type of injustice? Or will he become just another unfortunate castaway with no one but me to keep watch over him?

"GIVE ME A MINUTE to think about it," Anne said, leaning her elbows on her desk and supporting her head with her fingertips. It was just past ten o'clock and Dusty, Basil, and she, along with another attorney, Walt Wilcomb, had been at it for hours.

Dave had produced the tape, as he had said he would. They had the proof that they needed to bargain with.

What Anne didn't like was the choices that her son had to make.

Even after turning over the information to the grand jury he was still facing jail time. How much, they didn't know until they produced the evidence in court.

"Mom," Basil spoke up, "we're not going to get a better offer. Let's take it and hope for the best."

"You're sure?" she asked, raising her head wearily. "We might be able to—"

"I'm sure, Mom. Let's do it." Basil leaned over, gently touched his forehead against his mother's, and smiled. "Bette always said that I looked good in stripes."

Even in the middle of her tears, Basil managed to make his mother laugh, turning her distorted thoughts around in a few short minutes.

"Now, c'mon, Dusty, get your wife and let's go. It's time to get home and check on that grandson of yours."

When they returned home, Bentley had relieved the sitter and was waiting with good news.

"I've been hired by the *Detroit News*. They heard about Jada Pinkett's production company buying the screenplay." She shook her head in amazement. "Boy, am I lucky. Production on the six-week-long movie is set to begin in June. But until then, the *Detroit News* wants to start running *The Riverdocks* comic strip beginning in the March issue."

"Honey, hush. Does that mean you have to move?" Anne asked, picking up her grandson and giving him a big kiss.

"No. I can send my work in from here. I will have to invest in a fax machine, though. The salary is much lower than I was making at the *Appeal*, but I'm willing to start at the bottom and work my way back up."

"Here," Dusty said, taking Daniel from Anne, "let

me see if the little man has to use the bathroom. He tugged at Daniel's fat jaws. "What do you say, little fella? Do you have to use the potty?"

Daniel grimaced, and began to sniff. It was the familiar sign he gave them when he was ready to do number two.

"I swear that little boy has been here before," Bentley said, smiling. "I don't remember training Reo that early. He's only what, nineteen months old?"

"No," said Anne, putting on a pot of hot water on the stove. "He was two on December thirty-first."

"Gosh, I keep forgetting that. Reo's going to be eleven in May. You know, sometimes when I'm around Daniel I think about having another baby."

"You're still young enough. Why not?"

"I'd like to be married this time. I want a man like Dusty, Anne. You don't know how lucky you are. Dating sucks."

Anne prepared a pot of hot cider and took a seat across from Bentley at the kitchen table.

"Tell me if I'm being too nosy, but what about Corky? Are you two still seeing one another?"

"Yes, but not on a regular basis. We're both trying to get our lives back in order. We care about one another, but we're smart enough to know now that we need to be stable in our own lives first before we complicate it with a rushed relationship. Having a sex partner is one thing, and making a commitment is another."

"And Erik? Have you and he come to terms on your visiting Reo? I remember you telling me that he and Isabell split. Right?"

Bentley sipped her cider. "Yeah. He moved out two weeks ago. He's called me every day since. I don't know how I feel about Erik right now. But by him being my child's father, I think that I'll always have some kind of feeling for him. And these days he's acting like the old Erik I remembered way back when."

"How's Reo adjusting?"

"She's a trouper. Just like you and me. And the miracle is that she loves me, Aunt Anne. It's so amazing. She's old enough to know now that I'll always be there for her. That's the most important thing. It won't matter if her dad and I aren't together."

Anne lifted her cup and clinked it against Bentley's. "And I'll amen to that."

"We're back," Dusty announced from the hallway. "Mama," Daniel squealed and toddled toward Anne.

The telephone rang and Dusty answered it. "Anne, it's Basil."

While Anne spoke on the phone, Bentley asked Dusty how Basil's case was looking.

"It's hard to say. Anne and Basil seem to think that they've got an ace in the hole."

"And what do you think?" Bentley asked candidly. "Is my cousin going to jail?"

Dusty turned to look at his wife, who was frowning. "Personally, I think he'll be damn lucky if he gets out of it with less than three years."

The following morning, Basil had an appointment with the grand jury. Anne, along with her business associate, Walt Wilcomb, waited outside the closed chambers.

In what seemed like a lifetime, Basil and the attorney general, Bart Shivers, finally emerged from the room. Basil was handcuffed, but smiling.

One of Fox 13's field reporters, Tom McSwain, asked

the attorney general the first of many questions that were being shouted out.

"Are you satisfied with the grand jury's findings, Mr. Shivers?"

He replied, "I knew that there were some rats running around loose in the city of Memphis. I was planning on calling the FBI in to help trap them. But lo and behold, all it took was a little piece of cheese by the name of Basil Hamilton."

Another reporter from Channel 3, Stephanie Skurlock, asked, "Was there some kind of deal cut with Mr. Hamilton?"

The attorney general replied, "What would you think is the most important thing for the city to do—lock up one little mouse or let the big rats continue to corrupt the city?" Mr. Shivers pushed back the hoard of microphones and walked away.

Anne managed to get close to her son and give him a big hug. Tears threatened, but she held them in check.

"It's over, Mom."

Basil told his mother that he was given six months in a minimum-security prison and had to pay a $50,000 fine. It seemed that the prosecuting attorney was eager to make a deal that would eventually oust the Republican Orin Matthews, believing that seat could be filled by a Democrat.

After Basil had been taken away, Mr. Wilcomb confided in Anne that Senator Orin Matthews as well as three other Tennessee politicians were implicated in taking kickbacks from the day care centers. The fraud and racketeering trial for them was due to start the following month and the prosecutors, with Basil's testimony, felt that they had a solid case against at least one of them. It was expected that the first conviction would have a domino effect on the others.

It seemed that Basil's day care program wasn't the only business that Senator Orin Matthews had profited from. He allegedly headed a criminal enterprise that illegally profited from three state programs, the main one being fees earned by an insurance broker on workers' compensation policies sold to state school districts.

Two other state programs were also the focus: the Child Support Enforcement Program, which contracted with private lawyers to go after deadbeat parents to collect overdue child support payments, and a $3 million grant program to contract with lawyers to represent children in some disputed custody cases.

It helped that the senator admitted last week that he controlled child support collection operations in three judicial districts and skimmed up to $2,900 a month for himself from six lawyers.

No matter. For Basil, it was over.

But the problems for Anne were just beginning. The Internal Revenue Service still hadn't finished conducting their audit. They had scrupulously gone over every cent in all of her accounts, questioned the money left to her from Holly's will, and even questioned the money that Dusty was using to open up his novelty store.

Anne's name was in the papers nearly every day in January. An allegation about her involvement with the day care center's counterfeit business was a hot topic. It didn't matter that Basil had already gone to jail and that the charge had been reduced to possession of three $100 bills in counterfeit money. It seemed that someone at the *Hamilton Appeal* had a special vendetta against Anne and wouldn't let up.

She'd been so depressed that her attorneys had been unsuccessful in stopping the malicious articles, she didn't want to go out in public. Anne didn't tell Dusty that she didn't believe her attorneys when they assured her that her accounts would be cleared up in a matter of days. She just wasn't that optimistic.

ON JANUARY 15, Martin Luther King Day, Jacqueline Smith's one-woman campaign against the National Civil Rights Museum landed her in jail. She allegedly scuffled with police over the placement of protest signs during the Martin Luther King Day observation.

Her unique story made the front page of Tuesday's *Hamilton Appeal*.

Jacqueline had been camped across the street from the historical site where King was assassinated thirty-three years earlier. Her signs were draped over the "Road Closed" barricades on Mulberry Street. When police tried to remove the signs, Smith grabbed them back, manhandling the police, screaming and hollering about her rights.

The police officer said that he would allow the signs elsewhere, but not where they covered the Road Closed sign. Mulberry had been closed in recent weeks to accommodate an expansion project for the museum.

Smith was arrested for disorderly conduct. The forty-nine-year-old Smith was transported to the Jail East at Shelby County Correction Center, with a court appearance expected that same day.

Ms. Smith had worked at the old Lorraine Hotel and lived there seven years. She was forcibly evicted after it closed in 1988. Ever since, she has protested the motel's conversion into what she calls the "Civil

Wrong Museum," saying that the building instead should be used to shelter the homeless and help the poor. Signs on the wall carried such messages as "Disgrace to Rev. King." Jacqueline even touted her protest Web site.

Hours after her arrest and ultimate release, Jacqueline Smith's couch, chair, and signs remained in their usual spot.

The following day, Judith Black, the marketing director for the museum, said that the arrest had no effect on the "excellent turnout" of visitors during the King Day observance, and that her daily protests didn't hamper museum attendance.

The article in the *Hamilton Appeal* about Ms. Smith had amused Anne. She wasn't sure if she felt sympathy for the woman or not. But what she did feel now was weird. There was a strange kind of freezing sensation going on inside of her body and she didn't know how to explain it. She told herself to be optimistic. Be practical. She hadn't had any tremors in months. For all practical purposes she had begun to lose faith in the miracle that she was completely cured. But as fate would have it, Anne couldn't muddle in self-pity for long. On February 21, Representative John Lewis had come to town to sign copies of his book *Walking with the Wind* at Burke's Bookstore. Today marked his sixty-first birthday. John Lewis had been a member of SNCC, the Student Nonviolent Coordinating Committee, and Anne felt an instant kinship with him. Mr. Lewis had written a speech considered inflammatory in what were the last months of the Kennedy administration in 1963. It was the speech given before Dr. Martin Luther King's "I Have a Dream" speech.

The twenty-three-year-old John Lewis had said, "We come today with a great sense of misgiving. We are tired. We are tired of being beaten by policeman. We are tired of seeing our people locked up in jail over and over again. How long can we be patient? We want our freedom and we want it now. We don't want to go to jail because this is the price we must pay for love, brotherhood and true peace."

Anne listened to John Lewis speaking to the crowd now at Burke's. Near the conclusion of his talk, he told the standing-room-only crowd that his book was written partly out of concern about how those with no memory of the movement will regard what happened.

"I want this story to be told. I want people to know it's not ancient history. It's a book of hope—a book of faith. And it's saying that you must never give in, give out, or give up. Let the spirit of history be your guide."

Anne left the book-signing on cloud nine. She admitted to herself that she had been wallowing in self-pity. It didn't matter that the IRS was auditing her. She wasn't guilty. Why had she let this singular incident ruin the happiness that she'd felt all these months?

Back at home, she played with her grandson, had a conversation with her husband, and was ready for a long hot bath when the telephone rang.

"Hello?"

"Hi. Is this Anne?"

"Yes it is."

"Hello Anne. I'm Ike Preston. A friend of Nikkie's. I need your help."

Her heart raced. Bentley wasn't at home yet. "What's wrong?"

"Nikkie's just fine. I should have said that I'm Nikkie's fiancé. She wanted me to call you so that you could help us with the wedding. Nikkie didn't want to upset Bentley and make her sick again."

Anne breathed a sigh of relief. "Why, Ike, I'd love to help. Honey, hush. What would you like for me to do?" There were a ton of questions that Anne wanted to ask him. Was he mentally disabled? Did he live in the same complex? Could he afford to support her? Did they plan on having children?

"Thanks. Nikkie's got her heart set on getting married on March seventeenth. I realize it's short notice. But she wanted something small. You know, just the immediate family."

My God. Where was Kirk? And Wesley was halfway around the world. She had to think fast. Could she get everyone back home by then?

"Ike, I think I can manage it. We'll have the ceremony at my home—"

"No, that isn't necessary—"

"Excuse me, Ike. But this will be the first wedding in the Russell family when someone didn't elope. I'd like to make it special. Will you let me do that, please?"

Before she went to bed that night, she wrote letters to both Kirk and Wesley telling them that it was imperative that everyone be home in time for Nikkie's wedding in March. She even planned on following up the letter with a telegram to ensure that they would get the message.

The next day Anne went into her law office with a new attitude. In the four short months since her office had opened in September, it was literally overflowing with new cases. The top priority was police profiling. This afternoon a two-hour forum sponsored by the Black Law Students Association, the American Civil Liberties Union of Tennessee, and the city's Civilian Law Enforcement Review Board was held at the University of Memphis. Anne spoke on behalf of two of her clients. They had filed a suit with the federal courts urging passage of a bill now pending in the state legislature to bar racial profiling and requiring local and state police to track all stops.

Being back at work was the best therapy. Manny Goldsworth, one of the first attorneys she hired, was working on a case involving six female Germantown police officers. The officers filed a federal sexual discrimination lawsuit seeking lost wages and $1 million in punitive damages. Manny asked Anne if she would mind assisting him on the case when her profiling law suit concluded. She told him that she would and Anne couldn't have been happier. Keeping busy at work and planning Nikkie's wedding kept her mind off how her son was faring in prison. When she saw him the week before, he tried to be cheerful, but she knew he was scared.

Who wouldn't be?

BASIL SPENT HIS FIRST FEW DAYS housed in the Shelby County jail—a place where gladiator fights, slave labor, and other intricate forms of gang control were the norm. Gang members controlled everything from televisions to telephones, forced other inmates to do their laundry in the sink, swiped their commissary treats, and, for fun, forced inmates to fight each other.

Presently, attorneys for jail inmates wanted jumbo-sized fines from Shelby County and time behind bars for Sheriff A. C. Gilless if jail conditions didn't improve soon.

A two-time loser named Ralph Corruth was Basil's cellmate. Ralph was also waiting to be processed into the Shelby County Correctional Facility. Ralph bragged about the three years he had spent there six months earlier. He professed to know the entire goings-on inside the walls at Shelby and decided to share his knowledge with Basil.

On his first day at Shelby, Basil was assigned to cell-block M. He was looking forward to getting some exercise. He could hardly stand being cooped up like a human sardine. There were 150 inmates quartered in cellblock M; all were supposed to be serving time for nonviolent offenses. Basil knew what to expect, and how to survive if he could afford it. With no intention of being anybody's punk, and more than willing to fight to prove it, Basil met the leader of one of the toughest gangs in the prison—the Pharaohs.

Not the typical monster-looking guy, Avery stood five foot nine inches tall, was of medium brown complexion, and wore his hair neatly cut. Avery spoke very softly, barely above a whisper.

He told Basil that for fifty dollars a week he could have steak, chicken, and fresh fish for dinner every day. The money would also afford him the use of a television set and radio. Nobody would raise a finger toward him as long as he didn't bother anyone else. Basil shook hands with Avery and agreed to pay him the money.

In the cell next to Basil was a quiet guy approximately fifty years old. His name was Crocus McFadden. Basil had witnessed several guys beating him up during his first week at Shelby. Unable to sleep afterward, Basil had lain awake realizing how dangerous the environment was that he was living in.

The next night, the same three guys entered Crocus's cell and began slapping him around. This time Basil had had enough. He went into Crocus's cell and punched the biggest bully square in the nose and broke it. Before the other two guys could get to Basil, Avery was standing in the doorway. Avery didn't say a word. He just stared at the three guys until they started to apologize to Basil and Crocus. After Avery had gone, Crocus thanked Basil for saving him. He owed the three men money and couldn't pay it. His money tree from the outside had dried up.

"You look like a gambling man, Crocus. I was once involved with the bookies and they threatened to kill me if I didn't pay up. So I can relate to what you're going through, man."

Crocus gave him an odd look. "Man, I ain't shit up the creek because of some bookies. My troubles are with one woman. And you know what, I got enough shit on this woman to lock her up for life. Yeah, I wonder how her rich ass would feel if I spilled my guts."

"I don't get it. What are you talking about?"

"Look, Basil. I know who you are, dude. I know your mom, too."

The smile left Basil's face. "What you trying to pull? I don't play that shit with my mom. She ain't got nothing to do with none of this."

"That's where you're wrong, man. Tell me, do you love your mother?"

"Yes. Of course I do."

"Well, I'm only going to tell my story once. Call your

mother. Because what I have to say is meant for her. You saved my life in here, man, and I'm going to save hers out there."

ANNE WASN'T ABLE TO MAKE IT until Saturday afternoon. Basil hadn't been able to get a word out of Crocus until now.

Basil sat next to Crocus in the visitation area, nervously tapping his foot. He still couldn't imagine how this man could help his mother.

"I'll get straight to the point, Ms. Anne. I've worked for Isabell Ford for years. My main job was to find out everything I could about the Russell family. Isabell is a very unhappy woman. She blames you for destroying her life. And she took special pleasure in making your family suffer over the years."

"Wait a minute, Crocus. Why should I believe what you're telling me? I don't know you from a hobo on the street."

"I've got the times and dates of everything I'm going to tell you recorded on a journal in my safety deposit box."

"I'm still not getting what I have to do with you and Isabell. She married my niece's fiancé. I would hardly call that—"

"She wanted you to suffer. She wanted everyone related to you to suffer."

"Why?"

"It began way back in August of 1972. That's the day Isabell killed Leigh Hamilton. Scott found out and ended their relationship. When he married you, that's when Isabell decided to make your life miserable."

Anne was numb as she sat listening to this man tell her

the horrible circumstances that her family had endured over the years. When Scott was trying to sell the *Appeal,* Isabell used a dummy corporation to buy it for much less than it was worth. Mae's abortion that sterilized her wasn't a coincidence. Isabell paid a doctor to perform his magic. It was Isabell who corrupted Basil's mind at seventeen and ultimately destroyed his marriage. She was behind Bette's rape. She was the one who introduced Basil to the senator and had him set up in the day care business, knowing that he'd be in trouble soon. She nurtured his gambling habit that led to his ultimate transgression into counterfeiting. Isabell married Erik only to spite Bentley. She was also responsible for Bentley being fired at the *Appeal.* And she was the one who coerced Erik into letting her adopt Reo.

"This doesn't make sense!" But as Anne said the words, her gut instincts told her that this man was telling her the truth.

"I'll die with one thing on my conscience that I can't erase. The accidental death of your daughter."

Basil cringed. "You said accidental." His words were hollow. "They were sent there to get me."

"That's right."

Suddenly his voice came to her as if in a distance, for she was locked up in a cocoon of her own making. She shook her head and tried to clear it. Why was he telling her all of this now? Nothing would bring Holly and Dan back.

"She had one final request." Crocus turned to look at Anne. "Last week I was supposed to get rid of you at your office and make it look like a burglary. But I had an offer to make some extra money moonlighting. A high-profile hit. That didn't work out. I was caught and Isabell turned her back on me."

On Monday morning, Anne did as Crocus suggested. She went to his sister's house on Hollywood Street with a note written by him. Anne had permission to remove all contents from the safety deposit box except for the cash.

Anne and Dusty were horrified at what they read. Crocus was telling the truth. They couldn't believe that Isabell would commit murder and pursue a vendetta as a scorned lover for nearly thirty years.

The next step was to get this information into the authorities' hands. At nine the following morning, Anne and Dusty sat waiting to see the city prosecutor. They planned to turn over the journal and hoped that its contents would be enough to send Isabell to prison. Hopefully this would bring closure to the devastation that had plagued the Russell family dating back to her marriage to Scott.

Ignoring Dusty's advice, Anne felt her only relief would be to confront Isabell. She picked up the phone and dialed Isabell's number.

"You low-down dirty bitch. You smiled in my face and pretended to be my friend, when all the time you were planning to destroy my family. I've got the 411 on you, honey, and you're going to rot in hell."

"What the fuck are you talking about?"

"I had a conversation with your friend Crocus. The city attorney's office has his journal. I'm sure you'll be hearing from them."

After Isabell hung up she was petrified knowing that she would be ruined if what Anne said were true. Isabell had no intentions of spending the rest of her life in jail.

It was time to finish tying up all her loose ends. The

next thing she had to do was to get her daughter by any means possible. Figuring that she still had a little time, she called American Airlines in Little Rock, Arkansas, and booked a flight for two to Cancún, Mexico. From there she would plan her final destination.

Packing a single bag for herself and one for Reo, she put an extra carry-on bag in the trunk for the cash that she would draw out of the bank. She laid a .38 under her purse on the front seat just in case Erik gave her any problems.

Putting in a call to Brenda Ellis at People's Bank on her cell phone, she requested $250,000 in small bills.

Rushing into People's Bank on Summer Avenue and Stage Road, Brenda had the cash ready and waiting for her signature. They exchanged pleasantries and Isabell left.

By then it was four o'clock. She headed for Erik's apartment to pick up Reo. She knocked several times and no one answered. She decided to drive around to kill some time, figuring that he'd be back soon.

And as she drove around in unfamiliar territory, Isabell's thoughts drifted back to the day when it all started.

She first met Scott Hamilton when her stepfather died and she took his place on the board of the *Hamilton Appeal*.

Not long afterward, Scott had come on to her. The older man's advances and his powerful image in the Memphis community impressed Isabell. The first time she made love to him was on the thirty-foot-long table in the boardroom. That afternoon was Isabell's first introduction to a man's penis that wasn't circumcised.

"It's so pretty, Scott, like it's wearing a little bonnet," she had told him before taking him into her mouth. Her breath was warm and wet against his hardened member. She smiled when she felt him reach out and stroke her head, then touch the rhythmic hollow in her jaw. When she saw the impassioned look on his face, she lifted her hand quickly to tuck back a tendril of her black hair so that he might better see.

"Oooh, that's so good, baby," he'd murmured.

She began licking the thick vein from the edge of his little bonnet to the brim of his balls. When it looked as if his penis was about to explode, she backed off, massaging the loose skin up and over the tip. She kissed it lightly, once, twice, flicking the tip of her tongue up and down the long column until it appeared that she had to come up for air. "Such a serious little face," she crooned, nudging the edge of the bonnet with her teeth.

"Don't stop yet," Scott begged.

"God," Isabell sighed, "I've wanted to do that for so long. Suck you. Come. Come hard, Scott. Come in my mouth. Come in my mouth and all over my face and hands." She stopped to look at the little slit of his where a single cloudy tear had appeared. Smiling up at him, she licked it off.

"Wait, Isabell. I've got to take care of you first, sweetheart. At my age, if I come, it's all over."

"Not with me, Scott," she said, taking him back into her mouth, then kissing it gently. "If you come, I'll make sure you come again."

By now his organ was enormous. "May I come now?" he asked.

"Whenever you're ready, I'm ready."

And that afternoon, like so many more afterward,

Scott ejaculated in her face, mouth, and into the cups of her hands.

When they were together, Scott would have two and three orgasms. He told her that he hadn't felt so young in years.

From the very beginning Isabell wanted his wife, Leigh, out of the way. Scott had told her that he loved her, but he wouldn't divorce his wife. His loyalty merely fueled her desire to break his resistance down and succumb to her remonstrances.

"If you'll just give me some time—"

"Absolutely not! Fuck that bullshit, Scott. I've got my family screaming down my throat. I need you to show me some decency here! You've got to back me up. Tell everyone how much you love me."

"But Isabell. I do love you, dear. But Leigh will never give me a divorce. She's already hinted as much."

Those words haunted Isabell day and night. She had left the meeting that day with an agenda. She would talk to Leigh and convince her one way or another, she thought, slipping her Versace glove on and pounding her fist inside her palm, to let Scott go. When she paid a visit to the Hamilton home and saw the beautiful Leigh for the first time, the supercilious wife was adamant about keeping her marriage intact.

"I've known about the affair you were having with Scott for some time now, Isabell. I would have thought that he would have conveyed my thoughts to you at this point. Like I told him, the idea of a divorce isn't possible."

Her voice was in a pleasant middle range, slightly smoky, and it had the tone of easy self-assurance.

"Let's be frank, shall we? He did tell me in his own

way. But I thought that I'd make the effort to try and convince you myself that it would be in the best interest of everyone concerned if—"

At that moment Leigh had laughed at Isabell. She had a peculiar laugh. It sounded more like a snort than an expression of amusement, and it irritated the hell out her. Isabell felt that she had no other choice if she was ever going to marry Scott. She caught Leigh off guard when she was showing her out, and knocked the fragile woman down on the foyer floor.

"Laugh now, bitch," she said, clamping both her hands over Leigh's nose and mouth. She kept her hands firmly in place, warding off Leigh's kicking arms and legs until she stopped moving and lay perfectly still. When she removed her hands, Leigh was staring blankly up at her. Even so, she checked to make sure that Leigh wasn't breathing. Satisfied that she was dead, she gathered her purse, and after checking to make sure that the traffic was clear, she quickly exited out the side door.

Isabell hadn't known that Scott had been watching her that afternoon, which possibly led to his ultimate breakdown. Nearly three years later, Isabell was still in love with him. When he came out of the psychiatric hospital, she felt that it would be only fair to give him a few months to heal before she approached him again.

To her dismay, he was already seeing someone else. Needless to say, she was shocked shitless. She hadn't expected that he would be horny so soon.

It was Jim Walker, an editorial supervisor at the time, who had told Isabell that Scott had fallen for some young welfare whore.

"I don't want to see or hear about you talking to that

black bitch ever again," Isabell told Scott when they were alone in his office.

"You're not in a position to threaten me," he said in a slow, calculating manner.

When Scott retained his bored look, Isabell wasn't sure if it was due to pure ennui or his state of mind from having been institutionalized. Regardless, Isabell was scared. She was scared because he'd clasped his hands tightly together as if he were trying to squeeze the life out of his own hands. And when she looked into his cold eyes, she knew that she had made a costly mistake.

Does he know? He can't possibly know.

It all seemed so comical to her now. As a result, Scott had married Anne, and her plight of the scorned lover began all over again.

Back then and up to this point, she hated Anne Russell. She hated Bentley Russell. And now, she hated Scott Hamilton. She had even killed to get him.

Sixty

WHY DID IT HAVE TO COME TO THIS? Isabell thought as she drove aimlessly around Erik's apartment building. She'd had everything planned perfectly from the very beginning—the total annihilation of the Russell family—the family that took her lover away from her.

And up until recently when Isabell learned from her investigator of Anne's likely death from Parkinson's disease, she couldn't have been more pleased, and decided to let nature take its course. Watching her die a painful and humiliating death would be much more satisfying.

But now things had changed. Anne would have to die today, Isabell told herself. Hell, why should she be the only one in this world to feel pain? She began to wonder, did she deserve the cards that life had dealt her?

With a plan formulating in her mind, she screeched her tires and made a right turn on Farmington Road. Glancing at the clock on the dashboard, it was ten minutes after six. Anne's house was a short twelve miles away. But she was forgetting something, she told herself, when she made a left on Germantown Road.

Her husband, Dusty. Where was he?

Punching the numbers on the cell phone, she dialed Anne's number. Clearing her throat, she prepared to disguise her voice.

"Hello?"

Isabell spoke from the bellows of her stomach, "Hello. May I speak with Mr. Baker please?"

"Who's calling?"

"Raymond Messenger."

"I'm sorry, Mr. Messenger, but my husband is not available. What number should I—"

Click.

So she was home all alone. Good. Hopefully, she could get over there and back before her husband returned.

As she drove the short distance, her hatred for Anne fueled to monumental proportions. She had intended to get sweet revenge, but instead was left with feelings of failure.

You never do anything right. Why should you even be alive? You have no purpose now. No one loves you. You're all alone. You've got nothing to live for.

It was Anne who was responsible for Scott's leaving her pregnant and unmarried and causing the abortion that had left her sterile. And it was Anne who had revamped her life only to once again see happiness despite her present circumstances.

Yet, as she headed north on Germantown Road, it was Isabell's driving passion to kill that caused her to accelerate to fifty-five miles per hour in a thirty-five-mile-an-hour zone.

Removing the pistol from the bottom of her purse, she laid it on the seat. With her left hand on the wheel, she used her right hand to check the chamber and make sure the gun was fully loaded. Bitter tears filled her eyes and she wiped them away with a fist. Glancing into the rearview mirror she looked searchingly at her face. There's no use crying now, she told herself.

At 6:15 she admitted to herself that if she managed to get away with Anne's murder tonight, she would take extreme pleasure in killing Bentley and Erik, watching them suffer and plead for their lives. She felt a surge of sexual stimulation that startled her at first. Then she smiled.

It was so quiet. Just the way she liked it. She hadn't bothered to turn on the radio. She could hear only the rasping of her own breath.

By 6:22 she was two miles from Anne's home when she slowed down at the stoplight. Funny, she thought, she wasn't the least bit nervous.

When the light turned green, her foot pressed down on the accelerator. She was in a hurry to get the entire ordeal over with. Approaching the green light at Walnut Grove Road, she slowed down a tad and made a swift left turn. Picking up speed again she headed west, passing the Memphis Agricultural Center. It was pitch dark in that area and she pressed down on the accelerator once more. At 6:25 she felt a surge of adrenaline and at 6:28, merely a quarter of a mile away, she felt the palms of her hands begin to moisten. It was then that she looked into her rearview mirror and saw the flashing red and blue lights behind her.

Glancing down at the speedometer, she held her breath when she noticed how fast she was traveling. There was no one else around, so she knew that the police car was meant for her.

She told herself to be calm as she pulled over on the side of the road about fifty yards ahead on the right.

It seemed like it took forever for the officer to get out of his car. Just as he was approaching her door, she rolled down the window and checked to make sure the pistol was out of view.

"What's the problem, Officer?" she tried to say in a calm voice as he lowered his head to look inside her vehicle.

"You were speeding, ma'am."

When his probing eyes focused on her purse, her heart began to flutter like a prisoned bird.

Suddenly everything went quiet. It was a warning. She could smell the black coffee on his breath as he spoke to her, and began reading his lips.

I can't believe I'm sitting here so calmly. This isn't me. It's someone else.

Her cold heart began beating so furiously, she could

barely breathe. At that moment, it seemed as if the world was standing still and her life encapsulated in time.

Looking into his eyes, she strained to hear his voice, any sound, but couldn't. Finally, she made out the word *license.*

Not sure if she could speak, she opened her mouth. "Who in the hell do you think you're talking to? I'm Isabell Ford."

When the officer shone a flashlight in her face, she jerked back in the seat, her right arm accidentally nudging her purse.

She wasn't sure if he noticed the outline of the gun beneath her purse or not.

Cars began passing by them, but her mind still wouldn't compute the sound.

Turning to look at his mouth, she saw the angry expression on his face and tried to read the words once more.

"Keep your hands on the steering wheel, and away from the gun!"

This time she made out the word *gun.*

Automatically she reached for the pistol and swiveled her body toward him. Her panic accelerated to hysteria when she saw the officer pointing his gun at her chest. Reaching for her gun in an attempt to conceal it, she screamed when she felt the bullet rip through her body.

Sitting motionless, she felt as though she had swallowed a lit cigarette from the burning sensation after the 9mm caliber bullet had entered her chest. Every second seemed like a week. This was the first time she had a chance to see her life for what it was, and she didn't like it. Before she could open her mouth to speak, another bullet ripped through her neck. In a split second she went from feeling the warm blood running down her arms to freezing cold, then freezer dark.

Wait a second! Just let me breathe. Help! Scott, dear God, help me!

Isabell fought to aim the gun at the officer and managed to get it breast level when she felt the third shot. The pistol fell from her hand and onto the floor of the car.

The last thing she saw was her friend smiling at her in the mirror. She knew that the officer didn't want to shoot her. She knew that she had forced him to do it. And now, she had to admit to herself that Scott had never loved her, no matter what she told herself. And she knew that despite that fact, she would have still killed Anne, and Erik and Bentley, but of course, she hadn't figured on this . . .

Sixty-one

"MY FELLOW UNITED METHODISTS are talking about racism, repentance, reconciliation, and reunion. Talking is good, but wake me when we're really ready to do something."

Anne, Dusty, Daniel, Bentley, Mae, Nikkie, and Ike sat in the middle section of Hyperion United Methodist Church. The pastor, Reverend Eliza Merritt, was addressing the congregation.

"Haven't we done a lot already? Well let's see. At

our general conference in May, we formally confessed and apologized for our racist past. We called it an 'Act of Repentance' and plan to repeat it in local churches in the coming months. We pledged to 'confront and eliminate' individual and institutional racism in church and society. We agreed to begin studying racism and consider what United Methodists can and must do to repair the divisions caused by racism and disunity. And our leaders are still talking about 'union' with leaders of the three black Methodist denominations. The next meeting is in April. It sounds like we're serious about something. I doubt it."

Anne really liked this pastor. In two weeks, Reverend Merritt would be presiding over Nikkie and Ike's marriage. Nikkie and Ike had attended Hyperion Methodist for months and had recently been baptized. The church was split half and half with black and white worshipers. And to everyone's surprise, Mae decided to become a new member of the church. Anne was speechless. Mae hadn't been to church since their father died. But when Mae showed them the engagement ring from Charlie Mickens, she understood why Mae had had a sudden change of heart.

Anne adjusted Daniel's sleeping body on her lap and listened to the pastor.

"Repentance means more than saying we're sorry and we're considering changes. In this case, it means making changes in the system that caused and perpetuates the divisions and disparities. The damage of years of exploitation has not been erased. A system designed to meet the needs of one segment of the population cannot be the means to the development of a just society for all. The racist system in the United States today perpetuates the power and control of those of European ancestry.

"We European Americans don't like to admit that, but it's true. In the church as well as society at large. The three African American Methodist denominations—AME, AME Zion, and CME—have been struggling financially. Forever it seems.

"Because our sin of racism was built into the systems and patterns of our United Methodist church, and because white privilege has been institutionalized over hundreds of years, our repentance for racism is corporate."

When the service was over, Anne and her family stayed and shook hands with the pastor. She told her that she enjoyed her sermon today and was happy to know that there were such honest people preaching the word of God.

Afterward, they all went out to dinner at Perkins Family Restaurant. The conversation was light as everyone stuffed themselves to their hearts' content. Even Daniel enjoyed a second helping of mashed potatoes.

Throughout the meal no one had mentioned Isabell's name. Her picture and the story about the alleged murder of Scott's wife had been the talk around town for days now. Since all the parties were deceased there was no reason to have a trial. So rumors ran rampant. And when Anne read about the abuse she suffered as a child from her father and stepfather, she felt an ounce of pity for her. It seemed that the only thing that she'd try to do right in her life was to give her love to a child that belonged to someone else.

It was a shame. But it was over. Bentley was able to get her job back at the *Hamilton Appeal* scripting *The Riverdocks* comic strip. And Erik and Bentley were splitting custody of Reo and the arrangement seemed to be working out. Bentley wouldn't confirm if her relationship with Corky had ended. Anne knew that she needed time to find herself—to decide what was right for her and her child. And whomever Bentley decided as her choice, Anne would abide by it.

To everyone's surprise, Erik and Reo joined the group in time to have dessert. Afterward they split into three cars: Nikkie, Daniel, Ike, Mae, and Reo in Mae's car; Dusty and Erik in Erik's car; followed by Bentley and Anne.

Reo chose not to ride with her mother and Anne; she wanted to play with Daniel and tag along with her cousin, Nikkie, and her fiancé.

Mae's car was to pick up Kirk and his wife and daughter. His plane was arriving at 6:15 P.M. on United Airlines. Wesley's plane was due to land at 5:55 P.M. on Trans World Airlines, and the rest of the group would be there to welcome him home.

And now, as she and Bentley drove toward the airport, Anne felt the need to explain one more thing to her.

"I've been withholding some personal information for months now that I feel I need to share with you. I've got Parkinson's."

"My God, Aunt Anne. How could you keep something like that to yourself?"

"Honey, hush. It hasn't been easy," she said with mild humor, full of ruefulness and affection. "Ever since the first day I was diagnosed with Parkinson's disease, my only question to God was Why? Did I deserve this? Had I done something that terrible? I knew that this disease shortened your life, like you were on a timer and one day there will be no more hours, no more minutes. At first, I felt sorry for myself. I wanted everyone's sympathy, blaming my doctors and getting angry because they didn't understand. How could anyone understand the feeling of knowing that you only have a few more years to live? I lived day by day with anger and pity for myself. But as time went on, I finally saw that the most important person who needed to understand this problem was myself. I was right when I said no one knows what it's like unless they go through it too. So that told me that instead of trying to make everyone else see why this was happening, I started to take care of myself and understand that even though my faith in God wasn't as strong as it was before, I had to know that He had a reason for this and there was nothing I could do about it but to keep living and continue to love myself.

"But somehow I was lucky. For almost a year now, I haven't been on any medication. I believe I was able to overcome it because of my growing faith in God and the belief of my husband, Dusty. He made me believe in miracles again."

Bentley reached over and patted her aunt's shoulder. "I'm so happy for you, Aunt Anne. I'm grateful for what you've done for Nikkie, too. Without you, she might have never met Ike. And Wesley might not have agreed to finally come home."

There was a comfortable silence between them as they took the International Airport-Airways exit off I-240, heading south toward Memphis International Airport. It was four-thirty by the time they found a parking spot. They exited the car, with Dusty and Erik in deep discussion following a few feet behind them.

First they checked the monitors for a last-minute gate change. The light was blinking on Wesley's flight. It was delayed. As the four of them went through security, they caught a glimpse of Mae and her brood heading in the opposite direction.

The airport was crowded with colorful travelers coming and going. Most people seemed to be in a rush to get to the baggage claim or in a hurry to get to their gate. No matter, Anne and Bentley felt euphoric as they were hustled along the aisle way to Gate B-34.

At the gate they took a seat near the window and watched and waited along with the dozens of others awaiting their loved ones coming in from Dallas, Texas.

"Anne," Dusty called. "Erik and I are going to Baskin-Robbins. Do you girls want anything?"

"Not me." Bentley shook her head no.

Fifteen minutes later, the 727 taxied toward the gate. People began getting out of their seats the moment the flight attendant opened the lobby door. It seemed to take forever for someone to emerge from the endless hallway.

Anne and Bentley made their way to the end of the long line that had formed on each side of the opened doorway.

"Do you think you'll recognize him, Bentley?" Anne asked, craning her neck to look down the plane's long corridor.

"I'd know my brother anywhere."

As the passengers continued to deplane, Anne and Bentley searched each face for a medium-height black man wearing an army uniform. Wesley was bringing his Vietnamese wife and son and had even included their pictures in his last letter. The picture that he enclosed of himself had been in the shade and wasn't very clear.

Several minutes later, the waiting area around the gate was nearly empty. Dusty and Erik had finally come back. Both had made a purchase from the golf shop.

Finally, Bentley, jumping up and down, screamed, "That's him. There he is. Wesley! Hi!"

Anne was overwhelmed. She had expected to see Wesley looking like himself but a little heavier. But what she saw was a man. As he walked toward them he had a half-smile on his face. He looked poised and self-assured, dressed in a black blazer, turtleneck, and slacks.

"Hey there, Sis." Immediately he dropped his wife's hand and hugged her.

While they embraced, Wesley looked over at Anne and winked.

He'd recognized her.

It had been almost thirty-one years since she'd seen him, and looking at Wesley now, Anne couldn't believe her eyes. He'd grown a mustache and sideburns and wore a thin silver earring in his left ear, but he still had those wide-set Russell eyes that reminded her so much of her mother.

Finally, Bentley let him go. They both had tears in their eyes when they faced her.

"Hello, Aunt Anne. It's good to be home." Wesley hugged her and Anne had never felt such strength. She had her family back—all of them. There was nothing anyone could do from this day forward to break them up.

Wesley introduced his wife, Nihja, and his seventeen-year-old son, Colin. They seemed especially quiet, but Anne knew that once everyone was settled at her house, they'd feel right at home.

From a few feet behind them, Anne could hear Mae's voice. She turned and saw her sister, Reo, Daniel, Ike, Mae, Kirk, his wife, baby, and Nikkie coming toward them. Nikkie's face was a question mark as Ike led her over to where they all stood.

"Nikkie?" Wesley called out and began walking toward her.

Nikkie was silent. She looked around at everyone, and saw the wide smiles and looked again at the man who'd called her name.

"Wes? Is that you?" Nikkie said, looking intently into his eyes.

Wesley was staring at her now, taking in her short hair, her trim figure, and the man who held her hand in his. "It's me, Nikkie." He framed her face with his fingers, tenderly caressing her cheeks, and then laid his lips gently on her cheekbone. Nikkie reached out and let herself be folded into his arms.

"I love you, Wes."

"And I love you, Nikkie." He wiped away her tears. "It's okay, sweetheart. I'm home now." He brushed kisses over her hair. "And I'll never leave you again."

By then Anne was crying. And she noticed that Bentley was crying too. She felt Dusty come up behind her and felt his arms enclose around her waist.

"Aunt Anne," Reo said, frowning. "I think that Daniel's done number two. He smells something awful. And look at him. He's laughing like he thinks it's funny."

They all began to laugh, too.

"Honey, hush. Give him here, Reo," Anne said, extending her arms. "I'll change him."

After Anne came from the bathroom, everyone seemed to be talking at the same time. Kirk had center stage, showing off his rodeo gear.

"Hey everybody," Anne said, stepping in the middle of the conversations, "Dusty's got champagne on ice. Let's go home and celebrate!" She turned to Reo. "And we've even got sparkling cider for you, sweetheart."

"Mama," Reo said, taking her mother by the hand, "can't I have the real stuff, just this once?"

Bentley looked at Anne and smiled conspiratorially. "No, baby. If Aunt Anne says no, the answer is no."

Bemused, Anne shook her head. A new generation of Russells was emerging and by God, she'd make sure that they'd learn from their mistakes.

Anne was forty-five years old and new to life. New to herself. With a healthy baby, a loving husband, a supportive family, and faith in the Lord, she'd finally learned the difference between existing and living. Married to Scott, she was merely existing in an unrealistic world. But now, with peace of mind and finally putting the Lord first in her life, she was finally finding *her* life.

She'd given back to the community and felt that her organization was beneficial to ensuring equality for African Americans. Today, she could finally say that she had contributed to the civil rights movement—something that had been important to her ever since she was a child. No, she might not be remembered as Rosa Parks, Angela Davis, and Ellis Baker were, but still, the people who lived in her community would recognize that she helped open the way for underprivileged people's voices to be heard.

Her happiest memories as a child were at home in their kitchen. She and Mae would cook dinner for their father when he came home from work and they would sit and talk about school, the weather, politics, and hopes for their future.

No, they hadn't all gone to college like he'd hoped. But they had something more—love and faith. They were a real family in the full sense of the word. And now, as she felt little Daniel's arms looping around her neck, and took a moment to look at the smiling faces of everyone she loved, she knew that she would no longer look back. She'd look ahead to the future.

Once outside, the air felt like silk. And as the large brood headed for their respective cars, Anne thought about Mud Island. As soon as the weather permitted they'd have a picnic there, watch the boats go by, and sit and talk about nothing in particular.

Anne came to understand that every natural longing has its natural satisfaction. If we thirst, God has created liquids to gratify thirst. If we are susceptible of attachment, there are beings to gratify that love. It we thirst for life and love eternal, it is likely that there is an eternal life and an eternal love to satisfy that craving.

Finally, she understood the meaning behind Reverend Billy Graham's favorite phrase, *This side of Eternity.*

About the Author

Rosalyn McMillan is the author of *The Flip Side of Sin, One Better, Blue Collar Blues,* and the national bestseller *Knowing.* When she's not plotting her next novel, Rosalyn enjoys gardening, reading, and taking ceramic classes. She lives with her teenaged daughter, Jasmine, and her husband, John, in Memphis, Tennessee.

M.S. 10-17 37
43

3519